Jackie ... alpha heroes who ... only to have ...

... ble Dr Jax, two kids and ... rats. When she's not torturing alpha males and their gutsy heroines she can be found drinking chocolate martinis, reading anything she can lay her hands on, wasting time on social media or being forced to go mountain biking with her husband. To keep up to date with Jackie's new releases and other news sign up to her newsletter at jackieashenden.com.

USA TODAY bestseller **Lucy Monroe** lives and writes in the gorgeous Pacific Northwest. While she loves her home, she delights in experiencing different cultures and places on her travels, which she happily shares with her readers through her books. A lifelong devotee of the romance genre, Lucy can't imagine a more fulfilling career than writing the stories in her head for her readers to enjoy.

THE INNOCENT'S ONE-NIGHT PROPOSAL

JACKIE ASHENDEN

THE COST OF THEIR ROYAL FLING

LUCY MONROE

MIX
Paper from
responsible sources
FSC
FSC C007484

This book is produced from independently certified FSC™ paper
to ensure responsible forest management.
For more information visit www.harpercollins.co.uk/green

MILLS & BOON

First Published in Great Britain 2022
by Mills & Boon, an imprint of HarperCollins*Publishers* Ltd,
1 London Bridge Street, London, SE1 9GF

www.harpercollins.co.uk

HarperCollins*Publishers*
1st Floor, Watermarque Building,
Ringsend Road, Dublin 4, Ireland

The Innocent's One-Night Proposal © 2022 Jackie Ashenden

The Cost of Their Royal Fling © 2022 Lucy Monroe

ISBN: 978-0-263-30070-3

THE INNOCENT'S ONE-NIGHT PROPOSAL

JACKIE ASHENDEN

MILLS & BOON

To Jo, Ayesha, latte bowls, flat whites, espressos and grabbing the last savoury scone!

CHAPTER ONE

GLORY ALBRIGHT THOUGHT she might be in trouble when the first naked woman sauntered past her.

When a second followed, Glory realised she was totally out of her depth.

So. It appeared the rumours about how wild the parties at Castor Xenakis's Malibu mansion got were true.

Wild didn't even begin to cover it.

She pulled the cloak she wore tighter around her shoulders and concentrated very hard on the bookshelf in front of her rather than what was happening around her. There was a small sculpture sitting on one of the shelves. It was of a woman being embraced by a man and was carved out of white marble. The man had his hands…

Oh.

Glory blushed as she suddenly realised what kind of sculpture it was and wished she could turn around and find something else to look at, but since turning around might mean potentially seeing more naked people, the statue was clearly the lesser of the two evils.

This was a stupid idea. She shouldn't have come.

In the room at her back, she could hear people laughing and talking and shrieking. Music throbbed like a heartbeat. From elsewhere came the sounds of smashing glass and yet more loud laughter. Then a splash from the pool area.

Someone brushed against her as they walked past where she stood near the bookshelf, and she shrank away in discomfort.

Infamous parties/orgies at luxury Malibu beach houses were so far out of her comfort zone that she may as well have been on the moon, and if she'd had any choice in the matter she'd still be safely at home in the run-down apartment she shared with her sister, curled up in front of the TV watching reruns of *Friends* and eating ice cream.

But she didn't have a choice. Okay, perhaps that wasn't exactly true. She didn't *have* to decide she wanted to pay for her sister to have IVF treatment. And the plan she'd come up with didn't *need* to include gatecrashing the party of one of the most notorious playboys in the world. Neither did it *have* to involve her virginity, and selling said virginity to said playboy.

Then again, Annabel couldn't afford IVF and after the sacrifices she'd made in bringing Glory up after their parents' deaths, Glory thought helping her achieve her dream of having a family was a small price to pay.

Yes, the idea of selling her virginity to an infamous playboy might be a bit wild and wild wasn't Glory at all, but how else could she get a lot of money in a short space of time, and legally?

And this *was* Castor Xenakis after all. She hadn't spent months looking at the pictures of him in the gossip magazines for absolutely no reason. He might be a very bad man and she might tell herself she was doing this for Annabel's benefit, but the deeper truth beneath that was that she wanted him.

Those pictures had led to an obsession with him that

she couldn't deny. An obsession that she was tired of and was hoping a night in his bed would cure her of.

Anyway, it wasn't as if she'd just dreamed her plan up on the fly. It had come to her after months spent reading said magazines at her job behind the counter of Mr and Mrs Jessup's grocery store, and then paying quiet attention to the customers who visited the store. Customers who talked. Customers who let slip certain things…

The plan was utter madness, of course, and totally alien to Glory's quiet nature, but when you were a dirt-poor checkout girl and your beloved older sister had given up a lot of dreams for you, then you did what you could to give those dreams back to her.

Exactly. And you didn't come here to stand in front of the bookshelf staring at naughty statues.

No, she hadn't.

She'd come to one of Castor Xenakis's notorious Malibu parties to find the world's most debauched and dissolute playboy himself, then offer him her virginity.

For a price.

It wasn't totally out of the realms of possibility that he'd accept. She had, after all, read *a lot* about him in those magazines that stood on a stand near the counter, because he was in those magazines constantly. And if the rumours about his parties were true, then she might have a chance.

He was supposed to choose a woman for the night from amongst the partygoers and whichever woman he chose apparently didn't go away empty-handed the next day. Money, jewellery, expensive purses were some of the gifts he gave to his lovers. One was even rumoured to have been given some expensive sports car.

Glory had been in the middle of reading one of those gossipy articles when a couple of women had come in, chattering about all the work they had to do for the party coming up that weekend.

She had sat there quietly, not drawing attention to herself, which she was very good at, just listening. Being able to fade into the background was a useful skill, since if people didn't notice you, they'd talk about all kinds of stuff.

Such as how the party was going to be a big one and how the boss himself was going to be there, and how he did like everything to go smoothly.

The two women were regulars and Glory knew they worked at Castor Xenakis's Malibu beach house, so he must have been the boss they were talking about.

Castor Xenakis, CEO of CX Enterprises—a multinational with interests in finance, shipping, construction and various other industries—and party circuit regular, had been linked to all kinds of scandals and was reputedly one of the most infamous womanisers in the western world, if not the entire globe.

The one who made extravagant gifts to his lovers.

It was then that her idea was born. Her mad, wild and very un-Glory-like idea.

There was no guarantee he'd accept her offer, and why would he when he had a legion of A-list Hollywood stars, supermodels and even royalty at his beck and call? Then again, he might be in the market for novelty, for something different, and Glory could safely say that she *was* different. At least for him. She wasn't beautiful, but she'd been told on a number of occasions—or at least shouted at by men—that she had a great body. But mainly, she was a total virgin. She hadn't even been kissed before. Men got off on that, or so she'd heard, and she was hoping Castor Xenakis would get off on it.

And if he doesn't, Annabel won't get a chance at having a baby.

That was true. And she wouldn't get her chance at a night with him either, which was disappointing.

She had to be rid of this obsession. How would she ever find someone in her own league if she kept thinking about a man normally so far beyond her reach he might as well have been on the moon?

Whatever, standing here feeling sick with nerves wasn't going to help with either of those two things.

First, she had to find him.

Steeling herself, Glory turned around.

The room was huge, running the entire width of the house. One wall was entirely floor-to-ceiling windows that faced the beach. Low, white leather modular couches were scattered everywhere, along with low glass tables, and sleek bookshelves devoid of actual books. Huge artworks—mostly abstract—adorned the white walls, and a number of other sculptural artworks stood on tables or on the white carpet of the floor.

The effect was one of stark luxury but Glory, who was fond of clutter, found it rather soulless.

People were scattered around the room, the women dressed in couture cocktail dresses and statement jewellery, the men in designer suits. She thought she might recognise some of the guests since it was definitely a place for the rich and famous, but so far she hadn't.

There were still laughter and lots of conversation, the music thumping, but she could see that there was a couple in the corner who were…

Oh. Right.

Glory moved quickly out of the room, her heart beating very fast, and into the soaring atrium-style entranceway. Massive globes of frosted glass hung suspended from the ceiling, looking like planets floating in space.

There were also people out here, though mostly clothed, thank God.

Glory wished she had the courage to ask one of them where Castor Xenakis was, but she didn't want to draw attention to herself. They might realise she hadn't been invited—she'd snuck in with a group of people dressed in burlesque costumes—and might decide to have her kicked out since it was clear she didn't belong here.

And she really didn't. The nudity, the alcohol, the luxury setting, the crowds of people and the uninhibited atmosphere were all making her extremely uncomfortable. She didn't do parties, never had, not even as a teenager. She'd been too busy taking care of Annabel after her breast cancer diagnosis, and there hadn't been time for any of that kind of thing even if she'd wanted to.

Not that she wanted to. Her life was quiet and steady and predictable, and that's just how she preferred it.

Which makes being here a really dumb idea.

Probably. But that IVF wasn't going to pay for itself and she was here now, and so she at least had to try.

Skirting a group of sketchy-looking men who were talking seriously and radiating 'do not disturb' vibes, Glory found another long hallway and started down it.

Perhaps Xenakis had withdrawn from the main party and was in another room. He could be outside, of course, somewhere in the lush, tropical-style garden that surrounded the house, but she wanted to make sure he wasn't inside first before she braved whatever was going on outside.

Or perhaps she'd missed him? But no, he wasn't like her. He wasn't a man who would ever fade into the background and remain unnoticed.

Castor Xenakis couldn't remain unnoticed even if he tried.

He was phenomenally handsome and even in the photos Glory had pored over she'd been able to tell that he possessed the kind of charisma that drew people to him, that commanded attention simply by its very existence.

And you're hoping a man like that will choose you for the night? Are you actually insane?

Maybe. But as she'd sat reading about him in that magazine and then heard his two staff members chatting about the upcoming party, well…it had seemed like fate.

The throb of the party music was a little less down this corridor, but was now joined by the sound of a piano, which was odd.

She followed the sound, the notes cascading through the hallway, echoing off the hardwood floors and the white stone walls.

Abruptly the hallway opened out into a room that faced the lush, discreetly lit garden. A white grand piano stood near the windows, a woman in a silver gown seated at it, playing.

Grouped around the room were yet more of those long white couches, with people—women mostly, in beautiful dresses—sitting on them.

In the middle of the room was a big white armchair and sitting in the armchair was a man.

He had a woman curled in his lap while another draped herself over the arm of his chair, and he looked like a king on his throne. Or maybe a pasha sitting at his ease surrounded by his harem.

Glory stopped short in the doorway, transfixed.

He wore tailored black trousers and a white shirt open at the neck and he was quite simply the most beautiful man—no, person—she'd ever seen.

It was him. It was Castor Xenakis, and he was even more incredible in person than he was in his pictures.

His hair was a dark tawny colour, like a lion's pelt, and artfully tousled, his skin golden. His features looked like they'd been hand carved by Michelangelo himself, with an Attic profile, high cheekbones and a beautiful, sensual mouth.

His eyebrows were dark, his lashes thick and silky and streaked with gold, and his eyes were the same dark golden brown of fine brandy.

He was like an exquisite Renaissance sculpture that had been feathered with gilding and then given a light scatter of gold dust.

Glory quivered at the beauty of him.

He sat back in the chair, smiling at the blonde in his lap and curling a lock of her hair idly around one finger, while the brunette sitting on the arm of the chair leaned down to say something in his ear.

He laughed in response, the sound low and sexy, making a curious heat prickle all over Glory's skin.

Her breath caught, her stomach dropping right down into the red patent stiletto sandals that she'd picked up from a cheap chain store the day before, as something she'd already thought about but hadn't fully taken on board became clear.

He might be dissolute, dissipated and morally bankrupt, but he was also beautiful. Stunningly, heartbreakingly so, and she… She was not.

He was a Greek god while she was a small, brown church mouse, and there was no way—*no way*—in the world he'd ever consider her pathetic little offer. Not only did he possess a charisma that burned like a forest fire, he was also surrounded by the most beautiful women Glory had ever seen.

Why on earth had she ever thought he'd look twice at someone like her?

But what about Annabel? She needs treatment.

Oh, she did. But Glory was going to have to think of some other way of getting money because this obviously wasn't going to work. And as for her own secret obsession and her even more secret desire…well, she could forget about that too, because that wasn't going to happen.

She needed to leave now, before she made an utter fool of herself.

On the point of turning around and heading straight for the front door, Glory froze as a pair of heavy hands came down on her shoulders, gripping her lightly, and she was aware of someone standing behind her. A man wearing an overpowering aftershave that didn't do much to mask the odour of stale sweat, cigarette smoke and another, musky smell that made her shiver with distaste.

'Ah, there you are, Red Riding Hood,' the man said, his accent thick and Eastern European–sounding. 'I've been looking for you everywhere.'

Fear iced her veins, her heart beating suddenly very loudly in her ears.

You're an idiot coming to a party like this on your own, looking for the biggest womaniser in the world. What did you think was going to happen?

Okay, so yes, she'd been naive and being desperate hadn't helped either. And now some horrible man was going to drag her off God knew where and no one here would help her, she already knew that much.

Still, she wasn't going to stand there and let herself be taken. The stilettos might have been cheap, but she was betting that the man holding her wouldn't like it if she drove one of her heels into his foot.

Glory tensed, preparing to bolt. Then the breath stuck

in her throat as Castor Xenakis's gaze locked on hers and she was held captive by a pair of golden-brown eyes, the distaste she'd felt at being grabbed by the man behind her scattering in a shower of bonfire sparks.

An expression she couldn't name rippled over Xenakis's beautiful face before his gaze shifted to the man behind her. He smiled. 'Dimitri,' he said, his voice deep and rich and warm as melted honey. 'I think Red Riding Hood might be a bit too tame for your tastes. How about I find you someone more interesting, hmm?'

Castor was furious, though he didn't let even a hint of his fury escape. He prided himself on no one being able to tell what he was thinking, still less what he was feeling, especially in the middle of one of his parties.

Most especially not when that party was turning into a complete failure.

The people he'd invited—a group of known human traffickers from Eastern Europe—had decided at the last minute not to come, sending only Dimitri, a thug not only low on the totem pole but also low in intelligence, in their stead.

It was an insult, that was clear, and it meant they weren't taking any of his efforts to gain access to their inner circle seriously enough.

He'd been trying for months to get close to this particular group of traffickers, but it turned out that the terrible reputation he'd careful cultivated, that had enabled him to gain their trust as far as it went, was now working against him.

This group were staunch family men, all with wives and children, and they did not want someone of Castor's ilk joining them. It drew too much attention, apparently.

It was beginning to be clear to Castor that if he wanted

to become one of them, he was going to have to do something to change their opinion of him.

He wasn't sure quite what that something was yet, but he'd do it.

Once he was part of that inner circle, all he needed then was to get the location of their next 'shipment' and pass that on to the authorities so they could intercept it.

He was going to take those animals down and their loathsome organisation with them.

Starting with that bastard Dimitri.

Are you sure you want to go after them now? In public?

That was true. How disappointing. He would have to settle with discretion, then.

His gaze fell once again on the woman Dimitri was holding. She was very small and wrapped entirely in what was, indeed, a red cloak. Her face was pale and sharp and fox-like, and she had the largest, most liquid dark eyes he'd ever seen. Eyes that had been full of fear as they'd met his.

The people that came to his parties were carefully chosen. They had few boundaries and even fewer inhibitions, and if any of them were frightened at being handled by Dimitri, none would have been gauche enough to show it.

But not this woman. Her fear was written all over her face.

She doesn't belong here.

Castor's temper, already roused, began to seethe. He always checked his guest list rigorously and people who weren't on it didn't get in, and he was pretty sure this woman, whoever she was, hadn't been on it.

So what she was doing here and how she'd got in, he had no idea.

What he did know was that he needed to get her out

of Dimitri's clutches and fast. The man was a brutal thug and Marie—who was ex-military and one of his security staff—would know how to deal with him.

'Interesting?' Dimitri echoed, frowning. 'How interesting?'

Castor bent and murmured in Esme's ear, 'Off me, sweetheart. I'll come and find you later.'

Esme slid off his lap without a protest and he got up, sending Tyler, who was playing the piano, an apologetic look.

Then he turned and headed for the doorway where Dimitri stood with Red Riding Hood, those dark eyes of hers getting rounder and rounder the closer he got. As if she'd never seen anything like him before in her entire life.

A small pulse of…something went through him, though what it was, he couldn't tell. Strange. Lots of women looked at him that way. Women lovelier than she was, so why he should feel anything at all God only knew.

'Come,' he said easily, taking Dimitri by the arm. 'Let me tell you about Lola.'

Dimitri frowned, but let go of the dark-eyed woman. She was trembling slightly. Castor couldn't help but notice.

What on earth was she doing here? His parties were infamous, exclusive and wildly debauched, and they were not for the faint of heart.

What they were for was getting information from human traffickers about their operations so Castor could pass that on to the authorities.

It was not a place for someone who didn't know what they were doing.

Marie, luckily, was standing near the doorway, dressed in a tight black cocktail dress that showed off her magnificent figure at the same time as it gave her room to move if there were any threats.

Castor signalled her and she approached, smiling at Dimitri. 'Hi there,' she murmured, taking him by the arm. 'I'm Lola. Wanna go have some fun?'

Dimitri relaxed, letting her take him off down the hall, leaving Castor with Red Riding Hood in her cloak.

She was still very pale, staring up at him with those huge eyes. And he was conscious that his fury was in no way satisfied now Dimitri had been dealt with. In fact, for some reason he couldn't quite pinpoint, he was even angrier than he'd been a moment ago.

She wasn't one of his guests, which meant she'd somehow sneaked in. And that was dangerous not only for her, but for him as well. Especially if anything happened to her. He had an agreement with local law enforcement that they would leave his parties alone in return for the information he passed on, but if something happened to an innocent, even they wouldn't be able to ignore it. And that would put at risk everything he'd spent the last ten years working for.

'I—I—' she began.

'As for you.' Castor took her arm in an iron grip. 'You're coming with me.'

He didn't want to do this publicly. He would take her into his private study, where he could find out exactly who she was and what she was doing here, and then ensure she'd never make such a foolish mistake again.

She stiffened as he urged her down the hallway, but she was no match for his strength and was soon hurrying along beside him, her cloak fluttering out behind her.

His study wasn't far and it had a lock so no curious guests could blunder in.

He paused outside, pressed his finger to the fingerprint pad and heard the click as the door unlocked. Then he ushered her inside and shut the door behind them.

It was a pleasant room, not that he stayed in this house often since he spent most of his time in Europe. But he liked the windows that looked out over the garden rather than the sea. It had the same white walls; however, most of these were lined with sleek modern shelving housing the many books he liked to read. There were comfortable couches scattered around, plus a few roomy armchairs, and the lighting was all recessed and discreet.

The woman had pulled away to stand in the middle of the room, her cloak wrapped tightly around her, big eyes peering at him from the depths of her hood.

He couldn't tell what kind of figure she had, but she had an interesting face. Sharp chin, sharp nose, but the most gorgeously full mouth.

She looked scared so he put his hands in his pockets, keeping his posture loose and unthreatening, since although he was angry and determined to give her a piece of his mind, he wasn't going to hurt her.

That was the very last thing in the world he'd do.

'Sweetheart,' he said coolly. 'You shouldn't be here.'

She gazed at him warily, as if he was a rabid dog who might attack at any moment. 'I—I—I know. I wasn't invited.' Her voice was low, husky, and sent the most disturbing shiver of sexual awareness down his spine.

How inconvenient. Still, it wasn't an issue. He had Esme for tonight and she was always up for anything.

'No, of course you weren't invited. I know everyone on that guest list and you weren't on it. So tell me, who are you and what the hell are you doing in my house?'

She stared at him for a moment, then squared her shoulders as if bracing herself for a distasteful task and took a step towards him.

'Actually,' she said. 'I'm here to make you an offer.'

It wasn't unusual. Lots of people made him offers.

Castor raised an eyebrow. 'You gatecrashed my party to make me an offer? What kind of offer?'

'I'd like to offer you…' She lifted her chin as if she was facing down a firing squad, then dramatically threw off the cloak. 'My virginity.'

CHAPTER TWO

Surprise rippled over Castor Xenakis's phenomenally handsome face, and Glory might have found that satisfying if she hadn't been so utterly terrified.

First that awful man putting his hands on her and then the man she'd been obsessing about for months grabbing her arm and forcing her down a hallway into this room.

Now her heart was nearly coming out of her chest and she didn't know why she'd thrown off her cloak. Hadn't she decided she wasn't going through with this stupid plan?

It had only seemed as if now she was here, now she'd finally got him alone, she had to do it, because she didn't want to be a coward. Even if she had no hope of him ever accepting her offer.

A part of her even hoped he'd refuse. Mainly because Castor Xenakis as a picture in a magazine was a whole lot easier to deal with than Castor Xenakis in the flesh, standing right in front of her.

He was devastating. That was the only word for it. And he terrified her, though she wasn't sure why.

What she was sure of was that she wanted to get away from him as quickly as possible.

What about Annabel? What about the IVF? What about a night with him?

She would never get her night, that was clear to her now, and even if she did, she probably wouldn't be able to handle it anyway.

But Annabel…that was a different story.

'I beg your pardon?' he asked in his smooth, dark voice. 'You want to offer me your what?'

He'd been sexy in those pictures in the gossip magazines, been charming in all the interviews she'd read. He'd never denied his lavish parties or his exploits with his many lovers. And when he'd been accused of being shallow, he'd only smiled as if that was of no concern.

Yet while the man who stood in front of her was still sexy, he wasn't smiling now and the sexy charm he'd displayed out in the room with the piano was long gone. His gaze was razor sharp and there was no give in his fallen-angel face.

That should have made her more afraid, should have made her bolt from the room, because this man was harder and colder than the one in the magazines she'd read so avidly.

Yet she didn't move, standing there exposed in the skin-tight cheap red dress she'd bought in the hope it would showcase her figure, conscious of the strangest shiver of delicious anticipation running down her spine. As if part of her was relishing the chance to do battle with him.

'I—I w-want to offer you my virginity,' she repeated, annoyed with herself for stuttering. 'For a price.'

He stared at her and if she didn't know any better she would have said that he was slightly dumbfounded.

'Of course.' There were traces of a lilting, musical accent in his velvety voice. 'Your virginity, how novel.'

His obvious sarcasm generated a spark of anger inside her.

If he didn't want her, he should just say. He really didn't need to be quite so rude.

'Okay, fine,' she said, not stuttering now. 'It's clear you're not interested. Just forget I said anything and I'll be on my way.' Then she reached for her cloak.

Only to have warm fingers wrap around her wrist.

She took a sharp breath, realising belatedly that he'd moved, crossing to where she stood and so fast she'd barely had a chance to be aware of it let alone get away from him.

'No,' he said flatly. 'I don't think you will.'

Glory trembled, a strange combination of fear and excitement tangling inside her. 'L-let go of me.'

He didn't move and he didn't release her. 'Who are you? Tell me why you're really here.'

There was an odd intensity to him. He seemed…angry. Almost as if he thought she was lying to him.

'I did tell you.' She tried to pull her hand away. 'I came here to—'

'You really expect me to believe that nonsense?'

He looked so forbidding, his amber gaze cold. So very different to the man she'd seen talking to the woman in his lap just before, who'd smiled and then laughed that low, sexy laugh.

Yes, he was angry, she could see that. But did gatecrashing his stupid party really warrant scaring her like this? And what did he care anyway? He was rich and powerful, so why didn't he get his security to deal with her?

Glory hated confrontation so she didn't often allow herself to get angry. And when she couldn't avoid a confrontation, she usually dealt with it by staying quiet until the other person had finished ranting, before apologising profusely.

Yet for some reason, there was something about this man that made her usual apologies stick in her throat.

He was *very* angry, which didn't seem fair, plus there was the fact that he was completely, devastatingly good looking. She already knew about that—she'd been mooning over him and his looks for months after all—and yes, he had quite the sordid reputation, but did he have to be so unpleasant to her?

She was only an ordinary woman in the wrong place at the wrong time.

He could just let her go, not stand there interrogating her like she was a terrorist or something. Especially when all she'd done was gatecrash.

'It's not nonsense.' Glory felt compelled to point out, since it also wasn't fair he didn't believe her when she was telling the truth. 'That's what all the gossip magazines say. That you choose a woman to spend the night with and then you give her money or gifts or jewellery or whatever.'

He remained expressionless, his amber gaze never leaving her face. 'The gossip magazines. I see.' Unexpectedly, he let go of her hand. 'Your name, please.'

A small, rebellious part of her, the part that wanted to stand up to him, also didn't want to tell him, which made no sense, because it wasn't like her name was a state secret.

'Glory Albright,' Glory said with some dignity.

He nodded, then reached into his pocket and brought out a sleek-looking phone. Glancing down, he touched the screen, then turned, raising the phone to his ear as he took a few steps away from her.

Glory looked at the door, then back at the man standing not too far away from her, talking into his phone in a low voice. If she was quick, she could get to the door and get out of this room before he had a chance to move.

Except that won't help Annabel. Or get you what you want either.

It wouldn't, it was true. Then again, this whole virginity thing had clearly been a stupid idea from the start, and given his surprise when she'd offered it to him, either the rumours were wrong and he didn't choose lovers at his parties, or he didn't want her. Whichever it was, the outcome was still the same: Annabel would not be getting her IVF treatment and she'd remain a virgin.

An odd pain shifted inside her and she swallowed, glancing back at him. He wasn't speaking English, but some other language she didn't recognise, low and musical.

Greek maybe? That's where he was from, wasn't it? Or at least, that's where the magazines had said. Maybe they were wrong though.

You should have known better than to believe them.

Of course she should have. She prided herself on being practical and keeping her head down, doing what she had to do.

That's what she'd done when Annabel had got sick, the small college fund that she'd put aside for Glory having to be used to pay for the cancer treatment. Not that it covered even a minuscule proportion of it.

Glory had had to drop out of school and get a job so the two of them had money to live on, since Annabel had been too sick from the chemo to work. Not that Glory minded. She hadn't wanted to go to college anyway, and besides, her sister was more important.

It was very good luck that the Jessups' little grocery store wasn't far from where she and Annabel lived, so she could walk to work, and they hadn't minded that Glory had no qualifications. She was polite, quiet and a hard worker, and that's what mattered most.

Gatecrashing a billionaire playboy's party and offering him your virginity is hardly polite and quiet.

No, that was true, it wasn't. Nor was arguing with him. She didn't like making people angry or upsetting them, and clearly she'd done both, which meant she needed to apologise for that and for ruining his party.

Glory drew herself up, steeled her spine and turned to him.

Only to find he'd finished on the phone and was standing there with his arms folded, watching her with that intent, almost predatory gaze.

It was unnerving.

She opened her mouth to apologise.

'Your name is Glory Albright,' he said before she could get a word out. 'You're twenty-three years old. You live at number 2A in the Bella Vista apartments. You dropped out of school to work at Jessups' grocery store, where you've been for the past few years. You have an older sister called Annabel who is currently in remission from breast cancer; you have a large amount of medical debt and no insurance. Correct?'

Glory stared at him, dumbfounded.

His gaze glittered in the light and she had the oddest feeling that he hadn't really looked at her before and that he was looking at her now. *Really* looking at her.

Her in her cheap red dress and cheap red stilettos, and the stupid cloak she'd found in a sale bin in the thrift store. Her with her untidy, unmanageable curly hair that never did what it was told and was probably already coming down from the bun she'd tried to put it in.

Her in the cheap make-up she'd had to borrow from

Annabel, that she didn't know how to apply very well because she never wore it herself.

Glory Albright, the checkout girl who thought she had what it took to seduce a man as powerful as Castor Xenakis.

It was exposing having him know who she was. Know every little thing about her. It made her feel vulnerable and small, and vaguely ashamed of herself, though she had no idea why.

She wasn't ashamed of who she was or the life she and Annabel had managed to build after their parents' deaths. They had a roof over their heads and food on the table, and she had a job that while it didn't pay much, it was at least steady and the Jessups were nice people. And Annabel was in remission. That was far more than some people had.

Glory stared back. 'Yes,' she said. 'That's me. And for the record, if you'd wanted to know all of that, I would have told you. You only had to ask.'

His gaze flickered. 'I could, it's true. But forgive me, sweetheart. I don't know you from a bar of soap and you could have told me anything. A background check from a trusted source was necessary.'

He had a point. Still, she didn't really understand why that was necessary. Unless he thought she was a journalist or something. Perhaps he didn't want the media leaking details of his parties everywhere. Then again, those details were already in the public arena so what was he being so cagey about?

Why do you want to know at all?

Oh, she didn't want to know. What she wanted was to get out of here, get home and then figure out what other options there were as far as getting money for Annabel's treatment. And as for her obsession, she'd simply have to deal with it. Perhaps she'd find another man who could help her move on. A man who was more in her league.

'Well,' Glory said. 'Now you know. So can I go, please?'

'Not yet, I think,' he murmured, gesturing at the couch behind her. 'Take a seat, Miss Albright.'

An icy current snaked down her spine and she had to fold her arms over her thumping heart. Because why would he want her to do that? Why wasn't he just letting her go? What did he want from her?

His gaze narrowed. 'I'm not going to hurt you,' he said. 'I just want to talk to you.'

His tone needled her, though why she wasn't sure. Maybe it was only that he'd picked up on her fear and she didn't like it. It made her feel even more exposed.

'I know.' She tried to keep her voice level. 'What I don't know is what on earth could you possibly want to talk to me about.'

Once again, his amber gaze moved over her, more slowly this time. Then the hard expression on his face eased, one corner of his beautiful mouth curving in a slight smile, as if he'd seen something about her that amused him.

'Well, mainly,' he said. 'I'd like to reiterate the dangers of wandering around parties you weren't invited to and offering your virginity to complete strangers.'

Glory felt her cheeks heat, that smile of his catching on her temper. She didn't know what was going on with her or why she was suddenly acting out of character and arguing with people she shouldn't be arguing with, but it had to stop.

Yes, he was overwhelmingly attractive, but he'd frightened her. And now he was looking at her in a way that made her skin feel tight and prickly, and everything in her was telling her that this was one confrontation she didn't want and she should get away from him and quickly.

Except the rebel in her wouldn't let her run.

He tilted his head, studying her, dark brows drawing together slightly as if he found her puzzling.

Glory was disturbed to find that she liked that very much, since very few people found her puzzling. Very few people thought much about her at all.

'How impolite of me,' he murmured. 'I know all about you, but you don't know me, do you?'

'I kn-know who you are,' she said, hating how she kept stammering and not understanding why she was still standing here. 'You're Castor Xenakis.'

He inclined his head. 'I am. Pleased to meet you, Miss Albright.'

'Pleased to meet you too, Mr Xenakis.'

'Call me Castor.' He nodded at the couch. 'Please, sit.'

'Oh, I think it's probably time to—'

He gave her a pleasant smile. 'I'm afraid I'm going to have to insist.'

Glory Albright was very pale, her dark eyes almost black. She was still scared, undoubtedly, which had been his aim, even though he hadn't much enjoyed doing so. He didn't like scaring women.

Then again, she had to know what a phenomenally stupid thing it had been to gatecrash one of his parties, and then to add to the stupidity by offering him her virginity. An idea she'd somehow picked up from some ridiculous gossip magazines.

It was ridiculous. It was also a concern.

He cultivated the rumours about himself very carefully, making sure the press knew only what he allowed them know, which was that he was a playboy of the worst

kind, notorious for his appetite for women and wild parties. A man with few boundaries and no scruples who'd
sell his soul for a good time.

It was a careful front he'd maintained for the past
couple of years, which had allowed him to get close to
various crime lords and gain access to information that
would normally be impossible to get. Information that
pertained to human trafficking.

Personally, he didn't care about his terrible reputation,
that had ended up with him being tarred with the same
brush as those unsavoury people.

It was the mission goal that counted and his mission
goal was to help as many people affected by human trafficking as possible, in particular women. And if being
thought of as a dissolute playboy was the only way he
could help those women, then that's what he'd do. Without a second's thought.

However, what he didn't want was for innocents like
Glory Albright to start wandering into his parties thinking they could get money or kudos or whatever the rumours the gossip magazines were printing from him.

If anyone found out what he was really doing at his
parties, then there was the potential for his cover to be
blown, and the network of contacts and information he'd
so painstakingly built would be destroyed.

Which couldn't happen and especially not when he
was on the verge of gaining access to the biggest trafficking ring in Europe.

He needed to decide what to do with her that wouldn't
involve her talking to anyone else, or coming back here
with yet more ludicrous offers.

*Do you have to do anything with her? She's not going
to say anything. You could just let her go.*

He could. But if anything the last ten years of associating with the scum of humanity had taught him it was that you couldn't trust anyone. People lied all the time, which meant you had to be careful. So very careful.

He had to find out if she'd run into anyone else tonight, or whether she'd heard anything she shouldn't, because he didn't necessarily want her running to the media with lurid tales of human traffickers and criminals.

Not that she'd be believed, he suspected. She was just a checkout girl at a grocery store with a sick sister. No one notable or special. A nobody.

A nobody in a cheap, stretchy red dress who happened to have, now that he was looking, a knockout figure. Generous breasts and hips, and a small waist. A classic pin-up.

Her hair had been covered by the cloak and when she'd flung it off, glossy, chestnut curls had fallen out of the bun it had been pinned in, some falling behind her ear and some haphazardly down to her shoulder.

It should have looked untidy but it didn't. It looked sexy, as if she'd been pulled into an alcove and ravished within an inch of her life.

From out of nowhere came the absurd impulse to go over to her and start pulling the pins out of her bun so he could watch all those luscious curls fall down over her shoulders. Then maybe bury his fingers in it just to see what it would feel like.

But he wouldn't, of course. Getting excited about an ordinary young woman who'd been reading too many gossip magazines? What a ridiculous thought for a man of his jaded tastes.

He'd seen everything, done everything. Nothing surprised him these days, nothing delighted him. Because after all, you couldn't live as long as he had in filth before some of it touched you, no matter how careful you were.

She was giving him a deeply suspicious look, as if she knew exactly what was going on in his head, in which case no wonder. He deserved her suspicion.

You scared her quite a lot.

Perhaps more than necessary. Clearly he'd let his frustration at the lack of progress with this particular trafficking ring and his anger at Dimitri get the better of him.

Another reason—as if he needed another—for him to figure out an alternative plan. Normally keeping a tight leash on his emotions wasn't a problem, but if he was letting fools like Dimitri get to him, then he needed to do something.

'I'd like to offer you some refreshments,' he said more gently this time. 'By way of an apology for scaring you.'

Her dark, liquid gaze was wary. 'You didn't scare me,' she said.

A lie. Her fear had been obvious. Which meant that perhaps it was time to give her the charming playboy rather than the wolf's sharp teeth. After all, it wasn't her fault she didn't know what these parties were really all about.

Deliberately, he relaxed his posture, let the tension bleed out of him. Put on the mask he'd cultivated over the years, the easy smile and the warm expression that didn't come naturally to him, but that he'd been faking for so long it was now part of him.

'I suppose that's why you keep looking at me like I'm going to murder you at any second, hmm?' He let amusement colour his voice.

She frowned, clearly not finding his sudden change in mood convincing. 'You might,' she said slowly. 'I've heard a lot of things about you.'

She had a point. Still, he hadn't thought his reputation was quite *that* bad if people thought him capable of murdering innocent gatecrashers.

Didn't you though? All those years ago? Wasn't it essentially murder?

Deep inside, an old agony stirred and along with it an old fury. But with the ease of long practice, he ignored both emotions, keeping his smile firmly in place.

'It's true, I'm not at all trustworthy,' he said easily. 'But since I'm Greek and we would rather die than let a guest under our roof suffer even the most minor of discomforts, you can trust in my sense of national pride at least.'

She eyed him warily for a long moment, a deep crease between her brows. 'Okay,' she said at last. 'I suppose I can do that.'

Sitting on the couch he'd gestured to, she grimaced as the hem of her dress rode up before instantly tugging it back down again. But not quick enough to prevent him from catching a glimpse of a pair of rounded, creamy thighs.

Sudden and unexpected heat caught at him and all at once he was again far more aware of her lush little body than he should have been. Of the indentation of her waist and the swell of her hips and thighs, outlined to perfection by that cheap red dress.

An ordinary young woman she might have been, but there was nothing ordinary about her figure.

Still, if he wasn't as notorious as his reputation made him out to be, he wasn't far from it, and if he wanted a woman he had her. However, he had rules. He always found his lovers from amongst his own social circle, experienced women who were out for some fun and nothing more.

Innocents were out of bounds and he'd never found that to be an issue.

It wouldn't be one now.

He forced his gaze from her hips, pulled his phone from his pocket and sent a quick text to one of his staff members ordering that some refreshments be brought. Then he sat down on the couch opposite her.

'So, Miss Albright,' he said conversationally. 'I hope you didn't run into anyone else causing you trouble tonight?'

Her straight, dark brows drew down again. 'No. Should I have?'

'Some of my guests aren't entirely polite. I wouldn't want you to have been inconvenienced by any of them.'

She shook her head, another long russet curl coming loose from her bun, and he found himself watching it as it fell slowly over her shoulder. The reddish gleam in the strands contrasted beautifully with her creamy skin.

'I wasn't inconvenienced, but thank you for asking.'

He wouldn't have thought a gatecrasher come to sell him her virginity would have such manners. Apparently he was wrong. Politeness wasn't a common commodity in the circles he moved in and he found it refreshing.

Relaxing on the couch, he stretched his arms out over the back in a conscious effort to put her at her ease, noting how she followed the movement of his body.

Interesting. He knew what that surreptitious look was all about. He knew that very well. And he wasn't surprised. He had a certain effect on women, and no doubt for this little sharp-faced checkout girl, he was dazzling.

Perhaps you can use that?

It was a thought he'd had before. Many times, in fact. He'd used his looks and the charm he'd forced himself to learn to pull himself up out of the Athens tenement he'd come from. After Ismena had disappeared and his mother had died.

He'd been called manipulative in his time and if manipulative meant his cause was more important than people's feelings, then yes, he was manipulative. Especially when his cause was to save as many people as possible from the fate his sister had suffered.

But she has nothing to do with Ismena.

This was true. And besides, what could he use her for anyway? She was a nobody.

'And you didn't hear anything that frightened you?' he asked absently, turning over various plans in his head, trying to figure out what his next move would be.

He couldn't make any progress with taking down this particular trafficking ring if he couldn't get information about their shipments. And he couldn't get access to that information if he wasn't part of the inner circle of people who ran it. So how to get access to that inner circle? They were, bizarrely, all family men with wives and children, and apparently didn't trust playboys like him.

In which case perhaps he needed to find himself a wife. Any marriage would have to be legal, naturally enough, in case anyone got suspicious and investigated it, but it didn't need to be for ever. Just long enough for him to get the information he needed to take this trafficking ring down.

Yes, maybe that was an option. Finding a woman who'd agree to marry him wouldn't be an issue either, since he had women coming out of his ears. Then again, if he married, focus would fall on his wife, which could potentially put her in some danger and he didn't like the sound of that. A beautiful wife in particular would draw the wrong kind of attention, so if he was going to take that route, he'd have to find someone who was plain enough that people wouldn't bother. Someone who wasn't famous either, someone whom no one else knew.

Someone…ordinary.

Someone like her.

Castor blinked.

Her. Glory Albright, checkout girl. Who'd been trying to sell him her virginity.

Interesting. Very interesting indeed.

She was looking at him from underneath lashes caked thickly in cheap mascara, wary still, but also curious if he wasn't much mistaken.

'You must need money very badly,' he said abruptly. 'If you were willing to sell yourself to me.'

'Oh… I…um…yes.' She folded her hands nervously in her lap.

'To pay back all your medical debt?'

'Um…partly.' She folded her hands again. 'Does that really matter?'

It didn't, but he was curious. Because whatever the reason, it was important enough to her that she'd do something so obviously out of character as to wander into his lair.

You could use that.

Yes, he could. And he had no compunction about doing so, not when the lives of people taken by human traffickers were on the line.

Ignoring the question, he asked instead, 'Why did you think I would choose you? Why did you think I would even pay you?'

'That's what the gossip magazines said and that you never sent a lover away empty-handed.'

'It didn't occur to you that they might lie?'

'Of course.' Her nervously shifting hands stilled and she looked at him. 'But I thought it was worth trying.'

Something glowed in her eyes. Something he recognised: determination.

He liked that. He'd done a few things himself that were long shots, but he'd tried anyway, because he was determined. Because even though he'd found no trace of his sister in all the long years he'd been searching for her, he still wanted justice. To take down those responsible for her abduction.

Did this woman have a mission too? Perhaps he'd find out.

'Indeed,' he murmured. 'And what would you have done if I didn't pay you?'

Her expression became very serious. 'I would have appealed to your better side.'

Humour that he didn't have to force for once wound through him, and he smiled, because really, she was such an innocent. 'You're assuming I have a better side.'

'Everyone has a better side, Mr Xenakis,' she said in the same serious tone, her gaze holding his, dark and velvety and soft.

And he found himself wondering if she really believed that. If she could see past all the filth he'd buried himself in. See past the despair the years of false hope had given him. If she could see who he'd used to be before the mission had consumed his life, before he'd lost Ismena…

Then again, when hadn't his mission consumed his life? Everything he'd done, every decision he'd made since he was fifteen years old, had been entirely about finding his sister.

Who even was he without it? Perhaps she knew, perhaps she could see. Perhaps this plain woman, this nobody, could tell him…

No, you need to get back on track. Forget about what you need, this is about justice for Ismena.

That was true. In which case he had plans for Miss Glory Albright.

She was a plain woman with an ordinary life, not a celebrity, not famous and very definitely not rich. And she could be exactly who he needed.

Yet, when he spoke, it wasn't the proposition he'd intended that came out of his mouth, but something else instead. 'Do you really believe that?' he heard himself ask, his voice gone a little rough. 'Do you really think everyone has a better side?'

She didn't hesitate. 'Of course. Some people's are more hidden than others, but everyone has one.' Her sharp little face suddenly softened, her mouth getting full and lush, and she smiled. 'For example, yours is quite hidden, I think. But it's there. It's definitely there.'

He didn't believe her, but he liked that she so obviously did.

She's not for you, fool.

Oh, he knew that, not that he wanted her, of course. At least, not in that way. But he could definitely use her and he would.

Castor leaned forward, his elbows on his knees, hands clasped between them. 'That's good,' he said. 'Because I have a proposition for you.'

CHAPTER THREE

GLORY WAS UNNERVED. Castor Xenakis's intensity was back again, a fierce glitter in his eyes that made her breath catch.

She couldn't look away.

A moment before he'd seemed to relax, the hard look on his face easing, his mouth curving in a smile. He was once again the charming man she'd seen flirting with the woman in his lap out in that room.

Except she suspected his charm was a mask he wore, that he could put on and take off at will. How she knew that, she wasn't sure, especially when he was still a stranger to her. But that was the thing about being polite and quiet. You got good at observing people, and since they pretty much forgot you were there, it was interesting watching how they reacted and how they behaved when they thought no one was looking. You got good at seeing things in them they probably didn't mean to reveal, secrets they thought they could hide.

She could tell this man had secrets, just as she could tell that despite his infamous reputation, he wasn't a bad person. A bad person wouldn't have cared Dimitri had touched her. A bad person would have let Dimitri take her away, not interrupted his evening to save her.

It didn't mean he wasn't dangerous though, because

whatever secret he was hiding, it seemed…painful. And she couldn't help being drawn to people in pain. She wanted to help them, wanted to make them feel better, and that wasn't something she should be doing for him.

He was notorious, a powerful stranger, not to mention disturbing in a way she couldn't put her finger on, and if she was sensible, what she should be doing was getting out of here, not listening to his proposition.

Perhaps you could use it to help Annabel?

Well, that was true. Perhaps she could.

'What proposition?' Glory asked cautiously.

His posture was casual, his long-fingered hands loosely clasped between his knees. Yet he seemed to vibrate with an intense, leashed energy, as if he was barely holding himself back from exploding into movement.

She had no idea why she found that so attractive, but she did. Then again, everything about him seemed designed to appeal, and not only to her but women in general.

'How would you feel,' he said, 'about marrying me?'

Glory blinked. Marry him? What? Surely she'd misheard. 'Excuse me?' she asked. 'I'm not sure…'

'You heard right.' His dark golden stare and the sheer perfection of his face were far more mesmerising than they had any right to be. 'I'm asking you if you'd considering marrying me.'

She blinked again. He couldn't be serious. He couldn't.

'I… I don't understand,' she began hesitantly. 'Wh-why would you want to do that?'

He remained perfectly still, energy crackling around him. Looking at her as if the very fate of the universe depended on her answer.

She'd never been looked at that way before. Never had

anyone stare at her with so much intensity, seeing her. Really *seeing* her.

It was disturbing and thrilling and frightening, and she didn't know what to do with herself.

'I have a…project that's important to me.' His voice was coloured with that warm richness she'd heard out in the living area. 'And the success of it involves presenting a certain facade. However, that facade does not mesh with my current reputation, which means I need some way of improving it.'

Glory frowned, not understanding. 'What kind of project? And how is marriage going to improve your reputation?'

He made a dismissive gesture. 'The project itself is confidential for a number of reasons. And as for my reputation, I'm hoping marriage to someone like you will improve my standing with certain…people.'

She frowned, her brain somehow skipping over the vague parts of his statement and settling on the thing that probably didn't matter. 'What do you mean, someone like me?'

He smiled the fake smile that he probably thought was charming, that he probably thought no one saw through. 'I meant no offense. It's only that you're not famous or rich, or powerful. You're a perfectly ordinary young woman, which in my world makes you rather… extraordinary.'

Glory already knew she was nothing special, she'd always known that. But for some reason she didn't like this beautiful man pointing it out to her.

You want to be special. Special and not a burden.

She ignored that thought, unfamiliar anger gathering inside her. 'Um, thank you,' she said and then, before she could think better of it, added, 'Though that's not really a compliment, is it?'

His smile flickered like a flame, warm and bright. And maybe if she hadn't been as sensitive to people as she was, she would have been charmed by it. But she could see the darkness behind that smile. It didn't quite reach his eyes.

And it came to her suddenly that it wasn't that horrible Dimitri who was the wolf in this scenario.

It was this man sitting in front of her.

'I'm not looking to compliment you,' he said. 'I'm looking to pay you.'

'Pay me?'

'What? You think I'd ask you to marry me out of the goodness of your heart? No, sweetheart. I won't pay you for your virginity, but I'll certainly pay you any sum you care to name for your hand in marriage.'

Glory could feel her heart thumping painfully hard behind her breastbone, shock moving slowly throughout her entire body.

When she'd come to this party, she'd thought it would only involve one night. She'd thought that if she somehow managed to catch his eye and he agreed to her offer, she'd lose her virginity in the best way possible: to the man she'd been admiring and desiring for months now.

But this was…not that. This was marriage in aid of some project he'd said was confidential. It seemed bizarre and strange, and considering his reputation, she shouldn't touch this offer with a ten-foot pole. Especially when it was clear a night with him wasn't on the table, which she couldn't help feeling disappointed about.

Except…he was looking at her so intently. As if he was desperate for her to say yes. As if he even needed her, which was odd considering he could have any woman he chose. He didn't specifically have to have her.

Does it matter why he wants you to marry him? If it means Annabel can have her treatment, then it doesn't matter.

True. As long as it wasn't anything illegal, of course, or something that would end up hurting someone.

He didn't say anything more, watching her, leaving the ball clearly in her court.

When he'd asked her whether she really believed he had a good side, she'd got the impression it was something he wanted to believe himself but didn't. She did though, even if she wasn't quite sure why.

Annabel called her naive sometimes and too optimistic for her own good, and maybe that was true. But trying to make the best of things and always looking for the silver lining had helped make things easier for her sister, who wasn't a bright-side kind of person.

'Well,' she said at last, still doubtful, yet at the same time oddly reluctant to disappoint him by refusing, 'This project of yours isn't illegal, is it? And it's not going to hurt anyone?'

Slowly, he shook his head.

'Okay,' she murmured. 'So…how would it even work?'

The corner of his mouth curled in the most fascinating way and it felt genuine this time, as if her answer had amused him, though she wasn't sure why. 'It'll be a marriage of convenience only and for…say, a year or two, not for ever, if that's what you're worried about. This would purely be for show.'

'Does it need to be legal though? You need an actual marriage?'

'I do. The people involved in this project might investigate and so I will need documentation to prove I am actually married.'

A shiver of unease went through her. 'What people? Investigate how?'

'I can't tell you that. Or at least, not yet.' The fierce glitter in his eyes burned. 'Well?'

He was driven, she could see that immediately. It was clear by the look in his amber gaze and in the vibrating, leashed energy that crackled around him. Driven by what, she had no idea, but whatever it was, it certainly drove him hard.

Curiosity tightened way down deep inside her. What on earth would compel a man like this one? A man who had everything. Everything she didn't. Ah, but it must be to do with that secret she'd sensed in him, that aura of pain.

You shouldn't be quite *so fascinated by him.*

No, she shouldn't. Especially when all those questions she kept asking herself weren't going to help her obsession with him.

Yet…she couldn't help herself. There were so many terrible rumours swirling around him and yet he didn't seem to be quite so bad in person. And that intrigued her probably far more than it should.

You should refuse him.

Maybe. Then again, there was Annabel.

Her sister had always wanted a family of her own and while cancer and her treatment had interrupted her plans for finding a partner, it had also sharpened her desire. She wanted a child before when and if the cancer returned, and Glory wanted to help her get her wish. She wanted it desperately.

'So…' Glory said carefully. 'What exactly would it entail?'

A smile lingered around his mouth. 'I'd need you to ostensibly live with me—we can stay in LA if you'd prefer, so you can be close to your sister. And then after a year, we'd get a divorce. I would arrange everything, all you would have to do is pretend to be madly in love with me.'

She stared at him in shock. 'What? Why?'

He seemed to find her response even more amusing, because his smile deepened and this time it did reach his eyes, making her feel hot, as if her skin was too tight for her body. 'I did mention the word "pretend" did I not? I only need the appearance of love, *mikri alepou*. I need this to be believable. The story of an ordinary girl capturing my heart, making me change my wicked ways and become a good family man will do wonders for this project of mine.'

She swallowed. 'I don't know… What did you call me?'

His expression softened. 'Little fox. It's Greek.'

'F-fox?'

He ignored her. 'Think of the money, Miss Albright. This wouldn't involve your virginity. You wouldn't have to sleep with me. I won't demand anything from you but your signature on the register and your presence for a couple of weeks. Nothing too onerous.' He tilted his head, gazing at her from beneath gold-tipped lashes. 'I have an island in Greece that would make a lovely wedding venue, so wouldn't you like a vacation? Some time in the sun? Perhaps you'd even like to go to Europe for a honeymoon, see some monuments.'

Her head was spinning and she wasn't sure if it was his offer or just him and the way he looked at her. Not the charming smile or the practised warmth, but the ferocity she could sense just below the surface of him. The wolf hiding in the skin of a man.

Hungry, that was what he was, though what he was hungry for, she had no idea. It wasn't sexual, she didn't think, but then how would she be able to tell? No one had looked at her like that before. No one ever had.

What does it matter that he wants a marriage? It's not for ever. And you'll get a couple of nice weeks' vacation and Annabel will get her dream.

That was true, but he'd also mentioned how he wanted whoever these people were to think theirs was some kind of great love story. Which would involve her pretending she was in love with him, and how was she going to do that? She might be obsessed with him, sure, but that wasn't love. Plus, she'd never been good at pretending.

Aren't you though? Haven't you been pretending your whole life? Pretending you didn't mind that Annabel had to give up her dreams for you. That dropping out of school to care for her was exactly what you wanted. That working at the Jessups' was a good, steady job. That you didn't have dreams of your own...

Glory shut those thoughts down hard. Her dreams were of a steady job, earning enough to live on, paying off her debt and making sure Annabel was happy. That was it.

'I don't care about vacations,' she said flatly, because it felt important that he know that. 'I'm not doing this for me.'

His mouth quirked in a cynical smile. 'Of course you're not.'

'It isn't like that,' she insisted. 'All of this is for my sister. For IVF treatment. She wants a baby.'

'A baby,' he repeated, frowning, as if he didn't know what the word meant.

'Yes, she had breast cancer. It's in remission now and so she wants to try for a child. She brought me up after our parents died and so I'd... I'd like to do something nice for her.'

Why are you telling him all this?

She had no idea. The words just kept coming. 'I mean, she had to give up a lot of things for me and then she got cancer, which really wasn't fair so I thought I could make sure that at least one of us got what we wanted.'

Castor leaned back against the couch again, his long legs stretched out under the coffee table. Again, he seemed relaxed, but she knew he wasn't, not with those fierce wolf eyes looking at her.

'Only one of you?' he asked lazily. 'And what is it that you wanted?'

You want him. That's what you want.

'It doesn't matter what I want,' she said tartly, ignoring that thought too, because she certainly wasn't going to tell him that. 'Annabel wanted a child as soon as she could in case her cancer came back.'

He was quiet for a long moment, studying her. Then he said, 'I'll pay for your sister's IVF. As many rounds as it takes, and also for any follow-up treatment. I'll clear your medical debt and any other debt too. You have my word.'

Her mouth went dry. All those debts, that terrible mountain of money that there was no hope of her ever paying back in her lifetime, crushing her, crushing Annabel, just...gone.

She could hardly imagine it.

'It's a l-lot of m-money,' she croaked.

He smiled, practised and charming, as if it was no big deal. 'Then isn't it lucky I'm very rich?'

'You can't possibly—'

'Of course I can.' That brow lifted again. 'Well? Do we have a deal, Miss Albright?'

Glory's eyes had gone round with shock, her hands clenched on her thighs.

He couldn't blame her. Money solved a lot of problems and it was clear from the look on her face that those problems had been large ones. He knew that feeling though, where you realised that all the things that had been hanging over you, the insurmountable difficulties, were suddenly gone.

He'd felt that way after he'd made his first million. The heady rush of knowing there was only one direction to go in from here and that was up. More money, more power. He wasn't that fifteen-year-old boy trying to find his sister in the chaos of the Athens streets. Going from place to place hoping someone would help. But nobody had because nobody cared, not even the police.

He was poor and alone and probably lying, so why should they?

It had been in those dark days after Ismena's disappearance that he'd decided. He'd taken his eye off her for one second and she'd gone, so he wouldn't make that mistake again. He would be focused, intent, and he'd pull himself out of these streets. He'd get all the money and power, and then he would find her.

So that's what he'd done. And that's what he was doing even all these years later, still trying to find her. Still trying to save other people—women mainly—who'd been caught in the net. He wouldn't let any other brother, father, uncle go through what he had, and he'd use whatever he could to achieve that.

Including the young woman sitting opposite him.

Hope was a difficult commodity to hang on to, or so he'd found, but if marrying this woman was what he needed to do in order to take down that trafficking ring, then he'd do it without a second's thought.

This woman with her soft, dark eyes and her assurance that everyone had a good side…

She was certainly determined, and he'd liked very much how loyal she was to her sister. It made him think of himself and how far he'd gone for his, and how far he was still prepared to go if he could even find one hint that she was still alive.

Glory's pretty mouth had firmed, the wrestling match she was obviously having with herself clear in her expression.

Well, he hadn't expected her to agree immediately despite the incentive he'd offered. It was already plain she wasn't of his world where money ruled and people would do anything for a taste of power including selling themselves.

She'd come here to do the same thing, with no idea of the cost it would exact. No idea of the scars it would leave, because the things you did when you were desperate always left scars.

Are you sure you're that desperate? Marrying you will put her in danger.

It would, but he had the resources to protect her. And in a year or so, once the fuss of the marriage had died down, no one would even know who he was married to, he'd make sure of it. She could fade back into the obscurity she'd come from.

And yes, he was that desperate.

'You want an answer now?' There was a deep crease between her brows. 'I really need to think about it.'

Unfamiliar impatience twisted in his gut.

'What do you need to think about?' he asked. 'Fundamentally, *mikri alepou*, what it comes down to is this: it's either worth it for you or it isn't.'

Her hands clenched on her thighs again, drawing attention to the soft round shape of them beneath her dress. More hair had come down from her ridiculous bun, curls lying glossy and gleaming a deep reddish brown over her skin. She had little freckles scattered over one shoulder, disappearing under the strap of her dress and he was gripped by a sudden, intense urge to shift that strap to one side so he could see them better.

He shifted, impatience tangling with the heat collecting inside him, making him feel restless and agitated.

Really, what was it about this woman that got him so hot under the collar? He never normally had such problems ignoring what was basically a mere physical attraction.

She didn't seem to notice his tension, letting out a breath and catching her full lower lip between her teeth. And despite himself, he found his gaze drifting to the press of her white teeth against the soft, red fullness of her mouth.

If he were to bite her like that, would she taste as sweet as she seemed? Like honey? Or would she taste more like sugar?

Why don't you bite her and find out?

The thought drifted like smoke through his head and for half a second he found himself contemplating it. Of charming her, seducing her. Burying his hands in her curls, taking that soft lip between his teeth, and biting down. Not too hard. Just enough to make her gasp and maybe—

Theos, what the hell was he doing? That was *not* happening.

Glory huffed out a breath, her chin firming as if she'd made a decision.

Castor forcibly corralled his wayward thoughts and lifted a brow questioningly.

'Okay,' she said. 'Fine. I'll do it. I'll marry you.'

A spike of satisfaction caught him, sharp and bright, though he made sure not to let it show. 'Excellent. In that case, I'll get the necessary—'

'But I have some requirements.' She gave him a severe look, as if she expected him to argue.

He almost wanted to, just to tease her, but now was not the time for games. 'What requirements?' he asked instead, without inflection.

Glory held up a finger. 'First, I'd like the money for my sister's first round of IVF right away, because the sooner we start, the more chances she'll have. Secondly.' She held up another finger. 'I need your assurance that this is a marriage in name only. I d-don't want to…sleep with you.'

First a stutter, then a hesitation. What was that all about? She was a virgin so it could just be discomfort with the subject of sex. Then again, hadn't she come here intending to offer him sex? Yes, she'd been nervous in her offer, but it wasn't as if the thought of sleeping with him hadn't crossed her mind.

What did she think about that?

Why do you want to know? You're not going to sleep with her after all.

Well, no, he wasn't. Yet even though it wasn't the time for games, Castor couldn't help himself. The temptation to test her was too irresistible. 'Are you sure? You didn't seem to mind the prospect when you came here to sell your virginity to me.'

She reddened, but to her credit didn't look away. 'I

didn't want to sleep with you. I was prepared to do it for Annabel's sake, that's all.'

He might have believed her if she hadn't been blushing and if that protest hadn't sounded just a touch hollow.

'Quite the sacrificial lamb, aren't you?'

'Not at all,' she said with quiet dignity. 'I don't mind. My sister is important to me and I want her to have some of the things she missed out on.'

That sobered him. Because if there was one thing he understood, it was the importance of one's sister.

'Very well.' He dropped the teasing tone. 'The money issue won't be a problem, and I'm certainly not going to be demanding my marital rights from you. However, as I said, I want this to look as real as possible, and while that won't entail actual sex, it will require more than a handshake.'

The marriage had to look real even if it wasn't. It had to stand up to scrutiny in case anyone got suspicious of him and decided to investigate. Certainly once word got out, the press would be interested and if there had to be pictures, he wanted pictures of a couple in love. Nothing else would be convincing.

Her dark eyes narrowed. 'What more are we talking about?'

'Have you never watched a pair of lovers, *alepou mou*? Do you really not understand what's involved?'

Irritation flashed over her face, which intrigued him. She might have been afraid before, and definitely nervous now, but it seemed as if she was comfortable enough with him to be annoyed at him.

'I understand, Mr Xenakis.' A small, dark flame of temper burned in her eyes. 'I might be a virgin and rather naive, but I'm not stupid.'

He could feel another unexpected smile curving his

mouth, which was unheard of. How strange. Genuine amusement was something he thought he'd lost years ago.

'You should probably start calling me Castor,' he reminded her gently. 'I'm not sure many women outside a Regency novel call their husbands "mister."'

More colour flushed her cheeks, turning them a very pretty pink. 'No, I suppose not,' she muttered. 'C-Castor.'

He didn't know why he liked the way she stuttered slightly over his name, but he did.

'Much better,' he murmured. 'However, to answer your questions, I suspect you are not, in fact, stupid. And as to what more I require, obviously I'm going to need to touch you.'

The blush made her eyes seem even darker. 'Touch me? Touch me how?'

He was being deliberately opaque and he knew it. Mainly because he'd forgotten how delightful it was to fluster a woman. It certainly didn't happen with the women he associated with these days. Women who were as jaded as he was and who didn't get either shocked or surprised by much. Oh, he flirted with them, but it was all rote, both his responses and theirs.

This wasn't though. Her responses were natural and delightful, and that blush... She sparkled when she blushed. He liked it. He wanted more of it.

'Well,' he said, dropping his voice into a low, seductive purr. 'I'll probably want to hold your hand. And maybe put an arm around you, pulling you close. Then quite possibly I might put a finger under your chin and tilt your head back. Perhaps I may even kiss you. For the cameras, you understand. Just a light brush across your lips, nothing too risqué.'

The blush in her cheeks became deeper and deeper

as he spoke, but she didn't move, continuing to stare at him as if she'd never seen him before in her entire life.

'And after that, I might want you to do the same things to me. Hold my hand. Lean in close. Look at me as though you adore me. Kiss me as if you can't wait for a taste.' He met her gaze, held it. 'It's not sex. At the most it'll be a couple of kisses, I give you my word. So what do you think, *mikri alepou*? Is that something you'll be able to contemplate?'

Glory blinked. Raised a hand to her mouth and coughed. 'I'm not sure,' she said, her voice husky. 'I've never kissed anyone before.'

Surprise flickered through him. While it was clear she was inexperienced, he hadn't thought she'd be *that* inexperienced.

'No one?' he asked, more sharply than he'd intended. 'No one at all?'

She shifted on the couch in an irritated fashion. 'You don't have to sound *so* shocked. It's not that strange to not have kissed anyone before. I just never met anyone I was interested in. Anyway, I didn't have the time for boyfriends.'

'I'm not shocked. More surprised.'

'Why? It wasn't totally my fault. No one ever showed any interest in me. I mean, after all, you said yourself that I'm a very ordinary young woman.'

He heard it then, the soft edge of hurt in her voice.

You shouldn't have said that.

No and especially not when he was starting to suspect that it wasn't true. Because if she'd been a very ordinary young woman, he wouldn't find the idea of flustering her quite so delightful, or the idea of kissing her quite so erotic.

'Does it matter what I said?' he murmured, watching her.

'No.' She looked down at her hands, a silky curl slipping over one shoulder and over the swell of her breast.

She was lying through her teeth.

There were too many things in Castor's life that he regretted. Too many things that were broken beyond repair. But this small hurt he could fix.

'I was wrong,' he murmured. 'I don't think you're ordinary after all.'

'It's okay, you don't need to lie.'

'I'm not lying. In fact, if you come over here I'll show you just how ordinary I think you are.'

CHAPTER FOUR

CASTOR'S SMOKY AMBER gaze burned from beneath dark, gold-streaked lashes, making it difficult for Glory to look at him without her breath catching.

He was just too…male, too beautiful. Too much of everything.

Why did you ever think you could handle him?

She had no idea. What she did know was that agreeing to this preposterous idea was a terrible mistake.

Yet, what else could she do? She'd come here for Annabel and the thought of leaving empty-handed was impossible. She had no other ideas about how to get the money Annabel needed. This was it.

And you want him too, don't deny it.

Okay, so she did. But that thought scared her. *He* scared her. Not that he would hurt her, not when he'd had plenty of opportunity to take what he wanted from her and hadn't. No, it was more about how fast her heart was beating and how tight her skin felt.

How she'd argued with him instead of apologising and hadn't immediately done what he'd said without protest.

How hot her cheeks were when he'd talked to her about kissing her and about how she might kiss him in return.

She couldn't even imagine it.

Can't you? Can't you imagine getting up and moving over to him. Bending and kissing that beautiful mouth...

Her face flamed.

He tilted his head slightly, obviously taking note. 'What are you thinking about? Something nice? Perhaps something to do with me?'

'No. No, I—'

'Well?' One corner of his mouth lifted. 'Are you going to give me a chance to show you? Or are we going to do this at another time?'

'This?' Her brain wouldn't work. Nothing seemed to work, not with him staring at her like that.

'We need to be comfortable with each other.' His voice deepened into something that resembled a purr. 'Which means you're going to have to get used to me being close. I understand that this might be too soon, so if you don't want to do this now, we can leave it a couple of days.'

Him being close. The very idea of it...

I could hold your hand...tilt your head back...just a light brush across your lips...

She could almost feel it too, the press of his mouth to hers. It sent sparks cascading all over her skin.

No, this was insane. She was letting him get to her far too easily. She needed to pull herself together, not sit there staring at him with her mouth open like a landed fish.

And being totally practical about it, he wasn't wrong. She did have to get used to him being close, especially if he wanted it to look real. So perhaps she should stop thinking about it and just do it. Get it over with. Besides, a kiss was the very least thing she'd thought she'd end up having to deal with tonight.

'No,' she said, then cleared her throat and said it again. 'No. Tonight will be fine.'

He shifted, a subtle movement that drew her attention to the length of his muscular body. To the white cotton of his shirt pulling tight over the width of his wide shoulders and broad chest, and the wool of his trousers constricting around his powerful thighs.

Oh, holy…

'Are you sure?' His voice wrapped around her like warm velvet. 'Like I said, we can wait a day or two if you'd rather.'

He's putting it on, all this charm. You know that, right? He's trying to seduce you.

The thought caught at her like a thorn and she glanced at him, looking past the blinding charisma, directly into the dark amber of his gaze.

And she expected to see the same cold deliberation she'd seen when he'd smiled at her initially, how the warmth didn't touch his eyes.

She was even bracing herself for it.

But it came as a shock to find it wasn't there. Neither was the warmth. Instead there was something far hotter, an ember of that fierceness she'd seen lurking beneath the surface of his charm. An intensity that made her throat close.

Why though? And what did it mean? Was he attracted to her?

It seemed impossible that a man of his beauty and power could feel anything at all for an ordinary woman like her, yet she couldn't get rid of the thought. It made her feel good. Made her feel…strong. As if, perhaps, she might be able to handle him after all.

'No,' she said slowly, staring back at him. 'I think tonight is good.'

Then she pushed herself to her feet.

He watched her a moment, then slowly did the same, rising to his full height in a graceful, athletic movement.

Scraping together the remains of her courage, Glory took a couple of steps in his direction, then stopped, her heart thumping.

Amusement filled his gaze and it was genuine. 'You'll have to come closer than that, *mikri alepou.*'

Little fox...

She'd never had a nickname. Never had anyone use an endearment. Annabel called her 'Glor' sometimes, and that was okay, but it didn't make her shiver the way she shivered when Castor murmured in Greek.

'Yes, I do know that, thank you,' she said, then immediately felt bad for sounding cross. 'Sorry. That was rude.'

'You're very polite, aren't you?'

'Of course. It costs nothing and it makes people happy.'

'You like making people happy?'

'It's better than making them sad. There's enough sadness in this world already.' She wiped her palms surreptitiously against her thighs. 'So, what should I do first?'

'I think I suggested holding your hand.' He held his out, a hint of challenge in his eyes. 'Please tell me you've at least held hands with someone before.'

'No,' she said, because why bother lying?

The heat in his eyes wavered a second and he frowned, as if her answer had personally offended him somehow. 'What? Why the hell not?'

'Because I never met anyone I liked enough, I told you.' And it was true, she hadn't. Not when every single man she'd ever met had seemed to pale into insignificance compared to the Castor Xenakis she'd read about in her magazines.

'I see,' he said, sounding sceptical. 'Well, it's nothing

to be afraid of.' He held his hand out more insistently. 'Come, *mikri alepou.*'

This was silly. If she couldn't even get up the courage to hold his hand, then how was she ever supposed to pretend to be his new bride?

Why did you ever think you could do this at all? It was a stupid idea and you know it, and Annabel would be appalled. You're just going to create more problems for her, like you always do...

No. *No*, that wasn't true. She was going to help her sister and if holding hands with this man, if marrying him, was what she had to do, then she'd do it.

Glory took a silent breath, lifted her chin and reached for his hand.

And all the breath left her lungs as his long, strong fingers closed around hers.

His skin was warm, his grip firm, and it was strange, but the second he closed her hand in his, something inside her relaxed at the same moment as something else gave a little thrum of excitement.

She blinked at the sensation and stared at him, searching his beautiful face, wanting to know if he felt it too.

His expression was opaque and even though he seemed relaxed, there was a tension to him. She took a step closer, curious to know what was going on, but his lashes swept down, veiling his gaze. 'And now,' he murmured. 'I'm going to put my arm around you and pull you in close.'

Before she had a chance to move, he lifted his other hand, sliding his arm around her waist and drawing her into his side.

She tensed, waiting to feel uneasy at being so close to him. Yet the unease didn't come. Instead there was only a restless heat and a fluttering excitement that crowded in her throat.

Because beneath his lashes, his gaze had turned smokier, brighter gold glinting in the amber depths, a glimpse of the wolf.

The excitement fluttered harder, that rebellious part of her liking that she could rouse the predator in him. A scary thought, yet also thrilling.

Did he feel this too, then? This heat? This excitement? Or was it all only her?

Castor drew her in closer until she was barely inches away. He towered over her, all wide shoulders, broad chest and hard, masculine strength, and she should have felt threatened by it, but she didn't. She felt safe and almost…protected, which was a strange thing to feel when this man's reputation had him being a predator of the worst kind.

He smelled warm, of that exotic spice, and for absolutely no reason that she could see her mouth watered.

She blinked up at him, fascinated by that wolfish glint in his eyes.

'How is this?' His voice was soft and deep, a caress of rough velvet.

'G-good,' she stuttered breathlessly.

He kept his gaze on hers as he slowly lifted her hand and brought it to rest on his chest, holding it there in his own warm grip.

She took another shaky breath, aware of the warm cotton of his shirt and, beneath that, the rock-hard plane of his chest.

'And this?' He looked down at her, gauging her reaction.

She'd never been this close to a man before, let alone this man. Never had his arm around her waist, one palm resting gently in the small of her back, while his other hand held hers to his chest. Never been pressed lightly against the length of a hard, masculine body, never felt his heat.

She'd fantasised a little about what it would feel like to have him touch her—nothing beyond a few light kisses since she'd found the thought of anything else too overwhelming—but the reality was…different. So much hotter. So much more exciting.

If you feel like this now, what will a kiss do to you?

Oh, nothing but destroy her in the best possible way.

'It's good,' she whispered, because it was, and this time she didn't stutter at all.

Castor released her hand, but kept holding her. 'Now, what did I say I'd do? Oh, yes… I lift your chin and tilt your head back.'

There was a warm fingertip beneath her chin, exerting a light pressure, easing her head back so she was looking directly up into that fascinating dark golden gaze of his.

It was obvious now, that fierce glitter. That…hunger, and for some reason it was fixating on her. She didn't know why. What there was about her, plain old Glory Albright, a checkout girl in a tiny grocery store, that made him, one of the most notorious playboys in the world, look at her like that.

Whatever it was though, it terrified her. It also left her trembling with excitement and a hunger that came from somewhere deep inside. A hunger that was entirely selfish, and not at all quiet or polite. A hunger for what came next, because she knew what that was. He'd told her. A kiss.

She quivered, waiting.

Except he didn't move, his gaze glinting gold.

Glory took a breath, then another. But still he waited. And a surge of impatience went through her. Because she didn't know why he was holding back and she didn't want him to.

He was so very close. All she'd have to do to reach that beautiful mouth would be to go up on her tiptoes. It wasn't far, not very far at all...

She'd come here for Annabel, it was true. Yet right in this moment it wasn't Annabel she was thinking about, but herself and what she wanted.

She was thinking about all those months of obsession and desire for something she could never have. About how she could have that now if only she had the courage. And she did have it. That's why she was still here after all.

So Glory rose up on her toes and pressed her mouth to his.

He went very still.

His lips were warm and softer than she'd expected, and they felt as amazing against hers as she thought they would. He smelled delicious and she was fascinated by the heat seeping through the cotton of his shirt and into her hand. Was he as hot like that everywhere? Was he as hard?

Her breathing was coming very fast and she wasn't sure what to do next. How, exactly, did you kiss a man? She'd obviously seen kissing before on TV, but she was pretty sure that it wasn't actually like that. You were supposed to do something with your tongue, weren't you?

You idiot. You're going to make a total ass of yourself.

A sudden wave of embarrassment at her own inexperience washed through her. Annabel had always told her she was too impulsive, that she needed to be more restrained, and this was in no way restrained.

He probably hated the kiss. He probably thought she was ridiculous and silly.

Blushing, Glory came down off her tiptoes. 'Sorry,' she muttered and tried to pull away.

Except he didn't let her go. If anything his grip on her firmed, holding her right where she was.

'Glory, look at me.' His voice had gone very deep and even rougher than before, and this time there was an unmistakable command in it.

She didn't want to look at him, didn't want to see what she knew was going to be distaste in his expression, but she was helpless to resist the command.

His eyes had gone a deep, brilliant shade of gold. 'Kiss me again, *mikri alepou.*'

Castor stayed very still, every instinct screaming at him to let her go. That this was a mistake. This was *all* a mistake. And he'd known it the moment he'd taken her hand.

Her skin had felt so soft and warm, her hand small, fitting his palm to perfection. And she'd looked at him with such wide eyes, as if holding his hand had been the most amazing experience of her life.

Drawing her closer had felt natural and even with his instincts telling him not to, he hadn't been able to stop. He had to anyway, he'd told himself. They couldn't pretend to be in love without touching each other and she needed to be comfortable with him.

Now he was touching her, holding her, and she'd just about brought him to his knees with an expected kiss.

He couldn't believe it. It had hardly even been a kiss. And he wasn't sure why he'd responded to it so powerfully, yet the moment her soft mouth had pressed to his he'd felt as if she'd lit him with a match and he was about to go up in flames.

Chemistry, of course, though why he should have it

with this sweet little innocent who had no idea how to even kiss properly was a complete mystery.

As was why he was still holding her when he was close to breaking point.

As was also why he'd commanded her to kiss him again, as if another kiss was the answer to this dilemma.

Wonder glowed in her eyes as she looked up at him, her cheeks fiery with her blush, her freckles like stars scattered over her skin.

He'd thought her plain initially, yet now he was struggling to understand why when it was so obvious that she wasn't plain in the slightest. Unusual, yes, but not plain. Not with that creamy skin and those dark, velvety eyes. That determined chin and that full little mouth.

She gave him a worried look. 'Are you sure?'

He could see her pulse at the base of her throat. It was beating fast yet she wasn't scared. She'd been scared before, when he'd brought her in here, but she wasn't now.

She was warm in his arms, her soft curves pressing deliciously against his hard angles, her scent very feminine, sweet and citrusy. Was that her perfume? Body lotion? He liked it very much.

'Kiss me,' he said roughly, the impatience he'd been struggling to deal with getting the better of him. 'Now.'

'But I'm not very good at—'

He took her mouth again before she could finish and all thought left his head.

She didn't resist and automatically he firmed his grip on her chin and took control, at first staying still to let her get used to the feeling, before he moved his mouth on hers slowly, showing her how it was done.

She'd stilled, and not, he thought, out of shock, but as if she was simply waiting for more. So he gave her more.

His tongue touched her lips in a brief taste. And then a

couple more times. Touching the corner of her mouth and then the centre, before following the line of her lower lip. Then a few butterfly kisses, light brushes of his mouth on hers, tantalising her.

She trembled, her breath catching.

His hunger growled, but he ignored it. For some inexplicable reason he was close to the edge and he refused to let himself go over, not for one kiss given to him by a virgin.

No, he'd go carefully, show her a little more and then pull back. This was her first kiss after all, if what she'd told him was correct, and there was no point in scaring her.

But then Glory blew all his plans out of the water.

She slid both her arms around his neck and opened her mouth beneath his.

Heat engulfed him, the fire she'd lit leaping high, and slow and careful and gentle went abruptly out the window.

He pushed his tongue into her mouth, kissing her hard, chasing the sweet taste of her and finding yet more heat, yet more sweetness. He began to explore, hunger building inside him, and before he knew what was happening, his hands were where they'd wanted to be since she'd first thrown off that ridiculous cloak, buried deep in her hair. It was as soft as he'd imagined, like raw silk.

He closed his fingers in it, tugging her head back further, tasting her deeper as heat expanded between them. She melted, pressing all those soft, lush curves against him, making a desperate little sound, as if she wanted to get even closer to him, but still wasn't close enough.

In the back of his mind, something screamed at him that he was making an even bigger mistake, but somehow it got lost under the sudden explosion of desire that was

pulsing through him. The desire to push her up against
the wall, drag up the hem of her dress and bury himself
inside her. Lose himself and forget for a few brief minutes the mission that consumed his every waking thought
and the loss that wouldn't leave him alone.

Her arms tightened and he was achingly aware that
the soft heat between her thighs was pressing against
the front of his trousers. Against his aching sex. It made
him growl deep in his throat, made him let go of her hair
and put a hand to the small of her back, fitting her more
firmly against him.

She sighed into his mouth, kissing him back, still inexperienced, yet bolder now, with a sweet edge of demand that made him want to give her everything she
was asking for.

Then she gave a little gasp, wriggling against him, and
he realised with sudden shock that he *had* pushed her up
against the wall. But she wasn't wriggling to get away,
she was wriggling to get closer, pressing herself against
him in a way he knew well.

She wanted him. She was desperate for him.

*You can't do this. You can't take her. Where the hell
is your control?*

He didn't know. Somehow it was gone. One young,
inexperienced and ordinary young woman had made it
disappear with a kiss.

Appalled at himself, Castor grabbed what was left of
it—and it was disturbing how much strength even that
took—and let her go, shoving himself away from her.

He was breathing hard—too hard—and before he
knew what he was doing, he'd put a hand through his
hair and had begun adjusting his clothing like a prim
Regency miss who'd just been taken advantage of.

Glory was leaning against the wall, her eyes dark,

her cheeks flushed, her mouth full and red from the effects of that kiss.

She looked shell-shocked and he was gripped by a sudden, sickening doubt that she hadn't wanted this, that he'd taken advantage of her, that the company he kept had stained him irretrievably and he couldn't be trusted.

Yet before he could get a word out, she said, 'I'm so sorry, Castor. I shouldn't have done that.'

For a second he could only stare at her, not understanding what she was apologising for when all of this had been his fault.

'Why are you sorry?' He knew he should temper his voice, make it gentle, make it warm and charming. But there was no charm left in him. 'I shouldn't have pushed you up against the wall, and I shouldn't have asked for that kiss. And I should be the one apologising.'

Glory looked stricken. 'Why? What happened? Did I do it wrong? It was probably terrible. I've never kissed anyone before so no wonder—'

'Wait.' He held up a hand, trying to understand what on earth she was talking about. 'What do you mean "it was probably terrible"?'

She was making small fluttering gestures with her hands as if she didn't know what to do with them. 'I… well… It's just that it was no wonder you pushed me away. I'm not very good at this.'

'You think I ended the kiss because it was terrible?'

Her cheeks had gone even redder, making those pretty freckles stand out. 'Isn't that why? You didn't want my… uh…what I was trying to sell you earlier and then I just kind of k-kissed you and—'

'Stop,' he ordered and even though he knew it was probably better for both of them if he let her believe he hadn't been moved by that kiss, he couldn't lie to her like that. 'Let me be clear. I didn't end that kiss because I wanted to. I ended that kiss because I wanted to keep going.'

Her mouth opened, her gaze wide and shocked, as if she didn't quite believe what he was saying.

'And now,' he went on. 'Since I have a fair few things to organise, I'll let Corinna see you home. I'll be in touch, Glory Albright.'

Then before she could speak, he turned and strode from the room.

Before he changed his mind and continued where they'd left off.

CHAPTER FIVE

GLORY SPENT THE next couple of days half thinking what had happened in Castor Xenakis's mansion was a dream. That she hadn't really gone there offering to sell him her virginity. That he hadn't got angry and refused her, before suddenly turning around and asking her to marry him for…reasons he then wouldn't tell her. And that she hadn't taken his hand, risen up on her toes and kissed him.

A kiss that had set her entire world on fire.

It was too bright a memory. Like the sun, she couldn't look at it directly without being blinded by the heat of that moment.

His mouth on hers. The demand of it. His hands in her hair, exerting the most delicious pressure. The feel of his body, hard and strong and so hot. The way he'd kissed her, as if he wanted to consume her whole…

It was everything she'd ever imagined and her entire being shivered in response.

Then he'd looked at her like he'd never seen anything like her in his entire life. As if she was something totally new and different and he didn't know what to make of her.

She'd liked that. She'd never been new and different to

anyone before, still less a man as experienced and worldly as him. And yes, she'd liked that *very* much indeed.

She'd been delivered home that night in a sleek black car driven by one of Castor's staff members, and as she'd stumbled into the run-down apartment she shared with Annabel, she'd felt oddly like Cinderella. Except the car had disappeared into the LA night instead of turning back into a pumpkin, and her dress and shoes remained, looking as cheap and tacky as they had when she'd put them on at the beginning of the evening.

She'd told Annabel before she'd left that she was going out with friends, which her sister had been vaguely suspicious of since Glory didn't really have friends, but luckily Annabel had been asleep by the time she'd let herself inside, so she didn't get the third degree about her evening.

Half bracing herself for it the next morning, it was a relief to find Annabel too distracted about some email she'd just received to be concerned about Glory's night out. The email had apparently informed her that she was the lucky recipient of a special grant from a charity who helped cancer patients achieve their baby dreams with subsidised IVF.

Glory blinked in surprise as Annabel relayed all of this, because she'd never heard of such a charity. But as Annabel went on excitedly, Glory realised that there was only one person who could have organised it.

Castor. And he was making good on his promise.

Relief flooded through her and she had to look away so Annabel wouldn't see it. Because not only had he kept his word, he'd done it so that Glory wouldn't have to make any uncomfortable confessions.

Of course, the tricky thing now was that since he'd upheld his end of the bargain, she was going to have to uphold hers.

The thought made her feel scared and excited at the same time. Scared because it was marriage she'd promised him, and excited because he'd mentioned travel, which she'd always wanted to do, and…well…*him*.

'What's up?' Annabel asked. 'You're looking very pleased with yourself all of a sudden.'

Glory flushed. Great, now she'd have to think up some lie since she couldn't exactly tell her sister what was really happening. About how her IVF grant was really from an infamous playboy who was only paying for it because Glory had agreed to a marriage of convenience with him. *After* he'd refused to buy her virginity.

Yes, that would go down like a lead balloon.

'Oh,' she said, thinking frantically about what to say that Annabel would believe. 'I…um…entered a competition. To win a… European holiday. And I was just imagining winning it.'

Her sister, predictably, frowned. 'Oh, Glory. Really?' And there it was, the usual disappointment in her tone. 'I hope you didn't have to pay any money. You won't win, you do know that, don't you?'

How do you know that? Glory wanted to ask her sister. *The chances are small, yes, but just because they're small doesn't mean it won't happen.*

But this was an old argument. Her sister's glass-half-empty outlook and her determination to make sure Glory didn't 'get her hopes up' had been a constant in Glory's life. Normally she didn't bother quarrelling about it, since she didn't like upsetting Annabel, but for some reason today it needled her.

Because wasn't it better to have some hopes rather than none? Otherwise what was there to strive for?

Says the woman who has striven for nothing but working at the Jessups' grocery store.

Glory ignored that thought. There was nothing wrong with working at the Jessups' store. It was a good, steady job and it paid the bills. Perhaps one day she'd think about what else she wanted from her life, but that day was not today.

'No, I didn't pay any money,' she said, 'but you're probably right, I won't win.'

The next day, she was kneeling on the cracked lino of the tiny, narrow aisle of the store, stacking tinned vegetables, when she heard the bell above the door ring, signalling a customer.

Getting to her feet, Glory went down the aisle to the counter, only to come face to face with a man in an extremely expensive, elegant suit who gave her a judgmental up-and-down look before asking, 'Are you Miss Glory Albright?'

Trying to resist the urge to wipe her sweaty palms on her stained jeans, Glory nodded.

The man held out a white, thick-looking envelope. 'Your contract, Miss Albright. Mr. Xenakis wishes an immediate reply.'

She blinked at the envelope, reality suddenly crashing down hard. 'Oh,' she said stupidly. 'Immediately?'

The man inclined his head. 'Indeed. The contract has been looked over by an independent and neutral party, and Mr. Xenakis sends his assurances that it is all aboveboard.'

Glory took the envelope and stared at it.

You can't sign this. This is marriage you're talking about. Marriage to a man you don't even know, who could be every bad thing they say about him and more. It's a mistake and you know it.

It probably was. And as to marriage, well, he'd been clear it was a marriage of convenience only. It was almost like a…job. Yes, that's how she needed to look at it. Which meant that this was her employment contract. And anyway, she'd promised him she'd do this, and she always kept her promises.

Glory took the contract, signed it quickly and gave it back to the man, before she could second-guess herself.

There. It was done. No backing out now.

Not long after that, an email arrived in her inbox that contained nothing but a date and a time, a request for some details for a passport and an attached itinerary, detailing flights to Athens.

Athens. She was going to Athens.

Glory knew she should reply requesting more information, such as how long she'd be going and what to bring, and what about her passport since she didn't have one. But part of her didn't want to ask. Part of her was thrilled at the mystery of it, since mystery had been sorely lacking in her life up until this point.

She'd dreamed as a kid of princesses and castles, of dragons and white knights. She'd wanted adventures and expeditions, and fairy tales. But then her and Annabel's parents had died and all the adventures and fairy tales had died with them.

There had only been Annabel, tired and grief-stricken, trying to look after a flighty, dreamy and far too imaginative ten-year-old. Always telling Glory that she had to be quiet, behave, not talk to strangers, not sing in the hallways or fight pretend battles in the stairwells. That she had to stay in the background, keep her head down, stop being 'silly.' That dreams were nice, but reality was where everyone lived and that's where she had to live too.

Except not today. Because here was her adventure, staring her in the face. A fairy tale complete with a handsome prince. And while fairy tales weren't supposed to happen to ordinary people—as her sister liked to say—perhaps sometimes they did.

So Glory decided she wasn't going to ask for more information. She wasn't going to ruin it with boring, crappy reality. She was going to have her mysterious, thrilling adventure while she had the chance.

There were a few details she was going to have to figure out though, such as what to tell her sister. Annabel would definitely have words to say about a marriage of convenience to an infamous billionaire, but whatever those words were, Glory didn't want to hear them.

Annabel would worry and no doubt try to talk her out of it, and Glory didn't want to have to deal with either of those things. Plus, she didn't want to have to explain how she'd met Castor, not yet.

Which meant she was going to have to lie.

It wasn't ideal, because eventually her sister would find out the truth. But Glory needed some time to think about how to break the news that not only was she married, but she was going to be living in Castor's mansion. Then there was the question of her job and what she was going to do about that, but again, that was something she'd deal with later.

She took a couple of days to brace herself, then she asked the Jessups for some time off—which they grudgingly gave her—and then one night over dinner mentioned to Annabel that, actually, she'd won her competition and that she'd be flying to Greece next week.

Her sister was flabbergasted and Glory couldn't help feeling slightly smug, even though the whole competition thing was a lie.

'Well,' Annabel said after she'd spent some time grilling Glory on where, when and how. 'I'm pleased for you.

I really am. You deserve something nice, especially after the past few years.'

Warmth spilled through her. Her sister was genuine, Glory could see that.

'Thanks,' she said, impulsively reaching for Annabel's hand across the table and smiling. 'You get your dream and I get mine. Didn't I tell you it would all work out?'

But Annabel didn't smile back. She squeezed Glory's hand, then pulled away. 'Don't go building castles, Glor. Reality isn't quite that easy.'

It stung that Annabel persisted in talking to her like she was a child, but Glory didn't say anything. There wasn't any point. And besides, her sister was probably right. It wasn't as if this ridiculous idea of marrying Castor Xenakis would result in any kind of happy ending, not when he'd mentioned a divorce at the end of it.

As he'd said, it would be a nice vacation in an exotic location, nothing more.

Still, that didn't mean she couldn't enjoy it.

She was more than ready a week later when the same sleek, black car that had taken her home that night at the beach house drew up outside the apartment again, this time ready to take her to the airport.

Annabel had some errands to run and so Glory had already said goodbye by the time came for the driver to load her single, battered suitcase into the trunk. So she had no one to wave goodbye to as they drove away, not that Glory was sorry for that.

The lie she'd told Annabel ate away at her. Because Castor was famous and if this was supposed to look real, she'd probably end up in the same gossip magazines he did, and even though Annabel didn't pay much attention to celebrity gossip, there was a chance she'd find out about it before Glory had a chance to tell her the truth.

The thought made her anxious, adding to the anxiety that already gathered in the pit of her stomach, along with a very real fluttering feeling that was probably excitement and of course had nothing whatsoever to do with *him*.

She'd been very good at not thinking of him at all the past week, not even glancing at the magazines in the rack next to the counter. Very good at not thinking about the kiss the night at his mansion either or about what would happen if he kissed her again.

'I didn't end that kiss because I wanted to. I ended that kiss because I wanted to keep going.'

Glory stared down at her hands in her lap, her heart giving a little kick as she remembered what he'd told her. He'd pushed her away so forcefully after she'd clutched at him, and she'd automatically assumed it was because she'd overstepped. But no, it hadn't been. He'd liked that kiss every bit as much as she had.

What if he hadn't ended the kiss? What if he'd kept going?

Her heart kicked again, harder this time, a sudden rush of heat scalding her cheeks.

No, she couldn't think about that. It hadn't happened and it wasn't going to. She'd been very clear she wasn't going to sleep with him and not because she didn't want to. She *did* want to. But she was afraid he might decide he was mistaken when he'd told her that he didn't find her ordinary after all.

While he might have liked that kiss, a kiss wasn't sex, and she was *very* inexperienced. He'd be used to women who knew what they were doing, not checkout girls who didn't.

Not that this was about her in any case. This was about doing what she'd promised for Annabel's sake.

Glory found herself staring at a small stain on her

jeans and it suddenly occurred to her that she hadn't bothered to wear something nice. She hadn't even bothered with make-up. She'd flung on some jeans and a T-shirt, grabbed an old sweatshirt, put her hair in a ponytail and that was it.

Yes, ordinary, that's what you are.

Well, and what was wrong with being ordinary? Nothing. She wasn't ashamed of it, and anyway, that's what he'd wanted, wasn't it?

A perfectly ordinary woman.

Glory ignored her cycling thoughts since they weren't helping, staring out the window and watching the city go past instead. And then gradually realised that they weren't going to LAX as she'd expected, but somewhere else.

That somewhere else turned out to be a small, private airfield where the car drove straight onto the runway and pulled up to where a sleek-looking Learjet waited.

Beside the jet stood Castor chatting easily to a woman in a pilot's uniform.

He was casual today, dressed in a pair of faded blue jeans and a black T-shirt. The hot LA sun glinted off the gold strands in his dark tawny hair and made his skin look even more gilded than it already was. Sunglasses hid the smoky amber of his gaze, but she could still remember the fierce heat in it as he'd stared at her after that kiss.

Her mouth dried, her palms sweaty.

If he'd been beautiful in simple black trousers and a white shirt a week earlier, in casual jeans, a T-shirt and sunglasses he was devastating.

A nameless fear suddenly filled her and if she'd been driving she'd have hauled on the wheel, turned right back around and headed straight back home again.

But she wasn't in her own car and she had no time to

tell the driver she'd changed her mind and could he please take her home, because at that moment Castor turned his head, and even though the windows were opaque, it felt to Glory as if he was looking straight at her.

Her face flamed, memories of that night hitting her full force. The intense heat of his body. The warm, woody scent of his aftershave. The taste of his mouth, like brandy and dark chocolate and mint all rolled into one.

And her own response, the wild uprush of excitement and longing. A hunger for something she didn't have a name for, and the intense feeling of rightness, as if his arms were the place for her. As if he was the home she'd been fantasising about for so long.

No fantasies. No dreams. Stop it. You signed a contract. This is a job so do it.

Glory curled her fingers into fists in her lap as Castor broke off his conversation with the pilot, striding towards the limo with the intent, purposeful grace of the predator he hid behind that charming smile.

It made Glory's heart thump painfully with a complicated mix of fear and excitement, and the knowledge that she was going to have to interact with him and she had no idea how, not after that kiss.

Perhaps it would be better if she simply pretended it hadn't happened.

She plastered what she hoped was a natural smile on her face as Castor pulled open the door and then there he was, standing in front of her, as devastatingly handsome as he'd been that night at his mansion.

His beautiful mouth curved, his gaze remaining hidden behind his sunglasses. 'Good morning, Glory Albright.' His voice was exactly as she remembered it, deep and dark, like rough velvet rubbed against her bare skin. 'I hope you're ready for our flight. A press release has already gone out from my PR team and there are likely to be photographers around, so follow my lead as we walk to the jet.'

A press release. Photographers. Which meant she'd have to start acting like his lover right now.

All thoughts of the kiss and how she was going to handle interacting with him went by the wayside.

'The press?' She sounded squeaky. 'Here? Already?'

'Yes, already.' His smile shifted, a slight adjustment that made it seem less practised, more natural. 'Don't look so scared, *mikri alepou*.' There was a reassuring note in his voice. 'It's not far to the jet and I'll be with you.'

Glory pulled nervously at the denim of her jeans as the full reality of her situation descended on her in a way it hadn't before. There would be people watching her, people taking photos, and here she was, in a pair of old jeans and a T-shirt, her hair in a ragged ponytail...

'I'm s-sorry,' she stammered. 'I should have worn something nicer, put on some make-up or something. I just didn't think, and I don't have anything very nice to wear—'

'It's fine,' he interrupted, as if it wasn't a big deal. 'That's exactly how I want you to look for our first appearance together. Come on, let's get this over with.' And then he held out his hand to her.

It's not the photographers who are making you nervous.

No. It was the thought of taking his hand and how she'd feel once those warm, strong fingers closed around hers. Whether she'd lose her mind so completely the way she had before or...

'Glory.' His voice was very deep and very soft, jolting her.

She blinked, pulled herself together and took his hand. And once again as his fingers closed around hers, heat twisted inside her before erupting in little prickles all over her skin.

It almost made her jerk her hand out of his grip, but she managed to stop herself at the last minute. If he noticed, he gave no sign, pulling her out of the car and into the bright sun. Then she was being drawn slowly yet inexorably into the heat of his body, the scent of his aftershave surrounding her, making her mouth water.

Alarm must have shown on her face, because he bent his head as one powerful arm circled her waist, his hand resting lightly in the small of her back. 'I'm going to kiss you,' he murmured close to her ear. 'Just briefly, for cameras.'

Another kiss. Dear God, she better not embarrass herself again.

'Okay,' she croaked and closed her eyes, just to be safe. Being close to him was almost more than she could handle, let alone looking at him at the same time.

A fleeting warmth brushed over her lips and she found herself trembling. Wanting to go on her toes again and kiss him back, taste him the way she had a week earlier. Remind herself again of his rich, heady flavour. It would stay with her for ever, she knew, and even just thinking about it made her desperate for more.

Was there something wrong with her that she couldn't stop thinking about kissing him? That she couldn't stop thinking about wanting more? About exploring him to discover whether he was as hard as he looked, whether he was as hot. Whether his skin would taste—

'You look hot.' His voice had gone even deeper, a seductive roughness edging his tone. 'Perhaps we should get you somewhere cooler.'

Glory stiffened, feeling as if she'd let slip something she shouldn't. She wanted to pull away, but his arm remained securely around her and it wouldn't look good for anyone watching if she did, so she stayed where she was.

'I'm fine,' she said, her own voice sounding wooden in her ears.

He stared at her a second, his expression hidden by the sunglasses, then without another word, he turned for the jet, urging her along with him.

'That should give them a couple of good pictures,' he said. 'Thank you. You did well.'

There was a warmth in the words that made her stomach flip over, which was silly when he'd only said thank you.

'No problem,' she forced out.

This was crazy. Her mouth was tingling, every inch of her was exquisitely aware of him and there was an ache right down low inside her, between her thighs. A nagging, dragging kind of feeling.

She wanted to step away, put some distance between them. But she didn't dare, not when there were photographers around.

Castor ushered her up the stairs and into the jet, and for a second she was distracted from his disturbing physical presence by the realisation that she was actually standing in someone's private jet.

His private jet.

Because this was Castor Xenakis, head of a billion-dollar corporation, as renowned in the boardroom as he was in the bedroom, and of course he'd travel by private luxury jet.

The interior was all pale carpet and cream leather, with low coffee tables in a dark wood. A pleasant, smiling woman in a pale blue uniform greeted them, but Castor murmured something to her and she soon disappeared off down the back of the plane, leaving him to guide Glory to her seat himself.

'I can do it,' Glory muttered, achingly aware of him as he leaned over to help her with her seatbelt.

'I know you can.' He pulled the seatbelt across her. 'Humour me.'

She wasn't sure why she had to humour him, but she didn't want to argue, so she let him fasten the belt in place before he mercifully stepped back and sat down in the seat facing hers.

Ten minutes later they were in the air and the smiles he'd had for her earlier were gone. It was as if he was a different person, the person he'd been that night at his mansion, angry and fierce and driven.

She'd been fascinated by him then, but now, given her own uncertainty, she wouldn't have minded seeing one of his smiles, even the practised ones.

'So, *mikri alepou*,' he said. 'I suppose now I should tell you the truth about why I want to marry you.'

Glory's soft, red mouth opened, then shut, her russet brows drawing together in puzzlement. 'But you've already told me. Something to do with a project, I think you said.'

Castor wasn't sure why he was talking to her about this or what had prompted him to bring it up. It was only that dressed in a plain white T-shirt and jeans with a couple of stains on them, and her curls in a haphazard ponytail, he'd been struck anew by how painfully not of his world she was. How unpractised and innocent, and how irresponsible it was of him to use her the way he was doing.

Yes, but you're doing this for Ismena's sake. You can't forget that.

It was true, he was. Yet leaving Glory in the dark didn't sit well with him, especially given how young and vulnerable she was.

Or how attracted you are to her.

He let out a silent breath.

This whole week he'd busied himself with his wedding plans, trying to forget about that kiss and how haunted he was by the heat of her mouth and how sweet she'd tasted. How she'd pressed her lush little body against his and kissed him back, hungry for him. And how he'd found himself pushing her up against the wall without even being aware of it.

He'd told himself that his loss of control with her had been an aberration borne of frustration at his lack of progress and that when he saw her again, that strange, uncontrollable hunger would have disappeared.

Yet it hadn't.

The same surge of desire had risen up inside him again the moment he'd pulled open the door of the car and her gaze had met his. Wide and dark and soft, and full of emotion. The effect had been like a lightning strike.

For a good many years he'd built up his reputation as the corrupt, jaded playboy, slowly lowering himself deeper and deeper into the mud so he could get close to the real criminals, all the while thinking he could keep himself clean.

But that had been a comforting lie. He didn't feel clean, he never had, not since the mission had consumed him. He knew other people saw him that way too. In fact, he couldn't remember the last time a woman had looked pleased to see him, excited that he was here.

He'd been forced to attend too many occasions where

the bastards who trafficked in people displayed their 'wares.' It sickened him every time. And he'd had to bear the way those poor women had looked at him, as if he was like the men he was trying to take down. As if he was the enemy, the abuser, the brutaliser.

Yet he didn't see that in Glory's eyes. He saw desire and excitement, and yes, fear, but also a rising heat. The same heat he'd seen the night she'd kissed him.

It made him want to take her face between his hands and demand she tell him exactly what it was she saw in him, ask her what that good side of him was, because he was starting to forget he had one.

But of course he couldn't do that, so he'd tried to ignore the feeling. At least until she'd taken his hand and their physical chemistry had kicked into life. And he knew his loss of control that night hadn't been an aberration. That what he'd felt then, he felt now, and it was her.

It was all her.

He hadn't been able to resist drawing her in close or pressing his mouth to hers in a brief, insubstantial kiss. He'd said it was for the press, but it wasn't. It had been for him.

That's all you should have. You don't deserve more.

Oh, he was well aware. And he wasn't going to touch her again, that was for sure. But he hadn't treated her very well that night, and she deserved an explanation.

No one knew his real mission—no one apart from the authorities and a few of his staff—because if it ever got out, he'd immediately lose the trust of the people he was trying to take down.

But he didn't think she'd tell anyone. He didn't trust many people—if he trusted anyone at all—yet he had the feeling he could trust her. At least with this.

'Yes, that's correct,' he said. 'It is part of a project.'

'What project?'

Such a simple question with such a complicated answer.

You'll have to tell her about Ismena.

The thought made something growl deep inside him, the part of his heart he kept locked away. The part that felt too deeply, that had never recovered from the wound her disappearance had left and still prowled obsessively around it, guarding it, protecting it.

He didn't talk about Ismena, not to anyone, because while she had long since vanished, he was still her big brother and he was still protecting her even if it was only her memory.

Glory's dark gaze was expectant, waiting for him to continue. Then abruptly concern rippled over it and she leaned forward, putting one delicate hand over his where it was resting on the arm of his seat.

'What's wrong?' she asked.

Shock jolted through him, both from her question and from the gentle touch, a lightning strike of emotion that felt like it lit him up inside.

Automatically he pulled his hand away from hers, the smile he used too often to distract people from asking too many questions already curving his mouth.

'Nothing's wrong.' His voice even sounded normal. 'Why would you think there was?'

Or maybe it didn't sound normal, because instantly she drew her hand back, the concerned expression on her face flickering.

'I… I'm sorry. I didn't mean to intrude.'

There's no need to snap at her.

He hadn't thought he'd snapped, but clearly he had. And she'd picked up on his thoughts of Ismena somehow, which meant he needed to manage himself better.

Still, he didn't have to mention her. He could tell Glory about the project without having to reveal his motives.

'It's fine,' he said dismissively.

Mercifully at that moment the stewardess interrupted to take drink orders and organise other refreshments, giving Castor a moment to pull himself together.

He undid his seatbelt and shifted in his seat to get more comfortable, stretching his legs out, crossing them at the ankle.

Glory had undone her belt too and kept giving him wary glances from underneath her lashes. He didn't miss how her gaze kept dropping to his body either, which made all his muscles tighten, made him think that perhaps he should keep the conversation light, flirt with her, tease her, seduce her.

Make it all about her so he didn't have to deal with the prowling grief that ached in his heart.

But flirting was too dangerous when he was in this mood, especially with a woman he had this level of chemistry with. And most especially when she was someone he shouldn't ever touch.

Besides, there was a part of him that wanted to tell her. That wanted to tell *someone* and why shouldn't it be her? She'd seen something good in him without him even having to do anything, so why shouldn't she know?

He was tired of keeping it to himself.

'The project I'm talking about is something I've been doing for the past ten years,' he said without inflection. 'And that is using my wealth to infiltrate some well-known and notorious European human trafficking rings.'

Glory's eyes went wide. 'Human trafficking rings?'

'It's undercover work of a kind, I suppose. I pass on any information I'm able to get onto the authorities who can then rescue the people being trafficked. However, there is one ring in particular that I need access to so I can get the information I need and my reputation is working against me.'

She was staring at him in shock, not saying a word, so he went on. 'The inner circle of this particular ring are family men, as ironic as that sounds, and they are wary of admitting anyone who doesn't have the same values. Hence me marrying you. I'm hoping that a declaration of love and a wedding will help them change their minds.'

There was a dumbfounded expression on her face. 'You're…kidding, right?'

Of course she wouldn't believe him. Why would she? When the facade he presented to the rest of the world was so complete?

'No,' he said, holding her gaze and letting her see the truth in his eyes.

She was silent a long moment. Then she said at last, 'That's…amazing. Just…an incredible thing to do.'

He didn't know what he'd been expecting, but for her to not only take what he'd said at total face value but also think it was amazing was not it.

He shifted in his seat, uncomfortable for some reason. 'You believe me?'

She blinked. 'Why wouldn't I believe you?'

'People lie for all kinds of reasons, believe me, I know.'

'But you're not lying. I can see that you're not.' Abruptly she sat forward and her hand came out again, slender fingers resting on his knee. 'I told you that you had a good side.' Her dark eyes glowed. 'You're like… like the Scarlet Pimpernel.'

Castor had no idea what to say to that, especially when the light touch of her fingers was burning through the denim of his jeans, scattering his thoughts.

'Does anyone else know about this?' Glory went on, oblivious. 'The police obviously, but other people?'

'No. And the fewer people who know, the better.' He tried to ignore her hand. 'The only reason it works now is because the people who run the trafficking rings don't suspect me. I have such a terrible reputation for a reason.'

'Oh,' she breathed. 'So you look like one of them?'

'Yes.'

Her brow wrinkled. 'It must be awful having to pretend to be someone like…that. How do you do it?'

The unexpectedness of the question and the sympathy in her husky voice took his breath away, and for a second he didn't know how to answer. He could already feel himself wanting to smile, to make some dry remark to distance himself from grief inside him. But there was something so unguarded and genuine in her face that he couldn't do it.

So he went with the truth.

'I think about the lives affected by these men,' he said. 'And not just the lives of the people caught up in something like this, but the lives of those who love them. And how if I could even save one person, then that would be worth it.'

Her gaze was liquid, her touch gentle. 'It must be dangerous.'

'I keep myself mostly on the periphery, but it's a fine line. I let them think I'm harmless and not much interested in the business side of their organisation. Plus, I also have the money to manage my own security very well.' The way she was looking at him was making him even more uncomfortable. 'The danger is negligible. It's the people who get caught up with these men who suffer most.'

'Oh, yes, of course. But still. There aren't many men who'd do what you do.'

Her touch was too much, especially in combination with the way she was looking at him, so he shifted his knee, letting her hand slip off. 'I'm not a hero, *mikri alepou*,' he said, his voice rougher than it should have been. 'Some of the things they say about me are correct. If you live with a facade long enough it eventually becomes the truth.'

She folded her hands in her lap and looked down at them, her lashes veiling her gaze. 'I'm sorry,' she murmured. 'I didn't mean to make you uncomfortable.'

Theos, how did she pick up on his emotions so easily? He didn't like that she was able to read him, didn't like it at all. Nor did he like the way his own discomfort had obviously hurt her.

'It's fine,' he said dismissively. 'But I didn't tell you for praise. I told you so you'd understand how important this is and what's at stake.'

'Okay, but…' She hesitated, then went on. 'I know it's none of my business, but can I ask why you're doing this?'

This question at least he'd been expecting.

'You can ask,' he allowed. 'However, my reasons are my own.'

She gave a little nod, but didn't press.

The stewardess came back at that moment, laying out drinks and some snacks. Castor thanked her and picked up his scotch on the rocks, cradling it in his palms, very conscious of Glory's dark eyes on him.

You shouldn't have said anything.

Ah, but that was ridiculous. He'd wanted to tell someone, so he had. What he shouldn't be doing was letting the way she looked at him get under his skin, and he couldn't work out why.

She wasn't anyone special. Just an ordinary woman he happened to have some physical chemistry with, nothing more. Her opinion didn't matter, not at all.

Then Glory said softly, 'This is personal, isn't it?'

He went very still, shock rippling through him, and it was all he could do to keep his gaze level and not snap at her, the beast in him protective of the raw wound in his heart.

She was far too sharp, far too observant, for her own good, because yes, of course this was personal. But Ismena's memory was his to guard and he didn't want to share her, not with anyone.

Castor downed the scotch, then put his glass back on the table in front of him with a click. 'You're right, *mikri alepou*. It *is* none of your business. Now, if you'll excuse me, I have a great deal of work to catch up on.'

Then he got to his feet and without a word he strode down the other end of the plane.

CHAPTER SIX

GLORY STARED AT the deep, rare blue of the Mediterranean as the helicopter circled a perfect little island consisting of dark green trees, white stone buildings, sharp, rocky white stone cliffs and soft, powdery white sand beaches.

Castor's private island.

The beauty of it took her breath away in rather the same way as the man who owned it.

He sat beside her in the helicopter, talking to the pilot in melodic Greek. She had no idea what they were discussing, but the sound of his voice was soothing and she needed soothing, especially after over fifteen hours of travelling.

The journey from LA to Athens had been a long one, despite the luxuries of the private jet. The stewardess had shown Glory to the jet's bedroom—a novelty she hadn't been able to resist trying—but she hadn't slept very well, tossing and turning, and generally not being able to get comfortable.

She wasn't sure why. Probably something to do with Castor and everything he'd revealed after they'd taken off from LA.

He'd wanted to tell her all those things, that had been clear, and she'd even had the sense that he'd been desperate to talk about them. But only some things, as it turned out.

He'd been uncomfortable with her praise and he definitely had *not* wanted to talk about why taking down the trafficking rings was so important to him.

Not that taking down such things weren't important, she just wanted to know why *he* felt compelled to do so.

Why? What is he to you?

He wasn't anything. Her boss, maybe, if she was thinking of their marriage contract as a job. It was only that what he'd told her about what he was doing had fascinated her and she wanted to know more.

Such as what had led him to put everything he'd worked for—and to get where he was now, he would have had to have worked very hard—at risk. And not only what he'd worked for, but his life too.

What kind of man did that? That question had burned in her mind and the only answer she could come up with was the one thing she'd already noted about him: something was driving him. And it had to be personal somehow given the quiet ferocity in his voice and the glitter in his eyes.

Saving people was *very* important to him.

Not that she was surprised. Despite his anger with her the night at his mansion, she'd known he wasn't the corrupt, jaded womaniser the gossip magazines made him out to be.

He was a knight in shining armour instead.

That's not going to help your obsession with him.

No, it wouldn't, and marrying him wouldn't either. But then she wasn't marrying him for herself, was she? She was doing this for Annabel.

The helicopter descended, heading for the helipad on a flat piece of ground near the most beautiful house. It was constructed of white stone on the side of a cliff, over-looking the sea, and consisted of a series of boxes and terraces on different levels, the terraces bordered by low stone walls. Greenery surrounded it, olive trees and cypresses and all sorts of other trees and shrubs.

She should have been staring out the window at her first glimpse of it amazed, yet her attention kept getting drawn to the man beside her as the helicopter came into land. He wasn't looking at her, his attention out the window, and he was still talking to the pilot. His eyes were hidden behind his sunglasses again, the expression on his face giving no hint as to what he was thinking.

Why had he suddenly ended their conversation on the plane? Was the reason he was doing this painful? Because yes, it had to be, didn't it?

Why are you so curious? What does it matter?

Perhaps it didn't matter. Not that she had the right to demand answers from him anyway and she didn't want to pester him. Annabel used to get irritated with Glory constantly asking her how she was, and she didn't imagine Castor would take it any better than her sister had.

The helicopter came in to land and instantly Castor leapt out. A man was waiting on the helipad and Castor went over to speak to him. They chatted a few moments, then Castor was back, pulling open the door of the helicopter and helping her out.

'I have some things to attend to,' he murmured, his hand strong around hers as she got awkwardly out of the helicopter. 'But Nico here will show you around.'

Then before she could say anything, Castor let her go and strode off down one of the white gravel paths that wound through green lawn and low shrubs towards the house.

Nico, who apparently managed everything, introduced himself, then organised for her bag to be unloaded, picking it up and carrying it himself as he led the way to the house.

It really was a beautiful house, all whitewashed stone, the pretty terraces she'd seen from the air shaded by pergolas overlooking the deep, pristine blue of the ocean beyond. Inside it was white too, with white stone floors and white ceilings. The rooms were large and airy and full of light, with lots of white linen couches and jewel bright cushions scattered here and there. White gauzy curtains fluttered in the warm breeze coming through open windows, and the air was full of the scent of salt and sun and oranges.

The effect was of casual luxury with a rustic touch that Glory found incredibly appealing. As she did the little touches of art here—folk art sculptures, and paintings and hangings, along with the odd black-and-white photograph that were clearly of the island itself.

Nico showed her to a room in the upper part of the house, with a big bed facing a long line of French doors that opened out onto a private terrace. The room was as white as everywhere else in the villa, as was the en suite bathroom complete with a bath and shower before huge windows that looked out over the sea.

It was incredible, and after Nico had left her alone, with instructions to treat the house as if it were her own, Glory had to pinch herself to make sure she wasn't dreaming.

Used to the LA heat, grime and pollution, and the run-down decor of the apartment she shared with Annabel, being here, where even the air smelled different, was astonishing.

After all the hours spent travelling, she felt tired and gritty-eyed, so she treated herself to a shower, revelling in the huge, white-tiled space, then stood wrapped in a towel in front of her suitcase, pulling a face at her clothing choices. Not that she had many choices. Eventually she pulled out her only skirt—a denim one—along with a clean white T-shirt.

She wasn't sure what to do next and since Castor hadn't given her any instructions, she decided to explore the villa, wandering through a series of interconnecting white rooms and short corridors.

Of Castor himself there was no sign.

Eventually she found herself in one of the smaller rooms where the walls were lined with rustic bookshelves that looked hand carved, the shelves stuffed full of well-thumbed paperbacks in various different genres, plus hardbacks on art and history and science and all kinds of other things.

There were a couple of large, comfortable-looking chairs positioned near the shelves, plus a generous window seat covered in cushions that looked far too inviting to resist. So Glory didn't, curling up in it and gazing out the window at the afternoon sunlight bathing the island in a warm, golden glow.

She should probably call Annabel and tell her she'd arrived safely, but she didn't move, gazing at the view and enjoying being in this beautiful place, in the kind of house that graced expensive home and garden type magazines.

She didn't mean to fall asleep. She was just tired. And she only intended to close her eyes for a couple of moments. So it was very confusing when a deep, male voice said her name softly and she jolted awake, realising that view outside wasn't golden any more but dark, the night sky beyond glittering with stars.

Glory inhaled sharply and turned her head to find

Castor standing beside the window seat, looking down at her, his expression unreadable.

'You certainly know how to hide.' There was a faint edge in his voice. 'I've spent the last fifteen minutes searching everywhere for you.'

Heavy-headed with sleep, Glory pushed herself up from the cushions. 'I'm sorry,' she said thickly. 'I didn't mean to go to sleep.'

He made a tutting sound and reached out, gently pulling away some strands of hair that had been apparently stuck to her cheek. 'Jet lag. Happens to the best of us.'

The intimacy of the movement made her freeze in place, her breath catching, and she found herself staring into his eyes as something deep in them flared into life.

Very slowly, he reached out again, the tips of his fingers brushing her cheek, making everything inside her shiver.

All remaining sleep fled. She felt alive and awake, as if she was standing on the edge of a cliff caught between wanting to hurl herself over it or stay on the safety of her ledge.

For a long moment they stared at each other. Then abruptly he clenched his hand into a fist, the fierce glitter in his eyes extinguished. 'Come, *mikri alepou*.' He turned in the direction of the doorway, his voice casual, betraying nothing. 'Dinner is on the lower terrace and we have some arrangements to discuss.'

Glory tried to will her heartbeat to slow down, her skin tingling from where he'd touched her. Why had he done that? Clearly it hadn't been something he'd enjoyed since he'd then turned away as if she was the one who'd burned him. Like he had the night he'd kissed her.

Then again, had that been heat glittering momentarily in his eyes?

Ah, but she couldn't think about that. If he'd wanted to kiss her again, he would have done so already and he hadn't.

You want him to.

Glory swallowed and ignored that particular thought, just as she ignored the unmistakable lurch of disappointment that followed. Because she had no reason to be disappointed. He hadn't promised her anything but Annabel's IVF treatment and paying off their debt, and a two-week luxury vacation, and that's all.

Pleasant fantasies of kisses and maybe more weren't part of it and neither was wishful thinking.

Sliding off the window seat, she followed him.

The lower terrace was wide, with potted shrubs and various trees in tubs. There was also a long, rustic wooden table with rustic dining chairs and bright cushions on each seat. Food had been laid out—olives and fresh bread, cold meats and salad—along with a bottle of wine and a tall jug full of iced orange juice. Numerous candles in white stone holders had been lit, casting a diffuse and flickering light over the entire terrace.

It looked like a movie set or a scene out of someone else's life. Definitely not her life.

Castor moved over to the table and pulled out a chair, indicating she should sit.

She blushed as she sat down, very conscious of him standing behind her, tall and powerful and very, very warm.

'That's gentlemanly of you,' she said sincerely. 'For a notorious playboy, I mean.'

Castor pushed her chair in, then moved around the table to sit opposite her, giving her a fleeting glance as he did so. One of those practised smiles turned his mouth.

'I try.' His tone was casual as he reached for a napkin and flicked it over his lap.

'You don't have to do that,' she said without thinking. 'You don't have to pretend. Not with me. Not now I know the truth.'

He went still, his gaze flickering gold beneath his lashes. 'Pretend? Pretend what?'

Should you really have said that?

Why did she keep doing that? Why did she keep talking to him as if she knew him when she didn't? He might have told her his secret on the jet, but only because he wanted her to know what was at stake. It wasn't because he wanted to confide in her specifically. And then she'd pestered him for answers...

She was presuming too much on too little acquaintance.

'It doesn't matter,' she said quickly. 'I shouldn't have said it.'

He leaned back in his chair, his gaze narrowing, his expression opaque. 'But you did say it. So please continue.'

She didn't want to continue, but she also didn't want to argue, so she picked up her own napkin and fussed with it. 'Oh, you know, pretend to smile. Pretend to be charming. Pretend to be the playboy everyone thinks you are.'

'I see.' He gave her a steady and rather unnerving stare. 'And what makes you think I'm pretending?'

'Your s-smile doesn't quite reach your eyes.' Glory fiddled with her napkin. 'It seems kind of...fake. Especially when most of the time with me you don't smile at all.'

He said nothing, his gaze unblinking.

'Like you're doing right now, in fact,' she pointed out.

He stayed quiet.

'Anyway,' she went on quickly, trying to fill up the tense silence. 'All I wanted to say was that you don't have to smile or be charming or…or…anything else with me.'

The tension in the air gathered tighter.

Abruptly Castor reached for the open bottle of wine that stood on the table and with a certain amount of deliberation poured it into two wine glasses.

Glory looked down at the napkin in her lap, smoothing it while her heartbeat raced, anxiety twisting in her stomach.

She shouldn't have said anything. Why had she? She was better at observing people than talking with them and now she'd clearly offended him.

Does it matter if you offend him? He certainly doesn't seem to care if he offends you.

That was true. He had a couple of times and without apology, while she seemed to be apologising to him all the time.

'I'm not the only one who pretends.'

His voice came suddenly from across the table, low and deep, with that edge to it that she thought now was anger.

She looked up from her napkin to find him watching her, making her breath catch.

'Wh-what?'

'You pretend, Glory Albright.' His stare became intent. A predator's stare. 'Don't think I haven't noticed. You seem so shy and so afraid. Stammering like a child whenever you talk to me. Yet I see the way you look at me.' The gold in his eyes glittered as he pushed the wine glass in her direction. 'And I certainly felt it the night you kissed me. There's nothing really shy about you, is there?' He leaned forward slowly, the candlelight leaping and flickering over his fallen-angel beauty. 'You're hungry, *mikri alepou*. You're hungry, just like me.'

Glory was sitting there frozen, her dark eyes fixed on his. Her lush mouth had opened slightly, the pretty freckles dusting her nose standing out under the blush that had risen in her cheeks.

He shouldn't be angry with her. He had no right to be. Yet fury wound through him, hot and raw, coming from a place so deep inside him he hadn't known it was there.

A fury that had begun to climb as he'd spent fifteen minutes searching the villa for her. A fury in direct proportion to the cold thread of worry that had also began to build. Because she didn't seem to be anywhere around and yet no one had seen her leave. He'd ordered Nico to search the grounds while he did another search of the villa, the chill inside him gathering along with his anger.

How dare she make him worry about where she was? And how dare he worry about her at all? Because since when did he care?

The last decade of his life he'd had to cut his emotions off completely or else go mad, and he'd done so successfully. So successfully that sometimes he wondered if he still felt anything at all.

Yet in the space of a week, one ordinary young woman from LA had set alight something inside him and now here he was, frantically searching his villa as if she mattered in any way, and yes, he was furious about it.

And then when he'd gone into one of the smaller rooms he kept as a library, he'd found her lying on the couch fast asleep as if she didn't have a care in the world.

An intense relief had overcome him then, only to be overtaken by an equally intense fury, because why he should be *quite* so relieved he had no idea. She hadn't disappeared inexplicably or been taken by any of the people he was trying to bring down. She'd simply wandered off and fallen asleep on the couch as if he hadn't mobilised the entirety of the villa's staff to look for her.

As if she wasn't lying curled up on the couch with her hands beneath her chin like a child, pretty russet hair spread over the white linen, the denim miniskirt she wore pulled up to expose rounded thighs and smooth, pale silken skin.

Over the years he'd become so jaded that it took a lot to get him hard. But looking down at her lush feminine curves and her innocence, he felt his fury and relief transform into something burning, that ached, that made him hollow with hunger.

Every part of him had tightened with desire and he'd had to take a step out of the room to control himself. To not simply scoop her up in his arms, carry her straight to his bedroom and punish her for making him angry, for making him worry. For making him feel anything at all, because he didn't like it.

But of course he wasn't going to do that. He'd made his decision not to touch her and he couldn't. Yet the time it took to get himself in hand didn't help his temper, and by the time he'd gone back in to wake her up, he felt as if everything was strangely precarious. As if he was an explorer in unfamiliar territory constantly on the lookout for threats.

Maybe that was why he'd pulled her hair off her cheek and touched her cheekbone. Because he wanted to understand the nature of the threat she presented. Solve the mystery of why she should render his control as brittle as glass.

It had been a mistake though, because even now he could feel the warmth of her skin lingering on his fingertips, as if the very touch of her burned him. Just as it had been a mistake to have this dinner with her, to sit here with her velvety dark eyes focused on him, her deliciously husky voice telling him that now she knew the truth, he didn't have to pretend.

And all he could think about was how great a relief that would be. To have just one person he could be himself with, because he hadn't had that in years. *Theos*, if he'd *ever* had it.

Hungry, he'd said to her and he was. Hungry for someone who saw beneath that mask of his, who saw *him*.

Just as he saw her, no matter how hard she tried to hide it. She wanted him and it was obvious.

'I… I don't know what you mean,' she said thickly, grabbing her wine glass and taking a healthy sip.

He shoved his chair back from the table. 'Then come here and I'll show you.'

What are you doing? You don't want to go down this particular path.

No. This was a game he played with women who knew what they were doing and who liked a challenge just as he did, not with inexperienced innocents like her.

He should be walking away, putting some distance between them, not sitting here staring at her and challenging her to come closer.

Yet he didn't move and he didn't look away. Fury and hunger had him in its grip and he couldn't get free.

You don't want to get free. You want to feel something for the first time in years…

Yes, he did. He couldn't deny it.

Glory put her wine down, her expression turning wary. 'Why? What are you going to do?'

'I think you know exactly what I'm going to do.' He held himself very still, tension gripping every muscle.

There was no charm now and all his smiles had disappeared. She'd told him not to pretend and so here he was, not pretending. If she didn't like that after all, well, she knew where the door was.

A long, aching moment passed and then, strangely, concern filled her velvety gaze. 'You're angry with me.'

The sudden change of subject made him catch his breath. 'What?'

'You're angry with me—I can see it in your eyes. Was it something I did?' Her hands moved nervously in her lap, fiddling with her napkin again. 'I shouldn't have fallen asleep, should I? I'm sorry. I was just so tired.'

Theos, did she really think all of this was about anger? Could she not see the desire that burned in his eyes? Or was it simply that she didn't recognise it?

Why would she recognise it? She's had no experience with men, as you know very well.

Castor gritted his teeth. He didn't want to have to explain himself, but it wasn't fair to let her think she'd angered him. Especially when it was obvious that mattered to her since she kept apologising.

'Of course I'm angry with you,' he bit out. 'I'm angry with you for falling asleep and letting me find you all curled up, with your hair across the cushions and your denim skirt up around your thighs. Looking like Sleeping Beauty waiting for your prince to wake you with a kiss.'

'But I—'

'You made me want to do that, Glory. You made me want to kiss you and more. And yes, that made me angry. Because I wasn't going to touch you. Yet all I can think about right now is whether you still want your virginity.' His voice had deepened into a growl and he let it. 'Because if not, I'm quite happy to take it from you right here and now.'

Her eyes went very wide, her mouth opening. Her hands stilled and a tide of colour crept up her neck and over her cheeks, contrasting beautifully with the white of her T-shirt.

'You are?' Her voice had gone hoarse. 'Why? I'm not beautiful. I'm not special. I'm ordinary, remember?'

'I told you that I was wrong about that. And as to why, I don't know. What I do know is that I want you, *mikri alepou*, because you told me that I didn't have to pretend.' He paused, staring into those beautiful eyes of hers. 'So, I'm not pretending.'

Something shifted in her gaze and her mouth closed, her chin suddenly getting a determined slant to it.

She put her napkin down, pushed back her chair and rose to her feet. Then she moved around the table, coming closer to him.

He waited, anticipation tightening inside him, joining his hunger to create something thick and hot. This was a very bad idea and he knew it. He couldn't afford to indulge himself with someone like her, not when she was part of his mission. And certainly not when all he had to offer was a night of pleasure and nothing more.

Glory stopped beside his chair and looked down at him. She smelled of soap and a sweet, musky scent that was all her. It made his mouth water. He wanted to position her between his thighs and make her stand there as he ran his hands up her legs and over the curve of her bottom. Watch that hungry look turn to flame in her eyes and know that it was him she wanted. Really him.

Not the dissipated playboy he pretended to be, but the flawed man he actually was.

The man who couldn't even take care of his own sister.

The thought came and went as Glory laid her fingertips lightly on his hand where it rested on the arm of his chair and said, 'Perhaps you're right. Perhaps I have been pretending. And perhaps I don't want to pretend any more either.'

He stared at her small hand touching his, the heat from her fingertips pinning him there as if she'd run a spear straight through him. Then slowly he lifted his gaze to hers.

Her eyes were so beautiful, dark and full of emotion. Desire burned there, along with fear and excitement and hunger.

And a question she probably didn't even know she was asking.

He knew though, just as he knew the answer.

Castor turned his hand over and closed his fingers around hers. Then he tugged her closer, reaching up to tangle his free hand in her hair, pulling her head down. She didn't resist, her other hand coming down to rest on his shoulder, balancing herself as he tugged her down even further until her mouth brushed over his, his entire being held captive by the softness of her lips on his. He could taste the wine she'd been drinking, both tart and sweet at the same time, which was exactly like her too. Tart and sweet. Sharp and soft. And so warm, so very, very warm…

Her hair fell around him like a curtain and he wanted to bury his face in her curls. But then her mouth opened, her tongue touching his bottom lip, shyly exploring, making electricity crackle the length of his spine, and it abruptly became clear to him that if he didn't stop this he *would* take her virginity here and now.

Do you really have such little control over yourself that you'd ignore doing the responsible thing in favour of what you want instead? And all because of one kiss? Remember what happens when you do that.

A cold thread wound through the heat. Oh, yes, he remembered.

Ismena tugging on his hand, because she wanted him to take her to get ice cream. It was late and he still had a lot of homework to do, and he knew he should refuse. But the girl at the ice cream shop had been flirting with another boy, and he was jealous. He wanted to talk to her, ask her out before this other boy got to her.

So he'd taken Ismena out to get ice cream. And he'd talked to the girl in the ice cream shop. And by the time he'd finally managed to get her number, Ismena had disappeared...

No, he couldn't be so irresponsible again. He couldn't think only of himself. Glory wasn't a little girl and he wasn't fifteen any more, but she was still an innocent and he had the power to hurt her, which made it his job to protect her. Especially when sex was something he could easily get from someone else.

It didn't have to be from her, no matter what his brain insisted on telling him.

Castor released her and pulled away. She looked at him uncertainly, her luscious mouth red from his kiss, and he could feel the heat inside him wanting to break out of the cage he'd put it in.

It was a struggle to control it, but he did.

'Not tonight,' he said quietly, holding her gaze so she could see the decision he'd made in his. 'Not ever. Do you understand?'

Hurt flickered over her face. Then she turned away abruptly, going back to her seat and sitting down, looking down at her plate and saying nothing.

So much for not hurting her.

There was a dull ache in his chest for no reason that

he could see so he ignored it. Pain was fleeting and her pain would be fleeting too.

She'd eventually see his refusal as the lucky escape it was and would go on to find another, far more deserving man than he was to gift her virginity to.

Castor reached into his pocket and took out the box he'd put in there earlier that evening, laying it down on the table. 'This is an engagement ring,' he said casually. 'I want you to wear it tomorrow. It's large and expensive and I'd like some pictures of you wearing it.'

He didn't wait to see if she picked the box up.

He got to his feet, turned and walked away.

CHAPTER SEVEN

GLORY DIDN'T SEE him the next morning. Breakfast was served out on the terrace where dinner had been the night before, but there was no sign of Castor when she sat down to eat.

However, there was a note.

Forgive my absence, but I have a few details to attend to this morning.

The marriage ceremony will be conducted tomorrow in the villa's chapel—if you wish to see it, Nico will take you.

You may spend today as you like, but please be advised that I have leaked details of our wedding to the press so there may be some cameras around.

I will join you when I can.

C

Disappointment made her stomach dip, closely followed by a flare of uncharacteristic anger that made her screw the note up into a tight little ball and deposit it next to the ring box she'd left on the table the night before.

He was an ass, that's what he was, and she shouldn't have allowed him to get to her last night. Being honest with him, telling him she didn't want to pretend either, had been a mistake, as had coming around the table to kiss him. She should have shrugged when he'd rejected her, when he'd told her it would never happen between them. She should have told him she didn't care.

Yet she hadn't. She couldn't. She'd never been able to hide her hurt with Annabel either, when her sister had told her she was too busy to talk, too tired to help her with her homework and didn't want to play any of her silly games. That she had more important things to do.

Annabel hadn't had time for Glory's hurts, and since she had enough on her plate already, Glory had decided that it was easier to keep quiet. Easier for her and easier for Annabel too.

So that's what she'd done last night with Castor. She'd gone back to her seat and said nothing, too embarrassed and upset to even look at him. Then he'd simply got up and walked away without a word.

Was it her fault? Had she done something she shouldn't? Misinterpreted him somehow? But then how could she have misinterpreted what he'd said when he'd been very clear about what he'd wanted?

'All I can think about right now is whether you still want your virginity... Because if not, I'm quite happy to take it from you right here and now.'

Her. He'd wanted her. He'd said that.

Except he'd also said, *'Not tonight. Not ever.'*

Glory's hands clenched into fists in her lap, hurt catching inside her.

She didn't understand him. She didn't understand why this was painful either. Because why did she care if he didn't want to sleep with her? What did it matter? She'd told him back in LA that sex wasn't on the table and told herself that she was fine with it. Besides, she hadn't known him very long and he'd never promised her anything.

He just made her feel as if she was ten again, constantly pestering her sister for attention that Annabel was too tired to give.

Too tired because she spent every minute of the day working just so they both had a roof over their heads and food to eat.

She knew she shouldn't let Annabel's small rejections hurt. Her sister hadn't been doing it maliciously. She'd only been trying to look after Glory as best she could. Yet they'd hurt all the same, sitting like a splinter close to Glory's heart, and even now, even as an adult, she could feel that splinter throb inside her.

The only solution was to keep pretending it didn't matter. That this was merely a job she was doing, a vacation she was having. That she didn't want him and he wasn't fascinating and she didn't care at all that he wasn't here.

She left the ring box on the table after she'd finished breakfast, then sent an email to Annabel to let her know she'd arrived safely, since she couldn't bear the thought of actually talking to her.

Once that was accomplished, she settled into the task of doing some serious sightseeing on the island.

It was small, rocky, a little bit wild and utterly beautiful, and Glory loved it. She took a lot of photos on her phone, enjoying the hot Mediterranean sun on the back of her neck, the cloudless blue of the sky and white rocks against the deep turquoise of the sea.

She poked around the chapel where the wedding was going to be the next day; it was tiny and had to be centuries old. It smelled of cool stone and incense, light flooding the small space in front of the altar from the window high above.

Tomorrow, she would be getting married here.

Tomorrow, Castor would be her husband.

The thought shouldn't have made her feel anything since it wasn't even real, yet trepidation turned over inside her as she stared at the altar.

No, she wasn't going to allow herself any nerves. Or if she did, it would only be about what kind of attention it was going to draw, nothing else.

It certainly wasn't going to be about *him*. Because she didn't care about him at all.

She returned to the villa and spent the afternoon by the glorious blue infinity pool, sunning herself in her sagging old swimsuit while she read a book stolen from the library, determined not to notice Castor's absence.

Which turned out to be relatively easy since he remained absent the entire afternoon.

Even after the sun went down and another delicious dinner was served on the terrace, he didn't appear.

Nico, however, arrived with another note.

The ceremony will begin at ten and Nico will escort you to the chapel.

A gown has been laid out for you. Please leave your hair loose.

If you have any questions, Nico will be happy to answer them.

Once again, apologies for my absence.

C

Glory debated on screwing this note up as well and maybe throwing it off the terrace and into the ocean for good measure. But Nico was watching her so she didn't. There was nothing to be gained by being petulant. If he wanted to continue avoiding her, then he could. She certainly wasn't going to go chasing after him. And besides, she didn't care. She really didn't.

If Nico noticed her temper, he made no mention of it, but he glanced at the unopened ring box on the table. Again, though, he didn't say anything.

Rather to her own surprise Glory slept like a log that night, and in the morning woke to find a gown laid over the chair in her room. It was very simple, a shift dress of white silk, cut on the bias to emphasise her curves. She found the simplicity of it beautiful. Beside it was laid a simple wreath of glossy green laurel leaves that presumably she was to wear in her hair.

She showered, then dressed, anger at Castor for his rejection and at herself for caring still burning in her gut, so when two women arrived at her door armed with make-up cases and hair implements ready to help her look presentable, she almost sent them away.

But she'd never had anyone do her make-up, or style her hair, and why should she miss out on something lovely like that, just because Castor Xenakis was being a complete ass? Anyway, she shouldn't be angry. She was here on a beautiful Greek island, having an all-expenses-paid luxury vacation, when she could be back in LA in the grocery store, so really, she should just enjoy it.

Swallowing her anger, Glory let the women fuss around, styling her hair and doing her make-up. And half an hour later, when they were done, Glory barely recognised the woman in the mirror, glowing and fresh-faced and pretty, her dark eyes outlined in gold and looking huge with liberal coats of mascara. Her curls—usually frizzy—were cascading down her back, gleaming and beautiful, the little wreath of laurel and wildflowers laid gently on them.

For the first time in her life, not only did she look

beautiful, but she felt beautiful too, and she liked that. She liked that a lot.

It wasn't real, she knew that. She wasn't going to marry the man she loved and who loved her. It was only a job, a bargain she'd made, but she didn't care. Today she felt like a bride and that was enough.

Nico arrived and offered her his arm and together they walked down to the little stone chapel, the sound of helicopters in the air heralding the arrival of the promised media presence.

Glory decided her nerves couldn't deal with cameras so she didn't look up, keeping her attention on the chapel ahead.

Inside it was dark and cool, and smelled of incense and centuries of prayers. Light came down through a narrow window above the altar, shining on the tall figure of a man who was pacing back and forth, clearly restless. The priest was murmuring to him in Greek, while he said nothing.

And despite her best efforts, Glory's chest clenched tight, threads of anger and desire constricting inside her.

Castor was unspeakably gorgeous in perfectly tailored black trousers and a plain black shirt. He wore no tie and though his dress looked casual, it was elegant and simple, setting off his phenomenal good looks to perfection.

The light through the window picked up the gold strands in his dark hair and made his skin gleam, and when he stopped and turned his head, looking to where she stood in the doorway, his eyes glinted pure gold.

She swallowed, clutching onto her bouquet.

He turned to face her, all the restless energy that she'd seen in him as he'd paced before the altar draining away until he stood very still, his gaze focused with complete attention on her.

No one had ever looked at her that way before, as if she was the only thing in the world worth looking at, still less a man like him. As if she was so absorbing he couldn't look away from her in case he missed anything.

A wave of heat swept over her, along with another wash of anger, because how dare he look at her like that, when he'd told her nothing was going to happen between them? How dare he look at her like he wanted her, only to reject her small advances?

She'd always checked herself in the past, not wanting to make things difficult for Annabel, because life had been hard enough for her and she didn't need a little brat for a sister.

However, Castor wasn't Annabel. He might have been a white knight, but he was also rich, privileged, and while he might play these kinds of games with the women who customarily threw themselves at him, he wasn't going to play them with her. She wasn't going to let him.

She might not be one of the people he was trying to save with his mission, and she might be rather plain and her life rather ordinary, but she was still a person. And she had feelings.

And she was tired of being toyed with.

Glory lifted her chin, met Castor's brilliant gaze and slowly walked down the aisle towards him.

He watched her every step, his gaze roving from the wreath in her hair, to her shoulders, to the swell of her breasts, her hips and then down further, before making its way back up again.

She glared at him, angry that he should *still* be looking at her like that, making her heart beat faster and her palms damp where they clutched her bouquet. Angry at the electricity building in the space between them, a snapping, crackling energy that felt like it was bigger than the church they were standing in.

She came to a stop in front of the altar and stared straight into his eyes, more gold now than anything else. There were a million sharp words sitting inside her and she wanted to let them all fly. But to do so would be to let him know he'd hurt her and she didn't want to do that.

So she said nothing, merely stood there giving him what she hoped was a cool look.

The flames in his eyes leapt higher.

'Why weren't you wearing my ring?' he demanded.

It was a stupid thing to say and Castor knew it the second the words were out of his mouth. It betrayed too much. Yet anger was the only emotion that made any sense in that moment.

Anger that the instant she'd appeared in the doorway of the church, the posy he'd had put together clutched in one small hand, her lush, gorgeous figure wrapped in the simple gown of white silk he'd arranged for her to wear, everything he'd told himself about control and denial had gone straight out the window.

As he'd ordered, her glorious hair was loose in an exquisite cloud of curls, prettier than any veil. The flowers and deep green, glossy leaves of the wreath in her hair was the most perfect touch.

She looked young and innocent and heartbreakingly beautiful. Persephone, Goddess of Spring.

Which makes you Hades, dragging her down into the Underworld.

No. He wasn't dragging her anywhere.

He'd been careful to keep away from her the past day, busying himself with organising the details of the wedding and liaising with his PR people to make sure the news being disseminated to the press was exactly what he wanted. Enough of the appearance of reality to make everyone think it really was as real as it looked.

He'd also got in touch with certain contacts as to how the news of his engagement and impending wedding was being received by the leaders of the trafficking ring he was trying to infiltrate. Which was favourably, according to the reports he got back.

He'd hoped that a day would have given him some distance, that his desire for her would become less intense or his control over himself stronger. He had Nico keeping an eye on her, and everything had seemed fine. Then just before he'd walked into the chapel, Nico had mentioned noticing that she hadn't been wearing his engagement ring. And Castor had found himself consumed by the most ridiculous rage.

He couldn't understand why. She wasn't his actual fiancée, and whether she wore the ring or not didn't matter all that much. He'd needed her to wear it for pictures, but that could happen after they were married. It didn't have to be before.

Yet he was still angry.

And it seemed he wasn't the only one, because now she was close he could see fire glowing deep in her dark eyes, and her chin had lifted in a very determined way.

'I wasn't wearing your ring, because I didn't want to,' she said shortly.

Electricity pulsed through him in a hard jolt, the predator in him responding to her challenge.

This is not the time or the place for this argument.

No, and especially not when he was so on edge. Yet he couldn't stop himself. 'You agreed to be my loving fiancée.' He didn't bother to temper his tone. 'And that includes wearing my engagement ring.'

Glory's chin came up higher. 'I might have worn it if that loving fiancé had bothered to talk to me yesterday, but since he didn't, I decided not to wear his stupid ring.'

Ah, so she hadn't liked the distance he'd tried to put between them.

That shouldn't matter.

It shouldn't. But it did.

Her sharp-featured lovely face was flushed, the gold outlining her eyes making them seem ever darker, the anger glowing in them like tiny fires. And another jolt of electricity hit him hard, his anger twisting, the desire in him deepening.

A mistake to give in to this feeling. A mistake to let himself be at the mercy of it. Yet all he could think of was that it had been far too long since a woman had looked at him with anything but either fear or calculated lust, and Glory's honest anger thrilled him in a way it probably shouldn't have.

He didn't look away from her, holding her gaze with his. 'Give me your hand,' he ordered, reaching into his pocket for the box that contained the engagement ring.

For a second he thought she might disobey, and he half found himself wanting her to purely so he could have the excuse to do something, though what he'd do he wasn't sure. But she only pulled a face and extended her hand.

The priest was looking at them both with some disapproval, but Castor ignored him. He pulled out the ring box and opened it, took the engagement ring from it, discarded the box, then slid the ring onto her finger.

He'd ordered it back in LA and hadn't put too much thought into it, wanting only big and flashy. And flashy it certainly was, a blue diamond set in a platinum band and surrounded by smaller diamonds. It looked too big for her hand and the second he'd put it on, he wanted to take it off, get her something more suitable. Which was ridiculous when none of this was real. It was *all* pretend.

'You don't have to pretend, not with me...'

The memory of her voice from their aborted dinner wound around him and he found himself staring into the velvet darkness of her eyes, seeing the anger burning in them.

You hurt her that night.

Of course he'd hurt her. He knew he had. That's why she was so angry with him now, wasn't it? *Theos*, she had every right to be. He'd told her he wanted her, had kissed her, then had turned around and told her it wouldn't happen, before walking away without even giving her an explanation.

No wonder she was so upset with him.

Regret shifted in his gut, another emotion he never let himself feel these days.

She doesn't need your mission. She doesn't need rescuing. And her hurt is easy enough to heal. You can't fix what happened to Ismena, but you can fix the way you treated Glory. You could give her a wedding night.

The thought hit him like a lightning strike, stealing his breath. No. No, he couldn't. He'd told himself right from the start that he wasn't going to touch her. She was now part of this mission and he couldn't complicate it by sleeping with her.

She wants you. And once you put that ring on her finger, everyone will think you're sleeping with her anyway. If you make the boundaries clear, where's the harm? Besides, you want her too, don't lie to yourself.

The priest coughed, glaring at Castor's silence.

'Begin,' Castor ordered, his voice rough as the thought dug its claws into him. Because he could, couldn't he? He could give her one night.

It could be…a wedding present even. It wouldn't mean anything. He'd be clear about that.

Glory's chin jutted as the priest began the ceremony, but she said nothing.

Castor couldn't look away. And as the ceremony went on, he watched the blush in her cheeks deepen, the scattering of freckles across her nose looking like fallen stars, and her lush mouth soften. The anger died out of her eyes, something hotter and more intense shifting in the velvety darkness.

His heartbeat thumped in his head and when they took each other's hands to exchange rings, he felt her touch on his skin like a brand.

Then somehow the ceremony was at an end, the priest murmuring that they were husband and wife and that Castor could kiss his bride, and he found himself holding his breath.

He couldn't remember the last time he'd wanted to kiss a woman so badly.

'You don't have to,' Glory said, her cheeks flaming despite the edge in her voice. 'I know you didn't—'

But instinct had him in its grip and he didn't even think, taking her face gently between his palms, tilting her head back and covering her protests with his lips.

She went very still, but he could feel the shiver that shook her.

Her mouth was so soft and she tasted of mint, along with something sweet. Instinctively he deepened the kiss, because it felt like for the past couple of days he'd been holding himself rigid and yet now, with her lips under his, he could finally relax.

You don't need to pretend with me…

Yet pretending was all he'd been doing for years. Pretending to be someone he'd never wanted to be. Pretending he didn't feel all the emotions he'd tried to cut himself off from. Pretending he was fine with all the things he'd had to do in order to keep up this ridiculous act.

But he'd never been fine and the little girl he'd done it all for was gone. He'd lost her.

Glory wasn't though. She was here and kissing her felt like drinking a cold glass of water after years in the desert. Sheer relief.

He tasted her deeper, sliding his hands lower till they rested at the base of her throat, his fingers caressing her neck. Her skin was smooth and silky and warm, and he wanted to lay her down and discover if she was just as warm and silky everywhere else.

She trembled, then began to kiss him back, shyly at first and then bolder, her tongue exploring his mouth as he'd explored hers, winding his desire tighter and tighter.

She was so responsive. He'd been a fool to deny her. A fool to deny himself. He could teach her so many things, give her so much pleasure...

The priest cleared his throat once again, ostentatiously, and Castor belatedly remembered that he was in a church and he was kissing his new wife in a way that was probably not appropriate.

It was a struggle to drag his mouth from hers, but he managed it, lifting his head and looking down at her. Her face was rosy, her mouth red and soft from the effect of his kiss. Then as he watched, the desire faded from her gaze to be replaced again by a certain challenge.

'You didn't have to force yourself to kiss me,' she said tartly. 'This isn't real, remember?'

The priest was still standing there, but Castor didn't care.

'And if it was?' he asked. 'What if tonight it was all real?'

Surprise rippled over her face. 'What? What are you talking about?'

She is yours now. All yours.

He didn't want to get possessive. That was all too prevalent in the world he lived in, where people were seen as possessions, and he didn't want to turn into that kind of man. But that didn't change the feeling that had him by the throat.

He took her hand tightly in his. 'Come, wife. You and I need to have a little chat.'

'Castor, wait.'

But he didn't want to wait.

He pulled her down the aisle and outside, tugging her in close to shelter her as the sound of helicopters came from overhead. Out in the bay, yachts bobbed, dark figures moving on the decks.

Since the island was private, the media couldn't gain access to it; not that they needed to when they had telephoto lenses.

Automatically Castor put a possessive hand on Glory's hip, making it clear who she now belonged to, and it wasn't entirely for show this time.

She'd gone rigid, but made no attempt to pull away.

Nico was standing on the church steps, waiting to fulfil his witnessing duties as Castor had specified. It didn't take long to complete the legalities. Five minutes later Castor said, 'My wife and I are going back to the villa.' He gave his manager a very direct look. 'Alone.'

He didn't wait for Nico's response, merely firmed his grip on Glory and urged her along the white gravel path back up to the villa.

'Castor, what are you doing?' She sounded breathless. 'I know you didn't want to kiss me, so why did you?'

But he didn't want to have this discussion here, not

out in the open with unseen cameras trained on them, so he didn't reply, hurrying her along the path lined with olive trees and up through some terraces, until finally they were safely back inside the villa.

Glory was glaring at him as he shut the door of the living room firmly behind them. She still had the posy in one hand, a handful of white silk in the other since the gown was long and she had to lift the hem. The wreath in her hair was slightly askew, curls drifting over her shoulders, and he wanted to grab her, undress her, scatter the flowers everywhere around them and lay her down on the petals like the virgin sacrifice she was.

'What is this all about, Castor?' she demanded, before he could speak. 'You just walked out the night before last without even a word, then you spent the whole of yesterday avoiding me, sending me ridiculous notes—'

'Yes.' He took a couple of paces towards her, itching to take her in his arms. 'You're right, they were ridiculous. And yes, I was avoiding you.'

She blinked, obviously taken aback. 'Why?'

'I think you know why.' He took another few steps, getting closer. 'You offered me something precious and I refused you. Then I walked out without explanation. I shouldn't have.'

She gave him a wary look, but didn't move as he came closer still. 'No, you shouldn't have. Especially considering you kissed me back. I thought… I thought I did something wrong.'

'You didn't do anything wrong.' He was so close now, inches away from her, and he didn't hesitate, reaching for her, his hands settling on her hips and drawing her up against him.

She gasped, her bouquet dropping onto the floor as she

lifted her hands to his chest, her palms pressing against him, holding him away. 'What are you doing?'

The heat of her body seeped through the thin silk of her wedding gown and into his palms like the promise of a fire on a cold, dark night, and he wanted to sit in front of it, let it warm him right through.

'What am I doing?' He eased her closer, fitting her softness against all the hard, aching parts of him. 'I'm doing what I should have done that night instead of walking away.' He lifted one hand and slid his fingers into her hair, cupping the back of her head. Then he held her still as he bent and kissed her again.

She made a soft sound, the pressure of her palms increasing on his chest, but it wasn't to push him away. And when he pushed his tongue into her mouth, her fingers curled in his shirt as if she wanted to pull him closer.

He should talk, explain himself, but he was tired of talking. He was tired of denial. It felt like he'd been denying himself for years, and finally, now he had something he really wanted here in his hands, he couldn't deny himself any more.

He kissed her deeper, letting hunger stretch out inside him, exploring the sweetness of her mouth with care before turning the kiss hotter, letting it build until there was a fever to it, and she was trembling against him, gripping him tightly as if she needed to hold onto him to stop herself from falling.

It was only then that he lifted his head, not hiding the hunger in his eyes, letting her see it.

She was breathing very fast, her make-up smudged, the darkness of her eyes thick and soft as midnight in midsummer. 'C-Castor… I don't understand,' she said, all breathless and husky. 'I thought…you said it would… n-never happen.'

'I know what I said.' His hand was still in her hair, chestnut curls wound around his fingers, but his thumb was free and he used it to trace a line across the silky skin of her cheekbone. 'But I decided I was wrong. I want you, *mikri alepou*. And I want to give you a wedding night.'

Her mouth opened, then shut. 'A…wedding night?'

'Yes.' He ran his thumb over her cheek, down to the corner of her mouth, tracing the line of her lower lip. 'I can only offer you one night, that's all. But if you want it, all you need to do is say yes.'

The pulse at the base of her pretty throat was beating very fast, the expression on her face slightly dazed. She felt so good against him and the musky, sweet scent of her was making his mouth water.

'You made me so angry,' she whispered. 'You…hurt me.'

Regret pulled tight inside him. 'I'm sorry. I was…trying to protect you. You're too young and you're too innocent, and you shouldn't be getting tangled up with a man like me.' He bent and brushed his mouth over hers, feeling the heat of her stoke the flames already burning inside him. 'I didn't want to complicate this and I thought distance would be better.'

'No.' She leaned into him, trying to follow his mouth, her eyes half closed. 'No, distance is not better.' Her lashes lifted and abruptly he was lost in the warm sooty darkness of her eyes once again. 'I might be inexperienced, but you don't have to treat me like a child. I know what you can and can't give me, and I'm okay with that.'

'Glory, I—'

She lifted a hand and pressed a finger against his mouth, the touch stealing the words straight out of his head. 'If you want my virginity, Castor Xenakis, then stop talking and take it.'

CHAPTER EIGHT

GLORY SHIVERED AS gold fire ignited in Castor's eyes and her whole body gathered tight in preparation for another of those soul-destroying kisses.

But he didn't bend his head. Instead his grip on her changed and she was turned around so her back was to him. Then she felt the tug on the zip of her gown, the fabric loosening around her as he drew it down.

He touched the top of her spine gently before his fingers began a long, slow stroke down her exposed back.

She caught her breath. She wasn't sure exactly why he'd changed his mind about her, but she definitely wasn't going to argue with him.

If he wanted to give her a wedding night, then she was going to take it.

Is that really all you want from him?

But she didn't want to think about that so she ignored the thought, concentrating instead on the touch of Castor's fingers on her bare skin as he slid them beneath the straps of her gown, easing the fabric from her shoulders, leaving her standing in a puddle of white silk, wearing only the lacy underwear she'd put on that morning.

He pulled her close, her back against his front, his mouth nuzzling the soft curve of her shoulder and the tender place where it met her neck, nipping her there.

She gasped as electric shocks of pleasure jolted her, all her senses spinning at the heat of his hard body pressed to hers and the warm spice of his aftershave surrounding her.

It felt so good she couldn't breathe. She arched against him, tilting her head back and exposing her throat to him in wordless invitation. Which he took, his teeth against her skin, biting her gently, before soothing the nip with a soft rain of kisses.

Oh, she had no idea it would be like this. How good it felt to be held, to have a man's mouth on her skin and his tall, muscular body behind her, a delicious kind of threat that both excited her even as it scared her.

Just any man?

No, not just any man.

'Castor…'

His name was both a prayer and a demand for more and he answered it, flicking her bra open, pulling the delicate fabric away to leave her breasts bare, then sliding his large, strong hands around to cup them in his palms.

Heat swept through her, along with the most delicious pleasure, and she groaned, arching into his hands, wanting more. Part of her was horrified at how demanding she was being, but the rest of her simply didn't care.

She'd never been wanted like this before, and even though she'd been angry, she'd also loved the way he'd looked at her in the church. And then the way he'd pulled her in close on the way up to the villa, as if he wanted her all to himself.

It made her feel special and she hadn't realised quite how much she'd wanted to be special to someone. Special and not a burden the way she was with Annabel.

But Annabel doesn't get to fly to Greece or be wanted by a beautiful billionaire…

Glory pushed the thought away. No, Annabel was getting her dream, so why couldn't Glory have this for herself? She'd intended to do so back in LA that night in Castor's mansion after all. And besides, it was only a night, nothing more.

Castor's fingers tightened, his thumbs finding her nipples, circling them gently before giving each a little pinch, sending shock waves of pleasure through her, scattering all her doubts.

No one had ever made her feel the way he did and even if this would all end in heartache for her, she wasn't going to regret this. How could she? If she wanted to lose her virginity to someone, she couldn't have asked for a better man to lose it to.

His mouth was warm and seductive on her neck, his body against her back a wall of heat, hard muscle and power. She liked how protected she felt standing right here in his arms, how insulated against anything that would hurt her. It made her aware of how lonely her life had been up till now and how she hadn't known how much she'd wanted someone to hold her until he'd taken her in his arms.

There had only ever been her sister and all the sacrifices Annabel had had to make for her. Everything had a price, and that included love.

But not this. This was free. There was no guilt attached. It was just pleasure and so she'd take it.

Glory arched back against him, wanting more, wanting his hands on her, wanting to lose herself in his touch and in the thrill of being desired by someone like him.

He stroked her breasts gently once more before his hands slid down to her hips and he was easing down the panties she wore, undressing her completely.

She felt no embarrassment, no need to cover herself,

not when it was so obvious how much he wanted her, and so when he turned her in his arms to look at her, she met his gaze without shame.

He didn't speak, but that look in his eyes told her everything she needed to know, and when he lifted her in his arms and carried her to the couch, she could see the need in him.

'I want you, Castor,' she heard herself say as he laid her down. 'I want you so much.' She reached up to touch his cheek, loving the feel of his hot skin and the prickle of his whiskers.

He turned his head, kissing her fingertips before straightening, his hands going to the buttons of his shirt and beginning to undo it.

Glory pushed herself up, suddenly dry-mouthed and desperate to touch him, but too shy to ask.

He seemed to know what she wanted though, because he paused, his golden gaze catching hers. 'Would you like to do the honours?' he asked softly, his hands dropping away from the buttons.

She nodded jerkily, coming off the couch to stand before him, reaching for the buttons of his shirt and fumbling a little with them. But he helped her and slowly he was revealed, the black cotton parting to reveal golden skin and hard, carved muscle.

Her hands shook as she touched him reverently, because he was a work of art and works of art should be worshipped.

'Ah, *mikri alepou*…' His voice had got deep, the rough velvet becoming gravel as she ran her fingertips over his chest, tracing the lines of his pectorals before moving downward to the hard corrugations of his abs. 'You will be the death of me.'

But he didn't stop her as she pushed his shirt from his

broad shoulders or when she rose on her toes and pressed her mouth to his throat, tasting salt and musk and the essential flavour that was all him. It was only when her hands went to the buttons on his trousers and she undid them, sliding her fingers inside and finding the smooth hot skin of the hardest part of him, that he gave a rough curse in Greek and then moved suddenly.

And then she was on her back once more on the couch, pressed against the seat cushions by his naked body, surrounded by the scent of warm spice, the oiled silk of his skin moving against hers.

He was between her thighs, leaning over her, his hands on either side of her head, his hot gaze burning down into hers. 'You deserve better than this,' he said. 'You deserve time, but I'll make it up to you, I promise.'

She didn't know what he was talking about, mainly because she didn't want time. What she wanted was more of this pleasure, more of his touch, more his kisses, just… more.

And he gave it to her, his hand sliding beneath her hips and lifting her, then a deep, hard thrust that had her crying out. There was pain, but it wasn't bad, a fleeting hurt and then a feeling of fullness, of completeness.

He stilled deep inside her, looking down into her eyes, murmuring something soft in Greek that she didn't understand.

But she thought she knew, so she took a breath, adjusted herself to the feel of him inside her, to the rightness of it, then reached for him, bringing his mouth down to hers.

The kiss was deep and intense, a feverish, hungry kiss, turning even hungrier as he began to move, setting a rhythm that had her trembling and shuddering with pleasure.

She hadn't known it was possible to feel this way, to be so consumed by another person that she thought she might die if he didn't shift his hips in just that way, giving her the most exquisite source of friction that made her gasp in delight. If he didn't bite her bottom lip, or trail kisses down her throat, or slide so deep inside her he made pleasure echo through her entire being.

His arms came around her, his mouth becoming more demanding, the rhythm faster, harder, the pleasure pulling tight until it felt like she was going to snap like a rubber band stretched too far.

She writhed in his arms, gasping, and then his hand was between her thighs, stroking the most sensitive part of her, and everything abruptly came apart and she called his name, lost beneath the flood of an almost unbearable ecstasy. She was only dimly aware of his sudden, sharp movement and then the rough sound of his groan as he chased his own climax, before his body came down on hers.

She didn't mind, floating pleasantly in the aftermath, the hot weight of him like an anchor that kept her tethered and not floating away to be lost in the currents.

Then she felt him cupping her cheek and she realised her eyes were closed, so she opened them, looking straight up into his beautiful face.

His expression was warm, but not the forced, brittle charm she'd seen that night of the party. This was natural, his amber gaze smoky with heat. 'Are you okay? Nothing too sore?'

His body was a hot weight on her, pinning her to the couch, and while there were a few…tender spots, she'd never felt better in her entire life. 'Yes, I'm okay. No, wait.' She smiled. 'I'm better than okay. I think I might even be great.'

His thumb moved idly across her cheekbone in a caressing movement, and though he didn't smile back, his gaze had softened.

She liked the way he was looking at her, with warmth and a certain tenderness, as if her well-being was important to him. As if *she* was important to him and not a burden he had to carry.

'What about you?' she asked, stroking the broad plane of his chest. 'Are you okay?'

He did smile then and it made her feel as if she'd won a prize. 'Oh, you don't need to worry about me, *mikri alepou.*' His thumb moved down, along the line of her jaw. 'Phenomenal doesn't even being to cover it.'

She flushed with pleasure, then a sudden doubt gripped her. 'But if sex is always like that—'

'Sex is never like that,' he interrupted, his smile vanishing, leaving behind it the burning ferocity that lay at the heart of him. 'At least it's never been like that for me.'

Glory stared at him in surprise, because that surely couldn't be right. He was very experienced, had had a lot of women, so why would being with her be so different?

'Why not?' she asked. 'I'm not that special, Castor. I'm just an ordinary woman—'

'You're not an ordinary woman.' The gold in his eyes glinted brighter. 'Because if you were, you wouldn't drive me as mad as you do. I wouldn't be thinking about you, or trying to resist you, or arguing with you about wearing my ring in front of the altar. And I certainly wouldn't be lying naked with you on the couch and thinking about how I'd love to make you scream again, except louder this time.' He brushed his mouth over hers, nipping at her bottom lip. 'Glory, you're not ordinary, you're *extraordinary*, understand?'

When he looked at her like that, she did feel extraordinary. Not a simple checkout girl in a grocery store, the burden her sister had to bear, but someone beautiful and mysterious. Someone special.

She blushed. 'I don't feel it sometimes.'

He gave her another nip. 'Well, I hope you're feeling it now, because it's true.'

Glory shuddered in delight, then put her hands on his broad shoulders, stroking his skin as she looked up into his face. 'Yes, I do feel it. You make me feel it, Castor.'

'I'm glad, *mikri alepou.*' He stared down at her for a long moment, the fierce currents of his emotions shifting in his eyes. Then he turned his head in the direction of the windows, as if he'd heard a noise, the lines of his beautiful face hardening. 'A little privacy, I think.'

He pushed himself off the couch and strode over to the windows, apparently not caring that he was naked. He grabbed the curtains and jerked them closed, before turning and coming back to the couch.

Then he settled himself back on top of her, making her breath catch at the feel of his bare skin sliding against hers. 'There now,' he murmured. 'Where were we? Oh, yes…about here, I think…' He bent his head, nuzzling at the base of her throat, his lips brushing over her skin.

Glory shut her eyes and drew in a shaky breath, heat rippling throughout her entire body. 'Did you hear something?'

'No.' His breath ghosted over her skin as he moved lower, trailing kisses over her collarbones. 'Just keeping out any eavesdroppers.'

Glory wanted to ask him why he thought there'd be any eavesdroppers on a private island, especially when he'd told his staff to absent themselves, but then his lips closed around the aching tip of her nipple, and her thoughts fractured, everything lost but for the exquisite pressure of his mouth and the sparks of pleasure lighting her up inside.

She forgot about eavesdroppers. Forgot about how this wasn't real. She forgot about everything but him and his mouth on her body and his hands on her skin, him inside her, moving hard and deep and fierce, showing her how good he could make her feel.

He was amazing. She'd never experienced anything like him in her entire life.

Afterwards, when their hunger had been sated for the time being, he picked her up and carried her up to his bedroom and the huge, white-tiled shower in the adjoining bathroom, where he washed her gently and with a care that brought tears to her eyes.

She hadn't been looked after like this since she was a child, and even then, looking into Annabel's tired face every day, she knew what a burden taking care of her was. Even worse that Annabel *had* to do it because Glory was her sister.

But Castor didn't have to. There was no obligation on him at all. He was doing it because he wanted to, and while she made a cursory protest, he ignored it so she gave up, letting herself enjoy it and not feel guilty.

After they'd got out of the shower, he insisted on drying her, kneeling in front of her with a soft white towel and wiping the moisture from her skin. She watched him as he did so, wondering why he was doing it and what he was getting from it, because he was getting something, that was clear.

'You like taking care of people, don't you?' she asked, the question escaping before she could think better of it.

He didn't look at her, intent on what he was doing. 'What makes you say that?'

'I mean, you put food on my plate when we ate, and

then you insisted on washing me and now you're drying me. I can do all of those things myself.'

His hand ran down her calf to her heel, urging her foot up, and she had to put her hands on his broad shoulders to keep her balance. 'I know you can.' He held her foot in his hand and began to dry it, his touch making her shiver. 'But I want to do it.'

'Why?' His skin was hot underneath her hands, his muscles tensing and relaxing with his movements. He was so very strong—she could feel the power in him—yet he touched her carefully and with great gentleness. It made her heart feel tender for reasons she didn't understand. 'What do you get out of it?'

'I think you know what I get out of it.' He put her foot down, then reached for the other one, glancing up at her briefly, wickedness glowing in his eyes. 'Sex, of course.'

He sounded flippant, but the muscles beneath her hands were rock hard with tension. He didn't like this particular topic of conversation, did he?

Perhaps she shouldn't push it, make a nuisance of herself. Then again, she kind of wanted to know.

'That would make sense if we hadn't had sex,' she said. 'But we have. Yet you're still taking care of me like this, so…why?'

He finished with her foot, releasing it, then rising to his full height, wrapping the towel around her as if she was a child. 'You don't like it?' He lifted a brow. 'Shall I stop?'

Clearly he wasn't going to make this easy for her.

Glory frowned. 'You shouldn't answer a perfectly valid question with another question.'

He smiled faintly, putting a thumb between her brows and smoothing it like he had done earlier downstairs. 'You shouldn't frown like that. You'll get wrinkles.'

'I don't care about wrinkles and next you'll be telling me I should smile more.'

'You should.' He bent and picked her up in his arms, turning to the door and walking through it. 'You have a beautiful smile.' He glanced down, brandy-coloured gaze holding hers. 'I would like to make you smile more.'

Glory's chest went tight as some strange, powerful feeling coiled uncomfortably inside her.

'You do, Castor,' she murmured, touching the smooth skin of his chest. 'And I'd like to do the same for you too.' She stroked him. 'But I'm not sure I can. You hardly ever smile at me.'

His expression shifted, the fierce glow in his eyes becoming softer. 'Didn't you tell me that I didn't have to pretend with you? Well, I don't, *mikri alepou*. All that charm is what I do for them.'

She'd already worked that out for herself, but she liked that he'd told her that anyway. 'So, what? You're actually a pretty serious person, then?'

His expression shifted again, a bleak look crossing his face that made everything inside her clench tight. But then he glanced away, the bleakness vanishing as quickly as it had come. 'Well, now, that's for me to know and you to find out.'

He doesn't smile, not at all. Because something terrible happened to him.

The thought was instant and cold, like ice in her veins, and worse, it felt like the truth. It had to be, didn't it? Something was driving him to put himself at risk the way he did, and she'd already sensed it was personal.

And it could only be something terrible. Why would he choose to infiltrate those trafficking rings? Why pretend to be one of those awful people for nothing?

You can't ask him. You don't have the right.

No, it wasn't any of her business. She might be his wife and he might have decided to give her a wedding night, but it was only sex. It wasn't her place to demand his secrets, no matter how badly she wanted them.

She stayed silent as he carried her into the bedroom, setting her down on the huge bed, before turning and going over to a dresser that stood against one wall.

She stared at him as he pulled something out of a drawer, trying to distract herself from the sharp edge of worry that sat inside her, and his body was certainly a good distraction. Tanned, golden skin and carved muscle, with a narrow waist and long powerful legs.

Oh, she could stare at him all day.

'Y-you're quite extraordinary too,' she said at last, trying break the thick silence. 'I don't know if anyone's ever told you that, but it's true.'

Castor turned around, holding something in his hand. He didn't smile, but the flickering gold in his eyes leapt. 'What makes you say that?' He came back over to where she sat and pulled the towel carefully away from her. Goosebumps prickled all of her skin as he looked down at her, all his attention very focused.

'What you're doing,' she said quietly. 'Your…mission. You're helping people regardless of the cost to yourself and that…that's extraordinary.'

He reached out, touching her face gently. 'You would do the same in my place, I think. Because you want to help people too, don't you? Your sister, for example. There aren't many people who'd gatecrash a party in order to sell their virginity to a complete stranger, and all for someone else's benefit.'

Glory lifted a shoulder. 'Annabel and I lost our parents when we were young and she ended up having to look after me. She had to make a lot of sacrifices and then she

me. I wasn't her child, only her little sister. She got stuck with me. She had to make all these sacrifices for me and then she got cancer and I...' Glory stopped, the secret fear she'd never actually spoken of suddenly right there in her mouth.

'You what?' Castor prompted gently.

And she found herself saying, 'I wonder sometimes if her life would have been easier if I hadn't been in it.'

Glory's eyes were full of unshed tears, making them look even more liquid and dark, and Castor felt a primitive, fierce emotion gather inside him in response. He knew what it was like not to have his little sister in his life, he lived it every day, and it had damn near ruined him.

'No,' he said fiercely, gripping her. 'No, it would *not* be easier if you hadn't been in it. Why on earth would you think that?'

Glory tried to pull away, but he didn't release her. Instead her lashes fell, veiling her gaze. 'She didn't choose me. I wasn't her kid. I was only her sister. I wasn't anyone special. I didn't do anything to—'

'Glory,' he cut her off roughly. 'You didn't have to do anything. You were her sister, that's enough.'

Her lashes rose, droplets of tears sparkling on the ends. Yet a certain anger glowed there too along with the pain. 'How would you know? You weren't there and you don't know Annabel. You didn't see how tired she was. How she had to drop out of school to look after me. You didn't hear her crying at night or talking to a friend about how she didn't know how she was going to feed us for the next week. And you weren't there when she got sick, and all I could think about was how maybe her getting sick was my fault. If she hadn't worked herself into the ground trying to look after me, she might not have got cancer, and then she might have had the baby—'

Castor lifted his thumb and pressed it against her soft mouth, stopping the flood of words. He hadn't wanted to talk about Ismena, but the pain in Glory's eyes was too much to bear. He hated her thinking she was a burden, that somehow she wasn't the special woman he knew her to be. Warm and empathetic and giving. No wonder Annabel had made sacrifices for her. Who wouldn't?

Ismena had been the same, and he would have moved mountains for her.

'I had a little sister,' he said, the words coming out hoarse. 'And I often had to look after her. She was never a burden and I never regretted even a single moment of the things I had to do for her.'

Glory's eyes widened. Then she asked, her lips moving against his thumb, 'You had a sister?'

He shouldn't have said anything, but it was too late. He'd only wanted to make her feel better, nothing more, yet now he'd mentioned Ismena, he couldn't pretend he hadn't.

She was such a precious memory and he guarded her fiercely even now.

You want Glory to know what you're really like? How you were supposed to be the responsible older brother? How you were supposed to be keeping an eye on her?

The thought was barbed wire winding around his heart, cutting into him, the guilt eating away at him.

Yes, she should know. She should understand that the good side she'd apparently seen in him was a lie. That he wasn't any kind of hero. Just a selfish man who'd put his own feelings ahead of taking care of his little sister.

He let her go and straightened, staring down at her. Wearing nothing but his shirt, with her hair lying in damp, gleaming curls down her back, she looked stunningly beautiful. And it satisfied him on some deep level that she was wearing something of his. It made him feel territorial and possessive, feelings he should have buried the day Ismena disappeared.

Apparently though, he hadn't buried those feelings deep enough.

You can't let them rule you, not again.

Oh, he wouldn't. But one night he'd allow himself and so he'd give them free rein. Tomorrow he'd bury them back in the grave he'd put them in and this time he'd make sure they stayed buried.

'I had a little sister,' he said at last. 'Or maybe I still do, I don't know. Ismena disappeared twenty years ago.'

A crease appeared between Glory's brows, but this time he didn't smooth it away. 'What happened?'

'My father was never in the picture so my mother brought us up. We lived in Athens, in a tenement. My mother worked a lot so I ended up looking after Ismena most of the time. I was…fifteen, Ismena was eight.' He found himself fixating on one of the buttons of the shirt she was wearing. It wasn't in the buttonhole properly so he adjusted it. 'There was an ice cream shop nearby with a girl behind the counter that I was interested in. Another boy was also interested in her and I wanted to ask her out before this other boy did, so that night I told Ismena I'd take her out for ice cream.' His voice got rougher. 'There was a pet shop next door to the ice cream place and they had some new kittens, and Ismena wanted to look at them. So I told her she could while I got the ice cream, because I didn't want her listening in to my conversation. I was only gone a minute, but when I got back, Ismena wasn't there.'

A terrible sympathy stole over Glory's face, and he

knew all at once that if she spoke he wouldn't be able to bear it. He'd have to turn around and walk out. Because sympathy was something he didn't deserve.

But she didn't say a word. Instead she reached out and took his hand.

There was warmth in her fingers and a strength he hadn't expected, and he found himself holding her small hand in his.

He didn't want to keep admitting to all the things he'd failed to do, yet her touch seemed to lend him some of that strength, because he found himself going on. 'I searched all night. I searched everywhere. And I did the next day and the next, and the next. I searched for months. I searched for years. But… I never found her. There was a trafficking ring operating in the area at the time and the general consensus was that she'd been taken.'

'Is that—?' Glory stopped and cleared her throat, her fingers tightening around his. 'Is that why you're infiltrating those traffickers?'

It was a simple question and because it had a simple answer, he answered it. 'Yes. My mother and I were poor back then, completely disposable, and the police didn't do a thing to help us. So I swore I'd become rich and powerful enough that I'd find Ismena myself.' He turned her hand over in his, stroking the back of it with his thumb. 'I was single-minded in my intentions. I made myself rich and powerful. And even though I haven't managed to find Ismena, I'll take down these goddamn traffickers if it's the last thing I do.'

The words hung in the space between them and he couldn't say there wasn't a small measure of relief at being able to say her name to another person. At having the acknowledgement that she existed.

'Castor,' Glory said carefully. 'How long have you been searching for her?'

He looked down at their linked hands, her narrow, delicate fingers folded between his longer, larger ones. 'Since she disappeared,' he said. 'Twenty years, though I've only been infiltrating the trafficking rings for ten.'

Theos. Had it really been that long? Then again, searching for her had consumed his life to the point where he couldn't remember *not* searching for her. Couldn't remember a time when she hadn't been the first thing he thought of when he woke up and the last thing he thought of when he went to sleep.

She consumed his every waking thought. He didn't have room for anything else.

Glory was quiet. Then abruptly, she brought his hand to her mouth, kissing it, before releasing it and slipping off the bed to kneel at his feet.

He looked down at her, allowing himself this view because she was so pretty kneeling there with her hair all around her and her big dark eyes gazing up into his.

'I want to give you something,' she said. 'A wedding present of my own. Will you let me?'

He'd had many women kneel at his feet like this, but for some reason with Glory it was different. She wasn't looking at him like he was Castor Xenakis, playboy, but as if he was just Castor. A man she wanted. A man she even might care about.

You don't want her caring for you.

He didn't, but he was done walking away from her. He wasn't going to hurt her again and definitely not when she was offering herself to him.

'What kind of wedding present?' He reached down and took a lock of her hair, curling it around his fingers, liking the feel of it on his skin. Liking her at his feet too, as if she was his. As if she belonged to him.

You can't start thinking like that. She can't be yours. You can't let her matter, you know this.

Oh, he knew and normally he'd never permit himself such emotions. But he'd allowed himself this night with her, which meant he could allow himself the feelings that went with them, surely?

Is a night enough?

Glory put one hand on his thigh, the other sliding up to grip the rapidly hardening length of his sex. The feel of her fingers closing around his hot flesh, soft and cool, stole the breath from his lungs.

'This kind,' she murmured, squeezing him lightly. 'A night to forget.'

Shock rippled through him that she'd somehow guessed how consumed he was, that she saw what he didn't even know he needed himself.

Because yes, that's exactly what he wanted. A night to forget. A night where he didn't think of Ismena at all.

He wound the lock of hair tighter around his finger. 'Yes. You can try, *mikri alepou.* If you think you can.'

It was a challenge to her, he knew that, and he could see something light up in her dark eyes, the fierce part of her meeting his.

She didn't say anything, but when she put her mouth on him, he felt himself catch fire. Because if anyone could help him forget it was her, and what was more, he wanted her to.

He gripped her hair tighter as the heat of her mouth took him and even though she was inexperienced and this wasn't new to him, feeling her lips against his skin made him groan.

It felt new. It felt like a wonder, a delight he hadn't

expected, especially when he showed her what he liked and she set to doing it with a will.

He hadn't thought it was possible, but in the end she did it.

She made him forget, and for a few, blissful moments, he was free.

And afterwards, when he picked her up and had her back on the bed where she belonged, beneath him, he'd already decided: no, one night wasn't going to be enough.

He wanted more.

CHAPTER NINE

Two weeks later, Glory stood in front of the ornate, full-length mirror in the bedroom of Castor's Parisian mansion and smoothed her hands down her sides nervously.

Castor was taking her to a special gala at the Musée d'Orsay, and among all the things he'd bought for her over the past couple of weeks was the most beautiful formal gown. She'd been wary of putting on something so terrifyingly expensive, some part of her worried she'd tear it or ruin it, or somehow look awful in it.

But she didn't look awful in it. She looked…beautiful. She even felt beautiful.

Glory smiled at herself in the mirror.

He's going to love it. He's especially going to love taking it off.

A delicious shiver worked its way down her spine.

Two weeks of being in Castor's bed had certainly taught her many things, including how much he loved undressing her. Slowly and with care, paying meticulous attention to detail, running his fingers over every inch of her body. Treating her as if she was a precious object.

It made her feel worshipped.

He'd made her feel worshipped these whole two weeks, right from the moment she'd woken up in his bed the morning after their wedding.

He'd rolled over, pinned her to the bed, then said, 'How would you feel, *mikri alepou*, about a proper honeymoon?'

That he'd changed his mind about only offering her one night was obvious, and part of her had wanted to ask him why. But after what he'd told her the night before, about his sister, she didn't have the heart to push him for more. And anyway, maybe she didn't need to. Maybe it was obvious why he'd changed his mind. Maybe, like her, he just wanted to take what they had together, where they could forget about real life for a while.

So she'd agreed. Without hesitation.

The honeymoon, as it turned out, had involved a couple of days where they only left Castor's bedroom in the villa for sustenance. Then when their hunger for each other had been sated, Castor asked her where else she wanted to go.

Glory had no idea. She'd never imagined leaving LA and yet here she was on a private island in Greece, married to a beautiful billionaire. And when Castor suggested Italy, she said yes, because why not Italy?

She'd sent Annabel another email telling her that everything was okay and that she'd decided to extend her vacation by another couple of weeks. She'd half expected her sister to have seen the news about her marriage to Castor since the news sites were full of it, but Annabel had never taken much notice of celebrity gossip and her response, when it came, was only to hope Glory had a good time and to take care with her money.

Their first port of call had been Rome and since she didn't have any idea what she wanted to do, he'd organised various private tours of the city including the galleries, the ancient sites and the shopping districts. Glory loved all of it. Just being in a different country and especially one as old as Italy was the most wonderful experience.

She discovered she loved history, the ancient sites in particular holding a fascination for her, so much so that Castor organised for a historian to come on one of the tours with them.

At first Glory had worried that Castor might not enjoy this as much as she did, because surely all of this had to be old hat for him. But he gave no sign of being bored. He seemed to enjoy the tour with the historian particularly, peppering the man with all kinds of questions, before turning to Glory and asking her what she thought. He was always asking her what she thought, in fact, and he always listened intently when she told him, as if her opinion mattered to him.

It made her feel important and valued, and maybe it was then that she realised she was falling in love with him. Or maybe it was in Venice, when he took her on a gondola ride only to chat to the gondolier for half an hour, somehow getting the man from only answering questions in monosyllables, to a full-blown soliloquy about his beautiful wife and his lovely children, and how he worried sometimes that he didn't earn enough to care for them. As they left the gondola, without a word Castor gave the man a tip that left him speechless and made Glory's heart squeeze tight.

Or maybe it was in Milan, where he gave her a Cinderella moment in an exclusive designer's salon, having her try on gown after gown, and telling her how beautiful she looked in all of them. Before buying them all, much to Glory's shock, because she was never going to wear them. She told him so and he nodded seriously, then turned around and donated all but Glory's favourite to a charity who could sell the gowns off to make money for disadvantaged kids.

He was a good man. A very good man. Kind and thoughtful and generous. He was excellent company with a dry wit that she very much enjoyed, and even though he was quite serious, she found that she had the ability to make him smile after all. Rare, genuine smiles that she treasured like the gifts they were.

Really, Glory thought now as she looked at herself in the gown she'd chosen in Milan, it wasn't any wonder if she was falling for him, because what woman wouldn't? Especially when he was so irresistible.

She'd tried not to. Tried to tell herself that was a stupid thing to do, because there was no future for them, he'd been very clear about that. She might be married to him, but their marriage wasn't real. And this honeymoon would be over in a couple of weeks, and then she'd go on with her life.

A life without him in it.

But she didn't want to think about that, so she didn't, preferring to live in the moments they had together and not wishing for something that couldn't ever be. After all, he'd never promised her anything more and she didn't have the right to ask for it. He had his own burdens to bear and she couldn't add to them by demanding something from him that he wasn't going to give.

How could he? When it was clear that what had happened to his sister ruled his life? She'd thought it would be something terrible and indeed it was, just as it was obvious that he blamed himself. He hadn't said so explicitly, but she'd seen the pain glittering deep in his eyes. She understood what it was to feel responsible for another's hurt.

That night she'd sensed he didn't want to talk about

it so she hadn't pushed him, merely given him what distraction she could. But the look on his face haunted her, made her want to know more. For example, was this mission of his an atonement? Or was it a punishment? Or was it perhaps both?

Whatever it was, she couldn't get it out of her head and she wanted to help him. But she didn't know how.

You couldn't help Annabel. What makes you think you can help him?

The thought was a cold one, so she pushed it away. Tonight he'd planned another Cinderella moment for her, a ball, and so she wanted to enjoy it, not depress herself with doubts.

The gown she wore tonight was of gold silk, wrapping around her body like the kind of gown a Grecian goddess would wear, and it fitted perfectly. A stylist had come to do her hair and make-up, which she loved, because it made her feel like a princess and she'd had so few princess moments in her life that she couldn't help but enjoy it.

Castor had told her that he was going to wait downstairs for her and to take her time coming down, because he wanted to see her make a grand entrance.

Glory had never made a grand entrance to anything and she was a little nervous as she came to the sweeping marble staircase that led down to the mansion's entranceway.

Castor stood by the front door waiting for her, dressed in plain, unadorned black evening wear, nothing to compete with the astonishing beauty of his face. The stark colour highlighted the golden strands in his dark tawny hair and drew attention to the smoky amber of his eyes. He looked like a god out of Greek myth and she felt the oddest sense of dislocation, because how could a man like that be waiting for her?

How could you have all these nice things when Annabel, who had to give up so much for you, gets nothing?

No, she couldn't think those things, and besides, that's why she was here, wasn't it? So Annabel could get the one thing she'd always wanted.

These doubts were ridiculous, and she wasn't going to think about them any more.

Putting one hand on the banister, Glory moved slowly down the stairs to where Castor waited.

'I was right,' he murmured, the look in his eyes catching fire. 'You have the most appropriate name. Glory, you are glorious.'

She flushed, inordinately pleased with herself and not a little pleased with him too. 'So are you,' she said, coming to a stop in front of him. 'Glorious, I mean.'

She expected him to smile, but he didn't. Instead the fierce gleam in his gaze only seemed to burn hotter. It was familiar that look. As if he was a dragon and she was the treasure he guarded.

Not that she was *his* treasure. She was only a woman he'd signed a contract with to marry and whom he was currently sleeping with, so why he'd even look at her that way was anyone's guess.

What was worse, however, was that part of her liked how fiercely he looked at her, as if there was nothing more important in his world than she was. Part of her wanted it, and because she was going to have this moment, this night, and not worry about real life, she said nothing, taking his hand when he held it out to her and letting him lead her outside.

A limo waited in the street for them and Glory was too busy looking at that to notice there were rather more men in plain dark suits standing around than there usually were.

She'd spotted them first in Italy and had asked Castor about what they were doing. He'd shrugged as if it was no big deal, telling her it was his security team, and that he always had security with him whenever he was out in public.

She'd accepted this since it made sense, given the facade he projected and the people he associated with, and since the security team was discreet, she soon forgot about it.

But as she'd finished marvelling at the limo and prepared to get in, she realised that there were twice as many security staff as there normally were.

'There are a lot of men in suits standing around tonight,' she said, after Castor had got into the limo beside her and they'd pulled away into the traffic. 'Did you hire more security staff?'

'Just a few more.' He took her hand, warm strong fingers enfolding hers. 'Tell me, would you object if I decided to ravish you in the back of this limo?'

That he was distracting her, she understood, but since she wasn't sure why, she decided to let him, dismissing the issue of security for now.

The gala was being held at the Musée d'Orsay and she wasn't surprised to find a contingent of press outside the doors.

They'd been followed around Europe by a press pack and while she hadn't quite got used to it, she was at least less anxious about being photographed than she'd been the day they left LA.

Castor had helped, carefully orchestrating their photo opportunities so she was comfortable and so that it didn't feel like too much of an intrusion, and he did so now, taking her hand once again, the warmth of his touch steadying her. But he didn't speak as he drew her out of the limo. He didn't look at her either, his attention on the gathered press, his expression oddly grim.

Drawing her close to his side, he hurried her inside despite the pleas for a photo opportunity and questions shouted at him from the waiting media.

It puzzled her, as did the hard expression on his face. Other people were arriving, dressed in beautiful gowns and suits, a crowd beginning to build, and he kept scanning them as if looking for someone.

'Castor,' Glory murmured, as he hurried her down an echoing, white and gilt corridor to where the gala was being held. 'Is everything okay?'

He didn't stop, but his expression was hard. 'It's fine. Why do you ask?'

'You keep looking around like you're trying to find someone.'

'Just checking security.' His fingers tightened around hers. 'Come, the party is this way.'

Glory frowned. He was radiating tension and was clearly not fine, but there were people all around and this was not either the time or the place for that discussion, so all she did was nod and let him lead her into the gallery where the gala was being held.

It was all high, domed ceilings, gilded columns and vast chandeliers. Trees in tubs stood at intervals, the trunks and branches wound around with fairy lights, and at one end a woman in a long gown played a gilded harp, flooding the air with delicate music.

Crowds of people ebbed and flowed around the gallery, the women in beautiful gowns, the men in exquisitely tailored evening wear, while wait staff circulated with drinks.

Glory was sure she'd spotted several A-list actors in the crowds, as well as a politician or two. It felt like being in a dream.

Castor's grip on her hand tightened and she found herself pulled very firmly up against him. His arm slid possessively around her waist, his fingers spreading out on her hip.

She liked being held against him like this, it made her feel treasured, but that strange tension that gathered around him wasn't going away. She could feel it in the arm around her, in the hand that pressed into her hip, in the hot, hard torso she was being held against.

People were turning their heads in their direction, whispering and pointing. The tension in Castor's arm increased. Yet when he moved it was with that natural ease and grace she'd come to associate with him, the mask he wore, his charming smile, firmly in place.

It had been so long since she'd seen it she'd almost forgotten the persona he wore around other people. She didn't like it, she realised. She didn't like him having to hide himself, to pretend to be this other jaded, dissolute man, and she didn't like others thinking he was that same man too.

Because he wasn't. He was so many other wonderful things and she hated, all of a sudden, that he hid his true self away.

He has to do that, remember? He's playing a part.

Yes, his mission to take down those trafficking rings by infiltrating them. By turning himself into one of those men. And he'd been doing it for at least a decade…

A sudden grief constricted around her heart as Castor guided them around the gallery, greeting people, answering questions and receiving congratulations on their marriage.

She glanced up at him, the discomfort she'd had coming in deepening. His handsome features had become hard, almost cold, his gaze relentlessly scanning the room. She noticed the black-suited men moving through the room too, fanning out around her and Castor like a protective shield.

He'd been living like this for a long time, pretending to be someone else, pretending to be as awful as the people he associated with. And that had to have affected him. If there was one thing she'd learned about him in the past two weeks, it was that he was a protective, caring man and capable of great kindness. What had all this pretence done to him? Was he tired of it? Did he want to lay down the burden of having to do this just once?

If he was anything like Annabel and how she'd felt while caring for Glory, then yes, he probably did. Because that's why he was doing this, wasn't it? It was for his sister's sake.

The constriction of grief tightened inside her. It wasn't fair that had happened to him. And it was clear the night he'd told her what happened that he blamed himself for it and had been spending the last twenty years of his life trying to make up for it. Why else would he be driven?

She wanted to help him, but she didn't know how. He had a right to his feelings and she wasn't anything to him but one of his lovers. Who was she to try to give him comfort? When she hadn't even been able to comfort her own sister?

Still, she could perhaps try, in her own small way.

'Castor,' she murmured as they threaded their way through the crowds. 'It's okay. I'm not going to disappear or anything.'

He glanced down at her, his gaze narrowing into smoky amber slits. The charming man he'd been just seconds before vanishing and leaving behind a danger-ous-looking stranger. 'What are you talking about?'

As she'd told herself a number of times tonight al-ready, an exclusive gala wasn't the place for such a dis-cussion. But she couldn't stay silent. He was alone in this, she knew that. He'd told no one else, which made her the only one here who could offer any help. She couldn't turn away from him, no matter how little confidence she had in her ability to comfort him.

'You,' she said quietly. 'You're incredibly tense and you haven't let me go all evening.'

He looked away, giving the room another survey, his grip on her hand tightening. 'This place isn't safe for you.'

'Why not?'

'I had word that some of the guests here are part of that Eastern European trafficking ring.' He scanned over the crowds yet again. 'They wanted to see my bride for themselves, which means I have to protect you.'

Glory knew that should frighten her, but it didn't. What frightened her more was the tension in him. 'I'm okay.' She squeezed his hand. 'You don't have to—'

Very suddenly, before she could say a word, he pulled her aside into the shadow of a gilded column, out of the way of the rest of the crowd. Then with firm hands he pushed her up against a wall and caged her there with his body, his palms on either side of her head as he looked down at her, his gaze blazing.

'Don't question me,' he said in a low, rough voice. 'You're *my* wife. I am responsible for your care and pro-tection, and I will do it as I see fit.'

The ferocity in his voice shocked her as did the burn-ing look in his eyes. He was staring at her as if he was furious with her, looming over her, his powerful body keeping her caged. And if she hadn't known him, hadn't known about his sister, she would have been frightened.

But she did know him and she wasn't scared. Because he wasn't angry. He was afraid for her. He was trying to protect her.

It's not about you, come on. He's still trying to save his sister even after all those years.

Her heart ached with a complicated kind of pain. Pain for the grief that still had a hold on him. Pain for how hard he drove himself. And pain for herself, that it wasn't her specifically he was afraid for, because deep down, she wanted it to be.

But what a selfish thought that was. This man had too many burdens to bear already, he didn't need her adding to them. What she should be doing was lightening the load.

So she reached up and cupped his hard jaw, trying to reassure him. 'It's okay. We can go home if you like. If that's easier for you.'

The expression on his face didn't change, his fierce gaze burning into hers for one long, unaccountable second.

Then he leaned forward and took her mouth.

Castor knew this wasn't the place for such displays—not that he'd ever let it bother him in the past—but he couldn't stop himself.

Her hand was on his jaw, her touch a sweet relief, and she smelled so warm and sexy and familiar. And right here, in the circle of his arms, no one could touch her, no one could hurt her. She was completely his. The dread that had gripped him the moment he'd had word that people from the Eastern European ring were here to take a look at Glory themselves.

Three weeks ago, it wouldn't have concerned him. He knew his security was faultless and that she would be safe. But that was before he'd spent two weeks with her in his bed, holding her. Two weeks of her smile and her wonder and her simple joy at all the new things he'd introduced her to. Two weeks of taking care of someone and watching how it made a difference to them directly, instead of wondering if anything he did helped anyone. Because no matter how many people he helped, there were always more.

She gave him hope, that was the problem. For the first time in years, the weight he carried felt lighter when she was around, and that was dangerous. Because eventually he'd have to pick it back up again and he had to be strong when he did so. He couldn't afford any weakness, any chink in his armour.

He'd thought he was fine though. The gala appearance was to solidify Glory's presence as his wife, and his contact had already told him to expect an invitation from one of shadowy heads of the trafficking ring, which meant his ruse was working.

But what he hadn't expected was the dread that had gripped him the moment they'd stepped out of the limo. The dread that centred on Glory and something happening to her. Something he couldn't prevent or save her from.

He'd tried to brush it off, tried to ignore the cold fear the way he'd been ignoring all his emotions for the past twenty years. But it didn't work. And the longer the night went on, the more the dread tightened its grip until he could hardly breathe.

He had to ground himself somehow and her kiss was what he needed, her warmth and her touch, to keep that dread at bay.

You know why you're so afraid. You feel something for her.

Castor kissed her deeper, harder, fighting the truth. The truth he'd tried for the past two weeks to ignore, that made him feel like a man sinking into the ocean, and dragged down to the bottom, unable to get free.

He'd thought her so ordinary that she wouldn't be in any danger, that she'd be instantly forgotten, a nameless, faceless woman he could divorce in a year or so and no one would ever even be interested.

But he was wrong, as he'd been wrong about so many things. She wasn't ordinary, not in any way, and if he could see that, then so could others.

They could threaten her. They could take her from him. They could make her disappear like Ismena had disappeared, and if that happened a second time, he knew he wouldn't survive it.

Then you know what you have to do, don't you?

Oh, he did. And he'd have given anything not to feel this, not to care, but it was already too late for him. There was only one way out.

But first, he could have this.

Her mouth was soft under his and so very hot, her hands lifting to cup his face, and suddenly the most intense desperation filled him.

He pushed her harder against the wall, wanting her taste in his mouth, her soft curves against his body, her scent everywhere. Because there was only one way to save her and he just didn't want to do it. Not yet.

Castor broke the kiss, his breathing harsh in the small space between them. 'I need you, Glory,' he said roughly. 'Now.'

Her eyes were very wide, her face flushed. 'Here? But…'

He shoved himself away from the wall and took a

quick look around, but it seemed as if no one had seen them. Good.

Without a word, he took her hand in his, headed to one of the exits and down an echoing corridor. A door stood slightly ajar and so he pulled her into the room beyond it, shutting the door hard behind them and locking it for good measure.

It turned out to be an office of some kind, not that he cared.

Taking Glory by the hips, he pushed her gently up against the wall and bent once more, brushing his mouth against her. '*Mikri alepou*, will you let me have you? I have to... I need...' His breathing was getting out of control, the desperation winding in a tight band around his chest. Just once more to have her in his arms, once more to be inside her. Once more to hold her against his heart.

'Please, Glory...'

She was frowning up at him, concern in her eyes. 'What's going on?' Her hands were pressed to his chest and she was smoothing the cotton of his shirt absently as if trying to soothe him. 'You're upset.'

It felt like someone had grabbed his heart in their hands and were slowly squeezing it tight, and he didn't know what to do. He should talk to her, explain himself, but right now there was only one thing he could think of that would help.

He kissed her again, feeling her stiffen slightly, then relax against him, her hands spreading wide on his chest, then moving up to his shoulders, creeping around his neck.

Theos, she was such a gift.

This is the last time.

It would have to be. He couldn't put her in this danger, where associating with him would draw the wrong attention. And he couldn't allow her to get any closer to him than she already was. That integrity of his emotional detachment was under threat and he couldn't permit it to be weakened any further.

He should never have taken her on a honeymoon, never have spent the past two weeks with her. He should have walked away after their wedding and never seen her again.

The hand around his heart squeezed hard, making pain radiate throughout his entire body, but he ignored it.

Time to think about that later, now he just needed her.

Gently, he pulled her arms from around his neck, before dropping to his knees at her feet. Then he reached beneath the hem of her magnificent gown, his palms sliding behind her calves before moving higher, her skin smooth and warm and silky, drawing the hem of her gown up with it.

She trembled slightly, but he could hear the uneven sound of her breath, could see the look in her eyes as she stared down at him. There was heat in the deep brown of her gaze, the strong flame of the passion she kept hidden behind her sharp little face.

A passion that set him on fire.

He leaned in as he slid his hands up the backs of her thighs, stroking her and making her shake, then he touched the lacy front of her panties, stroking the soft heat of her until the fabric became damp and the scent of her arousal filled his senses.

He held her gaze as he pulled aside the fabric before covering her with his mouth, tasting her. She jerked in his grip, letting out a gasp, her hands coming to his shoulders and holding on for dear life. Her gaze turned dark and even smokier than it already was, her cheeks turning a deep rose.

Beautiful little fox.

He took her to the edge of pleasure and then tipped her over it, the taste of her sweet and musky in his mouth, her cries loud in his ears. Then as she was still trembling through the aftershocks, he rose to his feet and pushed her against the wall. He undid his fly, slid one hand beneath her thigh and hauled it up around his waist, dealt with the protection, positioned himself and thrust hard into her hot, slick sex.

She cried out, her hips lifting against his, clutching at him as he moved, hard and deep and fast, losing himself in the sweet grip of her body around his sex, in the sounds she made, in the scent of her everywhere around him.

Her like this would be a memory he would treasure for ever.

He wanted to make it last, wanted for this to be something she'd remember for ever too, but he was too desperate, and in the end he had to slip a hand between her thighs, stroking her until the sound of her climax echoed in his ears.

And then he followed her, losing himself in the dizzying rush of pleasure for just a few moments.

Yet real life was always going to intrude and it intruded now, rushing back on him, weighing him down, crushing him.

He didn't want to make this choice, but he had to. The only way he could continue his mission effectively was to detach himself fully from the intensity of his own emotions. And he couldn't do that with Glory around.

He would have to end this and quickly.

CHAPTER TEN

GLORY WAS BARELY aware of anything as Castor smoothed her gown over her shaking thighs, then adjusted his own clothing. Her heart was beating far too fast and the throb between her legs was an aching reminder of what had just happened between them.

Without a word, he took her hand and led them out of the room, moving fast down the corridor and out of the gallery.

She found the lights blinding, still processing the stunning effects of the orgasm he'd given her as he pulled her down the steps. His hand was strong and warm in hers, and it was a good thing he knew what he was doing, because she was still dazed.

The limo was waiting for them and soon they were both inside and pulling away into the late-night Parisian traffic. And it was only then that Glory began to process what was going on, because something was.

First he'd kissed her like he was desperate, and then he'd pushed her into an empty room. And when she'd asked him what was going on, he hadn't answered her. Only made love to her as if his life depended on it.

She didn't understand.

'Castor?' Her voice sounded a bit rough and scratchy. 'What's wrong?'

He was sitting opposite her in the limo, his elbows on his knees, his hands clasped. His attention was on the floor, the expression on his beautiful face shuttered.

He was silent for a long moment, then without looking up he said, 'I have to return to the States tomorrow. Some pressing work issues have come up.'

Her stomach lurched with a disappointment she tried to tell herself she didn't feel, because of course their time together had always been limited. This couldn't go on for ever. 'Okay. So are you going to tell me—?'

'You can stay in France as long as you wish. My staff will be at your complete disposal.'

She stared at his shuttered face. He'd been so desperate back there in that room, holding onto her tightly, as if he'd been afraid she'd slip away from him.

Or as if that was the last time...

A thread of ice wound through her. She didn't want to ask, but she had to know.

'Is this it?' Her voice sounded hoarse. 'Is this the end? Is this goodbye?'

He lifted his head, his amber gaze gone suddenly cold, as if there was a sheet of glass between them. 'Give some thought as to where you want to live as my wife. I'll have my property manager give you a list of suitable properties. There's a place in the Hollywood Hills you might like. Or if you'd prefer the east coast, I have a penthouse in New York that will suit.'

Yes, apparently so. This was goodbye.

Her eyes prickled, her throat closing.

You always knew that this wasn't real, that it was only temporary.

Yes, and she'd told herself so many times these past two weeks. But all of that hadn't helped her prepare for the moment when it would all end. And now that moment was here it was every bit as painful and terrible as she thought it would be.

Why are you so upset?

Oh, she knew why. She knew down to her soul. She wasn't falling for Castor Xenakis, she'd already fallen, hard and fast and irrevocably.

She was in love with him and she didn't know what to do about it.

'We can't…we can't have another week?' she asked, hating how desperate she sounded, yet unable to stop herself from asking.

Castor's gaze flickered, then he shook his head slowly. 'No, *mikri alepou*, I'm afraid that will not be happening.' Slowly, he sat up, his gaze unwavering. 'You're right though. This is where we part ways.'

She didn't want to be needy, didn't want to demand things of him that he couldn't give her, because as she'd told herself time and time again, she didn't have the right.

Yet she couldn't stop the words from coming out. 'What about another few days? Surely that's okay?'

'That will only be putting off the inevitable.' He let out a breath. 'This was never going to be real, Glory, I told you that. And it can't be, understand?'

She swallowed, her throat suddenly thick. 'Why not? Why can't it be real?'

The cold mask that had settled over his features rippled, revealing what lay underneath, that bleak expression and a rawness that made her chest feel like it was full of broken glass.

'Because I can't,' he said, suddenly fierce. 'Because it's too dangerous for you, and now that you're my wife, you'll be put in harm's way.'

'But I'm already in harm's way,' she said a little desperately. 'And you have a lot of security. And I don't mind—'

'You might not, but I do.' His gaze burned as he stared at her. '*I* can't do it, Glory. *I* can't let anything happen to you. You're too important to me already and you shouldn't be. You're a threat to my mission and I can't allow that to continue.'

Shock stole her breath. 'A threat? What are you talking about?'

His expression shifted for a moment, became softer, warmer. '*Mikri alepou*, you have no idea what the past two weeks have meant and how much I've enjoyed being with you. It was a…respite for me. Some time out from reality and I needed it. But I have a mission to get back to and I can't be effective if I'm worrying about someone. If I'm afraid for someone.'

She understood. She understood all too well. She was a burden to him, an obstacle preventing him from doing what he needed to do, the way she'd been with Annabel.

Seriously? So that's it? You're not even going to protest?

But how could she protest? How could she demand that he consider her feelings? He was trying to save people and she wasn't more important than all of them. She wasn't more important to his mission.

'I…get it,' she said huskily, her chest aching. 'I really do. I wouldn't want to get in the way of what you're doing.'

The warmth drained slowly from his expression, the lines of his face hardening once again. 'I have to do this, Glory. You understand that, don't you?'

She wasn't sure why he seemed to think she was arguing with him. 'Of course I understand.'

'It's for Ismena's sake.' Gold glittered in his eyes. 'It was my fault that night. I was the one who took her out and all because I wanted to talk to some girl. Because I put my own needs first.' A muscle jumped in the side of his jaw. 'I shouldn't have. I should have been watching out for her. I should have protected her. And I didn't.'

The broken glass in Glory's chest shifted around, cutting into her. There was so much pain in his beautiful voice, so much self-recrimination, that she forgot her own hurt, leaning across the space between them and reaching for his hand, taking it in hers.

'Stop punishing yourself, Castor,' she said thickly. 'Please, stop.'

He went still, his gaze flaring. 'Glory...'

'Don't think I can't see it,' she went on, because now the words were out she had to keep going. 'You were fifteen. You were a child. How were you to know what was going to happen? You couldn't have predicted—'

'No.' The word fell like a sword, heavy and edged and lethal. 'You think I can excuse myself simply because I was fifteen? Everyone knew there were traffickers about in our neighbourhood—it was common gossip. Do you think I took any notice? No, I didn't.' He spat out a curse in Greek then, rough and guttural, and ripped his hand from hers. 'I was her older brother and I should have protected her, and there is no forgiveness for my failure. None at all.'

The warmth of his fingers in hers lingered on her skin, but the pain of his withdrawal stung. She didn't know what to say or how to help him, because she'd never suffered a loss like he had, not something so terrible. It was true that she'd lost her parents but that was an old grief, and not one she'd ever blamed herself for the way he had.

You have something to offer him though.

Glory took a breath as realisation came to her. Because yes, she did. She might be a plain, ordinary checkout girl, but there was one thing that she was that he wasn't.

She was someone's little sister.

She braced herself, then met his gaze and held it, blinking back her tears. 'Your sister would forgive you. And she wouldn't want you punishing yourself. It would have broken her heart if she knew you'd spent the last twenty years torturing yourself for something that wasn't even your fault to begin with.'

His eyes blazed with sudden fury. 'What would you know about it? What would you know about what she would and wouldn't have done? Ismena wasn't your sister. She was mine!'

Glory didn't look away. 'What would I know? I know that I would have done anything to make Annabel's life better. Because watching my older sister run herself into the ground trying to take care of me just about broke my heart.' The tears she'd been holding back suddenly spilled out, running down her cheeks, but she didn't stop them. 'And if I was Ismena, that's exactly how I'd feel, watching you suffer for something you shouldn't take the blame for.'

He stared at her for a long moment, the anger dying out of his eyes, leaving behind it that terrible bleakness, that terrible grief. 'I don't know,' he said roughly, 'why you'd even care.'

Glory swallowed. 'Why? Because I'm in love with you.'

He'd thought, that after the last twenty years, he'd got rid of the last remnants of his own heart. But apparently he was wrong, because looking into Glory's eyes, he could feel the remains of it tearing itself apart.

He let it though, let it tear itself to pieces in his chest. Because he didn't want it. Love was another threat to his mission, another weakness he couldn't afford. Love was nothing but recrimination and grief and twenty years of grinding sorrow, and he didn't want anything to do with it.

Even her love?

Castor ignored the thought. There was no point in continuing this conversation and dragging this whole process out. He'd made his decision and it didn't matter if Glory didn't like it, just as it didn't matter what she felt for him.

He'd said goodbye in that room in the Musée d'Orsay, he'd taken his last fill of her, and now it was over.

Why? There is an alternative, you know. Your life doesn't have to be all about the mission.

A ridiculous thought. His life was *only* the mission. His sister demanded justice and he would give it to her somehow. Otherwise what would be the point of the past twenty years?

Castor stared at the warm, lovely woman sitting opposite; she wasn't so ordinary after all, and never had been. He felt…nothing. An echoing coldness in his chest where his heart had once been. It was comforting.

'I'm sorry,' he said flatly. 'That is not my problem.' He turned, hit the button on the intercom. 'Stop the car.'

Glory took a shaken breath. 'Castor…'

The limo came to a stop.

'Castor, please.'

He found himself pulling at his tie, trying to get some air, because it felt as if he could hardly breathe.

Already this whole scene had gone on too long. It was time to bring it to an end.

Ignoring her, Castor opened the door, got out and strode away.

He didn't return to the mansion that night. Instead he took the jet to London, then spent a week at his company's London office, before crossing the Atlantic to New

York. His staff informed him that Glory was still in Paris, which was fine. He told them to keep him posted.

Then he got the invite he'd been waiting for to an exclusive party thrown by the inner circle of the group he'd been trying to infiltrate. Apparently rumours of his wedding had been circulating and there had been 'approval' from certain quarters.

He would get his meeting.

Castor told himself he was pleased since obviously marrying her had been a good thing, but no matter the emptiness in the centre of his chest, the dread wouldn't leave him. He put extra men in the security team he still had watching her, already going over plans for how he could take her out of range of the people he was dealing with.

Somehow, he would do it. He was the one who'd put her in danger by dragging her into this mess, and so he would be the one who would protect her.

You hurt her.

Yes, he had. But better the wound to her heart than anything else. Besides, she deserved someone who would put her first, and that someone wasn't him.

His mission was more important and always would be.

Eventually he got word that Glory had returned to LA, but not to any of his residences. She'd gone back to her apartment, which he didn't understand, not when she could have had any property she wanted.

Then again, who was he to argue? He'd let her go. He'd put distance between them, and that distance would have to stay. He made sure his security team was keeping an eye on her though, not that it mattered any more.

Not now he'd finally stopped caring.

CHAPTER ELEVEN

GLORY SAT AT the kitchen table in the run-down apartment she shared with Annabel and waited.

The flight from Paris had taken it out of her, and not only was she heartbroken, she was also jet-lagged and exhausted, and the very last thing she felt like doing was fronting up to Annabel with the truth.

But she couldn't bear the thought of lying any longer.

She couldn't bear the thought of pretending either.

She'd tried to do that in Paris the whole past week, telling herself her heart wasn't broken in two, and that she didn't ache for him, or miss him, or wish he was with her every second of the day. And of course that hadn't worked. Being in his mansion, surrounded by the memories of the precious couple of weeks they'd had together, only made the pain in her heart more acute.

So she'd finally packed her bags and headed home, taking with her the knowledge that the only thing she had left was the truth.

She loved him, but he didn't love her. He'd walked away.

A part of her had wanted to go after him when he'd got out of the limo, to demand they discuss it, but it had taken all she had simply to tell him the truth and she hadn't had the strength to face him. Not when it was so obvious that her love was just another burden he had to bear.

Sure, keep telling yourself it's all about not having the right to push him or not wanting to be a burden, when the truth is you're just terrified you're not good enough for him.

She wasn't sure what to think about that, but then she heard the key in the lock of the front door and a couple of minutes later Annabel came into the kitchen.

Her sister's brown eyes widened and she stopped dead in the doorway. 'Glory? You're back!'

Glory sucked in a breath. 'Hi, Anna,' she said thickly. 'I…need to talk to you.'

'Where have you been?' Annabel demanded, taking a couple of steps into the room, her shock moving into anger. 'I've been worried sick—'

'I lied to you,' Glory interrupted, needing to get this over and done with as quickly as possible. 'I'm sure you know that already. I'm sure you've seen the news.'

'Lied to me about what? And no, I haven't seen anything on the news.'

Glory sighed. 'You haven't seen the news about me and Castor Xenakis?'

'That billionaire guy?' Her sister frowned. 'What about him? What's he got to do with this? And what have you been doing?'

So, Glory explained everything that had happened, starting with that night in Castor's mansion and detailing the wedding, the honeymoon and finally the gala in Paris and how he'd left her. The only thing she left out was his mission since that wasn't her secret to give.

When she was done, Annabel looked at her in dumbfounded silence, and just like that Glory decided she was done with avoiding confrontation and making things okay for her sister.

She'd been letting Annabel's opinion guide her life for far too long and she was over it. Just as she was over pretending she wasn't in love with a man out of her league and unsuitable for her in every way.

'Just so you know,' Glory said into the tense silence, 'I don't care if you're disappointed in me. And if you don't want to pursue the IVF because Castor paid for it, then that's up to you.' She drew herself up, finding inside her the same well of strength she'd discovered with Castor. 'But you should know that I don't regret marrying him and I don't regret spending two weeks with him in Europe. And most of all, I don't regret loving him, because I do.'

For a long moment there was silence and then Annabel sighed. 'I wasn't the best sister to you, was I?'

Glory blinked, not expecting this. 'What? Of course you were. You were the best. I couldn't have asked—'

'Because if I was,' Annabel went on as if Glory hadn't spoken. 'You would have told me the truth. You wouldn't have felt you had to lie.'

Glory stared at her. Because it wasn't an accusation. It sounded more like...regret. And it was on the tip of her tongue to tell Annabel that she'd lied to save her worry, but that would be doing both of them a disservice.

She wasn't a child any more. She wasn't the little sister Annabel had to look after. She was an adult and she could handle the truth. If anything, Castor had shown her that.

'I'm sorry I lied,' Glory said at last. 'I didn't want you to talk me out of it and I...didn't want to be treated like a child. As if I can't be trusted to make my own decisions.'

Annabel shook her head. 'Oh, Glor... I never meant... It wasn't...' She trailed off. 'All I wanted to do—all I *ever* wanted to do—was protect you. You understand that, don't you?'

'I do,' Glory said. 'And all I ever wanted to do was to save you from worry.'

For a long moment the two of them looked at each other. Then Annabel crossed the kitchen and wrapped her arms around Glory, giving her a giant hug. 'I'm so sorry he left,' she murmured as Glory hugged her back. 'For what it's worth, he's an idiot to walk away.'

A tension Glory hadn't even known she was feeling gradually ebbed. 'He had his reasons.'

Annabel released her, then stepped back. 'Why didn't you go after him?'

Glory sighed. 'I…couldn't.'

'Why not?' And then suddenly something fierce glowed in her sister's gaze. 'You love him, don't you?'

Glory swallowed. 'Well, yes…'

You know why you didn't go after him.

Oh, she did. And it wasn't so much a realisation as an admission.

She'd let him go. She hadn't stopped him from getting out of the limo and she hadn't gone after him the next day. She hadn't made any attempt to contact him afterwards; she'd simply drifted around Paris in a devastated fashion trying to pull herself together enough to get home.

And now she was home. Back in her old apartment, ready to resume her old life. Was that all there was? Was that what she was doomed to? Watching her sister finally get what she wanted, while she sat behind the counter with no dreams and no plans. Never allowing herself to think of all the things *she* wanted.

Because you never thought you deserved them. Because you never thought you were good enough for them.

It was true. And as Glory stared sightlessly at her sister, all she could think about was the time she'd had with Castor and all the things he'd showed her, the big wide world outside her narrow LA existence. A world she'd never thought would be within reach of a girl like her.

Yet she'd not only reached for it, she'd held it in her hands.

A world with Castor in it.

A world where she was good enough for him.

Glory took a ragged breath, pain curling around her heart. Pain because she hadn't held on to that world, she'd let it go. She'd been afraid and hurt, and so it was easier to open her fingers and release it, than to stay and fight for it.

Like Annabel had stayed and fought for her, even when things had been hard.

Like Castor had fought for his sister too, even through his grief.

Because that was love, wasn't it? It wasn't turning tail and running when things got hard; it was digging in and staying despite it.

Because it was worth it.

He was worth it.

Something rippled through her, a powerful wave of emotion, the same kind of emotion that had propelled her into Castor's mansion that first night a couple of months earlier.

She couldn't stay here, safe in her little world. She had to find the courage of her own convictions. She had to fight for the world she wanted, a world with Castor Xenakis in it, and she couldn't let him push her away.

She'd never ask him to give up his mission, never ask him to put her before his sister, but she needed him to know she was there. And she'd be there for him whenever he wanted her, and if he never did, then that was fine too.

He just needed to know that he wasn't alone.

'I…think I've changed my mind,' she said hoarsely. 'I think I might have to go after him after all.'

Annabel didn't look surprised, only nodding as if she'd expected Glory to do this all along. 'Of course you do. Well, you helped me get what I wanted. Now let me help you get you what you want.'

So they sat down with the very old laptop of Annabel's and did a few searches. And eventually uncovered a gossip site full of salacious details of his latest exploits. They were all lies—which she told Annabel, even though she suspected Annabel didn't believe her—but in the last paragraph she found what she was looking for, mention of a party that was to be held in New York.

She'd had one meeting with Castor's property manager before she'd decided that living in one of his residences was a mistake, and the apartment in New York had been one of the properties mentioned. She knew where it was.

All she had to do was get there.

'I'll pay for your ticket,' Annabel said, already bringing up the booking website. 'And don't even think about arguing, Glory Albright.'

So Glory didn't, and a couple of days later, she was on the red-eye to JFK. She bought herself a simple dress of red satin that clung to her curves. And over it she put a cloak she'd found in a thrift store, just the way she had that first time.

The party at the Park Avenue penthouse was a nightmare to get into, and she had to let one of his staff know who she was in order to get in, but eventually they let her take the elevator up to the penthouse suite.

It was like the party in Malibu where she'd met him months earlier, thumping music and crowds of people, lots of beautiful women in beautiful dresses and some of them naked. She ignored them all, moving through the crowd unseen, searching for the one man who out-shone all of them.

He was nowhere to be found.

Until she finally pushed open the door into a small office and there he was, standing in front of the floor-to-ceiling windows, looking out over the city skyline.

Her heart clenched at the sight of his tall, familiar figure.

He was alone and he felt alone, and in that moment, she felt it too. They were so similar, her alone in the shadows, him alone in the spotlight.

But it didn't have to be that way.

'Castor,' she murmured.

He went utterly still as if he'd been shot, then he turned around sharply, his face full of shock. 'Glory?'

She stepped into the room and shut the door, her heart thundering. 'I need to talk to you,' she said, then flung off the cloak.

The hollow space in Castor's chest where his heart should be tolled like a bell.

His little fox was here. His *mikri alepou*. And he couldn't seem to catch his breath.

He'd thought it would be easy not to think of her, and over the couple of weeks he'd thought he'd succeeded. Yet sometimes a glimpse of russet hair or a pair of wide, dark eyes would make his heart race and all his muscles tighten.

Then there were the dreams that left him aroused and aching and wanting more. As if unconsciousness was the only time he could let himself have her.

And as she stood there, so real and lovely with her curls hanging down to her waist and her gorgeous figure outlined to perfection in a red satin dress, he knew all at once he was wrong. That it didn't matter how many times he told himself to forget her or that he didn't care about her, she'd somehow found her way into the empty place inside him, the place where his heart should have been.

And he could feel it now, beating hard and fast as he stared at her, a wild rush of adrenaline pumping through him.

She shouldn't be here, not at one of these parties. It was dangerous.

'What are you doing here?' he demanded, resisting the urge to cross the space between them and drag her into his arms. Because he knew if he did that, he'd never let her go. 'I thought I told you that—'

'Give me five minutes,' she interrupted, her voice very level and very determined. 'I need to tell you something.'

His jaw was tight, everything ached. The music from the party was shuddering through the walls and he suddenly hated it with everything in him. She'd given him a taste of something more than the life he'd been living for the past twenty years, something better, and now he'd had that taste, going back to his mission was starting to feel more and more impossible.

He didn't need her here tempting him and weakening his resolve, not when there was still more he had to do.

'What?' he growled.

'It won't take long, I promise.' Without hesitation, she crossed the space between them and came right up to him, her dark eyes shining. 'I'm sorry,' she said softly. 'I'm sorry I told you that I loved you and then let you go.'

He felt something inside him lurch, as if he'd missed a step going up the stairs. 'What?' he asked, not understanding.

Strangely, her mouth curved in a warm, almost tender

smile that felt like it set something ablaze inside him. 'I let you go, Castor. I let you walk away from me without a fight. And I… I shouldn't have.'

She still made no sense to him. 'I don't know what you're talking about. You know this can't happen between us. I thought I made myself clear.'

'Oh, you did. Very clear. But I'm sorry, if you think you're getting rid of me that easily, you're mistaken.' She lifted a hand and touched the side of his face, her fingertips brushing his skin like falling sparks. 'I know what your mission means to you and I would never ask you to give it up. I would never ask you to choose. But I want you to know that the one thing I'm never giving up is loving you.' Her fingertips brushed the line of his jaw, so softly, so gently. 'I let you go, because I was afraid to fight for you, afraid because I thought I wasn't good enough for you. Afraid of being a burden the way I was for Annabel.'

He couldn't move. Her touch held him frozen the way her touch always had. Made his breath catch and the heart he was so sure was dead and gone race.

'But I'm not afraid any more, Castor.' Her gaze was black velvet, soft and deep. 'Love doesn't run away from a fight. It doesn't avoid confrontation. It doesn't break when things get hard either, and it was Annabel who showed me that.' Her fingertips brushed his lower lip. 'And you showed me that too.'

'Me?' His voice didn't even sound like his, so rough and guttural.

'Yes.' Her smile deepened. 'Annabel loved me, that's why she cared for me, even when things were hard, and that's what you're doing too. You loved Ismena. You didn't run away when things were hard, and you didn't break when you couldn't find her. You dug in and stayed strong and continued your mission. For her.'

'Glory—'

Her fingertips gently pressed his mouth, silencing him. 'I'm not here to demand things. I just came here to tell you that if you feel the need to keep walking this path, you won't be walking it alone. You'll always have someone in this world who loves you and who'll always be with you, even if the only way you'll allow them to be is in spirit.'

There were tears in her luminous eyes and as he watched, they spilled over and down her cheeks, but she was still smiling. Smiling at him.

Then she went up on her toes and pressed her mouth to his and before he could stop her, she'd let him go and stepped back, taking her warmth and her bright light with her.

'Goodbye, love,' she said softly.

And then she began to turn and walk away.

And with each step she took, he felt the pain inside him grow.

You will always have her, but she will never have you. Because you won't let her. Coward.

How could he give himself to her though? He'd dedicated his life to his sister and the justice she needed, and that would always come first.

No matter what he wanted.

She was nearly at the door now, her hand reaching for the handle.

'Your sister would forgive you. And she wouldn't want you punishing yourself. It would have broken her heart if she knew you'd spent the last twenty years torturing yourself for something that wasn't even your fault to begin with.'

Glory's voice from that night in the limo rang in his head with an insistence he couldn't avoid.

Perhaps he was punishing himself. And perhaps Ismena wouldn't want that for him, but even so, how would that change anything? That would mean the last twenty years of his life would have been for nothing.

'Glory,' he said hoarsely, not even knowing he was going to speak until the words were out.

She turned, tears still streaming down her cheeks, so beautiful and bright in her red dress. His Red Riding Hood. His little fox.

'I can't stop.' The words were ragged and rough and he didn't understand why he was speaking when the quickest way to end this was to let her leave. 'I can't…forgive myself for that night.'

Her hand dropped from the door handle, her dark eyes full of tears and yet unflinching. 'Ismena would.'

His sister's name pierced him like a sword. 'You can't know that.'

But Glory's expression didn't even flicker. 'Would you forgive her if she was you?'

The question cut through him, because he didn't even have to think. Of course he would.

And the answer must have showed on his face, because then she said, 'Don't you understand, Castor? She loved you. And that's what love is. It's forgiveness.'

Something shifted in his chest, pressing against the heart he kept telling himself was dead. That heart that was painfully, agonisingly alive after all.

'I can't remember,' he said raggedly. 'I can't remember…what that feels like.'

Glory stepped away from the door, then she held out her hand. 'Come to me,' she said softly. 'Come to me and I'll show you.'

He felt frozen then, on the edge of something immense, the feeling in his heart too big for words. Too big for anything.

And abruptly he was back in his house in Malibu a month earlier, only it had been him holding out his hand to her. Offering to show her what it was like to be close to a man.

It seemed appropriate now that she should be the one holding her hand out to him, offering to show him what love felt like.

Except he had a feeling he already knew.

Love was grief and pain and heartache. Love was Ismena.

But love was also joy and pleasure and contentment. Love was Glory in a red dress. Glory poking interestedly around the Colosseum in Rome. Glory coming down the stairs in a golden gown.

Glory throwing off her cloak and offering him her virginity.

Love was Glory.

And he could not walk away from her.

So he took a step. And then another. And then another. Then her hand was in his and he was pulling her against him, or she was pulling him, he wasn't sure. All he knew was that she was finally where she belonged, safe in his arms.

'I love you, Glory,' he whispered into her hair. 'I love you so much.'

She went still and then melted into him, burying her face against his chest, and for a long moment they stood there together in silence, just being together.

Then Glory looked up and said, 'She would have wanted you to be happy. You know that, don't you?'

And he did. Finally, with Glory against him, he could

even feel it. 'Yes. But you'll have to show me how happiness works, *mikri alepou*, because I think I've forgotten that too.'

She smiled, pressing herself against him, her eyes shining. 'Oh, you haven't forgotten, Castor Xenakis. In fact, if you kiss me, I guarantee you'll remember.'

So he kissed her and it turned out she was right, he did remember.

He remembered very well.

EPILOGUE

'Stop looking so nervous,' Glory murmured. 'You'll be fine.' Then she stretched out her hands for the baby currently in Castor's arms.

Castor gave his son a final kiss on the forehead before he reluctantly handed Lucas over to Glory.

He'd never been nervous in his entire life but he was nervous now.

The helicopter had landed and in another couple of moments she'd be here.

Castor took a moment to ground himself by looking at his wife and son, the joy of which he still couldn't believe was his.

The past year had been a busy one. First, he'd used the information he'd managed to get from the heads of the trafficking ring, passing it onto the authorities, and just in time for them to intercept one of the ring's biggest 'shipments' to date. Not only had the authorities managed to save all of the people trafficked, they'd also taken down the heads of the ring itself, just as Castor had hoped.

The news of their capture was a great source of satisfaction to him as he'd disentangled himself from the rest of the web of traffickers he'd once been part of, letting Castor Xenakis, playboy, fade slowly from public life. He was a family man now. He had no need for anything else.

But that didn't mean he'd stopped his mission. No, it had only changed direction. He and Glory had decided to make all his residences safe houses for women in dangerous situations. Any woman could turn up, no questions asked, and they would be taken care of. It had turned out to be a rousing success.

Then six months after he and Glory had been living together, a miracle happened. He'd received the phone call he'd never thought he'd get from a woman he'd thought had died long ago.

The front door of the villa opened and Glory shifted their son in her arms, before taking Castor's hand. And like it had a year ago, he felt her love and strength flow into him, settling him.

'I love you,' he said softly.

She smiled. 'I love you too.'

Then the door opened and a young woman came in. A young woman he'd last seen as a girl, looking at the kittens in a pet store.

A young woman who'd been lost for twenty years and now was found.

Ismena. And she was home.

All Castor's doubts left him.

'Izzy!' he said.

And opened his arms.

* * * * *

THE COST
OF THEIR
ROYAL FLING

LUCY MONROE

MILLS & BOON

For my amazing husband, who has always been my strongest advocate and most enthusiastic support.

You've given me over three decades of love and laughter, honey, and I'm looking toward many more.

CHAPTER ONE

FRANK SINATRA SINGING "My Way" startled Prince Dimitri from his perusal of the United Mining contract.

It was the most important deal of his career to date. Dimitri wasn't going to allow a single poorly worded sentence to remain in the entire thirty-two-page document.

He tapped the screen on his phone, accepting the video call before the crooner started singing again. "Isn't this a little early for you?" he asked by way of greeting to his middle brother.

Konstantin and his wife made their home in Seattle, a time zone three hours behind his in New York.

His brother made a scoffing sound, his expression disbelieving. "It's only seven thirty a.m. over there, but there you are, in your office, chained to your desk already."

Dimitri shrugged. "So? I would have thought *you* would still be in bed with your lovely wife."

He had no wife and children to keep him in his sleek penthouse apartment through breakfast, much less in bed once he'd woken. Dimitri had been in his office since six a.m. and would no doubt still be here at six p.m. His executive assistant and their team would show up at eight a.m. These hours on his own, without interruptions, were usually some of his most productive.

"You need a life outside work," his brother chided.

Dimitri leaned back in his chair, working the kinks out of his neck. "Being older doesn't give you license to play agony aunt."

Even on the small phone screen, his brother's offence showed clearly in his expression. "I am no one's agony aunt, but I am your big brother, and you should listen to me. Wisdom comes with age, you know."

"You're a whole eight years older. Hardly a generation," Dimitri scoffed.

"Dima, I'm serious." Kon was no longer smiling but looking concerned. "You need a life outside your job."

"I go to the gym six days a week." He broke his day up with exercise and strength training midmorning. "I have my triathlons."

He was highly competitive, but all that training had to have a purpose, and Dimitri competed in triathlons throughout the year.

"If you were on a team, that might mean something, but you're an independent competitor."

"It is still something besides work."

"You were such a friendly child, but you've grown up to be such an isolationist."

"We all grow up eventually." Dimitri had reveled in his role as youngest son and prince, making friends easily and being a hell of a lot more social than he was now, until he'd entered the military.

Unlike his older brothers who had served in roles that would not put them in active danger, as the youngest son, Dimitri had been allowed to see combat. That time had changed him. Losing his best friend and other comrades to the violence of war had changed him. Losing the woman he thought he would marry had changed him.

The lesson he'd started learning at the age of six when he lost his mother to cancer had solidified in his twenties. Life was about loss.

The more people you let into your life, the more people you lost.

It was that simple. The profit and loss statement was heavily balanced in one direction.

He let no one else in. His potential for emotional pain was minimized.

"How are the boys?" Dimitri asked, when his brother didn't immediately get to the point of his early morning phone call.

His nephew, Valentin, was six and half years younger than brother Mikhail, who was now nine. Having learned from one of the best, Konstantin's son was just as good an older brother as his father had always been to Dimitri.

Dimitri had lucked out with both of his older siblings, not that he would ever admit that to either of them.

"Mishka is frighteningly mature for his age, and Valentin is never happier than when he is exploring." Pride rang loud and clear in Konstantin's voice. "They both miss their uncle."

"I will schedule a trip to Seattle soon."

"That is the hope."

"I hardly think making sure I come to visit my nephews soon was worth you leaving Emma and a warm bed for this phone call."

The expression on Kon's face said he agreed. So what was going on?

Dimitri waited in silence to find out.

Kon frowned and rubbed his face. "Growing up does not mean cutting yourself off from the joy of relationships, friendship or otherwise."

Dimitri's inner radar blipped. "You've been talking to Dad."

"He just wants to see you happy."

Their father had too much time on his hands since his health had forced him to abdicate the throne to Nikolai.

"I am happy as I am."

"Are you?" Only family could put so much meaning into two simple words.

However, Dimitri refused to be drawn into that discussion. Moments of loneliness were to be expected and not something he would ever discuss with his father or brothers. Though royalty, they were a close family. That *did not* mean he wanted to have some emotion-laden conversation with his older brother.

Sarcasm and business were their language currency, and he was pleased to keep it that way. "I am."

"You could be happier."

Seriously? Dimitri gave his brother a disbelieving stare. "Says you."

"But this is not actually why I dragged myself from my wife's bed so freaking early and snuck off to make a phone call."

Could have fooled him.

"Snuck off? That sounds serious." Even more serious was the fact his brother had been putting off the real reason for his call.

Whatever it was, it wasn't something Kon wanted to talk about, and that put Dimitri's instincts on alert.

Nevertheless, he joked, "I don't see Emma monitoring your calls."

"No, but I don't want her to hear this." Kon grimaced. "She's practically as close to Jenna as Nataliya is at this point. They're like three sisters by different mothers."

"And?" What did the sexy best friend to his sister-in-law, the Queen of Mirrus, have to do with anything?

"Nataliya is all right?" His brain automatically went there.

His sister-in-law had had a life-risking miscarriage a month after Dimitri's return from deployment.

He hadn't even known she was pregnant. Still in their first trimester, Nataliya and Nikolai had shared the news with no one.

Except perhaps Jenna, the fashion journalist that was like a sister to Nataliya, and now apparently Kon's wife, Emma. Dimitri hadn't noticed the three women growing that close, but then, with his office on the other side of the continent from his brothers' as well as their island country of Mirrus, he did not spend as much time with his family as his father would have liked.

Work kept Dimitri busy, though. He was determined to ensure the future stability of the company Mirrus Global, and by extension the country to which he had been born prince. It was his honor and his duty.

"She's pregnant again," Konstantin answered, his expression anything but pleased.

"Surely that is good news."

Konstantin nodded. "Of course it is, but after the last time, it is imperative she be exposed to nothing stressful."

While Dimitri agreed, he did not know how realistic a goal

that was for the Queen of Mirrus. "And there is something you think I can do to minimize her stress?"

"Yes."

"I cannot imagine what," Dimitri answered honestly. "Though naturally, I will do whatever I can."

"I expected no less."

Nor should Kon have. All three brothers had been raised with a strong sense of duty. Dimitri's time in combat had only intensified his own sense of responsibility. Being the officer in charge when lives were lost had taught him how high the cost could be of making even the smallest error in judgment.

"Someone close to the family is leaking sensitive information to the press." Kon said it baldly, with no buildup.

Dimitri sat up straighter, barely holding himself back from leaping to his feet. He was careful not to reveal too much of his inner thoughts or feelings. The practice was so ingrained, it came as second nature to him, even with his family.

"Personal or business?" he asked Konstantin in an even tone.

He didn't ask if his brother was sure, or how he'd come to that conclusion. It was enough that he had.

"Both."

Dimitri very deliberately bit out an expletive.

"Exactly."

"You do not know who it is?"

He framed it as a question, but Dimitri had no doubt he was right. If Konstantin knew the name of the culprit, he would have named him.

"Not as such, no."

"What does that mean?"

"The leaks happen after Jenna has been to visit Nataliya."

Something inside Dimitri seized painfully. Jenna had been accepted into the inner circle of their family by all of them. If she had betrayed them, it would devastate more than Nataliya.

His father looked on the beautiful fashion journalist as a daughter, just as he did his daughter-in-law, Nataliya.

From the moment Nataliya and Nikolai became engaged,

Jenna had been a frequent visitor to the palace. She and his
father shared a love for reality television that frankly had the
rest of the family baffled. Dimitri had thought Jenna was hu-
moring the former king at first, but had soon realized she was
as interested in the lives of celebrity strangers as his father.

"Impossible," Dimitri said after a second's thought. "Jenna
would never betray the sister of her heart."

Jenna had shown her loyalty to Nataliya time and again.
She'd been vocal about how much she valued her place among
the royal family, if equally outspoken about how much she had
no desire to actually be one of them.

The woman with strongly feminist ideals had no desire to
be a princess.

Konstantin sighed, suddenly looking like a man who had
gotten up two hours early to make a secret phone call. "I would
have thought not, but the timing cannot be denied. It has happened too many times to be coincidence."

"Either she's leaking information," Dimitri mused, still not
convinced, "or someone she trusts enough to talk about us is
doing it."

The latter seemed far more likely.

"That was my thought."

"Have you asked her?"

"Are you kidding me? What do you think is the first thing
she would do after such a conversation?"

"Call Nataliya." And that would cause stress for the queen.
"You really think Jenna would upset Nataliya right now?"

"Perhaps not on purpose, but even if she just lets it slip
we suspected her, you don't think that will upset our sister-
in-law?"

"Sure, but I'm not convinced someone as intelligent and
caring as Jenna would let something like that slip to Nataliya
when the queen's health could be at risk from stress."

"If not Nataliya, then my wife."

And that would lead to major stress for Konstantin. Dimitri got it.

"I still do not think there is any way Jenna would leak privileged information to the media," Dimitri informed his brother. "Or even talk about us to someone she trusts. She's too savvy for that. She's a journalist, after all."

"The timing, Dima."

Enough occurrences that it could not be a coincidence. That was concerning. As was the timing of the leak.

"I'm in the middle of an important but potentially fragile negotiation bringing several small countries together in a joint business venture," Dimitri informed his brother.

"Why have I heard nothing about it?"

"Because I'm still going over the information packet before sending it on to you and Nikolai."

Konstantin nodded. "There are a lot of reasons why another leak could be damaging, but I'll number that among them."

"Agreed. What exactly is it you want from me?" Dimitri asked.

"Find out if Jenna is the leak, and if she's not, who is."

"That sounds like a job for a security consultant."

"Nikolai wants everything kept between us. If Jenna is the cause of the leak, he doesn't want there to be even a chance that information could be made public."

His brother, the king, wanted to protect his wife's feelings, whatever the circumstance. Dimitri admired Nikolai's concern for his wife but was glad he had no such relationship to navigate.

He preferred the freedom to pursue his interests with unfettered ruthlessness.

"You live in Seattle. Why am I being tasked with this?"

"I've done my best to discern the truth and cannot do so without making myself suspicious to my wife."

"You don't think Jenna would be suspicious if I just showed up on her doorstep asking questions?"

"I trust you are capable of a great deal more subtlety than that."

"You want me to date her?" He wasn't some undercover spy.

"Would that really be a hardship?"

Dimitri hid his knee-jerk reaction. Going to bed with the

beautiful woman would be no hardship at all. Dating her? That implied the kind of relationship he did not do.

And it smacked of dishonesty.

So maybe his honor had some fetters on his ruthlessness, but that wasn't something he needed to share with his older brother.

Konstantin sighed. "Look, Dima, I don't care if you date her or invite her to participate in one of your triathlons. Just figure out a way to get close enough to determine where the leak is coming from."

"She's not a triathlete."

"She runs. She swims. Teach her how to ride a bike competitively."

Dimitri just shook his head at his brother's ignorance.

"I'll be in Seattle at the end of the week." But he was handling this thing as he saw fit.

Jenna Beals put down her phone, equal parts excited and worried for her best friend.

Nataliya, Queen of Mirrus, was pregnant again. After her last pregnancy had ended in a miscarriage and her nearly hemorrhaging to death, Jenna had assumed the other woman wouldn't try to get pregnant again.

Silly her.

Although Nataliya had given birth to both the heir, six-year-old daughter Anna Yelena, and the spare, three-year-old Daniil, it turned out the queen adored being a mother and wanted more children.

Children. As in plural.

Since Nataliya's miscarriage and subsequent bleeding had been diagnosed as idiopathic, which meant they didn't *know* what caused it, there was as much chance it could happen again as not.

So Jenna worried, but she couldn't help being happy for her friend too. Because Nataliya? Was over the moon.

Jenna would have to plan a trip to Mirrus soon, just to confirm to herself that her friend was doing as well as she claimed. Her heart sped just a little with the usual fillip of excitement at the thought of seeing another certain member of the royal family. Prince Dimitri: Dima.

The youngest and, in her opinion, sexiest of the three Merikov brothers, the six-and-a-half-foot-tall triathlete had a gorgeous body. With brown hair and gorgeous gray eyes, he was her own personal brand of catnip, but the prince was five years younger than Jenna. He was also the brother-in-law of her best friend. Then there was that pesky *prince* thing.

He was off limits to Jenna's libido on so many levels, it would take a skyscraper elevator to reach him.

A trip she was in no way willing to take.

Forcing her thoughts away from the delectable man, Jenna went back to work on the spread for the sustainable fashion article her magazine was featuring that month. The plus-size model, who had opened her own wardrobe for the photo shoot, had a ginormous following that had only grown after she'd caught the notice of a pop icon.

The interview and photo spread had the potential to be one of their most popular to date, and that included the dating and wedding spreads she'd done on Nataliya.

"Hey, Jenna, there's someone here to see you."

Jenna looked up, about to ask who it was, only to look into the gray eyes she saw way too often in her dreams.

Dreams that left her feeling hot and breathless.

"Dima!" she exclaimed in shock. "What are you doing here?"

It was as if her thoughts of him had conjured up the one guy she could not let herself go for.

Casually, for him, dressed in a spring-weight designer suit sans tie, he stood in a relaxed pose opposite her desk. "Kon asked me to come visit the boys."

His security detail must be outside the door, only knowing Dima, he could as easily left them in the lobby, or downstairs. He took more liberties with them than his brothers.

There were benefits to being third in line, she supposed.

"I meant here in my office, not Seattle." Though Dima

didn't visit the West Coast as often as his family would have liked, the fact he was in the city wasn't that surprising.

That he was standing in front of her desk startled her usual cool right out of Jenna.

"I had some time on my hands."

"So you came here?" Why?

He gave her the charming smile that was featured so often in the papers when his picture was taken. Only she'd noticed how it no longer reached his eyes since his deployment. No one else in his royal family seemed to find Dima much changed.

Nataliya did, though.

She wanted to ask him about it, but knew doing so would draw them closer together, something she could not afford with her ridiculous sexual fixation on the man.

"So you came here? When you are in town to see the children?" His sister-in-law, Emma, would be delighted.

Dima was a favorite with his nephews, and Emma liked anything that made her sons happy.

"They are in school, and Emma and Kon are both working, so here I am."

He made it sound like the most natural thing in the world, but it couldn't be much further from that.

"Why aren't you?" she asked. "Working, I mean."

His smile this time reached his gaze, but those gray eyes were filled with humor. At her expense. "Perhaps you have not noticed, but it is lunchtime."

She flicked a gaze to her computer monitor. Sure enough, it was twelve thirty. "Maybe I don't take lunch until one."

"More like you don't take lunch at all and sit at your desk with one of those disgusting protein bars." The words reminded Jenna that they still had an audience.

Skylar, the editorial assistant who had led Dima to her office without giving Jenna a heads-up that a prince was here to see her. The woman would have made a lousy receptionist. It was a good thing she was more interested in the journalism side of working for the magazine.

Speaking of... "Where's Rose?"

The receptionist guarded her desk and the inner sanctum behind it with the tenacity of a trained secret service agent.

"She's at lunch," Jenna's assistant offered helpfully.

"As you should be." Oh, Dima might be the youngest, but he had the princely arrogance down pat.

"And you are here to make sure I eat?" she asked mockingly, not believing it for a minute.

"It sounds like someone needs to." He gave Skylar a conspiratorial look. "Protein bars? Really?"

"Some of us actually live our lives without a personal chef." Did that sound snide?

Maybe a little, but sarcasm came as naturally to Jenna as breathing. Dima had never been offended before by it.

If the wry tilt of his lips was any indication, he wasn't offended now either. "How long do you need to button things up?"

"You're assuming I'm coming to lunch with you."

"Not immediately." He sounded like he expected accolades for the accommodation.

"You are a piece of work, Your Highness."

"I prefer Dima."

"Since when?" She used the honorific as a barrier between them.

A reminder of their age gap and his familial relationship to Nataliya.

And because she'd always assumed it annoyed him. He'd corrected his brothers and Nataliya often enough over the years.

Not that his family took any notice. To them, Prince Dimitri was, and always would be, Dima.

"Since hearing it in that snarky tone you use. It sounds more like a pet name coming from you than a reminder of my role as youngest in my family." His honesty took her breath away.

It also let her know that she had achieved the opposite of her intent.

"Are you two like a thing?" Skylar asked, her interest practically vibrating off her.

The look Dima gave the woman could have frozen concrete. "Do you work for a fashion magazine, or for a gossip rag?"

The younger woman gave Dima a flirtatious smile. "Sometimes they're the same thing."

"Not this magazine," Jenna informed her. "We don't peddle gossip, and you should know better than to speculate about something like that, especially out loud."

Giving up any hope of getting more work done until *after* she'd had lunch with Dima, Jenna shut down her system and stood up. "For your information, His Highness and I are not dating. We are not sleeping together, and if I hear anything to the contrary, I'll know exactly who to yell at."

Not that Jenna was known for yelling, but hopefully Skylar would take note that in this case, she would be more than willing to.

The younger woman gave Jenna a disbelieving look. So, not intimidated. "I don't think I'm the only one who hasn't left for lunch who's wondering the same thing."

"You've got no sense of self-preservation, do you?" Dima asked, his own tone disbelieving.

"What? Jenna isn't the type of boss to bury me under bad assignments because I irritated her. She's not like that."

Jenna didn't mind the confirmation that she had a reputation for being fair-minded and practical. However, she didn't like knowing her editorial assistant thought that sense of fair play meant Jenna wouldn't come down on her like a ton of bricks. Because she so would.

"Good to know," Dima said calmly. "However, I am a man who takes my privacy very seriously, and I am not nearly so forgiving."

Jenna knew she could trust Dima with her life, and still she wouldn't have liked being on the receiving end of that look.

This was the ruthless prince that few had met, but those who knew him even remotely well would assume lived under his urbane exterior.

No way could Dima have done some of the deals he had

since taking over the New York office for Mirrus Global if he didn't have a deep and well-utilized ruthless streak.

"It's not like I was going to spread any rumors," Skylar assured them hastily, her expression not nearly so sanguine. "I was curious, that's all."

Dima didn't look like he bought it. Jenna wasn't sure she did either. This particular young editor was known for how much she liked to gossip.

Showing a recently wakened sense of self-preservation, though, Skylar gulped, gave a weak smile, and took herself off.

Jenna grabbed her purse and cardigan. "I think you intimidated her."

"I am a prince. She should have been intimidated from the moment of meeting me."

"I can't tell if you are serious or not."

"Why wouldn't I be serious?" He sounded genuinely curious. "Most people are awed to some degree by royalty."

"I guess that's reason one hundred and fifty-nine that I'm glad my BFF is the queen and not me."

What looked like satisfaction flashed in his gray gaze. "You are unique, Jenna. You have never been awed by my family. I remember when you called my brother King Yummy."

Jenna laughed. She still called him that sometimes, to tease Nataliya. To tease a king who seemed to take life more seriously the older he got.

CHAPTER TWO

THEY WALKED INTO a Michelin-starred Asian fusion restaurant on the waterfront. "Oh, I've heard amazing things about this place," Jenna said with approval.

Those royal pearly whites flashed. "Glad to know I pleased, but I'm surprised you have not been here before."

Jenna just smiled and shook her head. When lunch would probably cost more than her car payment, this was not someplace that could make it onto her restaurants to try list.

Not to mention the weeks-long wait on reservations, which begged the question: How had he gotten them in for an impromptu lunch?

Or had lunch not been impromptu at all?

Whoever had done the decor was a minimalist with a preference for Japanese artwork, green plants and teak wood. A water feature trickled down the center of one wall over flat natural stones.

Jenna's stress level went down several notches as they stepped into the peaceful dining area. The noise level was low despite every table being filled. The architect and interior designers had done their job and then some.

"You had to have made reservations," she remarked.

And still, he'd offered to wait while she finished what she was working on.

"The chef is an old friend," Dima said dismissively. Like that was no big deal. "He keeps this table for his guests."

The table they'd been led to was nearer the kitchens, but not even remotely poorly located. Though she had to admit that none of the tables were situated in a spot she would have considered less than ideal.

"You have *old* friends?" she teased. "You're barely thirty."

"Is that like being barely pregnant?" he asked sardonically.

"Either you are, or you aren't. I am in fact thirty. You were there for the ridiculous cake Nataliya insisted on."

Nataliya had done an Over the Hill party for Dima's thirtieth as a joke, since thirty was in no way over the hill and the man was the youngest adult in the family.

"The cake was supposed to be shaped like a hill."

"It looked like a pile of manure with green bits. Not at all appetizing."

The epic fail had been funnier than the party theme. "It tasted good, though."

He pulled her chair out for her, subtly maneuvering the maître d' out of the way. "It didn't taste like it looked, and for that I should probably be grateful."

"She was trying to give a new baker a chance." Jenna smiled up at Dima as she settled into her seat.

The maître d' placed her napkin over her lap, and Jenna murmured, "Thank you."

The woman moved away quietly after Dima had taken his seat. The table could seat four but was still intimate for two.

"Well, I don't see the bakery getting a lot of orders off of that monstrosity of a cake," Dima opined.

"Then you're very short-sighted," Jenna informed him. "Nataliya told me the baker has been inundated with orders for novelty cakes since pictures of your party went viral."

"To each their own."

She laughed. "You can be such a snob."

"Because I don't want to eat food that looks like it's already digested?"

"Don't be gross. I'd like to eat my lunch now without that image in my head, thank you."

"I beg your pardon. I did not mean to put you off your feed." Jenna burst into laughter. "I'm not a horse."

"No, you are not." The look he gave her was all male appreciation.

"Don't look at me like that. You are practically my own brother." Oh, that was such a lie.

"Again, either you are, or you are not," he informed her

wryly. "You and I share no blood relation, or any legal relation either, for that matter."

"You are my best friend's little brother-in-law." That felt less like the deterrent she'd always told herself it was.

He gave her another heated, purely adult look. "Hardly little."

"Oh, brother, you are laying it on thick." And it was working. Jenna's body was zinging with *want* and *now* and *give me some*. "The question is: Why?"

He shrugged. "Why look at you like you are a beautiful woman? Because you are. Why look at you like I want you? Because I do."

"What?" She looked around furtively, but no one was paying them any attention. "You can't just blurt stuff like that out."

"Why not?"

"Because."

"You're strangely lacking in words for a journalist."

"I shouldn't have to tell you. Wasn't Skylar's reaction earlier enough? Regardless of what either of us said, the rumors we are dating are going to be all over our offices by the time I go home tonight."

"So?"

"So? We aren't dating!"

"We could be."

"What are you saying? You want to date me?"

"Don't look so horrified. I didn't say I wanted to court you; I'm fully aware of your aversion to being a princess. We can date…" He paused, letting their eyes meet and hold while the sexual tension between them built. "And other things, if we want. You are single. I have no commitments of that nature. Neither of us is looking for marriage or expecting long-term commitment of any kind."

"We aren't?" she asked, thinking he took a lot for granted. "Why? Because I'm not some kind of nobility?"

He didn't even bother to look worried, just patient. "Because you've made it clear over and over again how little desire you have to be an actual part of a royal family," he spelled out. "No matter how close you are to mine."

"That's true." And he'd been listening.

The waiter approached their table and placed a starter in front of them both.

"I hope you do not mind, but I when I am here, the chef selects my food."

"I like the adventure of that, but it surprises me you cede the control," she replied with candor.

The barely there tilt of his lips couldn't quite be called a smile, but the expression reached his eyes, so Jenna took it as a win.

"Control is an illusion in most things."

"You did not just say that." Such a sentiment was not the type expressed by the men in his family.

The women either, for that matter.

"You learn a lot about what you do and do not control when lives are in the balance." He shrugged. "Besides, who better to select my food than the man who prepared it?"

"You said he was an old friend. You must trust him a lot."

"I've had to trust him with my life."

"He was in the military with you?"

"He was in an American unit that worked closely with our Mirrusian one."

"So, not such an *old* friend."

"My last combat tour was six years ago."

"That's not even a whole decade," she chided with humor.

"You can die in an instant and live a lifetime in a year."

Jenna couldn't argue that bit of wisdom.

"I have no desire to get married anytime soon either," Dima said, picking up the thread of their conversation before the waiter's arrival with their starter, like they hadn't had a whole other chat between times. "No matter what plans my father might have."

"You're saying Prince Evengi would never convince you to sign a contract like he got Konstantin to do."

"No."

"You're so sure." Jenna wasn't as certain as he was. "You are every bit as duty-driven as either of your brothers."

"And I will do my duty," he readily agreed. "On my own timetable."

Laughter burst out of her. "I did not think it was possible, but you are possibly even more stubborn and arrogant than your older brothers."

"The privilege of being the youngest." His tone was as good as a shrug.

"You don't deny being arrogant?"

"I would term it *confident*, but I do not see arrogance as an undesirable trait."

"You wouldn't."

"It takes confidence to achieve one's goals."

"Sometimes it takes patience."

"I have plenty of that when I need it as well."

She made a scoffing sound.

"If you doubt me, ask any of the men I served with. War requires a lot of waiting."

"Does it?" Jenna knew very little about life in the military.

"Yes. Especially on the types of missions my elite team was sent on."

"It always surprised me that you were actually in combat. Neither of your brothers was allowed."

"As the youngest, it was my duty."

The very concept horrified her, but Jenna did her best to keep her expression neutral. Royal families did things differently. "I don't understand. Why was that your duty?"

"Neither of my brothers could be risked by serving in a war zone, but not to have a member of our family serve in an active unit when we asked other members our military to do so would be cowardly."

"What if there had only been two brothers?"

"Then Konstantin would have waited to do his military service until after Nikolai had fathered his first child."

"Konstantin would have gone into combat, though?"

"Yes."

"Being royal has a lot of unseen expectations."

"Especially for a ruling royal family."

"You do realize that it is medieval to have ruling authority based solely on the circumstances of your birth."

He gave her a look that couldn't be termed anything but indulgent. "It is also twenty-first century. We are hardly the only royal ruling family in the world."

Okay, so he had a point. "Even so, I don't understand why your brother, who seems to be a very progressive thinker, hasn't instituted a constitutional monarchy."

"You might be surprised to know that my father considered doing so."

"Wow." That was surprising.

With uncanny prescience, Dima stopped talking again, and seconds later, the waiter approached to clear away their starter. Another of the waitstaff placed their lunches before them before stepping away without a word.

Dima took a bite of the soba noodles mixed with vegetables and chewed appreciatively. "That is good," he said after swallowing.

Jenna agreed, having tried it herself and loving the umami seasoning with a hint of lemongrass. "It's a mix of Vietnamese and Japanese flavors."

They ate in silence for a moment or two before Jenna asked about the surprising revelation Dima had made.

"It was before my birth. I had no part in the decision."

Though clearly it was something that had been talked about years later, or Dima wouldn't know about it. "But His Highness told you about it."

"Do you realize that my father is the only person in my family you consistently use formal address with?"

She shrugged. "I think he prefers it."

"Perhaps." Dima took a sip of his seltzer water. "In answer to your question, yes, Father told my brothers and me about it."

"Why didn't he do follow through? He wouldn't have considered it if he didn't think it was a good idea."

"You are right, but ultimately, Father and his advisors determined that the potential for instability to Mirrus was too great."

"Of course, they did." Her cynicism leaked into her voice, but Jenna had seen too many men, and women too, if she was being honest, refuse to let go of the power they had grown accustomed to wielding.

"You sound dismissive. I assure you, both he and, later, my brother examined the issue very closely."

"But holding on to power was easier."

"Holding on to power, as you term it, nearly cost my father his life. It was the main reason my eldest brother's first marriage was an unhappy one. The personal cost of maintaining the ruling monarchy has been great to my family, but ultimately the good of Mirrus must come first."

"The good as you define it."

"Yes."

She respected that he didn't try to dress up his agreement. One of the things she liked about Dima was that he didn't apologize for his beliefs.

He was a good man, but yes, a very arrogant one as well.

"I could never be part of making choices for other people without their say-so."

"Mirrus is no dictatorship. My brother holds court, listening to our citizens and their concerns for one entire day each week. Furthermore, unlike a dictatorship, our citizens have the ability to emigrate whenever they wish, and because of our diplomatic ties with other countries, options for many to settle in."

"That's still not the same as a democracy."

"Where oligarchs make most of the power decisions behind the scenes with money and deals that will never see the light of day?" Dima asked with heavy mockery.

"It's not always like that."

"Your optimism is charming."

"Your arrogance is showing again."

"I wasn't aware I had tucked it away at some point."

She just shook her head. Point to the prince.

"Have dinner with me tonight." Dima's expression left no doubt how he wanted the evening to end after their meal.

Or perhaps during. Honestly, the man looked hungry.

And Jenna liked it.

But she wasn't giving in that easily. Not to a man who was used to getting what he wanted, when he wanted it. Like all the Merikov princes.

They were wealthy, handsome and charismatic. A fatal combination for the hope of any level of humility.

"We haven't even eaten all of our lunch yet," she demurred.

"It's not food I'm thinking about."

"I'm not hopping into your bed, Dima." No matter how much her body might be urging her to do that very thing.

"But you want to."

"Are you always this blunt?"

"No."

"Why me?"

"Why do I want you?"

"No." She didn't think she'd survive a listing of what he found sexually appealing about her over lunch. "Why so blunt with me?"

"You appreciate honesty."

"I do." And once again, he'd noticed. He listened.

She liked it.

His dark brow lifted in sexy inquiry. "So?"

"So, you are honest to the point of bluntness."

"Would you rather I was more subtle?" he asked like he really wanted an answer.

Jenna realized that no, she didn't want that. "I prefer the bluntness."

It should be easier to combat. Just say *no.* Only she was struggling with that one small word.

"You're five years younger than me," she said instead.

His gray gaze pierced hers. "If I were a teenager, that might matter. At the age of thirty, it does not signify."

"To you."

"Does it bother you?" This time his question came out as more of a challenge.

It had. When they'd first met, and she was lusting after a twenty-two-year-old who hadn't ever had a serious girlfriend, as far as Jenna knew. And because he was a prince with a significant public profile, she thought she would have known.

When he'd started dating Galena, it had certainly gone public.

"Jenna?" he prompted. "Are you really bothered by such an insignificant thing?"

"No." At least not in the terms he'd outlined. Dating. Sex. Casual. "But if it did bother me, it would not be insignificant."

"Point taken." His smile was sexy and natural.

It was also really devastating to the one part of her she didn't want affected by this man.

Her heart.

The truth was, Jenna was enjoying lunch with Dima a lot more than was good for her. She'd always found the youngest Merikov brother likable, if arrogant, but in dating mode?

He was a force of nature, his animal magnetism drawing her.

Charming and urbane, he willingly discussed topics of interest to her, showing a wide breadth of knowledge on subjects she found surprising.

"You're well-read on sustainable fashion."

"The fast fashion industry feeds too many societal ills for me to ignore its impact. It is important that my brothers and I are aware of the societal and environmental impact of any company we choose to do business with."

"Not all CEOs feel the same."

As CEO, Dima's oldest brother, King Nikolai, was the nominal head of Mirrus Global, the family-owned international conglomeration. Konstantin was the chief operating officer, and Dima was the chief financial officer, but the truth was, all three brothers shared certain responsibilities while delineating others.

That delineation could be geographical, like Nikolai running the offices on Mirrus, Konstantin controlling those in Seattle, and Dima heading the New York office. Jenna knew the brothers also had certain assigned work responsibilities they trusted to each other, while still working closely together.

"Is it hard for you to live so far from your family?" His other brothers were a couple of hours' flight from each other.

Even with a private jet at his disposal, Dima had to travel a good portion of the day to reach his closest family in Seattle, though.

"No."

"But you're such a close knit family."

His gorgeous mouth twisted in a slight grimace. "Since my time in the military, I have preferred a certain amount of privacy that distance makes more possible."

"You are still in the military, aren't you?"

Something serious flashed in his gray eyes. "I should have said active deployment. Yes, I have followed tradition and retain an officer position in our country's military. When my father finally retires as brigadier general, it is expected I will be in a position to succeed him."

"Not Nikolai?" she asked.

"It has traditionally been the role of a younger son, but my father was an only child."

"Oh." Her dearest friend had been married to the King of Mirrus for the better part of a decade, and there was still so much about the royal family that Jenna did not know.

The alarm on her phone sounded. Regret at what it meant swept over Jenna as she swiped the screen before the chimes could annoy the other diners. "I have an afternoon editorial meeting. I have to go."

Dima stood immediately, grabbing his own phone and sending a text. "I'll drop you off."

"But what about paying?"

"Sorted before we arrived."

"It must be nice."

"Many aspects of my life are *nice*. Just as many are challenging."

She thought that wasn't something he admitted readily to others, so Jenna took the confidence for the honor that it was.

Dima drove her the few blocks back to her office but stayed her with a hand on her arm before she exited the car. "What time would you like me to pick you up?"

"For dinner?" she asked. Had she agreed to that?

His gray eyes sent messages likely to make breathing difficult. "To start."

"You are persistent."

"It goes with the stubborn arrogance." Charm. He had it.

And Prince Dimitri of Mirrus was fully aware of just how charming he was.

She gave him a wry look. "I'll say."

His smile sent tingles of arousal to places she couldn't focus on minutes before going into a conference room filled with her colleagues.

"Don't Emma and Konstantin expect you for dinner?" He was in town to visit his nephews, after all.

"Yes."

"Well then."

"Join us." His finger brushed over the pulse on her wrist. "Emma will be disappointed if you don't."

"I'm being maneuvered, I think."

He shrugged, clearly unrepentant.

"You'll tell her you invited me, won't you?"

"Naturally."

Jenna shook her head, but she was smiling.

"Is that a *no*?"

"That's a *you're too much* head shake, but I'll be there. Emma would be hurt if she found out you had invited me and I said no." If Jenna had had other plans, that would have been fine.

But she didn't, and Jenna made it a practice never to lie to her friends, not even to get out of doing things she didn't want to do. In this case, she wanted to have dinner with the charming man a little too much.

She tried not to lie at all, but sometimes finessing the truth saved a lot of hurt feelings. Especially in the fashion industry.

CHAPTER THREE

Jenna changed her outfit for the third time and said a word she didn't usually say. This should be no big deal. How many times had she shared a meal with Kon and Emma and their two adorable sons? Too many to count.

She had even done so when Dima was there as well. The only difference tonight was that she was arriving with him.

After spending lunch flirting.

He'd made his sexual interest in her known.

Blatantly.

It had been a lot easier to think of him as King Nikolai's kid brother when Jenna had thought the desire was one-sided. Not that she hadn't noticed him looking at her over the years, but she'd convinced herself she'd been mistaken about the heat she'd seen in his gaze.

Why would he be interested in a woman five years his senior and not the supermodel type that usually vied for his attention?

At five-foot-six, with an average figure and a little above average bra size, Jenna would never be described as tall and willowy. Elegant.

She could dress that way, of course, but her default was more relaxed fashion, not to mention sustainable. Jenna wouldn't be gracing the covers of any glossy magazines, but that didn't mean she wanted Dima to look at her and see nothing but average.

Not usually so lacking in confidence, Jenna glared ruefully at the pile of discarded clothes on her bed.

All of this for Dima? Her best friend's kid brother? Or as good as.

He was no less off-limits in terms of a relationship than ever, but then, Dima wasn't offering her a relationship.

He was offering sex.

And if her instincts were on target, he was offering really good, really satisfying sex.

The kind of sex she hadn't had in too long.

Maybe since meeting the youngest prince.

Not that Jenna had been celibate, but physical intimacy was never as satisfying as she expected it to be anymore.

She'd dated guys who were tall like Dima. Well-built like Dima. Even men with the same espresso-brown hair and gray eyes like Dima. Men who were older than Dima, more experienced.

Or so she convinced herself.

And not one of them had made it past a few dates and maybe a night or two in her bed.

None had held her interest. None invaded her dreams. None made her ache with wanting in the middle of the night when no one was there to see.

Not like Dima.

And today Dima had made it clear he was looking back. He wanted her.

He wasn't looking for long-term, and she was glad. Even if Jenna could stomach the idea of being royalty, she could never be the wife Dima needed her to be.

She would always be five years older than him.

Sterile, she would not be able to give him children, heirs the throne required.

Even as third son to the former king, Dima was expected to have children. His father, Prince Evengi, talked about it enough.

Dima had a responsibility to both the throne and to his family in that regard. Her sterility was something she simply could not and would not change.

So his lack of desire for anything serious was in her favor.

If a tiny part of her heart that Jenna had shut off long ago grieved that truth, she ignored it. Like she'd been doing for most of her adult life.

What she could not ignore was her need to look her best

tonight. She wanted to make it hard for Dima to keep his eyes off her.

She looked once again at her nineties-inspired outfit.

The vintage jeans she'd picked up at a consignment shop from a top-label designer had strategic rips and aging, but what they did to her butt was amazing. Her rust-colored short T-shirt clung to her body, but it was saved from being too sexy for a family dinner by the blue plaid shirt she wore over it.

Her jewelry wasn't vintage, but she loved the statement pieces made by female entrepreneurs in Vietnam. The doorbell rang and she tucked her hair behind her ear out of habit.

She'd brushed her blond hair to a sheen of soft waves falling to her shoulders and refreshed her natural-toned makeup. Nothing more to do to get ready for this date.

Family dinner as a date. She almost smiled at that, but the sudden advent of nervous butterflies in her tummy kept the smile from fruition.

Jenna shut the door on her now messy room, forcing down the urge to ask Dima to wait while she straightened things up a little.

She hated leaving dishes in the sink or clothes on the bed or floor when she went out.

Dima himself waited on the other side of her door, and that brought the aborted smile out in full force.

"You could have just texted, and I would have come down," she chided.

He leaned in and kissed both her cheeks. "Not my style."

She returned the familiar Mirrusian greeting, her entire body lighting up as she pressed chaste kisses to his cheeks.

They were in the parking garage, walking toward the car, when he said, "I like those jeans. Very retro."

"Thank you." She looked back over her shoulder and noticed his attention was firmly on her backside. She smiled. "I like the way they fit."

"I do too." He said it in an undertone, but one of the security men made a sound like a stifled laugh.

Dima gave him a sardonic look but didn't seem embarrassed

to be caught ogling her. Jenna was doing her own ogling, so she could hardly complain.

Dima wore a tight-fitting lightweight silk sweater and slacks cut to show off his gorgeous body.

He stepped around her and flicked a remote in his hand. The door on the passenger side of the high-end sports car opened. Black, of course, the car gleamed under the lights of the parking garage. Even with the powerful engine and sleek lines, no Mirrusian prince would go for a color as attention-grabbing as red.

Dinner with Dima's family was as fun as it usually was. Living in the same city, Emma and Jenna had become very good friends over the years. Jenna had learned to tolerate Konstantin, and she adored their two boys.

Emma was down-to-earth, just like Nataliya, her role as princess only part of who she was. She was an amazing artist and really involved mom. Not to mention head over heels in love with her husband, Prince Konstantin.

There was no accounting for taste. Sure, Konstantin was a pretty decent guy, but Jenna would probably never forgive him completely for treating Nataliya like he had.

He'd had his reasons, Emma being the biggest one, but Nataliya had nearly lost her family over her decision not to fulfill a contract Konstantin had no real intention of fulfilling either.

He might have lied to himself, but anyone who saw him with Emma would know he couldn't have married another woman and stuck it.

The boys, however, were adorable as ever, suckering Jenna into a game of hide-and-seek before dinner.

"Now, count to sixty and don't look."

"They want to see if you can figure out their latest hiding spot," Emma informed Jenna as the boys rushed away, being awfully light-footed for a twelve-and a seven-year-old.

She couldn't tell if they'd stayed on the main floor or gone up the mansion's staircase.

"I remember doing the same with my siblings." Jenna's

heart panged as it always did when she thought of the years before they'd lost her brother. "My sister and I were always trying to outguess our older brothers."

"I thought you only had one brother," Emma said, her brow furrowed.

"I do. Now." They'd lost Matt when she was sixteen.

"I'm sorry for your loss." The words might be a cliché, but Emma's tone was filled with sincerity.

"Thank you. I never stop missing him, you know?"

"I never had siblings," Emma said softly. "I can imagine, though. I love Dima, Nikolai and Nataliya like siblings and I cannot imagine losing one of them, much less one of the children."

"The princes all experienced loss early." The queen had died, and it had probably been the beginning of the end of Prince Evengi's reign.

He'd abdicated to his adult son after a near fatal heart attack almost two decades ago.

His willingness to do so had always impressed Jenna. While Prince Evengi had been a king who ultimately had refused the idea of a constitutional monarchy, he was not a man who put tradition and royal duty above all else.

He'd preserved his own life for the sake of his children.

The fact he'd lived long enough to woo and then marry Nataliya's mother, the former countess, was just one more reason that choice had been a good one.

"He and Solomia are coming to visit next month," Emma said, showing their thoughts had traveled down a similar path. "Will you come for dinner again? I know they'll want to see you."

"Of course, but right now I think I need to go searching for your sons."

"They're going to be thrilled it took you this long to find them," Emma said with warm humor in her tone.

In fact, it took Jenna another several minutes of searching before she discovered the boys tucked into what she would have thought was an impossibly small space behind storage boxes in an under-stairs closet she'd peeked into twice before the third time going to the far back on a hunch.

She took their teasing over dinner about how poorly she'd done finding them in good humor.

Mikhail, especially, reminded her of Matt. Jenna doubted she could ever be angry or even annoyed with the twelve-year-old.

"You're a fabulous auntie, you know?" Emma said when the boys had left the table. "They adore when you come to visit."

"They do." Konstantin managed to infuse his tone with a surfeit of disbelief.

She made a face at him. "Your sons have good taste."

"They have never been treated to the edge of your tongue." Konstantin's expression said he wasn't particularly worried he had.

"Sharp-tongued? Our Jenna?" Dima teased. "I don't believe it."

"Yes, well, you weren't the prince expected to marry her best friend as the result of in her words, a draconian contract that any adult man with an ounce of respect for women would never have signed."

"I did say that." Jenna grinned cheekily. "And I stick by it."

"She signed it too."

"She was a teenager, and she was under pressure."

"So was I." It was an old argument, and the prince didn't seem to be taking it any more seriously than she was.

"You weren't a teen," Emma said. "But you were under pressure. I love your dad, bless his heart, but he knows how to administer a guilt trip."

"He's a professional at them," Dima agreed ruefully.

Konstantin nodded vehemently. "So, how have you remained single with no *draconian* contracts on your horizon?"

"That contract caused a lot of grief for you, Emma and his grandson, not to mention for Nataliya. It didn't take much to extract a promise from Father not to try anything of the like with me."

"I hear a *but* in your voice."

"But I have agreed to allow him and Solomia to introduce me to what he deems appropriate women."

Jenna's stomach plummeted, though she could not have said why. She wasn't looking for long-term with Dima, and she for sure didn't want to join the royal family for real.

Emma flicked a quick glance Jenna's way, looking a little worried, though Jenna didn't know why she would. "You agreed to let him matchmake for you?"

"Not matchmake, introduce. I have no intention of getting married anytime soon, and I'm definitely not going to start dating a woman of his choosing."

"Good luck with that," Konstantin said with a laugh.

"I'm hardly on the bubble to marry soon, being the youngest. In centuries past, I would have made a career out of the military or the church."

"Orthodox priests can marry."

"Indeed. However, none of our ancestors who became priests did so."

"Really?" Emma asked with interest. "I wonder why?"

"I would love to sit around and chat about our ancestors, but it's time to get back to my hotel."

"If you don't want to leave, I can run you home later," Emma offered Jenna.

"Or have a driver do so," Konstantin drawled sardonically.

Emma blushed. "We've been married seven years and still, I forget."

"That you are a princess?"

Jenna still remembered when news of Emma and her four-year-old son had rocked the royal family. It had been a hard time for Prince Konstantin, realizing that his own actions and those of someone he considered a friend had kept the woman he loved and the child he had not known about from him.

"And obscenely wealthy." Emma rolled her eyes. "There's something to be said for being a starving artist."

"There's something to be said for being married to your soul mate," Konstantin instantly countered.

Emma smiled. "I'm willing to be convinced."

"And on that note, we are out of here," Dima said, sounding a lot more like a younger sibling than a prince, or a business tycoon.

"Hmm, what are we doing here, I wonder?" Jenna mused, her voice laced with humor.

Dimitri turned off the sports car's powerful engine but left the ignition remote in the console for the valet. "You are just now asking?"

It had to have been obvious to her that he wasn't returning Jenna to her home within the first two turns of their drive.

"You could have been taking the scenic route." She gave him a droll look.

"I told you my plans earlier."

"You implied you had plans for seduction," she acknowledged just as the hotel staff opened her door and offered her a hand.

She turned and smiled up at the porter with pure innocence. "Thank you."

Shaking his head, Dimitri got out of the car and left security to deal with the parking instructions.

Two of his current team of four followed at a discreet distance as he led Jenna to the bank of elevators. They slipped inside the car with them, though, and his head bodyguard swiped the key card that allowed access to the penthouse floor of suites.

Jenna chatted with the security men on the way up, asking about their families, if they enjoyed traveling for their jobs. Dimitri would have put it down to the natural curiosity of a reporter, but genuine interest shone in her brown eyes.

Jenna cared about people.

Once they were in the penthouse, Jenna dropped her bag and shrugged out of her coat. Springtime weather in Seattle was mercurial, but one thing could be relied on, a drop in temperature after sunset.

Jenna showed her native Northwest roots by bringing along a jacket, even on a surprisingly warm and sunny spring day.

He took her coat and hung it over a chair while she looked around, taking in their surroundings.

"One thing I can say about your family. You all know how to travel in style."

He looked around the modern suite that was the size of his apartment while at university and shrugged. "The level of security we need comes with its own standard of luxury."

"Does it?" Her chocolate gaze mocked him.

"Tease me at your peril, lady."

"Oh, I am not one of those. I'm just a garden variety woman and happy to be so."

He stepped right into her personal space but did not reach out to touch her as he was itching to do. "I would never classify you as garden variety anything."

"Compliments? Already?"

"Compliments always." Jenna Beals was an amazing woman, and he'd always thought so.

She was a good friend to Nataliya, as close as any sister. There was no way that Jenna was the knowing source of the information leaks. Which left two possibilities: she was confiding in the wrong person, or she was being spied on somehow.

Tonight his security detail would be searching her home for listening devices while she was with him at his hotel. He would need to search her handbag.

It was highly unlikely her phone had been compromised. Guests who did not submit to the mobile phone security protocols at the palace had their devices locked in a secure vault that blocked all signals for the duration of their stay.

To his knowledge, Jenna had never refused to have her phones upgraded with the latest security software and checked on every visit to the palace.

"You've got a strange look on your face."

He gave himself a mental shake. "Do I? Are you sure it's not just the look of a man who wants to kiss you?"

Which he did. Even without his brother's request, Dimitri would have come looking for Jenna. His desire for her only grew as the years went by.

He'd never acted on it when they were both visiting the palace. It hadn't felt right, but then, he'd never taken a lover to the palace, much less taken one while staying there from among the guests.

Too much opportunity for scandal, and really? His family had already had enough of that. He and his brothers had each brought their own kind of notoriety to the royal house, and not in a good way.

Dimitri had no intention of featuring in the scandal rags again if he could help it.

"You're doing it again," Jenna said.

"What?"

"Thinking."

"How can you tell?" He was genuinely curious. Controlling his emotions and expressions had been taught to Dimitri from the cradle.

"You get this look."

"What look?"

She sighed in exasperation. "The one you just had on your face."

"I do not have it now?"

"No. Now you look irritated."

"Wow."

"What?"

"I am irritated." And she could tell. Unbelievable.

He had better control than that.

"Why?" she asked.

"I don't like the idea of being so easily read by someone," he said with more honesty than he would usually offer.

"Oh, well, I've known you a long time," she said consolingly. "It is inevitable I would learn your tells."

"If you say so." Even his brothers weren't that adept at reading Dimitri.

"What were you thinking about so hard?"

"You'd rather talk than kiss?" he asked, a little offended.

She rolled her eyes. "Are you saying we can't do both?"

That was not a denial she wanted to kiss him, and he took

that as a win. "I was thinking about how my brothers and I have brought enough scandal to our family."

Which meant finding out how someone was mining Jenna for information was paramount. Especially now that Nataliya was pregnant again and *not* ready to go public with the knowledge.

"You can't be angry with Kon for not knowing about his son."

Dimitri gave a mental sigh. She really did want to talk.

And damn it, as much as he found it strange, he enjoyed their conversations enough to put off the kissing.

And other things.

For a little while anyway.

"No. Would you like something to drink?" He headed toward the wet bar.

"I'll take a whiskey."

"No white wine spritzer?" That seemed to be the drink du jour among the women in his family.

"If I were driving after, sure, but I plan on staying a while."

"You aren't nervous?" he asked, bothered that could be the case.

"Dutch courage, you mean?" She laughed as she kicked off her shoes, the sound going straight to his groin. "Not all. I learned to enjoy slow-sipping Scotch whiskey when I was on an assignment in Edinburgh."

"Edinburgh and fashion are not synonymous in my mind."

"Don't be a snob. Fashion isn't limited to New York, Milan and Paris, I promise you." She settled onto the sofa, her feet tucked up beside her.

Dimitri poured them both a scant shot of well-aged whiskey. He handed one to her before sitting beside her. "I'm learning all sorts of new things about you."

"I think before this night is over, you're going to know a lot of things you didn't." The look she gave him told him she wasn't talking about her preference in beverages.

Dimitri did nothing to stifle the smile that thought elicited. "I'm looking forward to it."

"So, if you don't blame Konstantin for the scandal he brought to the family, do you blame Nikolai?"

"I don't blame anyone. It is what it is."

"Really? You don't blame *anyone*?" Her tone was tinged with disbelief.

"You mean Tiana?" Nikolai's first wife had done damage to both his older brothers in her pursuit of what she wanted.

Or did not want.

Responsibility. Motherhood.

"She was a piece of work." Distaste showed on Jenna's lovely features. "I was actually thinking more about Galena."

Dimitri frowned. "I don't talk about her." His former fiancée was a part of his past he had no desire to revisit.

"Nataliya's dad has some blame for the months your family spent in the tabloids too," Jenna said, showing no signs she was bothered that he did not want to discuss Galena.

"He does, though Nikolai got out ahead of him with the media."

"Your brother is a smart man. He married Nataliya after all."

"Smartest thing he ever did," Dimitri readily agreed.

The woman who had been born into Volyarusian nobility made a damn fine queen.

"On the other hand, I thought my best friend had lost her mind when she agreed to marry a king."

Dimitri laughed. "They have two children and a country in common now."

"She wants more children. This pregnancy, she doesn't want it to be her last."

"You know she is pregnant?" he asked.

"Of course, I do. Who do you think she called first?"

"Her mother?"

Nataliya smile was wry. "Okay, yes, maybe. But of course she told me."

"You two are really close."

"I love her as much as I do my birth siblings."

"I cannot imagine trusting a friend as much as I do my brothers," he said truthfully.

"Not even the men you served with?"

Dimitri shook his head in negative without hesitation. "Trusting a man with your life is not the same as being able to trust him with your secrets."

"You have secrets, Your Highness? Do tell."

A much bigger laugh than he was used to allowing burst out of Dimitri. "Not a chance."

"Because I'm not family?"

"You're as much family as Nataliya and Emma." She might not be married into their family, but Jenna was definitely a part of it.

"You wouldn't share with them either, but you and Nataliya have been friends for years. She told me you used to text her when you were away at school."

"I did." He'd seen the Volyarusian as an imminent member of his family since she'd signed that crazy contract at the age of eighteen. "She convinced Nikolai and my father that the gap year I requested was a good idea."

"And still, you wouldn't tell her your secrets?"

"I don't make it a habit to confide in anyone."

"Not even your brothers?"

"Not about everything."

Hid dad came closest to being Dimitri's confidant, but even then, Dimitri had a habit of holding things back, for many reasons. The most important was that as great as his father was, the man had an agenda of seeing all his sons married, and Dimitri wasn't giving him any ammunition for salvos in that direction.

Dimitri had never shared with anyone all that he experienced in combat. The two men who had experienced it all with him had not survived their final mission.

"What about Galena? I'm not asking you to dissect your past relationship," she assured him before he could shut her down again. "I just want to know if you ever confided in her."

The name of his ex-fiancée did not bring warm, fuzzy feelings to Dimitri at the best of times. When he was sitting on the couch with the one woman he had wanted for years, it was like a bucket of ice water.

"What is this fixation you have on who I share my secrets with?"

"Because we all have to have someone, and it worries me that you don't."

That answer surprised him enough he blurted out, "You think a woman who cheated on me and eloped with another man while I was in hospital would have been a good candidate?"

Dimitri might be the youngest, but it had been a long time since anyone evinced that kind of worry over him. He would have hated it from someone else but found patience for it with Jenna.

She was just that kind of woman. Despite her sarcastic demeanor, she cared about everyone.

"Clearly not, but the fact you didn't trust the woman you asked to marry you says a lot."

He was not sure what she thought it said, but Dimitri was certain that right now, he wasn't interested in finding out. "I don't understand how we got sidetracked by this kind of heavy discussion."

This was not pre-kissing conversation. Not in his book.

"When you were just looking for a good night of bedroom gymnastics?" she teased, not sounding perturbed by the thought.

"A fantastic night, thank you."

Her smile was filled with the kind of heat he didn't mind getting burned by. "I could go for fantastic."

CHAPTER FOUR

HE REACHED OUT to do what he'd been wanting for a hell of a lot longer than he wanted to admit, and pulled her close, his body going from zero to Mach 1 in a single breath. "Fantastic it is."

She didn't wait for him to kiss her but leaned forward and pulled his head towards her at the same time. Her lips pressed against his, her body doing the same.

It was no tentative kiss, but pure sexual heat, their hands mapping each other's body with urgency he hadn't felt since he was still at university.

Sex was a necessary, delicious part of life.

This kind of sex made him feel like he *was* alive.

She climbed into his lap, spreading her thighs over his and kissing him with the kind of unfettered passion he'd only dreamed of finding in a lover.

Literally. He had dreamed about this woman, waking up hard and aching, craving just this kind of sensual abandon from her.

They didn't make it into the bedroom but stripped each other right there in the suite's sitting room. Her breasts were gorgeous and full, rosy-tipped peaks tempting him.

She cried out when he took one in his mouth and suckled, undulating her hips against him. He was steel hard and aching to be inside her. Rubbing his erection against her slick opening, up and down, but without shifting so he could penetrate.

He had to get a condom on. Now.

She gasped and jerked backward. "Condom," she gasped. "I've got one in my bag."

He didn't ask why. They'd both known how this night was going to end.

"Hurry," he urged.

She jumped up and rushed to her bag, and dug through it,

tossing things with abandon onto the table. She lifted a strip of condoms in her hand. "Yes!"

"Bring it here," he demanded.

"Bossy." But she complied, crossing the room quickly.

He put his hand out. "Give it to me."

"I want to put it on you."

"If you do, it may be over before it begins." He would have been loath to admit that to someone else. Probably wouldn't have done so.

But he knew she wouldn't take it as weakness, or lack of sexual prowess. Not with how hot she was too.

She didn't. In fact, her dark gaze glowed with increased desire as she handed over one of the foil packets. "Do it."

"Who is bossy?" he teased to cover the tremble of his hand as he tore the packet open and pulled out the protection.

Even sliding it on himself made him groan. She climbed back onto his lap without preamble, arranging their bodies so the head of his prick kissed her slick entrance.

Using all of his self-control, his body taut with need, Dimitri waited for her to take him inside her.

Jenna shifted down and then forward, her body taking him in an increment at a time. She kept shimmying, making sexy noises that had him so close to coming he started reciting the Cyrillic alphabet backwards in his head.

Dimitri surged upward, pulling her down toward him, and he was fully seated inside her. They both groaned. "So good. Why is it so good with you?" she asked.

He had no answer. He only knew it was perfect.

They began a rhythm as old as time, their bodies surging together again and again. The sound of skin slapping against skin, panting and moans filled the air around them.

"Yes, harder!" She followed that demand with a word he'd never heard her say before, but one that felt very appropriate to the moment.

He obeyed, using his core and thigh muscles to piston in and out of her, helping her tilt her pelvis so he pressed against the spot inside her that made her scream. Over and over.

He was shouting too, promising they would both come soon, telling her she was perfect, and the sort of stuff he would never say in his right mind.

Suddenly she was convulsing around him, her climax nearly silent after very noisy sex. Her face was fixed in a rictus of pleasure that was one of the most beautiful things he'd ever seen. Then he was coming too, and his arms locked around her.

Too tight, but he couldn't make himself let go. He had to hold her as he came inside her for the first time.

She held him too, her own arms nearly as tight, her face pressing into his shoulder as they both shook with the aftershocks of pleasure.

He did not know how long they remained like that, but eventually he said, "That was pretty good for round one."

Her laughter rippled through her and around his flesh still inside her, bringing round two closer than it had been a moment before.

"You're good for a second time?" she asked with a smile.

"It's a good thing. That one was pretty darn fast."

"Neither one of us was slowing down."

"No, we weren't."

He was careful to hold on to the condom as she disengaged.

She stood up and gave a rueful look to their clothes strewn around. "We didn't even make it to the bed."

"That sofa worked well." It had in fact been just the right angle and height to make their frenzied lovemaking work.

She grinned. "Maybe we'll have to use it again."

"I like that idea, but right now, how about the Jacuzzi?" he offered. He'd had dreams about making love to her in water more than once. Not that he was admitting that out loud.

Wet dreams were not something adult men suffered from. Unless they met a woman like Jenna.

"Your suite has its own hot tub?" she asked now. "Swank."

"As good as. Both the rooftop pool and hot tub are reserved for my private use while I am here."

"I thought this hotel had a pool on the ground floor."

"They do."

"And a rooftop pool?" she asked, heading into the bedroom.

He got up on legs that felt just a little shaky. "Only for guests on the penthouse level."

"Sucks to be another guest while you're here, then," she said from the bathroom.

She came out wearing one of the white Turkish robes provided by the hotel and carrying another. She held it out.

"My security staff are using the other penthouse." He shrugged on the robe. "They can make use of the pool area when I am not."

"Really?" she asked a little skeptically.

"Why ask that? You know how my family see our staff."

"As valuable. Yes, I know, but you told them they could use the pool."

"Not tonight. I thought you might enjoy a naked swim."

"Is that safe?" She couldn't be too concerned, wearing the robe and nothing else with every evidence of being willing to go with him to the roof.

"Hotel security cameras have been disabled on this floor and the rooftop for the duration of my stay," he assured her. "My own security measures have been installed."

"Sounds like a lot of work."

Sometimes it surprised him the things *she* didn't know about how his family lived. "You realize that in addition to being ruling royalty, my family is worth billions of dollars?"

"Um…" The look of consternation on her features said she hadn't really ever given it a lot of consideration. "I just thought Nataliya's security was because she was queen, you know?"

"Certainly, that's part of it."

They took a private set of stairs up to the roof. Half the pool was enclosed in a pool house, the other half exposed to the elements. The hot tub was outside, steam coming off the water in the springtime chill.

Lights bathed the rooftop oasis in a gentle low light that did not detract from the view of Seattle at night.

"It's beautiful up here."

"And all ours for the night."

Jenna was having trouble believing she was here. Well, not here exactly. As impressive as this private rooftop pool area was, she'd been to some pretty amazing places in her life. Not least of which since her BFF had married a king.

But Jenna had never expected to act on the attraction she felt for Dima. Yet, here they were, practically naked and planning more sexy times in this private oasis.

"I have to say, Dima, if you set out to impress me, you succeeded."

"Good to know." He pulled her around and slid his hand inside her robe, no lack of confidence in this man, despite their age difference. "Now, tell me, was it the amazing sex downstairs, or is it the pool that's done it?"

His hands on her naked skin were distracting her, so it took Jenna a second to answer. "The pool would be nothing but a fun diversion without the incredible sex that came before."

He didn't reply with words but leaned down and took her mouth in a delicious kiss while undoing the tie on her robe, and then slid it off her shoulders. She let it fall in a pool around her feet. There was something incredibly decadent about being naked and out in the open air, content in the knowledge that no one could see them.

She tugged at his robe, wanting skin against skin again.

He complied without breaking the kiss, pulling her body flush with his when his robe had joined hers around their feet. Dima's strong hands cupped her backside, and he lifted. Jenna took the hint and hopped up, wrapping her legs around his hips.

It put her most intimate flesh against his, and she pressed against him, reveling in the bliss of having his hardness pressed against her clitoris, that bundle of nerves that gave so much pleasure. It wasn't enough, but it was a lot.

He made a growly sound deep in his throat, and she reveled in that too.

She'd reduced the urbane prince to his primal nature, and Jenna loved knowing it.

He started walking, but she paid no attention to where they were going, her entire being focused on the kiss and the press of their naked bodies.

When her feet dipped into water, she gasped against his lips. A second later, the lower half of her body was in the lukewarm water.

The pool was heated, but it felt cool against her heated skin, and she gasped again, breaking the kiss. "What are you doing?"

"You need to ask? Really?"

She looked around them at the water that was now brushing against the underside of her breasts. "You want to go for a swim?"

"Not exactly, though we could certainly do that later." His smile was nothing short of devilish.

"Then what?" No way was he thinking of sexcapades in the water. Was he?

"This."

This was hands sliding over her body slickly, the water making the caresses feel different. *This* was him seducing her body with every wet touch, every slide of his limbs against hers under the water.

"Come, lie back and float. I promise you will like it."

Jenna allowed herself to be maneuvered onto her back to float, her wet nipples peaking with near painful arousal in the night air.

It was the strangest feeling to have part of her body exposed to the air and the rest in the water, but all open to his touch. Sensual in a way she'd never experienced before.

Jenna had had her fair share of lovers, but none had ever been this confident, this adventurous.

Dima slid his hands over her body, touching every dip and crevice, trailing his fingers with as much sensual care over her calves as he did her breasts. When he leaned down to take a nipple in his mouth, Jenna had to bite back a cry.

The naughty look he gave her said he knew exactly how hard it was for her to keep it down.

"I should be touching you too," she said, not sure she really believed it.

This felt too good.

"Believe me, I get all the pleasure I need touching you like this."

That was a heady thought, so Jenna went with it, relaxing in the water, letting her body float as he wanted. She had no idea how long she floated like that, with him touching her and telling her how sexy and beautiful she was, but at some point he'd moved them so the side of the pool was right there.

Dima ran his hands up her arms until their fingers meshed, and then he moved hers to the side of the pool. "Hold on."

"Don't drown me," she managed to tease.

"Never."

He glided through the water until he was between her legs, his hard sex pressing against her entrance. Dima stayed like that for several seconds, as if he was entranced by the moment.

Or waiting for her to beg.

She almost did just that, or at least demanded he enter, when she remembered protection.

"Condom!" She was proud of herself for remembering in her current state of intense arousal, if supremely frustrated for the necessity.

He cursed but did not shift away. "Are you on birth control?"

She knew what he was really asking and that he wouldn't do so if it wasn't safe.

"I have an IUD," Jenna offered without compunction. "But I don't do sex without condoms."

Never. Not once.

He gave her an unfathomable look. "I don't either."

She took those words in, let the implication settle deep inside her. He was asking for something with her he'd never had with another woman.

They were both so turned on that to stop would *hurt*, but neither was out of control. This was a decision they were both making with their brains as well as their bodies.

A decision she wanted to make. They weren't making promises. They'd both been clear from the start where this was going.

Nowhere serious. They were friends. With benefits.

Jenna had never actually had an arrangement like this with a man, but it was the only one she *could* have with a prince.

Maybe it was their longtime friendship. Maybe it was knowing he was part of her BFF's family, but Jenna wasn't worried about breaking her ironclad rule for Dima. She absolutely trusted him not to be putting her at risk.

She let her thighs float further apart in the water, the invitation obvious. "I'm safe."

"I never doubted it." His eyes were dark with need, his body rigid with control.

"Okay."

"You are sure?" he asked, though the sexual strain showed in how tightly he held his body, in how hard he was.

"Yes."

"Good." He pressed forward inside her, his hard flesh stretching hers, making room for himself in her body and somewhere deep in her heart.

Not that she was ever going to acknowledge that last bit.

Her body was buoyed by the water as he controlled the depth and speed of his thrusts. She had no hope of meeting him. Every time she tried to move, her hands would lose their grip, or her body would shift in the water, doing the opposite of what she'd intended.

He gripped her hips. "Just let it happen, Jenna. It will be good."

She was pretty sure *good* was a huge understatement. Trusting him to give her the blissful stimulation she needed, she concentrated on keeping her body relaxed and floating while he controlled their joining.

Sometime later, as she climaxed in wave after wave of pleasure, she had to admit he'd been right.

She loved it.

His shout as he came said he did too, and that he wasn't nearly as worried as she was about being overheard. Though who she thought was going to hear them, she wasn't sure. Only, rooftop or not, they *were* outside.

Dima carried her to the showers, and they washed each other's bodies, kissing in the way that lovers do after mind-shattering orgasms.

When Jenna found herself sliding into bed beside Dima, she acknowledged, if only to herself, that she was breaking another rule. She didn't sleep with men she wasn't committed to.

And again, she wanted to.

Dimitri waited until Jenna was sleeping soundly before sliding quietly from the bed. He went out to the living area on silent feet, pulling the door shut behind him. He found her purse, most of the contents still spilled out on the table.

He started going through it all, item by item, examining each for any kind of surveillance device. He wasn't actually expecting to find something in her handbag. It didn't make sense to plant a device in something Jenna switched out to compliment her mood and outfit.

So when he discovered a sophisticated micro listening device incorporated into the design of a portable phone stand, he cursed quietly in shock.

Well, that explained a lot. Jenna used the stand when she video chatted with Nataliya; Dimitri had seen her do it. Even when they were at the palace together, they would call each other when Nataliya's schedule allowed for a call but not to break away long enough to get together in person.

The Volyarusian palace covered three city blocks, certainly not a few seconds' walk from one area to another.

He'd always thought the two women's closeness was special, and it infuriated him that someone would use it against them.

As glad as he was to find the device, Dimitri knew Jenna

was going to be devastated when he told her someone had been spying on her.

He pulled out the remaining items in Jenna's bag, examining each one just as closely as before. He could not assume there was only one device. Although he found nothing.

He then examined the bag, and his anger grew when he found another device inserted under a buckle on the shoulder strap. How many of her accessories had been compromised like this?

Whoever had done this was serious about gathering intel on the royal family through Jenna.

"What are you doing?" Jenna's voice startled him.

He should have heard her get out of bed. What was wrong with him that he hadn't?

"You woke up," he said rather inelegantly as he turned to face her.

"You weren't there." She frowned, like that wasn't what she meant to say. "Why is everything scattered like that? I know I pulled stuff out earlier, but not all of it." She blinked, sounding a little out of it and very confused, her beautiful brown eyes looking unfocused.

His body and brain were at cross-purposes as he struggled with his instant, nearly overwhelming response to the sight of her tousled hair and naked body. She looked like she'd just come from bed, and he knew she had. His bed. That knowledge was doing crazy things to his libido.

"Let's talk about it in the morning, *milaya moy*. You're tired, and there are much more pleasurable things we can do with the night than talk."

Jenna's body shifted subtly, but suddenly she was alert and not looking nearly as sleepy. "What exactly do we need to talk about? And when did I become your *darling*?"

He'd called her *darling*? Dimitri played his words back in his own mind and realized not only had he called her *milaya*, but he'd added the possessive *moy*. My darling. Shrugging off how uncharacteristic that was for him, he answered the easier question first. "I'd say calling the woman I had sex with twice tonight *darling* might be expected."

She bit her lip but nodded. "Okay, but that doesn't tell me what this serious thing is we need to talk about."

"You are so sure it's serious?"

"Yes, or you would have simply taken me back to bed while explaining what you were doing rummaging through my—"

He put his hand up and shook his head before she could mention exactly what he'd been doing. At the same time, he cursed inwardly. He'd mentioned them having sex. If the person spying on Jenna was monitoring, they would know it too.

Damn it.

But that wasn't as bad as the conversation that was coming, because it was going to hurt her.

He was tempted to sigh, but princes did not expose their thoughts so easily. However, internally Dimitri wished he could avoid what he knew was coming. He hated thinking Jenna was going to be hurt by the spy's actions.

"If you want to talk, grab a robe," he informed her. "You'll be far too much of a distraction otherwise."

She gave him a look, but retreated to the bedroom, coming back seconds later, tying her robe. He was closing the door on the room's safe, the handbag and phone stand tucked safely inside in the lead compartment that would not allow any electronic transmission.

Jenna threw the robe she'd had tucked under her arm at him. "Cover yourself. The same goes."

Stifling the reply he wanted to give, Dimitri slipped into the robe, surprisingly resentful that he had to deal with family business before they could return to the bedroom. Dimitri never resented doing his duty.

Jenna was giving him a searching look, her brows drawn together. "Why did you put those things in the safe?"

"Did you buy that phone holder, or was it a gift?" he asked, rather than answering.

"It was a gift. Now tell me why you tucked my purse and

phone stand away like the crown jewels." She spoke more forcefully, her intention of getting answers clear in her tone.

Finessing around the subject wasn't going to do either of them any favors. "There were listening devices in both."

"What do you mean listening devices?"

"High-tech micro-sized microphones that transmit to a receiver."

"I know what a listening device is." She gave him a look that said she wasn't impressed. "I just don't understand how you're telling me there was one on my purse and phone stand."

"Someone has been spying on you."

Jenna's lovely features leached of color. "No. That's not possible."

"Yes."

"But how could you know?"

No doubt Konstantin would expect Dimitri to lie, but Dimitri knew that Jenna wasn't going to put her BFF at any more at risk than the rest of them would. She wasn't going to go calling Nataliya the moment he and she were done talking.

So he told her about the leaks and Konstantin's certainty they were somehow coming from her.

"You're saying Prince Konstantin thought *I* was leaking stuff to the press, about *your* family and Mirrus Global?" Jenna asked in a flat tone he'd never heard from her before.

"He wasn't convinced it was you personally, but yes, he knew it was coming via you. Somehow. And it did," he pointed out. She couldn't be offended at the truth.

Jenna was far too pragmatic a woman to be that dramatic.

"*You* thought I was the leak, and you slept with me?" Her tone wasn't flat now, but near shouting.

"Clearly not. I wouldn't have been searching your handbag if I did, or have my security searching your apartment." What did she think? That he didn't know her at all?

"You have security men searching my apartment?" she asked, sounding even angrier, certainly not mollified by that news. "How did they get in?"

He just looked at her.

"Fine, they have their ways." She stared around her like she was horrified, and having a difficult time taking his words in. "I can't believe you've had strangers pawing through my stuff without even telling me first."

Jenna was focusing on the wrong issue here, and it surprised him.

"They aren't strangers," he assured her. "It's my personal security team. You've met them before. You talk to them."

He didn't mention he couldn't risk telling her if she was the actual leak. Her current reaction indicated that wouldn't go over well. At all.

She was responding with unexpected emotion. He'd thought she would be hurt, but because she was being spied on, not because he was trying to figure out what was going on.

"Oh, that makes it so much better." Her tone said the exact opposite.

"Jenna, if you just look at this situation rationally, you'll see I took the best course of action."

"No. No. No." She shook her head. "You are not standing there telling me you had sex with me to figure out if I was some sort of spy and that it was the *best* you could come up with."

"Of course not. I had sex with you because I want you. You want me too."

"You used it as a diversion to get me out of my apartment."

He couldn't deny that, but it was not the whole truth, or even the most salient truth. What could he say that would not dig him deeper in this pit he had never thought he would find himself in?

"You and I were both done dancing around this attraction between us."

The expression on Jenna's face said those were not the right words.

CHAPTER FIVE

JENNA FELT LIKE ants were crawling along her skin.

Dima thought the fact that they wanted each other justified him using sex to keep her out of her apartment while it was searched?

She wanted to throw up.

"You don't look well. Sit down and I'll get you a brandy. I knew finding out you were being spied on was going to upset you." He offered his hand, like he really expected her to take it.

"I haven't even started to process that," she assured him. "I'm furious and hurt that you used sex between us as a tool." She spelled it out in case he still didn't get it. "I trusted you."

She'd thought they were friends. Friends could trust each other.

His dark brows drew together. "You can still trust me."

In what universe? "No. I can't."

"Don't be dramatic, Jenna. Nothing about tonight has changed other than I had to give you some upsetting news."

"You're talking about someone supposedly spying on me."

"Yes, of course. And there's no *supposedly* about it. I found two listening devices. I haven't heard from my team yet, but if your bag was bugged, chances are other frequently used accessories are as well."

Stomach acids suddenly too unruly to control, Jenna spun and rushed toward the en suite. She was retching into the sink moments later, trying hard not to actually throw up.

A cold cloth was placed gently on the back of her neck while a hand rubbed her back in a soothing motion.

The urge to elbow the arrogant prince away from her was almost overwhelming. "Don't touch me," she gritted out.

He stepped away and left the bathroom. Both grateful and angry that he'd left so easily, Jenna bathed her face with cool water and then dried it as she fought to get her feelings and body's response to Dima's revelations under control.

How could he have used her like that?

How could either he or Konstantin think she would ever knowingly betray their family's trust? Was Nikolai in on this?

These were people she'd considered family for more than half a decade.

And they thought she could betray a woman as close as a sister?

Jenna would never hurt Nataliya, and every single one of those arrogant, distrusting royals should know it.

Equally to the point, she was a fashion editor, not a tabloid reporter. Did they really think all journalists were the same?

Intent on finding her clothes and getting dressed, Jenna turned around and nearly ran into Dima. He was holding a brandy snifter with a good inch of amber liquid in it. "Drink this. It will help."

Ignoring him, she maneuvered around Dima without touching him and went in search of her clothes. They were scattered around the living area, and she grabbed each item with jerky movements, muttering to herself about untrusting, arrogant *jerks*.

"I did trust you. That is why I have my people searching your apartment."

She spun to face him, fury and hurt a maelstrom inside her. "Trust? You call that trust? If you trusted me, you would have told me what was going on."

He looked utterly shocked by the idea. Like he'd never even considered it. "I did tell you."

"When I caught you going through my purse, which, by the way, is considered a massive breach of trust by some women." Having grown up with a mother who routinely sent her children searching through her purse for everything from lunch money to allergy meds, Jenna wasn't one of them.

But that didn't make the fact any less true.

He managed to look a little uncomfortable at that reminder. "I apologize if that caused offense."

"Are you kidding me? First, that is a supremely lame apology. Second, you didn't just offend me, Your Highness. You hurt me!"

"That was not my intention. You must know that."

"No, I do not know that. I don't think you considered my feelings at all, to be honest, and that makes your *intentions* worth this." She snapped her fingers, signifying *nothing*.

"I planned to tell you everything in the morning." He spoke with exaggerated patience.

"Talking to me like you are trying to explain a complicated concept to a toddler is *not* digging you *out* of the pit you made." She glared at him, wishing she could at least singe his perfectly cut hair with the heat of her anger.

Who looked that good just climbing out of bed?

Jenna knew she didn't. Her hair was a mess, her makeup completely lost to their time in the shower and pool after.

So not the point, she reminded herself. Who cared how she looked to the Neanderthal standing in front of her?

"No, that's an insult to Neanderthals," she said aloud. "They were supposed to be intelligent and resourceful. You are a spoiled, distrusting *prince*."

"Being a prince is not a bad thing."

"You just keep believing that, Your Highness."

"Stop calling me Your Highness. I don't like it."

"I give this—" she paused and snapped her fingers again "—for what you like."

"You are very angry."

"And hurt." Jenna wasn't one of those people who thought hiding emotional pain made her stronger.

If someone hurt you, they should know it. If they *liked* that they hurt you, they had no business in any part of your life. Ever. At all.

Dima winced. "I am truly sorry I hurt you."

"That, at least, is a more sincere apology, but I don't forgive you, because you thought it was an okay thing to do. You *still* think it was acceptable to use sex as a tool of expedience and to investigate me behind my back." She deflated, her pain and disillusion overtaking her anger. "Not to mention the fact that you, or your brothers, could even suspect me of betraying Nataliya's confidence."

"I do not suspect you." His voice rang with truth, but it was way too little, too late.

"Well, certainly not now that you found the bugs." She shook her head. "You and Konstantin thought I could betray Nataliya. Does Nikolai?"

The expression on his features answered before he spoke. "I am sure he does not honestly believe it, but we had to be sure."

"You said you were sure before you searched my purse." Had he been lying?

"I was. Just as I'm sure neither of my brothers genuinely believed you could be culpable."

She shook her head again. "It doesn't matter."

Done talking about something that could not be changed and hurt too deeply for her to process in a matter of minutes, she went back into the bedroom, shutting the door behind her.

Jenna dressed as quickly as she could, leaving her jewelry off. She stared down at it in her hand and realized she couldn't just tuck it into her purse as she'd planned. Her purse was locked in the suite's safe. She went in search of something she could use to gather her possessions to take with her and found a leather satchel.

Opening it, she found some files. Most were clearly business files, and she took a second to wonder why Dima didn't use a locked briefcase. But then all thoughts of locked briefcases and better security flew from her mind as she found a dossier on herself.

It was thorough, she'd give him that. It listed her entire family, even her deceased brother. Not that Matt was a secret, but Jenna didn't often talk about his loss. Earlier that evening with Emma had been an anomaly.

Every coworker, friend and acquaintance was listed as well as the names of the men she'd dated in the past year and a half, with short backgrounds on each.

She discovered one of the men she'd dated had lied about his job and marital status. Divorced rather than never married. The lies didn't surprise her. She'd felt like that guy was off somehow. Not genuine. Her gut had been right.

So why hadn't it warned her about Dima?

That he could use her like this?

A peremptory knock sounded. "Are you coming back out?" Dima asked through the door.

It would serve him right if she didn't and left him to sleep on the sofa.

But Jenna was not a petty person. Never had been.

She marched over to the door and unlocked it, pulling it wide to glare up at the sneaky prince. "I found your file on me."

"You went through my things?" he asked, sounding and looking outraged.

That made her laugh. If it was more cynical than humorous, who could blame her? "Really? That's what you're going with?"

"There was no need. You could have asked, and I would have told you anything you wanted to know."

"I could say the same, though now, not so much. But I didn't go looking for answers to questions I'm not asking. I needed something to put the stuff from my purse in."

"So you decided to confiscate my briefcase?"

"Why doesn't it have a lock? For a family worried about security, yours is really lax."

"Without a lock, it looks less important, and since I travel with a security detail, locking my files away is unnecessary."

"Until you bring the wrong woman to your bed."

"You are not the wrong woman. You would do nothing with what you found in there."

"You're so sure about that?"

"You know I am. I was before I searched for surveillance devices, and I'm only more so now."

"Sure. I believe you." She let her tone tell him she actually felt the opposite.

His gorgeous face creased in a frown. "I don't bring other women to my home or personal suite when I'm traveling. They do not have access to sensitive information."

"So? Am I supposed to feel special?"

"I don't know. How you feel is up to you, but I will tell you that you are special."

She made a disbelieving sound.

"Jenna, you are part of our family."

"I used to think that too, but family members don't spy on each other."

"I was not spying on you."

"What would you call it?"

"Trying to find out how information was passing through you to someone else."

"Behind my back. That *is* spying."

He walked over to the pile of files she had discarded and picked them up, then laid them on the bed in front of her. "You see these files?"

"I could hardly miss them."

"Usually I find your sarcasm sexy, but right now I could do with a little less of it."

"I could do without everything that happened tonight, to be honest." There was no sarcasm in her tone.

His grimace said he understood she'd meant every word. "I am sorry. Perhaps I should have talked to you about what Konstantin had discovered."

"What exactly is that?"

"I will get to that in a minute. Look at those files."

"Why?"

"Because I trust you."

"And looking at your business files proves that, how?" she asked, curious despite herself.

"They pertain to the biggest deal I have ever put together for Mirrus Global. You can read them cover to cover. I know you won't do anything with the information."

Again, despite herself, Jenna was impressed. Not that she was going to admit it, but the offer would have shocked her before tonight's events. She was more shocked now that she knew somebody was leaking information about his family.

"How did you find out someone was leaking information about the family?"

"It isn't just about the family. It's about Mirrus Global too." He went on to tell her what Konstantin had put together and brought to him.

"Why didn't he just approach me?"

"He was worried asking you would offend you and that you would vent to Nataliya and upset her."

"And right now, any kind of stress is not a good idea for her, but how did he not realize I'm fully aware of that? I wouldn't vent to Nataliya about anything that might upset her right now."

This seemed to sink in. "You are right. We both made a bad call even entertaining the thought you might."

"But not that *I* might be the leak?" she demanded, angry all over again.

"The leaks always coincided with you and Nataliya visiting each other or having a video call."

"We video call at least twice a month." It had been hard to adjust to her BFF not being available for daily chats like they used to have, but they texted almost every day still. "That seems like a pretty long stretch to causation."

"We were right. Someone is spying on you," he pointed out, like that made everything okay.

And just like that, she was done. Done with this conversation. Done with tonight. She just wanted to go home and be alone. Jenna needed time to process all this.

Only she couldn't go home, could she? "Has your team contacted you yet?"

"Yes. While you were getting dressed and ransacking my room for a handbag replacement."

"You just keep harping on that. It will remind us both what double standards you have."

He let out a sigh, and she stared at him in shock. She wasn't sure she'd ever heard Dima make such a *human* sound. Although she found it surprisingly easy to read his expression when others seemed to find him rather stoic, he did not express emotions with the typical sounds others made.

No surprised laughter, sighs or even grunts of annoyance from him.

He was too polished.

"I was teasing you, but clearly my timing was bad. It is not my intention to propagate a double standard."

"You sound pretty formal for a man who was inside my body only a few hours ago."

"As you have pointed out so many times, I am a prince."

"But not a robot." She shook her head. "Never mind. I want to leave, but I need to know if it is okay for me to return home."

"My security team would like time to try to trace the listening devices back to their source."

"That's not necessary. My assistant ordered the phone stand and delivered it to me. She has access to a lot of my accessories, like the purse I was using tonight, because designers gift them in hopes they'll be featured in the magazine. Skylar is the conduit for all swag that comes to me."

"If she's the one, it shouldn't take much to find out, but we can't assume that she is guilty because of proximity."

But it was okay to assume that Jenna had been guilty because of *her* proximity? She didn't bother pointing out yet another flaw in his brothers' and his thinking.

"I just want to go home."

"If you will not stay here with me, please consider allowing me to get you a room in the hotel. If you give me a list of things you need, the security team can gather them for you."

She'd planned to stay the night, but now she wanted anything but.

"Fine. Get a room for me sorted and my things delivered. I'll text a list of what I want you can forward to your security people. I assume it will all be checked for any more bugs."

Jenna did her best to ignore Dima's presence beside her as she made her way to the room she would use for the night. He'd insisted on escorting her, and she had simply not been willing to argue. The sooner she got to her room, the sooner she could shut the door on him.

"I would feel better if you slept in my suite." His tone was supremely patient.

She didn't bother to respond. Jenna had no desire to spend any more time arguing with the arrogant prince.

They reached her door, and she stepped forward to swipe the key card that had been delivered by the helpful hotel staff.

"Jenna," he said, his tone now tinged with exasperation. "Are you just going to ignore me?"

She turned and glared up at him. "Yes." Then she stepped into the room and shut the door on his too handsome face.

She flipped the security lock, although she was sure his security people would be there shortly with her things. She stared around the room, not at all surprised that it was not a standard single, but a suite.

Albeit much, much smaller than the penthouse suite she'd just left, it had a living room and a bedroom, and presumably a bathroom through the open door beyond. There was even a tiny kitchenette area, though why she would need one for a single night's stay she could not imagine.

For that matter, the living area was surplus to requirements. Jenna just needed a bed and a few hours of privacy to sleep.

Her knees started to wobble, and she stumbled to the sofa, plopping down.

Someone had been spying on her for at least a year, and despite Dima's refusal to *jump to conclusions*, Jenna was pretty sure she knew who it was.

Listening to her phone conversations, listening to her meetings, maybe even when she talked to herself in her apartment when she cleaned or brainstormed a layout, as she was wont to do. It all felt so icky, like slime was dripping from the edges of her life.

Typically, Dima had only looked at it in terms of his family, but Jenna had access to fashion concepts sometimes months before they were made public. People and businesses who had trusted her with their time-sensitive information could have been scooped because of her, and she had no idea.

She remembered the debacle last year when an established design label who were notoriously unimaginative had come out with a brand-new line. It had all but mirrored the one a new designer had shared with Jenna in hopes of getting a spread in her magazine for its launch.

The established house had brought their line out two weeks before the new designer.

The designer had accused Jenna of revealing her designs. Jenna had denied it, of course. She'd known she'd done no such thing.

Not only had the designer's new line been stolen, but her reputation had been damaged because she'd come for someone who everyone knew was trustworthy. Jenna's reputation was longer-standing and unassailable.

It had been a mess.

And now? How could she not wonder if she had in fact been the source of the leak?

That designer had lost her startup money and been forced to go back to designing for someone else.

Jenna had felt bad for her, even when she thought she hadn't been responsible. Now?

The guilt lay like an anvil in her gut.

As horrible as it was to be spied on, knowing that nothing confidential she'd worked on the past year had been safe was even worse. Other people had been hurt because of her.

She remembered how Nataliya had felt when news of her miscarriage was leaked ahead of the planned announcement. Nataliya and Nikolai had just wanted time to grieve in peace, but that had been stolen from them.

Because someone had access to Jenna.

Tears burned Jenna's eyes, but she refused to let them fall. The security people would deliver her stuff soon, and she didn't want to be caught crying like an infant.

A confident knock on the door sounded. She swiped at her eyes and went to open the door.

Swinging it open, she put her hand out to take her bag. "Thank you, I…"

Her voice trailed off when she realized Dima stood there, not his security person. And he wasn't holding a suitcase.

She frowned. "What do you want, Your Highness?"

"Damn it." He reached out as if to touch her, but she stepped back. "You've been crying. I knew I shouldn't leave you alone."

"Go away."

"You don't need to be alone right now."

She stared at him. "Are you for real? I mean, as arrogant as you can be, how can you not see that the last person I would want comfort from right now is you?"

"Be honest, Jenna. You aren't going to look for comfort from anyone. You're used to being the strong one."

He was right. As the oldest surviving sibling, she'd always considered it her job to carry the emotional burdens for her loved ones, not the other way around.

Knowing he was right and acknowledging it were two different things, however. "If you think you know me so well, why didn't you know that having sex with me as an expedient would hurt me?"

Taking advantage of the space she'd created stepping back from him, he moved into her room, shutting the door behind him.

He met her gaze, his own gray one steady. "It wasn't expedience. It was desire." His lips tilted on one side in a wry look. "The timing could have been better."

"Really? You think maybe?" Jenna retreated further, once again sitting on the sofa, the coffee table between them.

"Yes." He had the grace to look discomfited. "Jenna, *milaya moy,* I know this is hard on you. I didn't intend to make it harder."

That *my darling* hit her on the raw, taking what was left of her patience. "You need to go back to your suite, Your Highness. I am tired, and I'm going to bed."

"Your things will be arriving any minute."

"Good."

"Jenna—"

"I mean it, Prince Dimitri. Go away."

"I'm not the one who spied on you," he pointed out.

"Aren't you? What do you call going through my bag? Having your people scour my apartment behind my back?"

"Protecting you, as I am doing my best to protect the rest of my family, our company and our country."

"Protecting me?" she asked, disbelief coursing through her like waves crashing on the beach.

Cold and powerful.

He made an impatient gesture with his hand. "As much as it bothers me that someone has used you to get information on my family and company, I'm sure it has occurred to you that other areas of your life have been exposed as well."

"Don't pretend you care." She'd assumed he hadn't even considered that aspect.

"I do care, *milaya*."

"Enough with the Russian endearments." More than enough. She could not hear that word one more time without bursting into tears, and she had no idea why, but she wasn't going to pretend to herself she had a better hold on her emotions than she did. "It's not as cute as you seem to think it is."

"I am not trying to be *cute*."

"At this point, I cannot figure out what you are trying to be."

Another knock sounded on her door. This one a lot quieter, and Jenna had to shake her head that she'd thought the earlier confident and demanding one had been anyone other than Dima.

She went to get up to answer, but the prince beat her to it, opening the door and taking possession of her bag with minimal words.

"I can answer my own door," she pointed out.

He gave her a look that questioned why she felt the need to point that out. "Have I implied otherwise?"

"Never mind. Dima, I'm tired, and now my things are here. I want to go to bed."

"Yes, of course." But he made no move to relinquish her bag. "I do not want to leave you alone."

"I spend most nights alone."

"Tonight is not most nights."

No, it had been the best sex of her life followed by some awful news. Not that it competed with the worst news of her life, but learning Dima had used sex with her for his own ends and that she'd been spied on hurt all around.

She just wanted time to herself to lick her wounds, but

the dense man seemed to think she needed company more. *His* company.

He put her suitcase down in the bedroom, coming back out immediately, his expression unhappy. Not something he would be happy to learn he expressed. He was so proud of his ability to hide his emotions.

All the princes were.

It was a thing.

A weird, royal thing.

She sat in silence, waiting for him to leave.

He stopped just before he reached the door and turned to face her again, his expression intent. "Sex between us was inevitable."

In that moment, she would have given anything to deny those words, but she couldn't. "Maybe, but it didn't have to happen tonight."

He inclined his head, like she'd made a point. "I am used to doing what I think is best."

"Arrogant."

"Probably."

"Good night, Your Highness."

He winced, as he'd done every time she used the title. She would figure out what that meant later, after she'd gotten some sleep. Maybe.

"Good night, Jenna. I will see you tomorrow."

"No."

"We have to discuss a plan for going forward."

"Call me." There was no reason they had to meet face-to-face.

While her mobile phone was still locked in his safe, he could call the phone in her hotel room, or her work phone. Hopefully, her cell phone would be cleared and returned to her soon regardless.

By security.

She wasn't sure when she'd be ready to see any of the brothers face-to-face again, but tomorrow would not be it.

CHAPTER SIX

THE NEXT MORNING, Jenna got into her office two hours before anyone else was expected.

She put her things away in her office and then stood staring around, wondering if there were bugs in here too. Refusing to worry about it, she went back out into the main area and began searching her assistant Skylar's cubicle.

When Jenna found extra copies of a photo shoot, she didn't immediately excuse it as explainable as she once would have. How easy had it been for Skylar to pilfer information and pass it on for profit?

Jenna wasn't the only one on staff who assumed the best about people, particularly those working for them. An attitude of trust and empowerment was built into the magazine's employment culture.

The knowledge that that had been tainted and taken advantage of made Jenna really angry. Not all media companies valued those things, and she'd always been proud to work for one that did.

With renewed determination, she continued her search. Even with righteous anger fueling her, she was unable to dismiss the similarities in her own behavior to Dima's.

Jenna had convinced herself that Skylar was responsible based on circumstantial evidence. However, they were *not* friends, and she had a lot less reason to trust the other woman than the Merikovs had to trust Jenna.

Not finding anything else suspicious in the cubicle, she went to her own office and started looking for bugs. She didn't think she'd recognize anything for what it was, but she *would* know what wasn't supposed to be there.

She searched her desk, her cabinets, behind the blinds on her coveted window, and bile rose in her stomach when she found a tiny black piece of technology attached to the inside of the shade on the standing lamp beside her desk.

She stared down at the small plastic disc in her hand.

Wasn't this all just a little over-the-top?

Okay. Corporate espionage was a thing. She knew that.

And sure, someone could get paid for the information on the Mirrusian royal family, but was it worth all this?

How many devices could there be?

She grabbed her phone and dialed Dima.

"Jenna. Have you had breakfast?" he asked, like everything was normal between them.

"What is it with you and feeding me?" She sighed. "Never mind. Can you have one of your security people come to my office? I found something."

"You are in the office already?"

"Not the issue here."

She was pretty sure he swore in Russian. "I did not expect you to leave the hotel."

"Hmm." She made a noncommittal sound because really? Why hadn't he?

"I thought you would sleep on it and realize that I had your best interests in mind. We should have had breakfast together and then discussed how best to approach what we discovered last night."

"Do you make it a habit of making plans without input from the people they include?"

"I thought we established last night that I do."

"That is not something to be proud of."

"Did I say I was proud of it?"

"Well, if you're not, maybe you should consider changing that habit."

"Perhaps I should. We can talk about it over breakfast."

"I'm already at work."

"You do not need to stay there."

"Yes, I do."

"I will send over the team to do a thorough search of your

office while we discuss what they found in your apartment last night."

"We can have that discussion over the phone."

"Please, Jenna, just meet me for breakfast."

"Are you begging me?" she asked with more mockery than she meant to, but the fact that he'd started that sentence with a sincere-sounding *please* was throwing her for a loop. "Why is this so important to you?"

"I'll tell you over breakfast."

"You assume I want to know enough to be swayed by that."

"You may not have the cutthroat nature of some journalists, but you have always had the professional curiosity of one."

"This is hardly a professional situation."

"Agreed, though it impacts your work, as it does mine."

He was right. As much as she hated admitting it. Her situation was impacting his work, and his family.

Though Jenna had not shared any secrets out of turn, sensitive information had leaked through her.

"Fine. Where do you want to meet?"

"I will be at your building in a few minutes to pick you up."

She sighed, not at all surprised that he was already on the way. If she had refused breakfast, the irritating man would have simply shown up in her office.

Like he had the day before.

"Send your team up. I'll let them in, and then I will come down." She didn't wait for his agreement before hanging up.

Dimitri waited impatiently for Jenna.

He had miscalculated about her leaving the hotel, but that wasn't the only miscalculation he'd made. He'd been so sure that once he told her what was going on, she would understand the need to search her apartment and handbag.

Instead, she'd assumed he'd instigated sex as a maneuver of expediency and was hurt that his family had doubted her at all.

He'd spent more time thinking about her reaction than sleeping the night before and had come to some conclusions. The first was that he should have told her what was going on before having sex with her.

The second was that his brother, Kon, could not seriously have doubted Jenna's innocence. Which raised the question, why had Kon implied that he did?

The passenger door opened, interrupting his thoughts. "We've only got an hour. I called my boss and gave her a heads-up about what is going on. She's meeting me to discuss this situation further when I get back."

Dimitri bit back a curse. "Why did you do that?"

"Because this problem isn't all about you, Your Highness."

Dimitri grimaced. "It never was."

"There's a food truck that has yummy breakfast burritos just around the corner. It's a little chilly, but sunny. We can sit outside and talk."

"A food truck?" he asked, trying to process the very idea. "I can get something delivered."

"To where?" she asked wryly. "The car? Don't be a snob."

Offended, he frowned. "I am not a snob."

"Have you ever eaten from a food truck?"

What difference did that make? "No."

"Then..." Her challenge was clear.

He said he wasn't a snob; prove it.

Grimly determined to do just that, he pulled into traffic, his detail right behind him.

As they walked toward the food truck, Jenna had to admit to herself that eating this way was a different proposition for him than for regular people like her. Jenna had no security detail needing to stay close.

Nor did she have to worry about a random photo shot with a cell phone ending up in the tabloids with some cheesy headline.

Nevertheless, her prince did not grumble as she ordered for them. They got their food and found a nearby bench to sit on.

They'd both taken a couple of bites of their breakfast, washing it down with coffee, when he looked up, his expression tinged with surprise. "This is pretty good."

He looked down at his burrito, like he was trying to figure out what all was in it.

She wished him luck. Jenna had been trying to recreate this particular deliciousness at home for the past two years and had yet to get it just right.

"Don't sound so surprised," she chided him.

"I am not surprised," he denied with dignity. "I am a prince, but I do not live under a rock. Even I know about the food truck craze."

"It's not really a craze anymore, but an established source of dining."

"If you say so."

And he said he wasn't a snob, but Jenna just said, "Tell me what they found in my apartment."

"The listening devices are limited to a few accessory items besides your handbag from last night."

Jenna wasn't sure if she felt relief at that or not. She had a habit of leaving her purse on the end of the sofa, which would have made her living room accessible to the listening device.

All she said was, "Since Skylar's never been to my home, that makes sense."

"Assuming it is your assistant might be premature."

"Like it was premature assuming it was me?" Jenna asked with her brows raised.

Really. These princes. What was okay for them was not okay for the rest of the world.

"I don't think Kon actually ever believed you were the source of the leak." Which made it sound like Dima *never* had, and she doubted that.

Though he'd been clear he didn't doubt her the night before. Jenna crumpled her wrapper and tossed it in a nearby trash can. She set her coffee on the bench beside her and then rubbed her suddenly pounding temples.

"Do you have a headache?"

She rolled her shoulders, the pain receding a bit. "Just a tension one. Are you surprised?"

"No. For what it is worth, Jenna, if I could have spared you knowledge of this, I would have."

"Not what I want to hear." She wasn't some hothouse violet who wanted stuff hidden from her. Not even really hard stuff.

She never had been.

"Why do you say that about Prince Konstantin?" She thought it was pretty obvious he had distrusted her and found it odd that Dima would try to deny it.

"You saw how natural he was with you at dinner. Yes, you two give each other a hard time, but he trusts you with his wife and his children. No way he believes you are a risk to them in any way."

"He came to you." Dima had said so.

"Yes, and I'm still trying to figure out why, but his reasons are not the ones he stated." The prince sounded very certain of his conclusions.

Jenna wasn't convinced. "Oh, I think he wants to know the source of the leaks, all right." Of course he did. Prince Konstantin, like the rest of his family, would never stand for a leak remaining once identified.

"Naturally, but while we both knew it was somehow related to you, I do not believe my brother ever considered you the direct source any more than I did."

"I want to believe that." It would hurt a lot less.

But she wouldn't lie to herself, even if it saved her emotional pain.

"Then believe. I am sure it is the truth." Dima tossed his own trash, his aim as good as hers had been. "If it makes you feel any better, he suggested a lot of ways for me to get the information that weren't dating."

"We didn't date. We had sex."

"Fantastic sex," he clarified, like it was really important. "The dates can come later."

"You think I'm going to date you?" she asked. Again, were they living in the same reality?

"We are not done with each other, Jenna."

"So you say." But she couldn't deny the truth of that statement, so she didn't try to refute it directly.

She still wanted him, even if he was a toad for using sex against her.

At least, that's how it felt.

And it worried her that she was having such an emotional reaction to the timing of them having sex for the first time, because she was feeling things she really, really, really didn't want to.

"Are you going to talk to Emma?" he asked after finishing his coffee.

"And cause an issue with her husband?" Jenna wasn't a monster. Emma and Konstantin had a good marriage, even if the man was a distrustful jerk. "I don't think so. I do have other people to vent to than your royal siblings' wives."

It still rankled they had thought she would have put any stress on Nataliya right now, for any reason.

Dima had the effrontery to look alarmed. "I think even Kon would prefer you kept your venting to Emma."

"Listen, buster, if I want to vent to my own sister, I will. If you don't think she's trustworthy, that's your problem. *She* didn't put a bug in my cell phone stand."

"No, I am sure you are right." They were the right words, but his expression didn't match them fully.

She nodded anyway. He *should* agree with her.

Unfortunately, righteous ire did nothing to diminish her body's response to his nearness. What was it about this man that turned her on so effectively?

He was so not the sort of man she usually dated.

One, he was royal. Two, he was arrogant. Three, he was younger than her. Four, he was a workaholic. Five, he wanted children.

The last caused a twinge in the area of her heart she'd long thought atrophied.

Jenna had stopped grieving what could have been before she'd even let herself start.

"What is the matter?" he asked.

"Nothing. Well, other than the obvious."

"You looked sad for a moment."

She shrugged. "It's nothing."

"If it upsets you, it is not nothing."

"Nice sentiment. Too bad you didn't stick by it last night."

"I should have told you about the possible spy in your life before we had sex." He spoke stiffly, like admitting wrong did not come easily to him.

Only she knew that Dima was better at it than his brothers, at least from what she'd seen. Not that he had much experience admitting mistakes.

He didn't usually make them.

He had last night, though. A big one. And it *had* hurt her. "Yes, you should have."

"I will not make the same call again."

"Good to know." Though how that applied to her, she had no idea, considering the deed was done.

His own nod was decisive. "My security team has had no luck so far tracing the surveillance equipment back to its source."

"I spoke to my boss, and we will be confiscating Skylar's laptop as soon as she arrives in the building." While they'd agreed to meet that morning to discuss how to handle the fallout, that had already been settled during their earlier phone call. "It's the property of the magazine and isn't supposed to have anything private on it, but everyone uses their work laptops for their home stuff too."

Jenna had no doubts that proof of her assistant's spying would be found on that laptop.

If she was wrong, she would apologize, but her instincts were telling her she wasn't. So many things that in and of themselves had not triggered wariness in Jenna now looked suspect in retrospect.

"Is this true?" he asked. "We have the same policy at Mirrus Global, and I assumed employees followed it."

"Uh…how do I point out that most people don't have the financial means to buy a second computer when they have one supplied from work? There's always something else the money needs to go to."

"You do not have a private system?" he asked, sounding shocked.

"Of course I do. Nataliya is my BFF. Long before she became a princess, then queen, she insisted I have the most up-to-date technology for personal use. I end up using my personal computer for work stuff because it's faster and more secure."

He nodded, like he approved.

Jenna didn't even try not to roll her eyes. "Believe it or not, I'm not really worried what you think of my tech practices."

He laughed. "You are so damn refreshing, Jenna."

"Because I don't care what you think?"

"I'm not sure that is entirely true, but yes. Because you are not and have never been in awe of my family."

"You're the family of my BFF. If I was in awe of you, it would be awkward for her and me." And Jenna wasn't letting any awkwardness get between her and Nataliya.

"You two are very close."

"And you thought I would go crying to her if you asked me about the leak." Jenna let her disgust at that reasoning shade her voice. "You and Prince Konstantin need to take a course in reading people, because you sure showed some illiteracy when it came to me."

"You are right, and for that I apologize."

"You apologize for that, but not for using sex against me?"

"I did say I was sorry for hurting you," he pointed out. "I have acknowledged I should have apprised you of the situation before we had sex. However, I will not lie and say I am sorry we had sex."

"You're honest, at least." If he'd been honest about his motives for the sex, she wouldn't be so hurt now.

His timing had been so wrong, and him acknowledging it didn't make it all better.

"I was honest last night too," he said, like he was reading her mind. "I wanted you. The fact that we had to search your apartment and your things didn't influence that."

"But if you'd told me about it before…" She let her voice trail off on a sigh.

He knew he was wrong. She needed to leave it at that.

"You might have been so focused on the leak, you would have said no to the sex."

Shocked, Jenna almost dropped what remained of her coffee. "That is quite an admission."

"That I wanted you so badly I was willing to compromise my own integrity in order to have you?" He did not sound happy. "And am just now realizing it? It is not my finest moment."

Okay, that right there made her feel better. He was too genuinely upset to be shining her on about this.

And for a guy who prided himself on his integrity, recognizing he'd compromised it wouldn't be easy. That could explain why he'd been so dense about it the night before.

"I accept your apology, but if it has something to do with me, you cannot hide it from me. You understand that now, right?"

"That is not how I usually operate. Filtering information is something I was taught from an early age."

"Like the whole don't show emotion thing?" Which he didn't seem to be so successful at with her.

"Yes."

"You can unlearn anything you have been taught."

"I am not sure that is true."

"Try it and see."

He put his hand out for her empty coffee cup and then tossed it. "I am not going to start being a fount of information or transparency."

"No doubt, but if it has to do with me, then you tell me. That's not hard."

He looked like he would argue.

She put up her hand, silencing him without words. "Listen, Dima, if you want me to trust you, you have to trust me."

"I do trust you." He grabbed her hand and then brought it to his mouth to kiss the backs of her fingers, his expression all about sexual intent and not at all about promising full disclosure. "We have established this."

In his mind, maybe.

"Fine," she conceded. "If you trust me, then you don't withhold information from me that relates to me. I'm not asking for state secrets here."

He stood up and drew her with him, heading back toward the cars. "Maybe."

"What do you mean, maybe?" That connection between them, her hand in his, was doing weird things to her.

Not just sexual things, either, and that had her biting her lip with worry.

"It could relate to you and still be a state secret," he explained.

"For crying out loud," she said with exasperation. "You do not need to conjure up every potential scenario. What are the chances of that, really?"

Color burnished his cheeks.

Oh, wow, he was embarrassed.

"It is my nature to look at all potential outcomes." He sounded almost humble.

"Or you were taught that too."

"Regardless, it is far too ingrained."

"I believe you, but maybe just accept that not all of them are going to come to pass and let them go."

"That is not my way."

"I know Nikolai is the oldest, and the king, but seriously, Dima, I swear you outdo him."

"What do you mean?"

"Well, I think you may be more arrogantly certain of your own ideas than even he is."

"My brother listens to counsel."

"While you keep your own."

Dima didn't say anything, possibly realizing the attempt to refute her words would force him to lie.

"You're also more of a worrier."

"I do not worry."

"What would you call going through every possible dooms-day scenario before you commit to a course of action?"

"Being responsible."

That surprised a laugh out of her. "Promise me anyway, Dima."

"I like when you use my name."

He'd said so, and maybe her use of his title had been as much to annoy him as establish emotional distance when she was so hurt and angry.

"Great. I'll make a deal with you. As long as you exhibit trust in me that is in line with being my friend—"

"And lover," he slotted in, interrupting her like he never interrupted anyone.

"That's still up for debate." Though she hadn't pulled her hand from his, had she? "Anyway, as long as you do that, then I will call you Dima."

"This includes telling you about things like the leak of confidential information that coincided with your visits and video calls with Nataliya?"

She'd thought they'd already established that, but she gave him verbal agreement anyway. "Yes."

He thought for several long seconds.

Jenna's tension grew with each one, and she realized this was way more important to her than it should be. She didn't even try and lie to herself that it was all about her relationship with Nataliya and her BFF's family. This was about Jenna and Dima, about him *being* Dima to her and not Prince Dimitri, like his brother would always be Prince Konstantin.

"I agree," he said solemnly.

Air whooshed out of her in relief, but she still went for casual with her tone. "Good."

CHAPTER SEVEN

THE NEXT FEW hours were more than a little stressful.

It turned out that Skylar had a lot more than just a link to audio files in the cloud from her listening devices that was incriminating on her laptop.

She had pictures of designs that Jenna had kept in a locked filing cabinet in her office, and information files about Mirrus Global and even Jenna's brother's company.

However, because neither the royal family nor Jenna's boss wanted the negative publicity it would bring, both were adamant about not pressing charges.

The magazine actually had a policy to the effect that if an employee was found doing this sort of thing, they were to be fired, but that was all.

Jenna was furious. "It was my privacy that was violated, and yours are not the only companies affected by her criminality."

Skylar just stood there looking smug. Like she knew she could be fired but wasn't facing anything worse.

"Let us be clear," Dima said coldly to Skylar. "If a single piece of sensitive information about my family or company gets leaked from this point, we will not only press charges here in the US, but we will charge you with espionage and file for extradition."

Skylar paled at this but did not reply. When the magazine's editorial director made a similar, if less impressive, threat in regard to information related to the magazine, the editorial assistant didn't even blink.

"They might be content not to file charges against you, but I'm not," Jenna informed the other woman, her fury renewed by Skylar's smug attitude. "And considering the information you had stored in regard to my brother's company, I doubt he will be either."

Both Dima and Jenna's boss went tense at Jenna's words.

She did not care. Yes, she understood that it could be damaging for the matter to go public, but this woman had spied on her and other people through her.

What was to stop Skylar from doing the same thing again, if there were no consequences?

"Jenna, surely you understand that would not be the best circumstance for the magazine?" her boss pointed out, her tone not nearly as autocratic as usual.

Because she had to realize it was Jenna's choice and not hers. She also must see the willingness in Jenna to deal with the fallout for going against company policy. Who had a policy about stuff like this?

Her magazine that she was just thinking that morning was so much better than other media companies, that's who.

"You and His Highness are acting like you are the only ones affected, and you are not." He wasn't Dima when he was trying to get Jenna to back down on something so important to her. He couldn't be.

A true friend would not ask her to sweep being stalked and spied on under the carpet like it had never happened.

"A promising new designer lost her company and her reputation because of this woman. *I* thought she was being ridiculous accusing me of selling me designs. You did that, and you knew what you were doing when you did."

Skylar looked almost bored. "New designers fail every day."

Jenna gasped at that cold response. "She didn't have to. She could have made it." Jenna had been certain she would. It was why she'd planned an entire spread on the designer's spring collection.

Dismissing the woman who clearly had no conscience, Jenna spoke to her boss. "I don't know what Skylar has passed on about my brother's company, but I aim to find out."

"What are you going to do, have me arrested for listening to you talk to your brother on the phone?" Skylar sneered now.

"Yes, that exactly." Jenna let her livid glare settle on Skylar again. "This state has stalking laws, and I'm pretty sure you've violated most of them."

That brought a look of consternation to her *former* assistant's face, but then she rallied. "I didn't harass you. That's not stalking. Regardless, the magazine has too much to lose to let you do that."

"Here's the thing you don't seem to get. It is not up to them. You spied on *me*, not the magazine." And if it wasn't stalking, it still wasn't legal. Jenna was sure of that.

"Jenna," Dima said in a flat tone.

She turned to him. "What?"

"Can we speak privately for a moment?"

"I don't know. It doesn't look like any of my conversations have been private for the past year or more."

Dima's head of security stepped forward. "Your office is clean."

Genuine gratitude washed over her at that knowledge, and she let it show in her eyes. "Thank you."

Dima gave his security guy a look and then indicated the direction of her office with his hand. "Shall we?"

Jenna nodded before leading him from the room.

They got to her office, and he shut the door behind them, then turned to face her, his expression bordering on sympathetic. "You know you cannot press charges."

"Um…no, I *do not* know that."

"What kind of stress do you think Nataliya will feel to find out that someone has been spying on you for a year?"

She couldn't believe he was playing the BFF health guilt card with her. "Don't tell her."

"You really expect her not to find out?"

He might not believe it, no matter what he'd said earlier, but no way would Jenna even consider going through with pressing charges if she thought it could lead to unhealthy stress for her friend. "You and your brothers are resourceful. I'm sure you can keep the news from her."

"Like anyone has ever been able to keep a secret from her. She's a hacker."

And a darn good one, but Nataliya was too busy with her

roles as queen, wife, and mom to indulge in her love for digging out secrets unless she needed to.

"If she was monitoring me that closely, she would already know, and she would have been the one to come to me. She only researches what she needs to know, and right now she's focused on a whole lot besides the nitty-gritty of her BFF's life."

"Without the threat of prosecution, that woman is not going to keep silent about any of this," Dima said, taking another tack. "For all we know, she is already aware of Nataliya's pregnancy, and it is not supposed to be made public for another month."

"How well do you know your sister-in-law?" Jenna asked Dima, her tone dry.

"I would say very well."

"Then you know that if it were left up to her, Nataliya would want Skylar prosecuted to the very extent of the law in order to protect others from being harmed. Besides, you can still threaten her with extradition and longer prison time."

"A conviction isn't going to stop a woman like her from doing this again," Dima said cynically. "She's found a way to augment her income, and she's not giving it up just because she goes to jail for a while."

"So I'll sue her in civil court and bankrupt her. Besides, a conviction *will* make it a heck of a lot harder for Skylar to get a job where she has access to sensitive information. If I'd known she had a sideline selling information, I wouldn't have let her near me or my work."

Jenna couldn't help feeling responsible for hiring the woman regardless. She'd *liked* Skylar and had planned to mentor her career as Jenna had been mentored back in the day.

Dima gave her a grim look. "Jenna, do you remember the NDA you signed after Nataliya and my brother became engaged?"

Where was he going with this? "Of course."

"It prevents you from pressing charges against Skylar, because to do so would require you to reveal sensitive information about my family and company."

"I don't have to reveal that she stole information about you all and Mirrus Global." She would be perfectly happy to keep that out of either a criminal or civil suit.

"Any investigation would do so in its natural course, and that would put you in breach of the agreement."

"I'm not sure a lawyer would agree."

"By all means, consult with one." He didn't sound superior but resigned.

And Jenna knew then that Dima was certain of his legal standing. Additionally, he was willing to use her own integrity against her, if it meant getting what he wanted. She'd signed that NDA in good faith, more than willing to promise to keep her friend's secrets.

"So my brother and his company don't matter?" Jenna asked, disillusioned in a way she had never been before.

Not even last night, when she'd thought he'd used sex as nothing more than a tool.

"We will determine if any harm has been done to his company and what can be done to mitigate it." Dima said that like his promise was worth anything to her, and moreover that such a promise should be enough.

But how could she trust him to care about her brother's company? Or her brother, for that matter, when it was so obvious he didn't care about Jenna?

Jenna wanted to call Nataliya more than anything in that moment.

And knew it really was the last thing she *could* do.

"Fine." Jenna had no other words.

Her own sense of honor wouldn't let her go forward with plans that might mean the world to her, but also violated a promise she'd made. Even if she hadn't understood that promise to include a situation like this when she'd made it.

"Fine? Does that mean we are in agreement, then?" he asked.

"If you mean, do we agree that you have my hands tied? Yes."

His jaw tautened, but he nodded. "Pressing charges would not have the all-encompassing benefit you seem to think."

"Justice is not just a benefit." It was something you either believed in, or you didn't.

He obviously didn't believe Jenna deserved it, or that the woman who had done her harm deserved to be served with it.

Dima frowned, but after a quick look at his watch, opened the door. "Shall we?"

"No."

That stopped him. "You agreed."

"You don't need me in there to tell Skylar that she's won and can go on to do exactly what she's done to me to someone else."

"That is not what is going to happen."

But Jenna wasn't listening. "Close the door on your way out."

"Jenna—"

"We're finished here. Now get out of my office, Your Highness."

"I understand that you are upset—"

"Save it," she interrupted again, absolutely done with this conversation.

The look on his face would have been funny if her heart wasn't so sore. How had she left herself open to him and his family hurting her? Again?

Twice in twenty-four hours. Ignoring that would make her beyond foolish.

Being friends with a queen had its ups and downs, but for the first time, Jenna questioned whether staying in Nataliya's life was worth it.

Instead of listening to her, Dima stepped back toward Jenna, like he was ready to talk this out.

Only she'd given him that kind of chance once already, and hours later he was betraying her again.

"No." She shook her head, emphasizing her refusal to go there. "You have not only just told me that can I not seek justice for a terrible violation of my trust and privacy, but you have informed me that I cannot even tell my brother or other family about it. Not for his sake, not for mine."

"We can arrange for a palace-approved therapist for you to

talk to," Dima said, sounding like he really thought that was some kind of solution.

"How about you arrange a way to tell my best friend that I can't be in her life anymore?"

"No, that's not—"

"Your choice." She glared at Dima, Jenna's eyes burning with tears, her heart cracking at the thought of losing Nataliya. "I won't put other people in my life at risk because I want to keep a dear person in my life."

"You don't mean that."

"Honestly? I don't know, but right now, I do know I don't want you in my office. Can you respect that, at least, Your Highness?"

"Jenna, I respect you."

The look she gave him let him know how much she believed that.

His frown of consternation said he got the message. "Your boss is just as committed to not pressing charges."

Like that mattered. It wasn't her boss in here pressing the advantage and giving Jenna a gag order.

"I didn't have sex with my boss last night. She's never claimed I was part of her family." She spoked slowly, so he did not miss a single word. "She didn't pretend to be my friend."

"It is no pretense. Do you think I would press charges if it had been me who was being spied on?" he asked. "Or one of my brothers?"

"Does it matter? It wasn't you. It was me, and I want Skylar to go to jail."

"You're not a vengeful person."

Justice was not vengeance, but if he couldn't see that, Jenna saying so wasn't going to open his eyes.

A knock sounded at the door.

Jenna made no move to answer it. Doing so would require her walking right by Dima, and she wasn't doing that.

After a second knock, the prince turned around and opened the door. His security guy said something in a low tone.

Dima nodded and replied in the same quiet tone, then turned back to her. "I have to leave."

Since that was what she'd been trying to get him to do for the last several minutes, Jenna did not bother to reply.

"There's a problem with the deal I'm working for Mirrus Global," he offered anyway.

"Okay."

"Can I pick you up for dinner?"

She didn't even ask herself what planet he lived on. He'd established it wasn't in her orbit. "No."

"Jenna, we have to talk."

"No."

"Yes." Then he left.

Jenna took a deep breath and then let it out. Everything just felt too heavy to hold right now.

So she did what she always did when emotion got too heavy. She focused on something else.

Back when her brother had been dying, she'd gotten straight A's and been named player of the year on her soccer team.

Right now, she had a magazine to get out.

Moving to her desk, she powered up her laptop and got to work.

The next couple of days, Jenna ignored several calls and texts from Dima.

She hid her feelings from Nataliya, but that was easy via text. They had a video call scheduled on the weekend, and Jenna was seriously considering coming up with an excuse to get out of it.

Even if she had to lie.

Jenna and her boss had spoken briefly about the situation, and while the older woman had been sorry for how violated Jenna must feel, she'd been adamant that the magazine's reputation would suffer terrible harm if it got out that they'd had such a serious and long-lasting breach in their confidentiality.

No one seemed to care about the designer who had lost her business over that breach, or what potential harm could come to Jenna's brother's company, or how many other people had been harmed by Skylar's information leaks.

Not to mention, the woman had profited by her perfidy and had gotten away with it.

Sure, she'd been fired, but the carefully worded reason for doing so had left it possible for her to file for unemployment benefits even.

Jenna was beyond livid, and that feeling wasn't going away.

Her relationship with Nataliya wasn't the only thing she was reevaluating in her life. She didn't know if she wanted to continue working for the magazine.

She was also hurt. Her life and privacy had been invaded, and that was going to go unanswered.

She couldn't even talk about it to her two dearest friends, much less her family, and that inability was making everything feel bigger and more ugly.

And under all of it was this pain in her heart that centered around Dima.

Something she didn't even want to acknowledge, because the sex was supposed to be just that and not emotionally driven. Only she felt deep and pain-filled emotion every time his name flashed on her phone screen.

Thankfully, he hadn't shown up unannounced to her work again.

Jenna didn't know what she was going to do about her friendship with Nataliya and Emma.

She'd never thought the cost for having them in her life would be so high, that her personal integrity would be compromised.

She felt guilty about the people whose secrets had been betrayed because of her and wanted to tell them it had happened.

The fact that she couldn't only added to the maelstrom of negative emotion swirling constantly inside her.

While she had no intention of going to a palace-approved therapist, Jenna thought finding a local one to talk to might not be a bad idea. She didn't want to keep feeling this way.

And she needed to talk to someone. Jenna loved Nataliya

like a sister, but she cared deeply for Emma too, and both their children were like nieces and nephews to Jenna.

Only how could she stay in their life if it meant she had to lie? To hide damaging truths?

And yet, how could Jenna leave their lives without causing Nataliya stress that would be dangerous to her and her unborn child right now?

Her phone rang, the ringtone her brother's, and guilt washed over her anew.

While she was perfectly happy to avoid Dima's calls, Jenna wasn't a coward, and she wasn't going to do the same for Luke. She swiped to answer. "Hey, little brother."

"I just got off the phone with Prince Dimitri."

"Oh?" she asked, wondering why Dima would have called Luke.

Had he been checking to make sure she hadn't spilled the truth to Luke?

"What the hell, Jenna? You had someone spying on you for over a year! Are you okay?" Her brother's tone left no doubt how worried about her he was.

It was like a balm to Jenna's soul.

"He told you that?" Jenna could barely believe it.

Why would Dima do that?

"He made me do an electronic signature on an NDA first, but yes. That guy is a year younger than me, but I don't mind admitting he intimidates me."

Jenna surprised herself with a laugh. She hadn't felt much like laughing the last few days. "He's a prince. It's in the job description."

"You think? I never got the impression anyone in that family intimidated you."

"They don't."

"Then why didn't you tell us what happened?"

Jenna grimaced. "I signed an NDA too, a long time ago. Telling you would have breached it."

"Like any of us would have let them know," her brother scoffed.

"My integrity was already ripped to shreds. I wasn't flushing it down the sewer too."

Her brother's sigh was long. "Jenna, you expect too much from yourself. You didn't do anything wrong."

"I hired the wrong person. I made friends with the wrong person."

"What the hell are you talking about?"

"Nataliya. Being friends with her painted a target on your back, and I didn't even know it."

"There is no target on my back. Has anyone ever told you that you take your role as the oldest way too seriously?"

"I'm not the oldest." Matt had died, but he'd lived too, and she'd never claim his spot in their family.

"No, I know." This sigh was a lot less gusty.

Luke understood how important that distinction was. She was the oldest surviving sibling, but she would never actually be the oldest.

"Listen, sis, you need to stop taking yourself so seriously. You weren't the only one who approved your assistant. In fact, I doubt she was hired right into her position."

"She wasn't." Oh, man, had they bothered to look into the two years Skylar had worked at the magazine before she'd become Jenna's assistant?

"Right," he said, like he'd had no doubt. "Skylar is an opportunist. She wasn't just selling information about the royal family, but about designers—"

"And your company. She had a file on it." That still bothered Jenna. A lot.

"Sure, but nothing really actionable to work with. You are about as interested in genetic research as I am in fashion. We don't talk business."

That was true. "But she had a file."

"A useless one with no information that isn't already public. Prince Dimitri made sure I got a copy so I could mitigate any potential damage. Stop feeling guilty about me and my company. We are both fine."

"Did Dima tell you to call me?" Jenna asked.

"Yes. He thought you needed someone to talk to because you aren't talking to any of them."

Okay, so she'd neglected to return Emma's latest phone call and her text trying to firm up plans for dinner again.

"I don't want to talk to them."

"Why? You're closer to Nataliya than Lisa," he said, mentioning their youngest sister.

"Lisa and I are close."

"I didn't say you weren't, just that you're closer to your BFF."

Jenna sighed. "I can't talk to her about this. She needs stress minimized in her life right now."

"Is she pregnant again?" her brother asked, no slouch in the thinking department.

"Yes."

"So why not Emma then?"

"I just don't know if being friends with their family is worth it."

"Worth what exactly?"

"Being forced to lie."

"About what?"

"This. All of it. I couldn't tell you that your privacy had been breached, and you're my brother!"

"So, Prince Dimitri made it so you could."

"He probably expects me to be grateful."

"Probably. He strikes me as the kind of man who thinks he knows what's best for everyone else."

"You wouldn't know anything about that, would you?"

Her brother laughed, but they both knew that described him too.

"Maybe you should take some time off."

"You think that will help?" she asked, not against the idea, just not convinced it would make any difference.

"You're a dweller, Jenna. You've had to come into that office where that opportunistic piece of work planted a listening device every day since you found out. Tell me you don't wonder if someone is listening in on your calls, if somehow somebody hasn't breached the security on that laptop Nataliya tricked out for you."

"I can honestly say that particular worry is a nonstarter."

"And the other."

"I hate being in my office. Hate it. And it's an exercise in willpower answering the phone. Every single time."

"Is that why you're ignoring Prince Dimitri's calls?"

"He told you that?"

"Sure. Everybody knows you two have feelings for each other. Just because you've never acted on them doesn't negate their existence."

Jenna gasped and flailed before sputtering out, "Lust is not a feeling."

"Sure it is, but I'm not talking about lust, and you know it."

"Who is everybody?" she demanded, rather than react to that bit of provocation.

"The family. And if our family sees it, I'm sure his does too."

"You all are delusional."

"The only one here not seeing reality is you, if you think the way you two feel about each other isn't obvious to the people who know you best."

"I would prefer my baby brother not speculate on my sex life."

He made a gagging sound. "Definitely not doing that."

"It can't be any more than that."

"It already is."

"It can't be," she emphasized. "And you know why."

Her brother was silent long enough she hoped he had dropped it.

"He's the youngest, not the oldest," Luke pointed out, though. "He doesn't have to have children for primogeniture."

"Ooh, big words."

"I use big words all the time. I run a genetic research lab."

More like a group of labs, but why quibble over terminology?

"Listen, brother mine, even if there was a chance that Dima

and I could have ever had something…" And she was convinced there was not. "There isn't one now. I can't trust him."

"Because he made you stay silent about what happened?"

"That's part of it." A big part of it.

"But here we are, talking about it because he made that possible."

"Stop. You probably think that's awesome of him, but you aren't the only one Skylar had a file on. I can't go to any of those other companies or designers and warn them."

"You'd get fired if you did."

"Maybe."

"Would it be worth it?"

"Maybe."

"Jenna, sometimes we have to do the hard thing because one set of priorities trumps another."

"His will always be his family. You think I want even a casual relationship with someone who will throw me under the bus so easily?"

"He didn't."

"That's how it feels."

"Again, take some time. You need to figure out what is reality and what is feeling."

Luke had a point. Though she could argue that feelings were as real as anything else in life. Only she knew Luke didn't share that viewpoint.

He was a scientist and a businessman.

He and Dima probably had more in common in how they thought than Jenna and the prince did.

Still, she felt the need to elaborate. "The fact Dima doesn't understand how important it is to me that Skylar be arrested for her crimes, that she be prevented from waltzing into another company and doing the exact same thing, shows how far apart our priorities are."

The royal family weren't the only ones who mattered. Not even Nataliya.

That's not the way the world became a better place, and Jenna believed in change.

She didn't mention the whole "sex to get her out of her apartment so it could be searched" thing. Jenna accepted that Dima really hadn't seen the sex as a convenient diversion, but something inevitable between them.

She could not deny that inevitability with any level of honesty either.

"You don't know what measures the prince has taken to protect the other people your assistant spied on through you. Maybe give him a chance to tell you before you write him off completely."

"I told you—"

"That you have no future because you can't have children."

She sucked in air, the truth something she hadn't needed to say out loud since her decision at the age of twenty-one to make sure the genetic disease that killed her brother could not be passed on through her.

When she and her two younger siblings had been tested for the gene, only she had been a carrier. For Jenna, no other decision could be made but to have a tubal ligation and prevent any chance of her passing the gene on to the next generation.

Luke cursed. "I didn't say that to hurt you."

"I know." She wished she could say it didn't hurt, but the wound she'd thought healed long ago felt fresh and new.

"My point is, it's not the roadblock to a future with Prince Dimitri you think it is."

"I know you believe that."

"But you don't."

"This is a nonsensical discussion. You do realize that, don't you?"

Luke let her change the subject, but Jenna kept thinking about her brother's suggestion that she take time off over the following week.

CHAPTER EIGHT

WITH EACH DAY, it grew harder for Jenna to go into her office, and the idea of taking time off became more appealing.

A last-minute emergency at work made it possible for her to avoid her video chat with Nataliya, but Jenna knew she couldn't avoid her BFF for long, and she needed to make some hard decisions about her relationship with the royal family.

Either she sucked it up and dealt with the compromises she had to make, or she walked away.

Her current level of exhaustion wasn't helping her apply rational thinking to it either. Jenna had had trouble sleeping ever since discovering she had been spied on. She would wake up in a cold sweat convinced she was being watched, only to have to convince herself it wasn't true before going back to sleep.

If she could go back to sleep.

Even though all her clothes and accessories had been cleared, she'd been dressing without her usual styling as well. She hadn't carried a purse since the night she'd made love with Dima.

She'd gone out and bought a new laptop bag, but for some reason couldn't make herself use a purse at all.

The job she had always loved was now a source of irritation and frustration. Jenna didn't want to return emails or calls from designers wanting to give her an early peek at their new collections.

Jenna wasn't just avoiding Emma's calls. She still found answering the phone nearly impossible.

No question, she needed a change of pace.

It started with asking for time off. If she came back with the intention of staying at the magazine, she would request a change of office locations. She would give up her window to get away from the sense of violation she felt every time she walked into her office.

Her boss approved the leave without a single argument, and Jenna went home, not sure if she was going to take a trip or just putter around her apartment for the next two weeks.

Her phone rang as she was walking in her door. Jenna grabbed it from her jacket pocket, where she'd been keeping it, and glanced at the caller ID.

Dima.

She swiped to answer. All sorts of snarky greetings went through her mind, but Jenna was a grown-up, so she went with, "Hello?"

"Jenna. You answered." He sounded shocked.

"Didn't you want me to?"

"I would not have called you otherwise."

"Okay."

"You talked to your brother."

"I did."

"Did it help?"

"With my feelings of guilt or betrayal?"

"Either?"

"Both actually." Though she also planned to take Luke's advice about asking Dima what he'd done to protect other people's information compromised by Skylar, since they couldn't be told about the leak.

"Then I am glad you spoke to him."

"That's not what you were saying in my office."

"I may have been overzealous in telling you not to speak to your family."

"Really? Because I reread that NDA your father had me sign, and it was pretty airtight. There were no exceptions."

"Yes, well, your family isn't going to blab to the press."

"No, they are not, but you still had my brother sign an NDA before you told him what happened."

"I'm a cautious guy."

"Is that part of being a prince too?"

"I wish you didn't say the word *prince* with such loathing," he said, his own tone almost wistful. "I am certain that caution is part of my nature and has little to do with my position as prince."

"You could be right," she acceded.

"I have to fly back to New York."

"You have been in Seattle all this time?" she asked, surprised as she dropped her wallet and other things she'd been carrying in her pockets in a small pile in the center of her table.

"No, I flew to Mirrus for a few days to meet with Nikolai and Konstantin."

"Emma texted that Konstantin was out of town."

Jenna had replied to her friend's texts but still avoided committing to getting together in person.

"He wants to apologize for allowing you to think he doubted your loyalty to Nataliya."

"Implying he didn't doubt it?" she asked with skepticism.

"I told you that he didn't."

"And yet you are also the one who told me he did."

"He did say so," Dima said, sounding a tad defensive. "When I confronted him about it, he admitted he'd never doubted you."

"Then why did he say he did?" she asked, still irked and, yes, hurt by it.

She'd cared about this family for a good part of a decade. Believing that some of them had not trusted her had been painful.

"He never really gave a straight answer, just that we'd needed the leak shored up, and he'd known I was the one to make that happen."

"Well, he was right," she acknowledged.

"You were hurt in the process."

"Yes." Why deny a truth they both knew?

"I am sorry."

She bit back a sigh. "I believe you."

"Because I called your brother?"

"Well, that and the fact you keep calling. You could have just let things go, but you didn't."

"You were thinking about giving up our family."

She had said she was considering ending her friendship with Nataliya. It was funny he put it that way, as if Jenna was walking away from all of them.

Which she would be, but still. Nataliya was her BFF. Jenna hadn't really thought the rest of the family saw her as part of *their* lives as well, despite claiming she was family.

People said stuff like that without meaning it all the time.

"I'm still thinking about it."

He said something under his breath.

"What did you say?" she asked.

"It is not important." His tone said otherwise. "I wanted to see you before I go back to New York."

"I'm not sure that's a good idea." Jenna needed a clear head to think about her future, and being around Dima clouded her mind and heart.

With lust, yes, but also with feelings she knew could go nowhere.

There was no win in that scenario for her.

Well, unless she considered mind-blowing orgasms a win. And in this case, she wasn't sure they wouldn't contribute to the problem.

"It is a good idea," he assured her with certainty ringing in his voice. "Me leaving town again without seeing you is not."

Knowing he couldn't see it, but unable to stop herself, Jenna shook her head in negation. She opened her mouth to say the denial out loud when her eyes flicked over a bunch of travel brochures she'd picked up in the middle of winter.

Dreaming about visiting sunny beaches had lifted her spirits when the skies were overcast and the never-ending rain of winter kept coming down in sheets so that even taking a walk was a challenge.

She loved Seattle, but sometimes when it rained nonstop for a week or more, she thought about what it would be like to *live* somewhere sunny. Not just visit.

"Unfortunately, I need to pack." Because she was going to pick one of those sunny destinations and go.

Wherever she could book for flight and accommodations

starting tomorrow. Jenna wasn't picky. She just wanted to get away.

"Pack for what?"

"I'm going on vacation."

"Where?"

"Not sure yet, but someplace sunny."

"You don't know where you are going?" he asked like the idea was beyond comprehension.

"No."

"But you are leaving tomorrow?" The disbelief in his voice came across loud and clear over their connection.

"Yes."

He was silent for a full five seconds. "Is that a good idea?" he asked, almost tentatively.

Imagine, Prince Dimitri of the House of Merikov tentative.

"Why wouldn't it be?"

"Perhaps you are reacting to what happened." He said the words slowly and carefully, like they were nitroglycerin he didn't want to detonate.

"I'm definitely reacting to it." And she had no trouble admitting that. "I want to get away, to enjoy some stress-free days on a beach somewhere."

And to think through what she should do going into the future, away from everything familiar.

"And you do not know where?" He was sounding almost panicked.

"Why does that bother you so much? Normal people go on spur-of-the-moment vacations all the time. That's why there's last-minute deals, for people like me."

She started sifting through the brochures and stopped at the one for Abu Dhabi. As funny as it might sound, she'd always wanted to go, ever since reading the *Garfield* comics as a child. The big orange cat was always threatening to ship Opie there.

As an adult, she'd learned it was the capital of the UAE, and that had only made it seem more intriguing and a place she wanted to go.

Jenna loved traveling, but her trips were usually dictated

by work. This time, she was going on vacation, and she could go anywhere she liked.

"I've got to go, Dima. I need to get my trip booked."

After a quick search, she'd discovered she didn't need a visa to travel the UAE as long as her passport was current, which it was.

"You aren't seriously booking a trip today that you plan to leave on tomorrow?" There was that odd near-panicked tone in the princely voice again.

"Well, yes." Or perhaps the next day, but she was really hoping for tomorrow.

"What if it is a scam?"

"I'm not booking on some random website. I'll use my usual links. You really need to get over this travel paranoia."

"I am not paranoid about travel," he said with stiff dignity.

"I'm glad to hear it. I was getting worried."

He made a strange sound, like he was choking, trying to talk and growling at the same time.

She laughed. She kind of liked eliciting that sound from the urbane prince.

"Where are you hoping to go?" he asked.

"I told you, I don't know. Someplace sunny." She didn't mention Abu Dhabi because that probably would sound like pie in the sky, and she realized her chances of booking anything for there in the immediate future were slim.

"Surely you have a destination you are hoping for?"

"I didn't," she said grudgingly.

"But now you do?"

"Abu Dhabi. I know I'll probably end up in Mexico." Last-minute bookings for cruises to Mexico and all-inclusive resorts were always being offered in the ads on the sidebars of her favorite travel sites. "But I'm going to look anyway."

"Do not let me keep you, then."

Jenna hung up, ignoring the disappointment she felt to be saying goodbye to the man she knew was not good for her. He'd hurt her, more than once.

Maintaining their friendship, much less pursuing something sexual with him, was not a good idea.

And yet, she didn't like that he'd given up so easily on the idea of seeing her before he left Seattle.

An hour later, Jenna was staring morosely at her computer. Not only were there no last-minute trips to Abu Dhabi she could get in on, but she'd realized that she didn't want to settle, and that left her not booking anything at all.

Dispirited, she got up to make herself a cup of tea when her doorbell rang.

Not expecting anyone, she checked the peephole in her door. Dima stood on the other side, his expression expectant.

She should be irritated, and she was, but she also felt pleasure at the sight of him. A small voice in the back of her mind rejoiced that he had refused to leave town without seeing her.

Even after everything.

And that was seriously scary.

She could not afford to catch deep feelings for a man she simply could *not* make a future with.

She opened the door to her small single-level ranch-style home. Her brother had suggested a condo in a secure building, but Jenna had wanted her own space, and she'd never regretted her decision to buy a single-dwelling house instead.

She pulled open the door. "Dima, what are you doing here?"

"Bringing you dinner." He held up a bag of takeaway from one of her favorite restaurants.

She had a choice. Jenna could refuse him entrance, or she could let him in. If she let him in, she was tacitly agreeing to talk to him.

That did not mean she was agreeing to continuing their sexual relationship, she reminded herself. And she had not yet asked him if he had done anything to protect others from Skylar's willingness to sell secrets to the highest bidder.

"Come in." She stepped back to let him inside.

One of his security guys came first, taking *the tour*, as she thought of it before declaring the house clear. He left, pulling the door shut behind them.

"Won't he be conspicuous standing on my stoop?" she asked.

"My security does not stand on stoops. They will take up noninvasive positions that allow them to watch your house from all approachable angles."

"Do you ever get tired of all of that?" she asked, leading the way into the L-shaped living and dining area.

He set the takeout bag on the dining table. "Security, you mean?"

"Yes. You can't ever just run down to the corner store and buy a candy bar."

"I've mostly always had them." There was a shrug in his voice even if he was too controlled to follow through with his shoulders. "I've never once *wanted* to run down to the corner store for anything. And as we discussed before, it's as much about my wealth as my royal lineage."

Jenna shook her head, and swept the brochures into a pile and removed them from her dining table, where she'd had them spread out in hopeful array. "I would hate living like that."

"You would be surprised what you can become accustomed to." The look he gave her said there was more than the surface message in those words.

Though she had no clue what it was meant to be.

"Maybe," she said noncommittally as she pulled out plates and cutlery. "What if I'd already eaten?"

"Have you?"

"No."

"Then the point is moot."

"I suppose. I'm sure I told you I would be busy packing."

"You need to eat."

Her stomach chose that moment to growl, and she didn't even bother trying to deny it. "I'll plate up."

It took only a minute or so to do just that, and then she cleared away the detritus of the takeaway, something she'd always done when eating takeout at home.

She liked sitting at the table and eating off plates, using real forks.

He settled in one of her dining chairs, and the table that was large enough to accommodate her family for holiday dinners suddenly felt intimate. "Have you booked your vacation yet?"

"No." She took a bite of her pasta, savoring it and realizing at once how hungry she'd gotten. "There are tons of trips I could take to Southern Cali, or Mexico."

"But nothing for Abu Dhabi?"

"Nothing." Well, not nothing, but no trips in her price range.

He gave her a warm look. "Perhaps I can help."

"Have you taken up travel bookings in all that spare time you don't have?" she asked while doing her best to pretend her entire body wasn't responding to that look.

"Not personally, but I have staff."

"And you asked them to look into a trip for me?" she asked, surprised.

"For *us*."

Warning bells started clanging in her head. "What do you mean?"

"A tsunami of bad timing hit us last week, but we were far from done with each other, *milaya*."

He was talking about sex. Jenna's body gave a big *whomp* of response to the thought. "I thought you were in the middle of a huge deal."

"We finalized it last week when I was in Mirrus. It will make the company millions and provide additional infrastructure on Mirrus."

"That's amazing." It couldn't be easy to provide local jobs for an island country that limited tourism.

"Thank you. I thought so. My brothers were both pleased, as well."

And that would be important to a man who was every bit as alpha as either of his older brothers but would always be the youngest sibling.

"I deserve to celebrate," Dima proclaimed.

"You seem like the kind of man who celebrates one good

deal by starting another one, not going on a trip with your current casual sexual partner."

"Usually you would be right, but you see, this woman I cannot get out of my system, she wants to go on a vacation."

"That's a pretty big admission."

"You led me to believe last-minute vacations are quite normal for people."

"People who aren't royalty, yes, or, you know…workaholic tycoons, but that's not what I meant."

"Oh?"

"Stop playing naive," she instructed him with just a tinge of annoyance. "You know what I'm talking about. You admitted that you can't get me out of your system."

"Are you saying I am out of yours?"

"Tell me what you've done to mitigate the damage to the other companies and people Skylar spied on through me," Jenna said rather than answer that loaded question.

"You are so sure I have done something?" he asked.

She hadn't been, but her brother's call had made Jenna take a step back from her roiling emotions and consider. "Not sure, but hopeful."

Something flicked in his gaze. Disappointment, maybe. "First, I have set our best fixers on the task of making sure that Skylar's actions follow her in her reputation, without bringing your magazine, my family or Mirrus Global into it."

Unsure how successful that endeavor could be with those caveats, Jenna nodded without enthusiasm.

This time it was easy to read the disappointment. "That does not please?"

"Let's just say I doubt how well it can work without revealing what she did to me." Jenna sighed, wondering if she was just expecting too much.

"You're assuming you are the first person she targeted this way."

Jenna had, but it was clear Dima hadn't. "You don't think I was."

"The magazine was not her first job out of university, so no."

"You think she's always done this?" Jenna's mind boggled at the idea.

Dima met her gaze, his gray eyes serious. "She was too proficient at it for you to have been the first employer she exploited."

"So you're willing to reveal another company's embarrassment?" Jenna asked, not really thrilled by that idea either.

"Rather than see you or my family hurt? Yes."

There was that streak of ruthlessness. And he showed no remorse about it either. Dima would do what he thought best.

"You were perfectly content to see me hurt," she said, not willing to let him pretend otherwise.

"No. I was not."

"Don't shine me on, Dima. When it was a choice between hurting me and protecting your royal family, you didn't hesitate."

"But I was not in any way content with the outcome. Your pain and disillusionment mattered. And that really is an admission of note if you care to take it."

CHAPTER NINE

JENNA DIDN'T ACTUALLY know what to do with Dima's admission.

If he meant it, and she thought maybe he did, then as ruthless as Dima might be, he *had* regretted hurting her when he made it a point not to regret any action he considered necessary.

"And the people she's already leaked information on?" Jenna asked, rather than dwell on something so emotionally explosive. "The ones she *still* has confidential information on that is worth selling?"

"My people went through all her electronic devices and her home for printed documentation. They took anything and everything that could be compromising to someone else. They also wiped her cloud accounts."

"She let you do that?"

"Rather than face prison? Yes."

"But you wouldn't have pressed charges."

"She could not be sure of that, could she? You did a good job convincing her you were willing to do just that, come what may."

"You used *me* as a threat?" Jenna felt a certain amount of satisfaction at that.

"Yes. Skylar also signed a confession admitting to planting the listening devices and the corporate espionage which she believes will be given to the DA if she is caught doing the same thing again."

"She could move to another state, change her name."

"She could, but she's on our radar, and she knows it."

"I…" Jenna wasn't sure exactly how she felt about all of that. "That helps."

"Good."

"But it doesn't change the fact that I couldn't do what I thought was right."

"Life is filled with compromise, and sometimes you must trust others to make sure your priorities are taken care of."

"Like you ever do that," she scoffed.

"You would be surprised at how often I've been forced to do that very thing." The look he gave her was all sober sincerity.

Jenna sighed. "I forget that you have to compromise too. Nataliya has had to often enough."

"Yes. You do not think she wanted to share the tragedy of her miscarriage with the world, do you?"

"No, I know she didn't."

And yet, even if the news hadn't been leaked early, it would have been shared. Because Nataliya's life could never be entirely private. No matter how much more comfortable that might be for the Queen of Mirrus.

He leaned back in his chair, his attention fully on Jenna, as it had been since his arrival. "So, Abu Dhabi."

She pushed her plate away and returned that attention. "You really want to go with me to the UAE?" Had he ever taken a vacation that she knew of?

Jenna couldn't remember one if he had.

"I prefer you go with me." He gave her a charming smile. "On my plane, and stay at our property there."

"You have a house in the UAE?"

"It is a condominium in an exclusive community, but yes, we have properties in most major markets."

"And it's empty right now?"

"Unless one of us is using it, the place is always empty. Allowing others to use it would be a security issue."

"That seems like a waste, doesn't it?" Even as she asked, she realized how little she cared.

She was just making conversation to give her brain a chance to process everything. The fact he'd neutralized Skylar, maybe not with the transparency Jenna would have preferred, but he'd done it all the same.

The fact he wanted sex again with her enough to go on a last-minute trip *with* her to make that happen.

Overkill?

Maybe. But better than the overkill of multiple listening devices hidden in her accessories.

"It cannot be helped," he said, a shrug in his tone.

It took her a second to remember what he was talking about. Oh, yes, responding to her question.

"Why are you doing this?" she asked, needing him to tell her again.

Maybe it would make more sense the second time around.

"I told you."

"We aren't done yet." He meant sex. "You are going on vacation, at the last minute, *you*, just so you can get more sex?"

"Not vacation exactly."

"What then?"

"I will have to work part of each day, and since I am there, I will move forward meetings that were to be scheduled with other companies for next month."

"Can they be moved?" Just because he wanted to change his travel schedule?

"It would be the best interest of the companies to do so."

"Mirrus isn't a major world power."

"No, it is a small island country with some very important natural resources. Mirrus Global, however, is a multibillion-dollar corporation with powerful connections worldwide."

"The company protects the country," she said, making sense of something she'd wondered about for a while.

How Mirrus had maintained its independence.

"Yes. We have powerful business partners with deeply felt political influence in most major markets."

"Don't you mean countries?"

"It is my brother's job to think in terms of country. I make money."

"And use it to exert influence."

"Yes, but also to build infrastructure and improve education and employment for my people."

"It doesn't bother you to use your control over money to wield power in other countries?"

"No."

"You are so sure of yourself and your path."

"Are you trying to imply you are not? Because we both know that is not true."

His words shocked her. She wasn't like that. "I'm not sure what you mean."

"You have pushed your sustainable fashion agenda to the point you are now influencing not only your magazine, but designers and even clothing manufacturers."

"I am trying to take care of our planet." And her influence at her magazine wasn't nearly as far-reaching as she would like.

Their focus was still almost entirely on traditional fast fashion.

"That is a laudable goal," he said, approval warm in his voice. "I am taking care of my country."

"You said that was your brother's job."

"No, I said it was his job to pay attention to country distinctions. It is mine to know markets."

"You're splitting hairs."

"I do not see it that way."

"Stubborn."

He gave her a devastating smile. "Like is drawn to like."

"I'm not stubborn," she lied.

"I can imagine those who know you well laughing at the hilarity of that statement."

"Maybe." She shook her head and pulled her plate back toward her, resuming eating her dinner, her appetite stronger than it had been in days.

She *was* stubborn. And liked herself that way, so she didn't see it changing.

Jenna thought too many people lived without the things that gave them joy because they were not stubborn enough. If that was a self-justification for a personality trait that could be both weakness and strength, so be it.

"We will need to have a layover in New York so I can take an in-person meeting that could not be moved."

"You're assuming I'm going to Abu Dhabi with you."

"Yes, I am."

"Arrogant."

"Undoubtedly."

"At least you didn't try to say I am too."

"You have your own arrogance, but it is tempered by your compassion."

"And yours?"

"No doubt could use some tempering."

"You're very honest with yourself and about yourself." It was one of the things that drew her to Dima.

More than his brothers, he could admit to what others might consider flaws, but maybe that was because he didn't see them as flaws?

Of course, he probably couldn't imagine anything worse than lacking confidence like any other mere mortal.

"What is that look?" he asked her.

"What look?"

"If I knew, I would not have asked."

"I was just thinking that you don't suffer from the crises of confidence that plague most of us."

They finished dinner without much more discussion, like Dima was giving her some time to think. Which surprised her, but she liked it too.

When they were done eating, Dima helped her clear the table.

"You're awfully well domesticated for a prince."

"I had no domestic help in university, graduate school or my two years of active duty in the military."

"None?" she asked doubtfully.

"None. I could have had a cleaning service, at least at university and grad school, but I wanted to experience life as most of my country's citizens do while I still had the chance of doing so."

"You went without security too?" This time she was more horrified than questioning.

"As much as possible, yes. You don't imagine I had security in my military unit. We *were* the security."

"I didn't realize. Did your brothers do the same thing?"

"Not as such."

Which means what? she wondered.

"You really want to go to Abu Dhabi together, just so we can have some more uncomplicated sex?"

"The sex so far has not been without its complications."

She could not disagree. "But the understanding still stands? We are having sex, not starting a relationship."

"We already have a relationship. We are friends, and you are part of my family."

She couldn't help the grimace that twisted her mouth.

"Don't," he ordered.

"Don't what?"

"Think your life would be better without Nataliya and the rest of us Merikovs in it."

"You don't know that's what I was thinking."

"Don't I?"

"No, Mr. Smarty-pants. I could never think my life would be *better* without my BFF." Just easier. More straightforward.

"And yet you are considering breaking off your friendship."

"Not because I think my life would be better."

"If not better, then what?"

"More honest."

"In what way is your life dishonest?"

"Not telling the people that Skylar hurt by selling information about them, that it had happened."

"You would be fired if you did so."

"You sound very sure of that." She wasn't denying it, but Jenna wasn't positive that would be the outcome either.

She hadn't been allowed to put it to the test. In the end, it hadn't been the magazine that put a gag on her.

"That kind of admission would make the magazine vulnerable to expensive liability," Dima pointed out, clearly in a different headspace about it. "Not to mention seriously undermining its reputation in the fashion industry."

"Even so, it's my relationship with you all that has taken my choices away."

"Some of them. Being born into my family took away many of mine." He didn't sound particularly bothered by that truth.

But then he'd had an entire lifetime to come to terms with it.

"You can't change the role you were born into, but I can determine who I am friends with."

"Can you?"

"What do you mean?"

"Could you really walk away from Nataliya, who is like a sister to you, simply because the friendship isn't always convenient?" The look he gave her said he doubted it.

"I don't know." She had no trouble admitting that. "It's one of the things I planned to think about while I'm on vacation."

"One of them?"

She shrugged. "I'm in a life-assessing frame of mind right now, I guess."

"And what else do you want to assess in your life, besides your role in my family?"

"I'm not sure I want to stay at the magazine." Like usual, Jenna found it way too easy to talk to Dima.

Like her brother Luke. Only her other feelings toward Dima were anything but familial.

Shock flashed in Dima's gray gaze. "Why?"

"The industry has changed a lot in the last decade, but especially for print media." Which was an answer, but not the whole answer.

"Are you saying you've been considering this move for a while?"

"Not consciously." But what had happened with Skylar, and the magazine's reaction to it, had brought what had been nebulous feelings of discontent into stark relief.

"And subconsciously?" he asked leadingly.

"The magazine is never going to give as much attention to sustainable fashion and all size models as I want it to."

"Your activism is as important to you as your job?"

"It is," Jenna admitted, maybe even finally to herself. "I just don't know if I can make a living doing what I want to do."

She wasn't interested in being rich, but Jenna did need to provide for her own basic needs, like food and shelter.

"You were the contributing editor of a very successful adjunct blog before being promoted into your current position."

"You know a lot about me. Should I be flattered?"

"Do you know any less about me?"

"Maybe not." Jenna may have asked Nataliya more than her fair share of questions about Dima over the years.

She'd kept track of where he was and how he was doing when he was deployed. She had alerts set up for him too, and they were friends on social media.

"I'm not stalking you."

"No, you are not. We live in an information age, and keeping up with those nearest to us includes things like search engine alerts."

"Are you reading my mind?"

"I simply know what I do to keep up with my family, to keep up with you."

"You have an alert set for me?"

"And I subscribe to your magazine."

He was suspiciously as enthralled by her as she was by him. That was a dangerous situation. "We can't ever be more than friends with benefits, Dima. You know that, right?"

"We are friends. The benefits are what concern me right now. Jenna, I want you. Too damn much. If two weeks in Abu Dhabi will get this craving out of my system, I am willing to make them happen."

Another admission she wasn't sure she would have had the courage to voice. But then, Jenna was not even going to try to convince herself that two weeks together would be enough to get Dima out of her system.

The fact that he thought it would work with him for her was both a relief and a little bit of a letdown.

"All right. I'll go."

His smile was a little predatory, and too darn sexy. "I am very pleased to hear that." He moved toward her, making the kitchen feel smaller than it was. "Perhaps we should celebrate."

"I need to pack."

"I will help you."

"You'll help me?" she asked, unable to stifle the laugh that burbled up. "This I have got to see."

"If it gets us to the celebrating more quickly, I can fold clothes with crease-free precision."

He didn't just fold clothes, but offered advice on what she should bring, and it wasn't all lingerie. Not that the man didn't have a heyday with her nightie drawer, asking oh, so casually if she wouldn't bring the blue silk chemise that barely covered her butt cheeks.

Jenna made room for the lingerie and found that packing actually went really quickly with two people putting her clothes and things together. She kept a permanently packed roll-up with all her skin products, face mask for sleeping and the like, which she tossed in her case first thing.

"I have to say, I'm impressed." Jenna surveyed her neatly packed suitcase and matching garment bag with satisfaction. "That went much faster than usual."

"Two sets of hands make light the work."

"I think that adage is *many hands*, but you are right." It was also easier because she hadn't needed to style several outfits for particular fashion events she would be attending.

Jenna had brought mostly clothes for relaxing and sightseeing, but her garment bag held three gorgeous outfits in case she and Dima decided to sample the nightlife or go out to an elite restaurant.

He'd suggested she bring at least two swimsuits since the Merikov-owned property had a private pool.

Sexually stimulating memories of her last time in a pool with him made her all too eager to comply with that request. Though honestly, Jenna questioned just how much time she would end up wearing either swimsuit.

"Now, we celebrate."

"What about your packing?" she asked even as her body moved toward him of its own volition.

He reached out and cupped her nape, his gray gaze burning her with intensity. "I have people who will do that for me."

She would have said something about it being nice to be him, but his lips were covering hers, and she was enjoying the kiss too much.

This time should have been less frantic then that first night. They'd done this before, but Jenna was starving for the feel of his skin against hers, as if it had been months, not days since they'd shared passion in his hotel room.

With the way Dima shed his clothes so quickly, he felt the same.

They fell onto the bed, not even bothering to pull the comforter back and continued their passionate kiss, their hands everywhere.

He'd learned her erogenous zones the other night and again paid them special attention while seemingly intent on showing her that she had more spots on her body that sent sensual pleasure zinging through her than she'd ever known.

She returned touch for touch, undulating against him, aching for the intimacy of joining while relearning the feel of his muscular body under her hands.

They rolled across the bed, laughing when they nearly fell off together. The laughter didn't last long in the face of their mutual sexual need, and he shifted so he was between her legs, his erection pressing against her entrance.

"Okay?" he asked.

She nodded frantically.

He didn't immediately enter her, though. "No condom?"

"We don't need one." They'd talked about it before. "Right?"

"Right."

But there was something going on here. "Why?" she asked.

"Trust."

"I trust you." In this, at least. Maybe even in a heck of a lot more.

He hadn't made her priorities to be honest to those who had been affected and to make sure Skylar couldn't just go on her way, spying on her next employer, his top consideration, but he hadn't ignored them either. Jenna could fall in love with this man if she let herself.

All thoughts of taboo emotions splintered as he pressed inside her. They moved together as if they had known this intimacy a lifetime, not a single night. She climaxed first, but only by a few seconds, and then they were heaving with spent passion together.

Jenna's eyelids were growing ridiculously heavy, but she hadn't been sleeping much lately, and right this moment, she felt safe.

She fell asleep before he pulled out of her.

Dimitri would have been insulted if any other woman had fallen asleep that fast after making love, but he'd seen the tiredness in Jenna's eyes when he arrived. He doubted she'd been sleeping these past two weeks.

Not if she was *still* considering breaking ties with his family, not to mention the career she'd spent her adult life building.

He leaned down and kissed her forehead, and then, because he simply could not help himself, her temples. Finally gave a soft buss to her passion-swollen lips.

Something in the region of his heart squeezed as he carefully disengaged from her body, and she did nothing more than give a soft sigh.

She trusted him. Probably more than she realized.

That trust was humbling.

He knew she'd felt let down when he'd reminded her of the NDA and effectively tied her hands in the matter of her assistant's spying.

Jenna had to have been devastated to find out someone she'd trusted had betrayed her so badly. Dimitri hadn't taken that into consideration at first, but after talking to Kon, he'd realized what a mistake he'd made.

Jenna's refusal to answer his calls and most of his texts had been a pretty good indicator as well. Dimitri had spent his entire life being told there were few he could trust and even fewer who would never betray him.

He hadn't accounted for the fact that Jenna had not been raised as he had been. She was not part of the royal family; she wasn't even nobility.

Her parents were not wealthy, but middle class Americans who had never even made it into the papers before their three surviving children succeeded in careers that put them at different epicenters of the public eye.

As much as he might despise it, Dimitri's own father was used to being featured in both tabloids and the legitimate press. The Merikovs were accustomed to being spied on, but that didn't mean they didn't do what they needed to in order to protect the most sensitive information in their lives and business.

Jenna had to be hurting at Skylar's betrayal. She was hurting enough at not being able to press charges and *make it right* that she was considering ending a friendship that was as close as family.

Dimitri should have considered all of that before his heavy-handed insistence she keep her own counsel about the spying.

He'd hoped his actions with her brother would show Jenna that her needs were important to him, that Dimitri cared about her emotional well-being.

Not that he made it a habit of considering that aspect of most of his friendships.

Jenna was different, though.

She was special.

And Dimitri wanted her in his bed. Permanently.

He could acknowledge that to himself, if not to the skittish fashion editor.

He'd barely kept a straight face telling her he planned to get her out of his system.

But if he'd told her the truth, that Abu Dhabi was the first volley in a princely courtship, she would have run fast and far.

Jenna didn't want to be a princess. She didn't want to get more embroiled in the lives of the Merikov family than she already was.

It was Dimitri's job to convince her differently.

Kon had done it with Emma, and frankly, Dimitri thought his brother had a lot more to overcome than he did.

Though to hear Kon tell it, the opposite was true.

Kon and Nikolai both thought that how Dimitri had handled things so far had been disastrous. Unused to being censured by his brothers, Dimitri had withdrawn from any further personal discussions while he was in Mirrus.

Until his father had cornered him and reminded him that he'd promised to attend an event where potential partners for him had been invited. Unwilling to get into who he was hoping to align his life with, Dimitri had gone.

If he was lucky, the pictures of him talking and dancing with a princess would hit the news cycle while they were in Abu Dhabi, and Jenna would never even see them.

Jenna would deny that she cared, but Dimitri did not need to remind her that his father thought other women were potential wives for him. She was skittish enough as it was, but they connected in a way he'd never thought to with a woman.

Dimitri had no desire to fall in love like his brothers.

What both Kon and Nikolai had gone through because they loved the women they'd married wasn't something Dimitri ever wanted to experience himself. He and Jenna got along well, and their sexual chemistry was off the charts. She fit in with the rest of his family and had been doing so for several years.

She was perfect for him.

Now, he just had to show her how perfect he could be for her as well.

It started with a last-minute trip to Abu Dhabi.

CHAPTER TEN

JENNA WOKE SURROUNDED by warmth and feeling more rested than she had since discovering Skylar's penchant for spying.

A heavy masculine arm rested over her body at her waist, heated strength all along her back.

She turned to face him, inhaling his scent. "Mmm…" she practically purred. "You smell good."

"I had a video meeting, so I showered."

And yet, he'd undressed again and returned to her bed. Pleasure at that knowledge coursed through her.

"When is our takeoff?"

"We have two hours. Just enough time."

"For?" As if she didn't know.

"This." He nuzzled in, kissing her neck and sending shivers of delight cascading along her nerve endings.

They barely made their takeoff time.

Jenna settled comfortably in her seat beside Dima, accepting the flight attendant's offer of her favorite bubbly water infused with citrus.

"You're used to flying by private jet," he observed.

"Only to Mirrus."

"That's a short flight."

"It is." She'd taken both jets and helicopters to the island country to visit Nataliya. "Abu Dhabi will take much longer to reach."

"With a layover in New York."

"How long will we be there?"

"We arrive this evening and fly out again tomorrow evening."

"The red-eye?"

"Better to sleep on such a long flight."

"I've never found that particularly helpful with jet lag, though I know some people do."

"Then I won't feel guilty if I keep you awake."

There could be no question what he meant by that, and Jenna wasn't complaining. Not even a little.

"I think I'll take in some sights when we're in New York."

"But you have been to the city many times."

"For Fashion Weeks, and other work-related stuff. There's never time to go to the Met, or visit the Empire State Building, or just take a harbor cruise."

"I will be finished with business by two. Save the harbor cruise for me. I will arrange everything."

"*You* will?"

"I'll have it arranged. How is that?"

"More truthful and honestly? Wonderful! I'm really looking forward to it."

His smile said he was looking forward to something too, but it had nothing to do with taking a boat ride to see the sights.

Whatever he might have rather been doing, and Jenna had little doubt what that was—her body was pleasantly sore from sensual use—Dima had to work on most of the flight. However, he'd arranged for her to view a first-run movie Jenna had mentioned she wanted to see.

The noise-canceling headphones and large screen that dropped down from the ceiling made it a totally immersive experience.

When it was over, he asked, "Did you enjoy it?"

"Yes, very much. Only…"

"What?"

"I cannot see either you or your brothers watching movies on a long flight."

"What can you see us doing?"

"Working, just like you are right now."

"Good call. I do not believe I have ever watched a movie on a long flight. I am either sleeping or working."

"I can think of something else you could do to pass the

time." She'd noticed this jet had a bedroom in the back when she'd used the restroom earlier.

"Can you?" Dima moved into her personal space, his mouth hovering over hers. "What might that be?"

"Come with me and find out," she taunted, before sliding out of her seat and away from him.

She didn't have to turn around to know he followed her. She could feel him right behind her.

The bed took up most of the small room, but it was made up with luxurious silk coverlet and sheets and piled high with pillows all the colors of the royal house. The silk duvet cover had the royal house coat of arms embroidered in the center.

An impressionist painting of the palace in Mirrus hung on the wall opposite the bed. Soft cove lighting loaned the room a romantic air, though she was sure it had been designed the way it had to encourage peaceful slumber.

The room was so clearly meant to impress and remind the occupant of the connection to the royal house.

But Jenna loved the colors and the lighting, and it just added to her sense of anticipation for what was to come.

She turned to face Dimitri. "It's so regal in here, but I don't feel like I don't belong."

"I am very glad to hear that." He shrugged out of his suit jacket and hung it up.

"Oh, very fastidious of you, Your Highness."

"Now, if you always used that tone when you call me that, it would never bother me." He tugged his tie loose. "I'm not sloppy by nature, you may have noticed, and in a room this small, there simply is no place for haphazardly discarded clothing."

"Why do I find it charming you think about stuff like that? I should be offended you're more worried about the aesthetics of the room than you are about getting naked with me."

"Perhaps because you know with certainty that there is *nothing* short of family or country emergency that takes precedence over that with me."

"You know? I believe you."

He continued undressing but gave her a heated look.

Jenna took that as her cue to get rid of her own clothes. Following his example, she hung them up in the closet. She was reaching around her back to unhook her bra when she felt hands there, helping her.

"Your skin is so soft, silky and warm." His hands brushed over her back.

Shivers cascaded down her spine, her body shaking with desire so strong, her knees wanted to give way.

He reached around and cupped both her breasts as she pulled her bra away and let it drop. Uncluttered floors not making it on her list of priorities in the moment.

He brushed over her nipples, awakening pleasure with the first touch. After their lovemaking the night before and that morning, Jenna's skin was super sensitized. Her nipples beaded with pleasure that bordered on pain. Atavistic anticipation sent throbbing warmth between her legs.

Dimitri pressed her nipples between his thumbs and forefingers, gently squeezing and releasing before rolling them.

Every tiny touch sent ecstasy shooting to her very core, and Jenna was ready for him before they even lay down on the bed. He hadn't even touched her clitoris, but Jenna knew climax was imminent.

He seemed to know too, because Dimitri pulled her to the bed, laying her down before disappearing between her legs, his mouth working sensual magic that had her crying out in seconds.

She'd had three orgasms by the time he came inside her, his shout triumphant.

She couldn't even begrudge him that victorious sound. He'd conquered her body like an invading army intent on building up rather than destroying.

Wrecked, Jenna snuggled into Dima like she never did with men in her bed and slipped once again into slumber without a second thought.

Dima's penthouse apartment was all modern and sleek. That did not surprise Jenna.

How at home she felt in it did.

"Your artwork is amazing." The paintings on the wall were not anonymous prints, but carefully chosen pieces that reflected both his taste and the aesthetic of the apartment.

One was by an artist Jenna knew only put out two to three pieces a year, all of which sold for at least a high six figures. She knew that because the artist was one of her favorites and entirely out of her price range.

"I didn't realize you were an art collector," Jenna said, doing nothing to hide her admiration for the beautiful pieces that graced his walls.

Dima was sifting through a stack of papers his admin had greeted him with at the airport. He dictated instructions into his phone for some and signed others.

He placed one in the flat document box he was using for them all as he finished with them. "I know what I like."

"What you like is high-end and high-quality."

"I am glad you approve." He dropped the last sheaf into the box and flipped the lid shut, then turned to face her. "I believe art is an extension of not only the creator, but the person who seeks to possess it."

"I agree. You have excellent taste."

He gave her one of those heated looks that sent her nerve endings zinging. "I would say your presence here is a testament to that."

"You're very complimentary."

"Honest. Jenna, I am honest. You are a unique and intriguing woman."

"I'm just me."

"I like you."

"I've noticed." She smiled. "I like you too."

"Not when I'm stopping you doing what you think is right."

That was Dima, a man confident enough in himself he would never shy away from talking about the hard stuff.

"Not so much then, no."

"Do you want to eat dinner out, or have something delivered?" he asked, clearly uninterested in belaboring the point.

Jenna kicked off her shoes, feeling a certain satisfaction

in mussing up his perfect living space just that little bit, and headed into his state-of-the-art kitchen. "Do you have anything to cook?"

"I doubt it. My housekeeper keeps my favorite beverages and sandwich makings stocked."

"So much for being domesticated. You have all this—" she indicated the kitchen a chef would envy "—and you only use it for snacks and drinks."

"Yes." Dima didn't seem embarrassed by the admission either.

"Did you cook for yourself during university and graduate school?"

"I did, but I have no time to do so now and no one to cook for besides myself. Most of my meals are taken up with business meetings and are either catered or at restaurants."

"You're awfully fit for all that eating out."

"I work out every day, and I use farm-to-table caterers."

"What about lovers?"

"What about them?"

"Do you at least cook for them? Or let them cook for you?" Jenna loved cooking to relax, following along with her favorite celebrity chefs as best she could.

"I don't do lovers. Therefore I do not cook for them."

He wasn't a monk. So, what was he saying?

"Then what am I? A friend with benefits," she said, answering her own question.

But he shook his head. "We will call it by its name. This is not cute, casual sex together when no one else is available."

"You're not an afterthought," she agreed. He was the one man she wanted badly enough to ignore her own rules and even her instinct for self-preservation.

"You are my lover, Jenna. And until you tell me otherwise, you will be the only woman in my bed."

"Same." She wasn't going to belabor the point, not least of which because the knowledge wasn't something *she* wanted to dwell on.

"Good to know."

"If we eat out, can we go someplace totally touristy, like a celebrity chef restaurant or something?" she asked as much because she hungry as she wanted to change the subject.

"You're really intent on making this a full-on vacation, aren't you?"

"Yes," she responded without apology.

The only vacation time she'd taken in ten years was for family stuff. The only travel she'd done was for work. These two weeks were going to be neither.

No family stuff. No work. Jenna was going to play tourist to the hilt.

"Freshen up, and I'll get us a table somewhere."

"You will?" she teased, not sure why she always pushed that point.

Was it because she needed the reminder that he had staff to do stuff like that for him, and she did not? That they came from completely disparate worlds?

Despite her friendship with his queenly sister-in-law, Jenna herself was not royal, or rich, or even moderately famous. Her brother was more well-known by the media.

Both Jenna and Nataliya liked it that way.

"I will call my people."

"Okay." She gave him a cheeky grin and then headed off to find the bedroom and the en suite bathroom so she could do what he suggested.

Freshen up.

She'd like to think the time away from him might give her some perspective, but she knew that was a lost cause. She had not just had sex with the prince, but even more telling, Jenna had fallen asleep on the man. Twice.

Feeling secure like she never did, and after the past weeks, that was really strange. Like really, *really* strange.

He'd hidden things from her, forced her to back off on her own sense of integrity and hurt her. Yet she still trusted him on a deep, visceral level that allowed her to rest with him when sleep had been so hard to come by otherwise.

She'd like to believe she'd just been tired enough and the

sex had relaxed her sufficiently to make it happen. But that wouldn't account for the sense of well-being Jenna had both before falling asleep and upon waking.

Dimitri smiled at Jenna's delighted response as the driver pulled their car into the spot in front of the building where one of her favorite celebrity chefs had a restaurant. Getting a table was usually at least a month-long wait, but he had strings to pull and no compunction about tugging them. Hard.

"I'd say I can't believe you got us in here, but I can."

"So doing so doesn't impress you?" he asked as he helped her out of the car, subtly maneuvering his driver out of the way to do so.

"Did I say that?" Jenna gave him a wide-eyed smile. "I'm *very* impressed and really, really pleased you were thoughtful enough to pick this restaurant."

He *had* pushed for this particular eatery when his social assistant had told him it would be easier to get a table at a different one. "The chef owed my brother a favor. I cashed it in."

"Which brother?" Jenna asked suspiciously.

"Does it matter?"

"I'm still angry with Prince Konstantin."

"I told you, he never really suspected you."

"Sure."

"You two are going to have to talk."

"Not for the next two weeks, we aren't."

"But won't knowing with certainty that he didn't suspect you impact your decision about your friendship with our family?"

"Nataliya is my BFF, not the rest of you."

They'd entered the building, and his security made sure they were the only occupants of the elevator taking them to the rooftop restaurant.

"But over the years, you have forged friendships with all of us. You and Emma are almost as close as you and Nataliya."

"Well, despite her taste in men, she's a wonderful person."

Dima ran his finger down her beautiful jaw, reveling in

how she shivered at that small contact. "Now, see, I can't tell if you are teasing as you usually do about Kon, or are serious."

"Oh, really? You can't tell?" Jenna asked, sounding far too pleased by that state of affairs.

"No."

"You are more likely to influence my feelings about staying in the royal orbit than your brother. You do realize that, don't you?"

Dimitri felt those words like a punch to his heart. "No, I had not realized."

"This between us might not be long-term." She leaned up and kissed the corner of his mouth. "But it isn't *nothing* either."

He turned and caught her mouth in a real kiss, deeply satisfied when she melted into him. Definitely not nothing. And he thought it was going to be long-term, but he was smart enough to use his mouth to deepen the kiss rather than say that out loud.

The sound of a throat clearing reminded Dimitri that they were not alone. He broke the kiss and felt his lips curve into a smile at the sight of Jenna looking disoriented from the connection. She turned him on by walking into a room. It was only fair he should impact her body with equal urgency.

The restaurant's decor was exactly like Jenna had seen on television, the clientele dressed by designers she knew well.

Jenna was used to seeing celebrities and dignitaries alike in her job and her role as a queen's BFF, but seeing one of her favorite actors out with a group of friends still required concentration not to gawp.

It did not help that Dima had kissed her silly in the elevator.

A bouquet of yellow irises graced their table, a standing ice bucket with chilling champagne beside it. Jenna wanted to remain unmoved by the show of romance, but she couldn't.

After showing kind of spectacularly that he was not as aware of her feelings as she would have liked, it meant a lot that Dima had taken the time to have the flowers delivered. It indicated that he *did* think of her when he wasn't with her.

How far that would take them, she did not know.

They had no future, but neither did she want their time together marred by incidents like the ones that had hurt her so badly already.

Dima pulled her chair out for her before taking his own.

It was all over-the-top, and in her secret heart, Jenna loved the sense of wooing and romance.

She reached out to touch an iris petal. "These are my favorite spring flowers."

"I know."

"How?"

"You are not the only one who notices things."

"You think I'm observant?" she asked him, feeling pleased and not really sure why.

"I do. If you wanted to sell secrets, you would have so many more at your disposal tucked away in your agile brain."

"That's a compliment, I think." Not that he was gaining points in the boyfriend column with bringing up that particular issue.

"It is."

"Thank you." She sighed, realizing she wasn't going to stay silent about his lack of tact, though. "Bringing up the situation that made me wonder if I wanted to ever see you again isn't your best move right now."

"I cannot pretend to be other than I am."

"What does that mean?"

"You cannot be with me only because you've chosen to ignore the harder side of spending time with a prince. This thing between us has no chance in those circumstances."

"This thing between us?" she asked carefully, suddenly feeling that an emotional minefield surrounded her.

"Whatever you want to call it, we are friends. We are having sex. I don't want to lose either of those things because another situation arises that shows the limits being connected to a family like mine brings."

"You are so unapologetic about those limits."

"On the contrary. I feel regret just like the next man."

"But you still do what you need to."

"Some consider me ruthless."

"I am sure they do."

"And you? Do you think I am ruthless?"

"I think you can be." She just had to decide if she could live with the knowledge that ruthlessness could be turned on her, just like anyone else.

"Does it help to know that whenever possible, I will give you what *you* need?"

"This is getting really heavy for a relationship based on sex." She said it quietly, not wanting to be overheard.

"And friendship."

"But *not* friends with benefits." He'd been adamant that did not describe them adequately.

"No. We have a commitment to exclusivity until we agree that we don't." His words were no different than they had been at his penthouse.

But suddenly they felt weightier, like that *until they both agreed they didn't* clause was some kind of long-term commitment. Was that because of his attitude, or hers?

Jenna was very much afraid that the feeling of emotional weight came from inside her.

Needing a moment, Jenna picked up her menu and began perusing the offerings. Dishes she'd seen prepared, some she'd never heard of, all sounding beyond delicious.

Dima pressed down on the menu with his hand, his expression telling her he knew exactly what she was doing. And typically, in Dima fashion, he was pushing past the barrier. "We can order off the menu, or we can allow the chef to decide."

Shock coursed through her. "He's here?" Jenna looked around furtively, sure she hadn't seen the celebrated chef when they arrived.

"He is. We are sitting at a table he reserved for us, in fact."

It had been a long time since Jenna had fangirled out, but she was on the verge. She was sitting at her favorite chef's table. "That is so cool."

"I am glad that you think so." Humor laced his tone.

She made a face at him. "You're too sophisticated to get excited about stuff like this?"

"Not at all. My celebrity crushes aren't chefs, though."

"You have celebrity crushes? You?" Who would an Adonis crush on?

"Sure. Doesn't everybody?"

Right until this very minute, she would have said *no*. "So, spill."

"You are acknowledging, then, that the owner of this establishment is yours?" he asked.

Heat climbed the back of her neck, but she nodded. "I do so acknowledge."

His sexy smile reminded her that crushes were all well and good, but real-life passion was something else entirely. Something she never wanted to give up.

Which did not change the unalterable fact that at some point she would have to.

"Queen Bey."

Jenna stared in amazement for several seconds. "Beyoncé? She's your celebrity crush?" To be fair, the pop star was a lot of people's crush, but he was a prince. "I didn't know you even knew who she was."

"Everyone knows Queen Bey. Even a prince. I've seen her in concert."

"You have not."

"I did."

Jenna guessed she didn't need to worry about him getting serious over *them*. Not when his feminine ideal was that beautiful and talented.

Mere mortal women could not measure up.

"You've got a *look* again."

"I was just thinking that would be a lot to live up to for a woman who wanted a relationship with you."

"Worried, *milaya moy*? Don't be. No fantasy could live up to the very real pleasure between us."

Jenna opened her mouth to assure him she was *not* worried, but a British voice asking how they were doing froze her vocal cords.

She knew that voice.

She turned her head in what felt like slow motion to see the man in the flesh.

He was wearing his chef's whites, his face creased in a smile.

Jenna nearly swallowed her tongue.

"I was just asking Jenna if she wanted to order off the menu, or let you choose our food."

"Is there really a question?" the chef asked, raising a single brow like she'd never been able to do.

"No. I...you *want* to?"

"Of course. It is my pleasure to feed my friends, and I count the Merikov princes among them."

"He said he had to call in a favor to get the table." Jenna slapped her hand over her mouth.

But both men were laughing.

"The favor was me staying long enough to make your food personally. My table is always at his and his brothers' disposal."

"Oh," Jenna breathed. Dima had arranged for the chef to be there, to cook for her.

"I think you made major brownie points with that move, son."

"Well, then I guess it was a good thing you could stay up long enough to cook our dinner, old man."

Listening to the two tease back and forth was surreal, and really, really cool. Jenna couldn't believe she was getting the chance to do just that, much less that her favorite chef ever was going to make her dinner.

The food was amazing, but Dima's company was the best part of the night. Not that she was going to tell him that.

The man had enough personal confidence.

"I am not sure if it will be me in your bed tonight, or dreams of your crush," he teased her as she swooned over dessert.

She shook her head, too serious about this to tease. "It can only ever be you if you are the one that is there, Dima."

She'd wanted him so long. How many sexy times dreams had she had about this man? Even more disturbing, how many regular life dreams had she had about him?

Despite the sure and certain knowledge she would never have a child, she had dreamed about having a baby with him every few months for the past few years. She'd never told a soul. Not Nataliya. Not Luke or Lisa.

It was no use sharing dreams that could never come true. And Jenna had no desire to be pitied.

CHAPTER ELEVEN

THAT NIGHT THEY made love in the shower, but Jenna went to bed alone because Dima had work he had to do.

She woke in the middle of the night to his naked body wrapped around hers, and it felt so right. She could have pulled away on principle.

It wasn't supposed to feel this good to sleep with another person. In fact, Jenna had never liked having someone else in her bed. Not a lover, not a friend, not her sister.

She liked her space, but with Dima, she gravitated to him in her sleep.

Deciding it wasn't worth worrying about when they only had two weeks together, she snuggled in and let herself go back to sleep.

Jenna next woke to an empty bed beside her, but the sound of the shower running indicated Dima hadn't been gone long. She threw back the covers and padded naked into the bathroom.

He stood under the shower, hot water cascading down over his golden body.

Jenna throbbed between her legs, her nipples beading with need.

He turned, like he knew she was there, and his welcoming smile drew her like a magnet.

Jenna stepped into the shower and right into a good-morning kiss that curled her toes.

They didn't have penetrative sex but used their hands to give one another pleasure before he jumped out, reminding her to save the harbor cruise for him.

Jenna stood under the hot water way too long for conscience's sake. She wasn't saving any dolphins with this long shower.

Grimacing at the thought, she finally turned off the water

and got out to dry off. She had the whole morning to sightsee, and she planned to make the most of it.

She discovered that Dima had left a car and driver at her disposal. Jenna took advantage, loving that this driver was both friendly and clearly enamored of his adopted city. He told her stories about many of the buildings they passed as well as his own life in New York.

He insisted she have a hot dog from a vendor for lunch. Jenna was so glad she did. She'd never had one with that much flavor and dressed so perfectly.

At two o'clock, he took her to the harbor, but not the docks where the boats that hosted the harbor cruises were moored.

This dock had row after row of yachts.

A man dressed in crisp sailor blues stepped forward to open her door when the driver pulled the luxurious sedan to a stop beside the curb.

He offered her a hand out of the car. "Miss Beals, His Highness is waiting for you on the yacht."

She accepted the man's help but turned to lean back into the car. "Thank you so much, Jackie. You gave me a wonderful tour of the city today. I've never seen it in the same way all the times I've been here for Fashion Week."

"It was my pleasure, Jenna." He winked. "My sister is going to think I'm a hero when I give her those tickets to Fashion Week you arranged for me."

"I'm glad. Tell her to shoot me an email and let me know what she thought." Jenna knew a budding fashion designer would leap at the chance to talk to someone with her contacts.

And she was happy to help when she could.

Jackie was fantastic as a driver for Mirrus Global but was only doing it while he finished up his engineering degree.

His younger sister had different aspirations. She'd already gotten into a top fashion design school, and that showed Jenna the young woman was serious about pursuing a career as a designer.

Jenna remembered that time in her life when she'd been going to university for her degree in journalism. She'd had so many plans for what she wanted to do with it, and honestly? Jenna had achieved her goals.

Now she was thirty-five and wondering if she needed new dreams to pursue.

She followed the sailor to a large gleaming yacht. Stepping aboard, she looked around for Dima, but was unsurprised not to find him on the deck.

Most likely he was getting some work in while waiting.

The sailor led her to a large living room where she did indeed find Dima working away on his laptop.

However, he looked up immediately upon her entrance, and his expression said he was glad to see her. "Hello, *milaya moy.* Did you have a good day?"

"It was fantastic. Jackie is an amazing guide to the city, and that young man is wicked smart."

"He'll make a good engineer."

"You know who he is?" she asked, surprised.

Dima's dark brows drew together. "You think I would send you out in the city for the day with someone I did not?"

"If I say yes, will that get me in trouble?"

"No trouble, but let me assure you that it is true." His tone said maybe a *little* trouble.

"I believe you now. I just would not have thought that before," she said in all honesty.

He stood up and moved toward her. "You do not think enough of your own importance."

"It's not that I don't think I'm important. It's that I can't be that important to *you.*" Still, she didn't move away from him, did she?

He stopped so his big body was only a breath away from hers. "There you are wrong, Jenna. You are very important to me."

"Watch it," she said, fear making her voice harsh. "We aren't in that kind of relationship, Dima."

"Jenna, the number of people allowed to call me that name is a very short list and includes only family." He cupped her nape, his expression showing no hint of humor. "Yet you are on it. What kind of relationship do you think we need for you to be important to me?"

"I just…this can't be more than what it is."

"Why is that?" He brushed his lips over hers.

"I…" Telling him would build the intimacy between them. Not telling him could leave him believing there was a chance.

Only, they'd agreed they weren't doing anything more than sex.

She stepped back from him, forcing his hands to drop from her neck. "Why are we having this discussion? We agreed this was just sex."

Why did it feel like she was running?

"But we are also friends. Whatever makes you think you cannot have a life with me, or amongst my family, is naturally of concern to me."

"You speak so formally sometimes."

"I admit it. That is in fact a prince thing, as you like to call it." His eyes teased her.

"I figured." She bit her lip, thinking.

Talk, or don't talk?

"Tell me."

"What?" She gave him her best guileless look.

The look was wasted on him. He just stared at her, clearly unwilling to allow prevarication about this.

She sighed, part of her wanting to share her past and part of her knowing that no matter how many years had passed, it never stopped hurting to do so.

"I'm not the oldest child in my family." That's where it started. With her brother, Matt.

He took her hand and led her to the large horseshoe-shaped sofa. "I thought you were." Dima sat down and despite all that room, pulled her into his lap.

"No. Matt was two years older than me." She let her head rest against his chest. This was easier to talk about without making eye contact. "He was the best big brother. He never made me feel like I was in the way."

Dima's arms tightened around her. "What happened to him?"

"He got sick when I was ten. At first, we didn't know what it was, you know?" Pain welled, like it always did. "But it turns out that my mom carried a gene for a degenerative disease."

Dima went very still. "Your mother is not sick."

"Neither am I."

He let out a breath she hadn't realized he was holding. "However, you *do* have this gene?"

"Yes." Inactive, but there in her genetic makeup, just waiting to be passed on to the next generation, which she would never allow. "Matt died when I was sixteen after years of pain and slowly, inexorably losing more and more of himself to the disease."

"I am very sorry."

Jenna nodded, acknowledging the sincerity of his sentiment. "We were all tested for it." She lifted her head so their gazes met. "I was the only other child carrying the gene."

"Could you still get sick?"

"No. It would have come on during adolescence. It didn't, but my parents were watching for it. We were all scared, though, until I aged past the window when it would have manifested." Looking back, she realized how that had shaped her and her siblings.

Her parents too. Though she honestly didn't remember what they'd been like before Matt had gotten sick. Her memory had melded it all together.

But her brother Luke had gone from being a determined boy to a driven man who'd built nothing short of an empire by the time he was thirty. Lisa, their baby sister, had rejected college and gotten married young, having four children in six years. She and her husband were happy living their organic, off-the-grid lifestyle.

"Explain why this terrible tragedy means you and I cannot have a future."

"I had a tubal ligation the day after my twenty-first birthday."

"So that you could not pass on this gene that had wreaked such terrible pain on your family," he guessed.

Though he sure sounded like he had no doubt about being right.

"It took my brother from me. I could never risk it taking a

child. Also, it stops with me. This disease will not make it to the next generation of my family."

"No cousins who have it?"

"Only one, and he took the same permanent measures, having a vasectomy."

"You are both very courageous."

"I didn't feel courageous at twenty-one. I felt desperate." She'd still been grieving the loss of her brother.

He rubbed her back, the touch consoling and yet…enticing too.

So much about Dima and her feelings for him were like that. Complicated.

"So you cannot get pregnant by conventional means."

"I *will not* get pregnant by any means."

"That is your choice."

She relaxed against him. "Yes."

"And this is why you believe we have no future."

"The main reason, but there are others."

"I am a prince."

"That is one of them."

"What are the others?" he asked, not sounding particularly stressed by her revelations.

So he hadn't been thinking of a future with her. Not really.

But Dima, being Dima, wanted to know everything.

"You're younger than me."

"Five years at our ages hardly matters. Both my brothers have a bigger age gap with their wives."

"It's not the same."

"In what way?"

"Everyone accepts that kind of thing when the man is older."

His laughter shocked her.

She sat up in offense. "What's so funny?"

"I never thought I would live to see the day that a die-hard feminist like yourself would make a statement like that."

"I didn't say I felt that way."

"Then what does it matter what others think?"

"The tabloids are going to have a field day with us as it is. Can you imagine if we got engaged?"

"I do not live my life by what the tabloids decide to print about me."

"Really? You've worked really hard to stay out of them, especially since Galena's very public split with you."

"None of us likes to be featured in the gutter press, but I'm not going to live my life by giving up what I want to avoid it."

"Clearly, or you wouldn't be going to Abu Dhabi with me."

"Exactly."

"Still, a lover is not the same thing as a potential partner."

"Sometimes they are one and the same."

"Well, now is not one of those times."

"So you say."

"And so you should know as well, Dima. I can't give you children, and even if I could, I wouldn't want my children growing up in a palace."

"I do not live in a palace. I live in a penthouse."

She opened her mouth to argue, but he forestalled her with a kiss.

A very nice, thought-stealing move of his lips over hers with just a tiny swipe of his tongue along the seam of her lips before he pulled back. "Kon and Emma do not live in a palace either."

"They do part of the year."

"They visit Mirrus. That is not the same thing."

"If you say so."

"I do."

"Okay."

"You can be maddening, Jenna."

"You think so? I thought I was just being pragmatic."

He shook his head, but he didn't say anything. Just stood up, lifting her with him, and headed out of the room.

"Where are we going?"

"I would like it to be bed, but in fact we are headed for the observation deck. Your harbor cruise has started."

The yacht was moving, and Jenna hadn't even noticed, she was so intent on her conversation with Dima.

He let her down when they reached the deck. A voice sounded over the state-of-the-art speaker system, giving a running commentary on the landmarks that could be seen from the water as well as tidbits of New York history she had never heard.

She and Dima stood at the rail for the first hour, taking everything in, but eventually they moved to sit together on an outdoor love seat, where they sipped their bubbly water and enjoyed the views while their bodies touched from shoulder to thigh.

It was odd.

And Jenna wasn't sure how she felt about that. Nataliya was bound to learn about the shared vacation.

Jenna had a hard time believing Dima was willing to feature in gossip columns for the chance at spending this time together.

And yet, hadn't he said he would be working her out of his system?

"What other objections do you have to a relationship with me?" he asked, like their conversation had not paused for the tour.

"The last couple of weeks have been brutal. I cannot imagine a lifetime of compromising my integrity."

"That is a harsh indictment."

"You did hear me say the last two weeks have been brutal?"

He didn't reply, but then the question had been rhetorical.

Jenna got lost in the commentary of the tour once again, so another hour passed before she realized it. They were pulling into a slip near the Statue of Liberty.

"What are we doing?" she asked.

"You said you wanted to play tourist. Nothing could be more iconic than the Statue of Liberty."

A prince visiting the Statue of Liberty was a little different than the average person. They didn't shut it down or anything. She didn't imagine they had time to arrange it, but the bodyguards managed to create space around them. When they got inside, he'd arranged for access all the way up the ladder to the inside of the flame.

There was a small hatch they climbed through to the walkway used to service the spotlights that were directed at the flame at night.

Wind whipped Jenna's blond hair around her head and her clothes around her body, but the view was magnificent.

"This is incredible." She had to practically shout to be heard.

Dima wrapped an arm around her, pulling her in to his body. "It is impressive."

Jenna felt safe in his arms, regardless of the wind and the way it felt like the narrow platform swayed under her feet.

"Your Highness." That was all the security head said.

But the way Dima's body stiffened told her he knew what the prompt meant. "We have to go down again, *milaya*. I did not give them enough time to arrange proper security protocols, so we have to keep the visit short."

Jenna didn't mind. She loved that he'd made this happen at all. The climb down was a heck of a lot easier than the climb up had been. When they got back out to the plaza, she stared up at the statue. "It feels heavy being here."

"I imagine it does." He took her hand, uncaring of all the people surrounding them with camera phones. "I feel a great profundity when I stand inside the original home built by my family."

"It wasn't the palace?" she asked.

"No. When my family left Russia, they did so in secret and with few of their possessions."

"So there's a log cabin out there somewhere your ancestors lived in?"

"Not a log cabin, but nothing like a palace either. It was turned into a museum after the palace was built by my great-grandfather."

"I never knew."

"I am surprised Nataliya has never spoken of it. She has taken a personal interest in preserving the history of our country."

Jenna had known that, but her BFF had never mentioned the house turned museum. "I'd like to see it."

"I will take you the next time we are in Mirrus."

She pointed out that chances were they wouldn't be there together. If she ever returned to the small island country.

Dima insisted on having their photo taken in the middle of the plaza, like all the other tourists. Of course, unlike the other tourists, their picture was taken by a bodyguard, while the other three managed a decent gap between her and Dima and the rest of the people intent on visiting the Statue of Liberty.

They made it back to the yacht, and Jenna didn't mind that Dima led her back inside. She kicked off her shoes and sat on the sofa, her legs curled under her. "I'm wiped."

Dima gave some instructions to someone just outside the door before joining her. "No club before we fly out?"

"No." The very idea of pounding bass and crushing bodies made her shiver in revulsion. "I need some downtime."

"You are not a party girl."

"Never have been. I spend Fashion Weeks *on* or holed up in my hotel room, rejuvenating."

"You're so honest. I like that about you."

"You're the same."

"And?" he prompted, sitting beside her.

"I like it too, as if you didn't know."

"Considering how much you do *not* like about me, affirmation of what you do is not a bad thing."

"What are you talking about?"

"I am a prince. I am ruthless. I am rich. I am royal."

"Prince and royal are the same thing."

"You've mentioned it in regard to both roles."

"I never said I didn't like you." Even when she'd been hurting so badly.

"Not in so many words."

"Not in any words."

"That is good to know."

She was totally lost as far as this conversation went, and just on the side of too tired and mentally exhausted to figure it out.

Dima patted his own thigh. "Here."

"Here what?" she asked.

"Your feet. You should have worn tennis shoes today."

"My sandals were perfectly comfortable." For the first hours of sightseeing anyway. Her feet ached now.

"Give them to me."

"You asked for it." She wasn't turning down a foot rub, even by a prince.

Maybe especially by a prince.

It turned out that Prince Dimitri of Mirrus gave a magnificent foot massage.

"How soon will we be back at the dock?" she asked.

"We'll have dinner on board and then dock in time to make our flight."

"I didn't repack before leaving your apartment this morning."

"My people will take care of it."

"I should insist on doing it for myself."

"Why?"

"Because I'm an independent woman."

"Allowing someone else to repack your things compromises that how?"

"It doesn't?"

"I should hope not. I am a man who makes his own decisions, but am content to allow others to do things for me if it saves me time to do what I am best at."

"Dominating the business world?"

"Only on days that end in a *y*."

The joke was old, but she laughed anyway. Because it was also true.

"You're not dominating the business world right now."

"No. I am giving you a much-needed foot rub."

"You're very good at it."

"I took a course on massage during my university days."

"Why?"

"I was dating a woman who told me that if a man was serious about giving pleasure in the bedroom, he had to learn to give pleasure out of it."

"She sounds pretty sure of herself."

"I am drawn to strong women."

"I guess so. You're going on vacation with me." Jenna had no doubts about her own inner strength.

"That I am." His massage technique changed.

Jenna started having some very different responses to Dima's moving fingers. "Please tell me this yacht has a bedroom."

"Need a shower before dinner, *milaya moy*?"

"After."

"After?" he teased as his fingers did something that went straight to her core.

Jenna gasped and jerked, but did she pull her foot away? No, she did not.

His laughter was low and oh, so very sexy.

"Dima, we need to take this someplace no one is going to walk in on us."

He nodded without any more teasing, the sexual energy coming off of him intense and powerful.

He stood up and offered his hand.

She took it without hesitation.

He led her out of the living room, down a hall and a set of stairs that ended in a set of double doors. He opened one and pulled her inside.

The cabin was as luxurious a bedroom as any she had ever seen, including the one she stayed in at the palace. Spacious and decorated with warm, rich colors and fabrics, it screamed wealth and privilege.

In another situation, Jenna would probably find it over-the-top, but in that moment, she was only thankful it had a door that could be shut and locked.

Which they did before wrecking the bed in a way she would have been certain only thirty minutes before she was too tired to do.

CHAPTER TWELVE

THEY DID TAKE a shower before dinner, and Jenna was delighted to find that he'd had her cases put on the yacht before her arrival.

She changed into a loose maxi dress that clung to her in elegant lines but would also be comfortable for travel later.

Dima's eyes warmed with approval before he crossed the room to kiss her. "Time to eat, but I would rather muss the bed again."

Staff had come in while they were in the shower, and the bed looked as pristine as when they first arrived. "That is kind of scary, you know?"

"Scary?"

"Having staff so efficient they change the bed while you are in the shower."

Dima made a noncommittal sound, but it was clear he was used to that kind of invasive pampering.

Jenna wondered if she could get used to it and shook her head.

"What are you saying no to in your mind?" he asked, showing yet again how good he was at reading her.

She was always pleased when he was stumped at what she was thinking.

"I don't think I could get used to having staff that invasively efficient."

"So give instructions for them not to enter our quarters when we are still in them." He said it like that was a no-brainer.

"I can't give instructions to your staff."

"Of course you can."

"I wouldn't feel right."

"Jenna, we are going to be spending two weeks together in Abu Dhabi. If you do not make your wishes known to the staff, it will not be the vacation either of us wants it to be."

"You said you weren't taking a vacation."

"Only working a few hours a day *is* vacation for me."

"You are a workaholic."

"Hmm…and what does that make you?"

"My family says I am a workaholic." Especially Lisa, who was content to live by the schedule of the farm but found any other pressure to conform to a calendar or timetable anathema.

"You are driven."

"I have been. Luke is worse."

"He would have had to put in hours longer than even I do to build his company as quickly as he did."

"I worry about him."

"Why exactly?"

"You think you know, but you want to hear what I say," she guessed. She loved…*liked* that about him. He might think he could read her mind, but he still asked.

"Yes."

"He's so determined to build an empire; he forgets that his life is more than his company."

"Perhaps for him, it isn't."

"He lost one marriage because of it."

"He was married?"

"Yes. He married his high school sweetheart right out of college, but two years later, she left." Luke hadn't had a relationship since.

He didn't date. If he had lovers, he was discreet about them.

"You worry about him being alone?"

"Not really. That's Mom and Dad's job, and they harp on it enough for both of us, but I do worry he's going to have a heart attack before forty from the stress of his lifestyle."

"Have you talked to him about it?"

"No. I know he works out, has a personal chef focused on nutrition. I just…"

"Worry. You are a good sister."

"I love him." She would not lose another brother.

"Family."

Jenna smiled. "You sound like yours gives you fits."

"Can you doubt it?"

"No." She knew how pushy his father, the former king, could be.

And his brothers were every bit as arrogant as he was. Being the youngest in that crowd could not be easy, but Dima held his own.

A huge bouquet of irises, these purple, were on the sideboard by the table.

Jenna felt moisture well in her eyes, unsure why it touched her so much. "You got me flowers, again."

"You like flowers."

"I do. Especially irises this time of year, as you know."

"Yes."

"But…"

"What?"

"You keep getting me these really gorgeous bouquets."

"They are a small symbol of the value I place on your company."

"You're a romantic guy, Dima. Who knew?"

"Blame my father. He passed that trait down to all his sons."

"Even Prince Konstantin?" she asked doubtfully.

"Don't tell me that Emma has never mentioned it."

"She says your brother spoils her. I've always been skeptical."

"Jenna."

She laughed. "I'm just teasing. Mostly." She took the chair Dima pulled out for her. "He would go into shock if I stopped."

"You could be right, but know that he values your friendship, not only to his wife and sister-in-law, but to himself and the care you show his children. He speaks of you as an aunt to them."

"Putting a plug in for me staying on the periphery of the royal family?" she asked with some humor.

"Something like that."

They talked about everything from history to the latest scientific discoveries over dinner. Jenna enjoyed Dima's intelligent conversation but liked the way he respected her opinions and actively listened to her even more.

This man might be used to bossing people around, but he'd been raised to respect women, and Jenna thought maybe his father deserved recognition for doing such a good job. But the person sparking emotion in her heart she'd been so determined not to feel?

That was all Dima.

As they sat on the deck watching the city lights sparkle like manmade stars, the answer to why Jenna had agreed to travel with Dima, why she wanted this time with him regardless of what being with him had already cost her emotions, became too big to ignore.

Jenna had never been in love. She'd had relationships, but none worth making the compromises necessary to keep them going.

Because that all-consuming feeling had not been there.

Love.

Looking at Dima hurt in the best way. Touching Dima brought pleasure that had nothing to do with sex. Being touched by the prince did the same.

Sex with him was so mind-shattering, it would be easy to dismiss her feelings as sensual thrall. Only, they weren't having sex right now. They weren't even touching, and yet the connection between them was stronger than corded steel.

She didn't just want Dima. She needed him.

As terrifying as that reality was, even more so was the tiny kernel of hope that maybe, just maybe, they could make this thing between them work. Despite the fact he was a prince. Despite her age and sterility.

Her practical mind told her not to be a fool, but her heart thrummed with a love so deep she wasn't sure it had an end.

She had been slowly and surely falling in love with this man for eight years. Taking him as a lover had only cemented those feelings, making them permanent and inescapable. And no amount of telling herself it was a bad idea was going to change that.

His reaction to her list of reasons why they could not be to-gether was ambiguous at best. If he *were* interested in a long-term relationship, shouldn't he have tried to convince her that what she saw as barriers weren't?

He hadn't seemed upset, *but* he had brought the subject up a second time to make sure he had the complete list.

Why?

Jenna had no more of an answer to that question as they boarded his private jet later than when she'd first asked it.

They'd had time to cruise the harbor and enjoy the view of the Statue of Liberty lit before docking and taking a limousine to the airport. The whole time, they'd talked about anything and everything, except the one thing Jenna could not stop thinking about.

Was Dima still set on a no-strings affair? She'd said she was too, but she'd been lying to herself and him. Had he been doing the same, or was she in this emotional quagmire on her own?

Dima led her back to the bedroom, starting to undress without even asking if she was ready for bed. But maybe her drooping eyes and frequent yawns had given her away.

While he seemed intent on being naked together, he made no effort to initiate sex, but pulled Jenna's body close to his before giving her a sweet and entirely chaste kiss good-night.

Considering how her mind was spinning, it should have been impossible for Jenna to sleep.

It wasn't.

For the first time ever, Jenna had no trouble sleeping on the plane. Of course, the fact she was doing it in an actual bed while snuggled closely to Dima's warm body could have something to do with it.

Dima woke her with a kiss. "You need to get up, *milaya moy*. We are landing momentarily. If you want a shower, now is the time to take it."

Feeling wonderfully rested, Jenna sat up. "I slept the whole trip?"

How could that be possible? Jenna never slept longer than nine hours, and that was only when she was full-on exhausted.

"You needed the rest."

"I bet you didn't sleep for twelve hours." She could not imagine it.

"No, but I enjoyed a full night's rest."

Full night for him, maybe.

She grimaced. "I won't sleep a wink tonight."

"I will not mind." The look he gave her said Dima had plans for their nighttime hours, and they didn't include a lot of sleeping regardless.

She laughed and shook her head. "I would ask if you think of anything else, but I know you do. I really enjoyed our time on the yacht."

"I did too, Jenna. You and I fit very well."

"Yes, we do."

His eyes widened in surprise, his body jerking in shock like her agreement had stunned him. Then he frowned. "Where real life does not intrude, you mean."

"I didn't say that."

But he was standing. "We touch down in thirty minutes." Then he left the bedroom.

What had just happened?

Jenna didn't know, but she didn't like feeling as if she was missing something elemental.

She did take a shower, though it was a quick one. She dressed appropriately for Abu Dhabi, her shoulders covered, and a casual scarf looped around her neck that could be used as a head covering if necessary.

Not that she thought they'd be going anywhere between the airport and the Merikov condo, but it was better to be prepared.

The royal condo was nothing like any condominium Jenna had ever seen. The seven-thousand-square-foot structure surrounded by palms and stone walls topped by decorative wrought-iron felt more like a stand-alone mansion than anything in a complex.

She said as much to Dima.

"We share a wall with two other smaller units used to house domestic and security staff." He shed his jacket and tie, hanging both over one arm. "The complex has its own security as well, which makes using the gym, private golf course and the like less problematic for residents."

It sounded like the perfect getaway spot for his royal family. "So what you are saying is that this very private complex offers additional security and amenities for the rich and famous."

"Yes." He frowned but seemed to shake off whatever was bothering him. "There is an Olympic-sized swimming pool that is fantastic for laps, but I prefer our private infinitely pool for relaxation."

"And other things, I bet," she teased, wanting the warm, bantering Dima from the evening before back.

This brooding alpha male was very sexy, but he made her feel sad, and she didn't know why.

"I've never brought another woman here." His tone implied he found the very thought obscene. "I don't bring lovers to my family's properties."

"I'm the exception?" Because she was definitely his lover.

"Can you doubt it?"

She didn't want to, especially now she had acknowledged the truth of her feelings for him, but she wasn't about to get into that. "One thing I don't doubt is that even if I'd gotten the deal of the century, I wouldn't be staying in accommodations nearly as nice as this."

The foyer opened to three different reception rooms through archways. One was a large living room, another a dining room that could easily accommodate sixteen if not twenty at the table. The other was a library that rivaled anything she'd ever seen in a private residence, even royal ones.

Beautiful furniture in dark wood graced each room, the upholstery different shades of the sunset. It was impressive and luxurious but didn't feel like a hotel.

"This reminds me of Piper Nikos's designs, but I thought she only did the properties her husband's company developed."

"You have a good eye. She did the decor when she was still running her private design firm."

"It's stood the test of time this long?" Jenna was impressed.

"There are six bedrooms, but we will only be using one of them."

"That library...this place doesn't feel like a property used for the occasional business meeting."

"It was my mother's favorite vacation spot."

And he'd brought Jenna to this clearly very private family oasis?

"You rarely mention her," she said softly, laying her hand on his arm.

Dima's handsome face showed old grief. "I was only a child when we lost her, but I still remember her smile."

"And that hurts?"

"Yes."

"Thank you."

He turned to face her. "For?"

"Not playing stoic he-man. Sharing your real emotions with me."

"According to you, I am no good at hiding them from you, regardless."

"I know you better than most people," she said consolingly.

He laughed. "Believe me when I tell you that my ego is not so fragile that your ability to read what most people do not bothers me."

He said that, but he'd brought up her ability to read him more than once.

It had to bother him at least a little.

She slid her hand down his arm to take his hand. "Let's explore."

The condo had a private media room. Unsurprising. And game room filled with board games from the antique to the latest offerings. Surprising. Six bedrooms, all with their own en suite bathrooms. Unsurprising. A small breakfast nook that opened onto a secluded outdoor garden with another eating area as well as a conversation grouping of cushioned outdoor furniture. A little surprising.

But the most surprising thing was how at home Jenna felt from the moment of crossing the condo's threshold. She could fit her own house into this condo several times over, and yet it felt warm and welcoming to her.

Or was that just the glow from realizing she was in love with the man she would be sleeping with that night?

Later, he took her on an evening kayak ride through the mangrove forest. It was amazing and magical, the smell of mangroves mixing with the scent of water teeming with wildlife and fauna. The sound of nightlife in the waterlogged forest was so not something she had expected to experience here.

When they landed back on the dock, Jenna was not at all surprised to discover he had dinner plans at one of the city's hottest restaurants.

They were shown to their table, and when she saw the mixed iris bouquet there, Jenna felt tears burn at the back of her eyes. "They're beautiful."

"Their recipient is even more beautiful."

"If I didn't know better, I would think you were wooing me, my prince." She leaned close to him, but not so close it would scandalize the other diners. "I'm a sure thing, Dima."

His even, white teeth flashed in a gorgeous smile, his gray eyes smoldering like molten metal. "As am I."

Dima seemed in an unusually good mood over dinner, and Jenna let herself relax and enjoy his company. She did not know what was coming, but she knew that right now, she was happy to be here, with this man.

As if by unspoken agreement, they were silent on the ride back to the condo.

When they got there, he made good on his promise to keep her awake late into the night, but it wasn't just making love. They played naked Parcheesi in the game room and snuck into the kitchen to make a snack in the wee hours of the morning before finally succumbing to sleep.

The next day, they both woke pretty early and enjoyed a leisurely swim in the infinity pool before breakfast. Contrary to what she'd expected, Dima was happy to play in the water with her, without getting sexual.

Which made sense when the housekeeper came out to tell him he had a call.

They were surrounded by staff, even if that staff were adept at being unobtrusive. That phone call started Dima's workday, and Jenna decided to relax and read one of the books from her towering to-be-read stack.

Well, metaphorically. She'd brought her electronic reader with her, and it was loaded with the books she'd been too busy to read in the last year.

Jenna spent the next few hours taking turns reading in the sun, cooling off in the pool, and finally reading in the shade as the sun rose to its zenith.

Completely relaxed, she was startled when her phone rang with Emma's ringtone.

Grabbing it, Jenna found herself answering without any of the hesitation she'd been feeling the past couple of weeks. "Hi, Emma, what's up?"

"My husband does not think you betrayed his family's secrets."

"Okay, that's direct. What happened?"

"Kon admitted his attempt at matchmaking to me, and, well, we might be not speaking at the moment. The big, dumb prince didn't realize how hurt your feelings would be by the accusation."

"He didn't actually accuse me."

"Tell me you weren't hurt," Emma said, like she was daring Jenna to lie.

"I can't."

"And you still are, or you would have been answering my calls."

Jenna couldn't deny that either. "I answered now."

"Yes, you did. It makes me wonder what has changed. I was fully prepared to stalker-call you."

Jenna laughed at the reference to both Emma and Nataliya's habits of repeatedly calling when she didn't pick up right away. They didn't do it often, but both women could be a bit impatient about getting ahold of her when they felt they had something important to impart or discuss.

That laughter released something inside Jenna, and she realized she could and probably *should* talk to Emma about what had happened.

Nataliya was still off limits as a confidant, but once she'd passed her first trimester of pregnancy, the risk of miscarriage diminished considerably, and Jenna would be shocked if Nikolai didn't confess all to his wife.

Relieved she could talk this out with someone who knew all the players well, Jenna told Emma the whole story. She finished off by telling her how she'd had to step back from doing what she believed to be right because of her relationship with the royal family.

"You probably wouldn't even have been a target for that deceitful B-I-T-Charlie if you weren't our friend."

Jenna had to smile at Emma's avoidance of using the term she made it clear she was thinking. "No, Skylar would have targeted me regardless. She was an equal opportunity thief of information. She must have thought she hit the mother lode with my contacts, though."

"Your brother's company is working on some very sensitive stuff."

"Exactly. It's a good thing we don't talk about his business much."

"Yes. Listen, Jenna, I'm sorry."

"Why are you sorry? You didn't accuse me of divulging sensitive information."

"Kon didn't either. Not really. He just wanted to get you and Dima together."

"Are you serious?" It was the second time Emma had made such a claim, so Jenna thought maybe she was, but it was so out there.

"Well, yes. I mean it was obvious to everyone you two had a thing for each other."

"My brother said the same."

"See?" Emma said like that settled it.

"We have a lot of chemistry," Jenna conceded.

"Oh, my gosh, are you admitting it? Nataliya owes me five bucks."

"You bet on it?"

"She bet me that you would never allow yourself to admit what you were feeling toward Dima because he's a prince."

"You took the bet?" Nataliya had been right, and Jenna hadn't actually ever planned to act on her overwhelming attraction to the youngest Merikov.

"Sure. I said that kind of sexual tension was going to explode sometime, and I bet it would happen before Prince Evengi's campaign to marry off his youngest son bore any fruit."

"Dima said he agreed to meet women his father introduced him to."

"I'm glad that doesn't bother you. You know it doesn't mean anything. Sometimes with my father-in-law, it's easier to just go along in the short run while holding out for your own plans in the long term."

"It sounds like you made five bucks on me. I think you owe me a coffee."

"But that's the whole profit."

Jenna laughed. Like the princess couldn't afford to buy her coffee. "Get my coffee money from Prince Konstantin. He owes me."

"That he does," Emma said with fervent agreement.

A week ago, Jenna would have been happy to keep rehashing everything, but she had bigger fish to fry now. "How do you handle it?"

"What? Having an arrogant husband who thinks he knows best?" Emma asked wryly.

Jenna laughed as she was meant to, but it was funny. Prince Konstantin had met his match in Emma, just as his kingly brother had in Nataliya. Neither woman was a pushover, and neither man would be happy if they were.

"Having people around all the time," Jenna explained her question. "Never being alone, even in your own home."

"I won't say it's not that bad. When you weren't raised to it like they were, it really is hard."

"And?"

"And you have to decide if it's worth it to you to change your life to be with someone who can't change theirs." Emma's words made it clear she knew this was about more than Jenna admitting she was attracted to Dima.

"You don't do all the compromising." Jenna had seen Emma put her foot down about things that were important to her.

"No, of course not. Kon really struggled at first with my insistence on what I call *family dinners* at least twice a week."

"But he works really hard to be there for dinner." Jenna had seen the prince in action, cutting off phone calls and taking meetings late so he could be there for dinner with his wife and two boys.

Nikolai and Nataliya did the same thing. Jenna had always assumed it was a family tradition, even for the Merikovs.

"You've probably noticed it is their family tradition, but for me family dinner means him and me cooking together in the kitchen, letting the boys help where they can and then sitting down to eat together as well."

"He didn't understand the need to cook together?" Jenna guessed.

"Exactly, but I wanted my children to understand that food doesn't magically come from the kitchen. Someone has to prepare it, and if you want to be self-sufficient, sometimes that someone needs to be you."

"Even if your father is a billionaire prince."

"Even then." Emma made a humming sound, like she was gathering her thoughts. "On family dinner nights, the staff are given time off."

"You all wash your own dishes?"

"Yes. Again, teaching our children that dishes and tables don't magically clean themselves."

"While giving your little family a couple of nights of privacy. Only you still have security."

"Not in the family quarters. Privacy is at a premium, I will not lie, but there are ways to prevent you from feeling like you live in a fishbowl."

"I'm pretty sure the media contributes to that feeling." The fear of scandal had played a major part in Jenna not being able to file charges against Skylar.

"Yes, but Mirrus is a small country, and the Merikovs aren't of nearly as much interest to the paparazzi as more well-known royals."

"They're of enough interest that news of Nataliya's miscarriage got leaked."

"Yes, and Dima got dumped in a very public manner, which the news cycle ran with," Emma agreed. "But honestly? I drop my children off at school like all the other parents, and there aren't a bunch of photographers hanging around, hoping to get a picture."

"Like every other parent with a security detail," Jenna teased.

"Sure, but I'm willing to live with that to know my children are safe, that my husband is safe. That I am safe."

"That's one thing I'll say for the Merikovs. They don't distinguish when it comes to security between the brothers."

"No. But they're all billionaires in their own right, because they each own one third of Mirrus Global."

"I don't think Prince Evengi would settle for anything less than the strongest security measures for any of them regardless." Jenna had seen how protective the sometimes interfering former king was toward his family.

"It's not really his call anymore, but I agree. Nikolai is pretty adamant."

"Tell me about it." There had been times over the past years that Jenna had been assigned her own temporary security detail, and that was all down to Nikolai.

She'd dealt with the inconvenience for the sake of Nataliya's peace of mind and that of Jenna's own parents, who worried about her connection to a royal family. Jenna had also always known it was temporary.

The prospect of taking on that sort of thing permanently couldn't be dismissed just because she recognized the feelings she had for Dima.

However, neither could Jenna deny that she was more open to it than she had ever been before.

Love was a terribly powerful emotion. Her love for her brother Matt, and debilitating pain at losing him, had dictated choices in her life that might well impact her ability to have a long-term relationship with Dima.

CHAPTER THIRTEEN

JENNA WAS STILL mulling over her conversation with Emma when the scrape of sandals on the stone surround of the pool brought her head up.

Dima was dressed in chinos and a short-sleeved button-up. And yes, he was wearing sandals.

"Those aren't swim trunks," she said, a little stunned at this casually dressed Dima.

"No. I thought we could go to the Old Fort this afternoon."

She nodded, but her gaze was fixed on him, and her body wasn't moving.

"That hungry look in your eyes would make more sense if I *was* wearing swim trunks." His voice was laced with laughter.

"You mean European trunks, like swimmers wear?" she asked, her mind immediately going there and her tone husky from desire she made no attempt to hide.

"I believe I have a pair with me, yes."

He'd worn regular board shorts while swimming with her that morning.

Jenna fanned herself. "I'd like to see that."

"I'll change and join you," he said with alacrity.

"Yes." They could go to the museum tomorrow.

He was back in only a few minutes, wearing the promised swimsuit. The tight black fabric outlined his semi-erection and showcased his muscular thighs. Jenna sucked in air, trying to catch her breath.

Dima was hands down the sexiest man she had ever seen. Ever. Ever. Ever.

He dove into the water, coming up at the edge near where she sat under a shade tree. "Are you going to join me?"

She nodded, her mouth cotton-dry with anticipation. How did this man affect her so strongly, so quickly?

She dropped the gauzy swim wrap she'd been wearing to protect her skin from the sun.

His gray gaze remained steadily on her as she moved toward the pool and then sat down to slide in from the side. He was there before she even started sliding in, his body so close their skin touched as she let herself into the perfectly temperate water.

He pulled her in to him. "The thought of you out here in nothing but your bikini has been driving me mad all day."

"I was just reading, and swimming. Nothing exciting."

"You are exciting." He kissed her with a passion that gave truth to his words.

She responded, her entire body straining toward him in primal response.

His hands got busy at the back of her bikini top while he deepened the kiss. The thought of baring her breasts to him sent thrills through her and then chills.

Breaking her mouth from his, Jenna pressed against his chest. "You can't do that! Someone will see."

"We are alone."

"But what about the staff? Security?" The very people she was trying to decide if she could live with on a daily basis.

"I sent them to their condos."

"We're really alone?"

"The alarm system is armed, and all the cameras are monitored."

"Is there a camera back here?"

"There is, but I told them to turn it off until dark. There is no approach to the condo that is not monitored. They do not need to watch us now."

"You're sure?"

"I promise you, *milaya moy*. We are entirely private here."

"In that case…" She dove back into the kiss.

He peeled away her bikini and threw the top onto the stone surround. Then he cupped her breasts, brushing his thumbs over her nipples.

She shivered against him, running her hands up his back,

oving the feel of his rippling muscles under her fingers. It excited her that he'd changed his plans so easily when she showed interest in him.

Being wanted like that was heady.

One of his hands slid down her back and into her bikini bottoms until his blunt fingertip pressed against her entrance. He traced her labia, sending sensation pulsing through her core.

She ran her hands along his backside, squeezing tight muscles and making him groan. But she wanted something more, needed to touch another part of him.

Jenna brought her hands between them to caress his length. He pressed into her hands with another pleasure-filled groan.

Jenna tugged his hard-on out of its Lycra confines. It was hot and big, bobbing in the water, even as she curled her fingers around it.

Her fingertips didn't quite meet, but she used both hands to compensate as she'd learned to do in her short time as his lover. They touched each other, building the pleasure between them until the need to join was pulsing through her.

But it was Dima who broke the kiss this time to say, "I need to be in you, now."

"Yes."

She shoved her bikini bottoms down her legs and kicked them off, not caring where they went. Then she hopped up, spreading her legs so her thighs were on either side of him, and she crossed her ankles.

The head of his erection brushed her opening, and they both shuddered.

Desire was pulsating through her, but so was emotion. Jenna felt connected to Dima like she'd never been to anyone else. She'd spent years keeping people, even Nataliya, at a certain distance.

And somehow this prince had made it past barriers forged in the pain of loss and fear of her own body's genetics.

She needed him inside her, but even just being held like this, their connection reached to the core of her soul and held on tight.

Jenna used the water to shift easily as she settled over his erection, explosions of ecstasy going off inside her as she lowered herself onto him.

"Yes, just like that, *milaya moy*." Dima held on to her hips with both hands, helping her to stay close even as they began to move.

The water made her buoyant, but it also increased the friction, not as silky smooth as her own natural wetness. It all added to the moment, and they strained together, chasing that pinnacle of pleasure. He came first, his shout loud and his body going rigid.

The way he swelled inside her as he came was the final stimulation she needed to go over, and Jenna cried out as she climaxed too.

The water moved them together, causing pleasant aftershocks until Jenna let her head fall forward to rest against his neck.

"You did say you wanted to work me out of your system," she said, teasing. Mostly.

Part of her wanted him to deny it.

What he said was, "I'm not sure that will ever be possible, but we can keep trying."

He sounded like he was teasing too, but right then Jenna could not be sure. It was the worst time for her ability to read him to go on the fritz.

The pang in her heart needed him to be joking.

If he was still intent on sexing her out of his system, Jenna was in for a world of hurt. But then, she'd never acknowledged things had changed for her either.

She wasn't sure that either of them had the courage it took for complete emotional honesty, but at least when they were making love, they both offered nothing but raw truth and their need-tinged ecstasy.

Dimitri lay awake, Jenna held close to his body.

She had a list of reasons why marriage between them would not work. He was a prince and active member of a royal family.

If she would just admit it, she would see that she too was an active member of a royal family and had been since Nataliya agreed to marry Nikolai.

His status as a billionaire who required staff and security would be a plus to a lot of women, and men, but for his Jenna? Not so much.

He was five years younger, and that could not be changed, but it was hardly the barrier she thought it was. Jenna was the woman he wanted at his side, and he did not care that she was thirty-five, rather than twenty-five and primed to have children.

Her self-imposed sterility was something he admired, because it showed how much she was willing to give up to protect future generations. How could he feel anything but respect at that? It was certainly no reason for them not to marry. If they decided they wanted children, there were options.

How could she not see how perfectly they fit together? Not only in the bedroom, but outside of it.

She'd been hurt when he'd had to stop her pressing charges against Skylar, but he thought Jenna had come to terms with that.

He was damn lucky, and he knew it. Looking back, he'd messed up on a huge scale with the timing of their first time making love too, but again...she'd forgiven him.

Now, he just had to show her that he was more than his title. That he was a man capable of enhancing her life, not only making it more difficult.

There was nothing he could change about most of her reservations about a future with him, other than show her that they were not the barrier she believed them to be. Except for one thing.

And he had to think long and hard how much he was willing to give up to be with the woman he had decided was perfect for him. But if he took the step he was considering, it could well wash away her concerns about her sterility as well.

He had just under two weeks to show her that all her misgivings were about things that were not as important as how much they needed each other.

And she did need him. Just as he needed her.

Jenna's phone range, interrupting her doze beside the pool. She pulled it up and noted it was a video call. From Nataliya.

She swiped to answer immediately.

"When were you going to tell me you were dating my youngest brother-in-law?" Nataliya demanded as soon as the call connected.

Jenna was in too good a mood to even work up some worry about discussing this with her BFF. "There wasn't any chance of me dating the other one," she teased rather than answering.

Nataliya's lovely face twisted in distaste. "No kidding. Even if the guy wasn't so gone on Emma, you two would have murdered each other in your sleep if you tried to actually sleep together."

Still not completely over Prince Konstantin's matchmaking methods, Jenna could only agree. "Yep."

"So, you and Dima?"

"He's kind of perfect for me."

"Even though he's a prince with a pretty high-handed way of handling life?" Nataliya didn't pull any punches.

"No one is perfect." Jenna shifted in her lounge chair and pulled her wrap on, using the new portable phone stand Dima had gotten her without compunction.

She was carrying a purse again too. It helped that he'd asked his security team to go through all the stuff she'd brought with her one last time to set her mind at ease.

Relaxed in the certainty no one was spying on her, Jenna was thoroughly enjoying her holiday.

"No," Nataliya said with alacrity. "Though Dima is a good guy, even if he isn't perfect."

"He really is." One of the best actually.

"You know, I was sure you'd never give in to your feelings for him." Nataliya peered at her phone screen like she was trying to look inside Jenna's head.

Jenna just shrugged. "He can be very persuasive."

"In other words, you could fight your own needs, but not his too."

"You're so wise, oh, pregnant one."

Nataliya grimaced. "I'm so nauseated, it's ridiculous, but my doctor assures me that's a good sign."

"Can they give you anything for it?"

"Stop worrying about me. I'll be fine. Women have been dealing with pregnancy nausea throughout history."

"Yes, but—"

"Don't. The miscarriage was an anomaly, and there's no reason to suspect it will happen again, but if it does? I know you'll be there for me, just like last time."

Jenna nodded fast.

Nataliya's brown eyes warmed with compassion. "You never talk about it."

"About what?"

"Your sterility."

No point in talking about what could not be changed. "It was my choice."

"But that doesn't mean you never wanted to be a mom." Nataliya bit her lip, her gaze sheening over. "I never asked. I'm sorry."

"Oh, no, pregnancy hormones are making you maudlin."

"Don't joke. I'm a bad friend."

"You're the best of friends, and you're right, there's a part of me that will always grieve not having children. I know some people are just as happy not to have them, and my life is full, but being an aunt gives me more joy than just about anything."

"Like Dima?"

"Like Dima."

Nataliya put her hand over her heart and fake swooned. "You admit it?"

"I'm vacationing with him. I wouldn't think much of my own decision-making skills if I were doing that and didn't find happiness in his company."

Nataliya's eyes widened, and she gasped. "You're in love with him!"

"No comment."

Suddenly her royal bestie went all serious compassion. "Are you going to let yourself be with him?"

"I am with him." What did Nataliya think, they had separate bedrooms?

"You know what I mean."

And just that quickly, Jenna did. "We went into this saying no strings. Neither of us has verbalized a change to that status quo. Well, other than to promise fidelity as long as we are together."

"I'd say that was a commitment."

Jenna shrugged. "It is and it isn't."

"Do you want a future with Dima?"

"We're really compatible," Jenna hedged.

"That's not an answer."

"I don't know. I think I do, but everything here is so idyllic."

Jenna spent her mornings by the pool, swimming, reading and catching up on her shows on her phone. Then Dima joined her either before or after lunch, and they spent the rest of the day and evening together.

They'd gone to the Old Fort, shopping and dining on the waterfront. Yesterday, he'd surprised her by not going to work after their morning swim and breakfast. He'd taken her to Yas, a small, exclusive island off the coast, where they'd spent the whole day in a private cabana, enjoying the sun, the sand and the water.

They had plans to visit the Grand Mosque later that day.

But none of this was real life.

"Vacation isn't real life," Nataliya said, like she was reading Jenna's mind.

Considering how close they were, it wasn't a stretch.

"No, it's not," Jenna agreed.

Nataliya nodded, like she'd made up her mind about something. "Do you remember what you told me when I thought Nikolai was too good to be true?"

"To tap that?" Jenna joked.

Nataliya's laugh and the joy on her BFF's face warmed Jenna's heart.

"Something like that. You definitely said go for it."

"But you knew Nikolai wanted to marry you."

"What do you know about Dima?"

"He wants my body. A lot."

Nataliya rolled her eyes. "We *all* know that. What do *you* know?"

"He's ruthless, but he cares about my feelings. He's arrogant, but he's not impossible to reason with."

"Sounds like Dima."

"You two have been friends a long time."

"We have, but Jenna, I've never been his lover."

The light went on. "I know he's vulnerable in ways he'll never show. I know that his time in the military changed him. I know that protecting his family is paramount, but he considers me part of that family."

"Now we're getting somewhere."

She knew that he wanted sex without barriers between them and had taken that step with her when he had not done so with any other lover, but that was too private to share, even with Nataliya.

"I know he doesn't think any of the obstacles I see to us being together are insurmountable." And that was why he hadn't belabored them.

Because Dima had not seen any of her concerns as things that could not be addressed. Though how he thought to get past her aversion to being part of a royal family in actual fact, she did not know.

"I know he took time off to spend with me here, when he never takes time off." She smiled at that knowledge.

"You're going to have to negotiate yearly vacations, or you won't get them," Nataliya warned.

"He *is* a workaholic. He's a prince and he's a billionaire, but that's not all he is."

"Isn't it?" Nataliya goaded, maybe because she'd said something similar a time or two about her own husband to Jenna.

"No. He's funny and educated, and he is always learning new things. He can be harsh, but he can be really compassionate too. He loves his nieces and nephews."

"So do you."

"I do." How Jenna had even entertained for a minute, much less a couple of days, the idea that she could cut ties with this family, she did not know.

They were as much Jenna's people as Luke, Lisa and her family and their parents.

"I love you, Nataliya."

"I love you too, friend. You're my sister in all the ways that matter. I won't lie and say making that official wouldn't thrill me to bits."

"You're getting ahead of yourself," Jenna warned. "I haven't said anything about marriage." But she was thinking it.

"Maybe you should." Nataliya's words hung there between them for several silent seconds.

Finally, Jenna asked, "What?"

"Maybe *you* should propose to Dima."

Jenna felt her lungs seize, and then she gasped, her lungs filling again. "You're not serious."

"Why not?" Nataliya got a mischievous look on her face. "I'll leave you to chew on that. I need to go eat some soda crackers, or I'm going to puke."

Jenna was still pondering that *Why not?* as she dressed for lunch. Dima was supposed to be done with his video conference calls in time to join her.

She'd donned a flowy nineties retro dress with wedge sandals and chunky jewelry. Her blond hair hung loose around her shoulders, silky and smooth from her trip to the salon after her phone call with Nataliya.

Dima had told her to dress nice because they were going someplace special for dinner.

So far, everything they'd done had been special.

She couldn't find the scarf she'd brought to wear with this dress, so she pulled her case out to see if it had gotten left inside.

"You are not leaving me over this!" Dima's cold, autocratic tone had her spinning around to face him.

His expression closed, he stood in the doorway, a brooding and physical barrier.

"I'm not leaving." But what did he mean by *this*?

"You're packing."

"Um, no. I'm looking for my scarf. Why would I be packing?" Jenna finally focused on the tabloid in his hand.

From where she stood, she could see a picture of her and Dima while they walked along the Corniche. "We knew word would get out. We've hardly been discreet about this vacation."

He'd held her hand wherever they went, when it was acceptable to do so. They arrived and departed in the same car. They'd made no effort to obfuscate her presence in his family's home.

More to the point, why would she leave Abu Dhabi just because the inevitable had happened?

"I have no desire to hide that we are dating," he assured her, though his tone said anything but.

She nodded, agreeing. "So what has you so upset?"

"I am not upset."

"Okay." Honestly? He didn't look so much upset as, well, angry. "Are you mad about something?"

"I thought you were leaving." He glared at her suitcase.

Why would he think that? Even if she had her case out? "Because the media picked up on the fact we're dating? I'm not that thin-skinned."

Besides, the only people she worried about finding out already knew. And they didn't care. Not her family. Not his.

Nataliya had been sending Jenna teasing texts about Dima, and humorous memes about morning sickness, ever since they got off the phone.

"We're not just dating," he said firmly. "We are lovers."

That would feel more romantic if he had said it with a smidge more emotion and less chilly factualism.

"True." She reached for the paper. Something in the article had to be the reason he was acting like this. "Here, let me see."

He held tight to the newspaper. "If you haven't seen it, you don't need to."

Was he kidding? "That's not how it works, Dima. Not for me, anyway."

"You said you understood."

"What did I say I understood?"

"Me seeing the women my father picked out for me. You knew it wasn't going anywhere." He spoke dismissively, like it was a nonissue.

Only she didn't know what the issue was, and now she wanted to, badly.

"That's what you said." She couldn't pretend to be thrilled his father was looking elsewhere for a bride for Dima, though.

However, the older man had no idea that the relationship between Jenna and Dima had changed. So the only people they could blame for Prince Evengi's attempts at matchmaking were themselves.

"It is what I said, and I expect you to trust me," Dima assured her, all arrogance.

That trust thing was still a bit of a sticking point, and Jenna never reacted well to being told what she was supposed to do, much less feel.

"Let me see," she said again, this time her own tone matching his more closely.

"Fine, if you insist." He handed the paper over, but even under all that chill, she could read his reluctance to do so. "We made the front cover."

His disdain for that reality dripped from his voice. Then, without another word, he spun on his heel and walked from the room.

For a moment, staring at the empty room where he'd just been, Jenna forgot the tabloid. Didn't he care how she reacted to whatever it was that had him acting so strangely? Wasn't she important enough for him to stick around and have it out, whatever *it* was?

Uncertainty filled her, feeding her fears that despite her change of heart, they had no real future. Her prince did not care if she was upset by what she was about to read.

If he did, he would have stuck around. Wouldn't he?

Only, the first thing he'd said was, *You're not leaving me.* Not, *You're not leaving Abu Dhabi.* Was that because Dima was a possessive alpha male who expected everyone around him to fall into his plans?

Or because *she* mattered to *him*? Jenna knew what she needed to be true, but she was a mature woman, who could and would accept the *real* truth, whatever it was.

Even if it meant coming to terms with a prince who was seeing his father's matchmaking candidates because Dima saw those women as better potential life partners than her.

She lifted the paper and focused on the front cover.

It was a European tabloid, so that they were featured on the front cover was kind of surprising. Until Jenna saw the rest of the front-page splash.

Prince Dimitri Already Cheating on Princess Sophia!

Two pictures were side by side on the cover with a diagonal split. In one, Dima danced with a beautiful twentysomething woman wearing a formal gown. The background was familiar to Jenna. It was in the grand ballroom at the palace in Mirrus.

Dima and Princess Sophia were both smiling and looking into each other's eyes.

The other photo showed Jenna and Dima walking hand in hand along the waterfront, as she'd noted. What she hadn't been able to see from across the room was their expressions.

Jenna was looking out over the water, a half smile on her face. Dima was looking at her, his expression intent. If she could believe what her eyes were telling her, there was a wealth of emotion in that intent gaze too.

Jenna flipped open the scandal rag and found the article.

Speculation had been rife since Dima's latest trip to Mirrus, when he had singled Princess Sophia out at a formal function to dance and chat with.

There were several pictures of them together, but Jenna gave those photos nothing more than a glance. It was the pictures of her and Dima that caught her attention and would not let go.

They looked like two people in love. While the paper painted her as *the other woman* in a nonexistent love triangle, their photographer had captured the truth. Dima looked at her like he looked at no one else.

Jenna wasn't immune either. She had a particularly besotted expression in one of the shots, but her affection for him shone through in all of the pictures, if you knew what to look for.

Had Dima seen her love for him? Was that what really had him riled?

Only, again…he'd told her she wasn't leaving him. And he'd said it in that ruthless way that he usually reserved for business. He'd meant it.

Could it really simply be about sex for him?

The pictures said otherwise, because if they showed Jenna's love, they were equally revealing about an amount of emotion coming from Dima that did not jibe with their relationship being nothing more than friendship and sex.

He'd been adamant when he said they were lovers, and she couldn't help wondering…hoping…that meant they were two people in love as well as sexual partners.

The only way to find out the truth would be to talk to him. One thing Jenna knew. She wasn't walking away from this thing with Dima without having a real conversation about real feelings.

She found him sitting sideways on a lounger by the pool, his head bent, his focus on the empty, sparkling water, a whiskey in his hand.

It was a Dima as she had never seen him. His tie was askew, the top button undone on his shirt. His jacket had been discarded entirely, and his hair looked like he'd been in a windstorm. Or, you know, running his fingers through it and tugging at it in agitation.

So not like Dima.

"I'd like the originals." She stopped beside him, letting her knee bump his leg. "Do you think we could get them?"

He looked up, his expression grim. "They're already online. Even I can't put that genie back in the box."

Suddenly far more sure of herself than she had been in the bedroom, Jenna smiled. "Even you?"

His bleak expression didn't lighten.

Jenna shook her head. "Have a look at those pictures, Dima."

"I have looked."

"Then you know they answer a question I've been asking myself since we got to Abu Dhabi."

"What question?"

"Set yourself to rights and I'll tell you over dinner."

"We were to go to the Grand Mosque first."

"Then let's go to the Grand Mosque," she agreed easily.

"That's why you were looking for your scarf."

"Yes. It would not be appropriate to enter the mosque without a head covering."

He stood up, but arrogant, autocratic Dima was gone. Her prince looked like he didn't know what to do with himself.

Jenna stepped right up into his space and leaned up to kiss the underside of his jaw. "Go take a shower. You'll feel better for it."

"Join me."

"If I do, we won't leave the condo, and I have plans for tonight."

"I did too. Have plans for tonight."

"Well, then..." She indicated the bathroom with a tilt of her chin.

CHAPTER FOURTEEN

JENNA FINISHED READING the article while Dima was in the shower.

The sheer amount of lies and speculation might have staggered her if she hadn't been Nataliya's BFF.

But Jenna had been best friends since university to a lady who lived like a normal person, who married and became a princess and then, finally a queen.

This article was no worse than most and better than some. Yes, they implied Dima and the princess had some kind of family merger deal, like the contract Nataliya had signed so many years ago. They had even dug up old dirt on Prince Konstantin, during the years when he'd had a lot of one-night stands. Comparisons were implied. Dirt was slung, but really?

It wasn't the end of the world.

Not for her. Not for Dima.

By tacit agreement, they did not discuss the article while they visited the Grand Mosque. Neither did they dwell on it while driving through the city.

The special dinner he'd had planned later was at the end of a pretty long drive into the desert. A large Turkish rug had been laid out for a picnic on the sand.

Flaming torches positioned around it cast a soft golden glow over the piled pillows and delicious-smelling dishes arranged in the center on a low table. The stars and moon glowed in the night sky like they never did in the city.

"This is amazing, Dima. Thank you for setting this up."

"You said you wanted to come into the desert. I was going to take you on a Bedouin experience, but realized I wanted privacy more."

"I love it." She kicked off her sandals and found a seat among the plump cushions.

After removing his own shoes, Dima joined her.

"I know the security people and whoever set this up are around, but it feels so private out here."

"After securing the perimeter, they have all gone to the other side of that dune." Dima sounded very satisfied by that and proud of himself. "If we are loud, our sounds will carry, but other than that, we are effectively alone."

"You think we are going to do something that could make us loud?" she teased, but the reminder that sex was his primary reason for being with her reared its ugly head again.

He gave her a look. "That was the plan, before I found you packing."

"I wasn't packing."

"I thought you were."

Jenna laid her hand over his. "Don't you know? I'm too stubborn and vocal to just take off without shouting it out first?"

"Shouting?"

"If I'm angry enough to leave you, there will be shouting."

"You read the article."

"I did."

"You do not seem angry."

"Well, I know the truth."

"You do?"

She nearly rolled her eyes but realized this was too serious to downplay in any way. "Yes, I do. If you want me to trust you, Dima, you have to trust me as well."

"I do trust you."

"Then trust me when I say that no tabloid article is going to make me question the truth that I know."

"What truth is that?" he asked, sounding cautious.

She'd get there, but they were doing some talking first.

"Don't you think it's funny that it never even occurred to that tabloid journalist that you are wooing me?" she asked, rather than answering.

Wooing was such an old-fashioned term, but it fit. He *had* been courting her.

"Lack of imagination and foresight," Dima said with a shrug in his tone.

She smiled up at him. "You don't deny that you've been courting me."

"Why would I deny the truth?"

"I don't know. Why tell me you were just trying to get me out of your system?"

Even in the muted light cast by the torches, she could see the color that burnished his chiseled features. "You did not want to hear the truth."

"You might be right."

"But now you claim to know it."

"Oh, I know all right. Have you looked at those photos?"

"The ones in the tabloid?" he asked, his dark brows furrowed.

"Yes."

"For a moment."

"You should have looked longer."

"Why?"

"They show the truth of the situation, no matter what lascivious lies the reporter claims."

"They show that I am wholly into you and not interested in other women, regardless of their status," he said skeptically.

"Yes."

Clearly startled, he asked, "They do?"

"Why do you think I wanted the originals?"

"To destroy them."

"Not on your life. They're going in an album along with all the other snaps I've taken since we arrived in the UAE."

"You're a strange woman, Jenna."

"Maybe, but you like me this way." Those pictures had given her a confidence she had not felt until seeing them, and she was beginning to believe it was a certainty of her place in his life that could never again be taken away.

"I do."

"Why?" she asked.

"Because you are smart and lovely. I can't keep my hands off you, but I enjoy every moment I spend with you in and out of the bedroom."

"I meant why do you want to marry me?" Though his list of reasons why he liked her was very nice.

"Who said I did?"

"You, with your wooing."

"I think it's just called *dating* in this century."

"No."

"No?"

"No. Dating can be casual. You even tried to pretend it *was* casual, but there's nothing casual about how we feel about each other."

"Admitting we're not casual is as good as you calling me *your* prince," he said with satisfaction.

"I do that?"

"You have, on very rare occasions."

"I do think of you as mine."

His expression was growing more and more deliciously predatory. "The possessiveness is entirely mutual."

"Good to know."

"We fit. Even though I am a billionaire prince who cannot take a full vacation, we fit."

"Even though I cannot give you children?" she asked, old pain as close to the surface as it had ever been.

"If we want children, we can adopt, or use a surrogate. Or if you want the experience of carrying my child, we can use IVF with your sister's egg, or, if she does not want to do that, with eggs donated to a fertility clinic."

"You've thought a lot about this," she said faintly, finding it hard to get a breath to speak. "Really a lot."

"Naturally. I do not have to have children for the line. You need to accept that my place in the family means any children we might have would not carry high nobility titles, but if you want it, I would love to be a father."

Tears burned Jenna's eyes. "You would make a really good father."

"I like to think so. You would be an ideal mother. Strong and a great role model for both our sons and daughters."

"You sound like you want a lot of children. You do realize I'm thirty-five."

"Women are having children later in life, but if you do not want to do that, it is not a deal breaker for me."

"You would not resent me if I never wanted children at all?"

"No. *Milaya moy*, I want *you*. I think I need you."

She nodded to herself. "Are you afraid of the *L*-word?"

"I…" He tugged at the collar of his silk dress shirt, his expression guarded. "I thought love was off the table."

"Did you?" He had a rude awakening coming then.

"I thought you were perfect for me. I didn't need to consider beyond that."

That's what he thought. Jenna did not agree, even a little. The *L*-word would be spoken.

"I was perfect for you even if you did have a list of things you thought were wrong with me," he added.

"Not you, your role as a prince."

"I can give that up," he said as casually as he might tell her the time. Only that was not a casual statement. Not at all. "I cannot change the billionaire thing, or that I am my father's son, but I can abdicate my role as prince."

Jenna felt like all the air had been squeezed out of her surroundings, which of course was impossible. But had he just offered to repudiate his role as a prince in the House of Merikov?

"You don't mean that."

"I do. I spoke to my brother Nikolai. It is not without precedence. Other Merikovs have chosen the life of a commoner over that of royalty."

"I would like to hear those stories."

"Ask my father. He loves to expound on family history."

"You *do* love me."

"I must, because I have always been very proud to be a Prince of Mirrus."

"I would never ask you to give that up." Jenna shifted so she was on her knees in front of Dima. She reached out and took his hand.

His usually confident expression bemused, he let her.

She started to speak, but found she had to clear her suddenly dry throat. "I love you, and don't think I'll ever let you forget I said it first."

"I am sure my words tonight have been infused with my love for you. What are three little words in the face of all I will do to bring you happiness?"

"Those three little words *are* happiness, Dima." He should never doubt how important they were.

"Then I shall say them."

"There you go being all formal again."

"It happens when I am feeling nervous."

"Good to know."

"As if you need anything else in the way of telling my secrets."

She didn't reply, just waited, because her prince was no coward.

"I love you, Jenna mine. I do not care about the age difference, or your sterility, or how different our lives are. I need you to complete my life."

"I need you to complete mine." Sure, Jenna could live the rest of her life without Dima, but it would not be as rich, as full, as it would be *with* him. "Will you marry me, Dima?"

He went utterly still, and then the most beautiful smile broke over his gorgeous features. "I suppose you will never let me forget you asked first either?"

"I'm telling our children this story every year on our anniversary."

He pulled her up and against him, his mouth hovering a breath away from hers. "Yes, *milaya moy*. I will marry you."

They kissed to seal the deal, and that kiss held something none of theirs had before, a certainty of each other. It was like adding cinnamon to coffee, making the kiss better than any they had shared.

"Just tell your brother that I don't want to be a princess," she instructed when they were settled against the cushions, arms wrapped around each other.

"I can tell him, but unless I abdicate my role, I cannot stop him bestowing the honor on you."

"If he does it, I'll start lobbying for a constitutional monarchy."

"You will do that anyway."

Joy bubbling like champagne inside her, she laughed. "I will."

The kiss that followed was incendiary. Soon, they were making love and doing their best not to be overheard, but ultimately, Jenna couldn't care less who knew she and her prince had just promised each other a lifetime.

EPILOGUE

Six months after they'd eloped, Jenna patted her barely protruding tummy and smiled to herself.

It had taken only one round of IVF, since her uterus was entirely viable, for her to get pregnant with Dima's baby. Having a tubal ligation had not impacted her other otherwise healthy reproductive system. They had decided to use donated eggs from a donor who shared Jenna's physical characteristics, but not her genes.

The donors at the clinic were all screened for genetic diseases, and Jenna could be confident she wasn't passing anything on to the next generation that would devastate a family like hers had been.

It still felt like a miracle.

She'd never thought to be pregnant, and she wasn't sure she wanted to carry another child.

This one had come with aching pain in her back and hips as well as nausea every day, all day long for the first four months. She had finally stopped throwing up, and now she could be around her BFF again, who was pregnant with her fourth child.

Nataliya had given birth to a healthy baby a couple of months before Dima and Jenna decided that they would elope rather than deal with the rigmarole of a royal wedding. Jenna knew it was more for her sake than his and loved him for it.

Nataliya's fourth pregnancy had come as a shock to everyone. Their baby was only a few months old, but other than the nausea, Nataliya's pregnancy was progressing fine.

Unfortunately, she and Jenna had set each other off with their nausea and had to settle for texts for weeks.

Now they were getting together on Mirrus to celebrate Prince Evengi's birthday.

The former king was delighted all of his sons were happily married, but even more happy with his own lovely wife.

Nataliya's mother had blossomed here on Mirrus, and Jenna loved seeing that.

She remembered the woman from when Jenna and Nataliya had first become friends. There had always been a sad look in Princess Solomia's eyes when she thought her daughter wasn't looking.

That sadness was gone. Being a grandmother suited the woman to the bone, and had done since the birth of Anna Yelena. Being married to her own arrogant prince had done wonders as well.

Nikolai and Nataliya were still sickeningly in love and the happy proud parents of three children, with a fourth on the way. Nataliya had finally determined four might be enough.

Emma and Konstantin were here with their boys for the birthday celebration as well. Jenna and Konstantin had finally made up, after sufficient groveling on the prince's part.

Konstantin's idea of matchmaking left a lot to be desired and she'd told him so.

Strong arms slid around her from behind, Dima's hands coming to rest against her stomach. "How is she doing today?"

"Active. Can you feel her?"

The baby kicked, and Dima made a sound of wonder as he always did. "I can. To think in only a few months' time we will be able to hold her."

"Can you believe Nataliya is having her fourth baby?"

"I can, but I admit I like our plan of adopting our next child."

"I do too." Jenna had this deep feeling that they were supposed to adopt their next child, and not a baby.

Dima had been all for it.

"We have a good life, Jenna."

"The best," she agreed with a happy hum.

"My brother is doing another study on the feasibility of shifting to a constitutional monarchy."

Jenna spun in her husband's arms. "Are you serious?"

He smiled down at her. "How can you doubt it? You, Nataliya and Emma make very persuasive advocates."

"Oh, I'm so happy."

"There is no guarantee he will shift our government in that direction."

"Nikolai is a good and fair man. Once he sees it will help and not hurt Mirrus, he will go for it."

"I love your confidence."

"I love you."

"Never stop saying that."

"I won't. Even if I did…"

"Have to say it first," he finished for her and then kissed her.

Love flowed around them as their mouths joined, as it always did. Her prince loved her with his whole great heart, and she loved him the same.

Even if it *was* his fault she had been bestowed with the title of Princess.

* * * * *

COMING SOON!

We really hope you enjoyed reading this book. If you're looking for more romance, be sure to head to the shops when new books are available on

Thursday 3rd March

To see which titles are coming soon, please visit

millsandboon.co.uk/nextmonth

MILLS & BOON ®

Coming next month

REVEALING HER NINE-MONTH SECRET
Natalie Anderson

She needed him to turn. Would she see those disturbingly green eyes? Would she see a sensual mouth? If he stepped closer would she hear a voice that whispered wicked invitation and wilful temptation? All those months ago she'd been so seduced by him she'd abandoned all caution, all reticence for a single night of silken ecstasy only to then—

A sharp pain lanced, shocking her back to the present. Winded, she pressed her hand to her stomach. How the mind could wreak havoc on the body. The stabbing sensation was a visceral reminder of the desolate emptiness she'd been trying to ignore for so long.

She'd recovered from that heartbreak. She was living her best life here—free and adventurous, bathing in the warm, brilliant waters of the Pacific. Her confusion was because she was tired. But she couldn't resist stepping closer—even as another sharp pain stole her breath.

'That's interesting.' He addressed the man beside him. 'Why are—'

Shock deadened her senses, muting both him and the pain still squeezing her to the point where she couldn't breathe. That *voice*? That low tone that invited such confidence and tempted the listener to share their deepest secrets?

Massimo hadn't just spoken to her. He'd offered the sort of attention that simply stupefied her mind and left her able only to say *yes*. And she had. Like all the women who'd come before her. And doubtless all those after.

Now his brief laugh was deep and infectious. Despite her distance, it was as if he had his head intimately close to hers, his arm around her waist, his lips brushing her highly sensitised skin—

Pain tore through her muscles forcing her to the present again. She gasped as it seared from her insides and radiated out with increasingly harsh intensity. She stared, helpless to the power of it as that dark head turned in her direction. His green-eyed gaze arrowed on her.

Massimo.

'Carrie?' Sereana materialised, blocking him from her view. 'Are you okay?' Her boss looked as alarmed as she sounded.

Carrie crumpled as the cramp intensified. It was as if she'd been grabbed by a ginormous shark and he was trying to tear her in two. 'Maybe I ate something...'

Her vision tunnelled as she tumbled to the ground.

'Carrie?'

Not Sereana.

She opened her eyes and stared straight into his. 'Massimo?'

It couldn't really be him. She was hallucinating, surely? But she felt strong arms close about her. She felt herself lifted and pressed to his broad, hard chest. He was hot and she could hear the thud of his racing heart. Or maybe it was only her own.

If this were just a dream? Fine. She closed her eyes and kept them closed. She would sleep and this awful agony would stop. She really needed it to stop.

'*Carrie!*'

Continue reading
Revealing Her Nine-Month Secret
Natalie Anderson

Available next month
www.millsandboon.co.uk

MILLS & BOON

THE HEART OF ROMANCE

A ROMANCE FOR EVERY READER

MODERN

Prepare to be swept off your feet by sophisticated, sexy and seductive heroes, in some of the world's most glamourous and romantic locations, where power and passion collide.

HISTORICAL

Escape with historical heroes from time gone by. Whether your passion is for wicked Regency Rakes, muscled Vikings or rugged Highlanders, the romance of the past.

MEDICAL

Set your pulse racing with dedicated, delectable doctors in the high-pressure world of medicine, where emotions run high and passion, comfort and love are the best medicine.

True Love

Celebrate true love with tender stories of heartfelt romance, from the rush of falling in love to the joy a new baby can bring, and a focus on the emotional heart of a relationship.

Desire

Indulge in secrets and scandal, intense drama and plenty of sizzling hot action with powerful and passionate heroes who have it all: wealth, status, good looks…everything but the right woman.

HEROES

Experience all the excitement of a gripping thriller, with an intense romance at its heart. Resourceful, true-to-life women and strong, fearless men face danger and desire - a killer combination!

JOIN US ON SOCIAL MEDIA!

Stay up to date with our latest releases, author
news and gossip, special offers and discounts, and
all the behind-the-scenes action
from Mills & Boon...

 millsandboon

 millsandboonuk

 millsandboon

might just be true love...

MILLS & BOON

HEROES

At Your Service

Experience all the excitement of a
gripping thriller, with an intense romance
at its heart. Resourceful, true-to-life
women and strong, fearless men face
danger and desire - a killer combination!